PROMISES TO KEEP

PROMISES TO KEEP

Malcolm Macdonald

This first world edition published 2012
in Great Britain and in the USA by
SEVERN HOUSE PUBLISHERS LTD of
9–15 High Street, Sutton, Surrey, England, SM1 1DF.

British Library Cataloguing in Publication Data

Macdonald, Malcolm, 1932-
  Promises to keep.
  1. Breit, Felix (Fictitious character)--Fiction.
  2. Hertfordshire (England)--Fiction.
  I. Title
  823.9'14-dc23

ISBN-13: 978-0-7278-8212-7 (cased)

All Severn House titles are printed on acid-free paper.

Severn House Publishers support The Forest Stewardship Council [FSC],
the leading international forest certification organisation. All our titles that
are printed on Greenpeace-approved FSC-certified paper carry the FSC logo.

Typeset by Palimpsest Book Production Ltd.,
Falkirk, Stirlingshire, Scotland.
Printed and bound in Great Britain by
MPG Books Ltd., Bodmin, Cornwall.

To Ingrid
There from first to last and always

Who lives where
in November 1956

A: The Old Tithe Barn: Felix Breit, 44 (German-born leading European sculptor; survivor of Mauthausen concentration camp), Angela, 36 (German-born electronic recording expert; survivor of Ravensbrück camp) Pippin, 7, Andrew, 5, Douglas, 3, Susan (newborn).

B: The Head Lad's Cottage: Alex Findlater, 47 (head of BBC Overseas Service) and his wife Faith Bullen-ffitch, 41 (publishing executive at Manutius Press and Felix's ex-lover) Jasmine, 9 (Alex's), Tarquin, 5 (theirs).

C: Tudor-style Victorian annexe: Adam and Sally Wilson (41, 42 – architects and co-founders of the Dower House community; partners of Tony Palmer – below), Theo, 9, Rachel, 7.

D: Upper floor of genuine Tudor remnant of original manor house: Chris and Debbie Riley-Potter (29, 24 – artists) Amanda 3, Hector, 2.

E: Ground and first floor back: Tony Palmer, 39 (architect, co-founder of the community and partner of Adam and Sally Wilson) Nicole, 36 (his French-born wife) Andrew, 9, Guy, 6, Constance, 4.

F: Entire attic floor: Willard A Johnson, 46 (American born, high-flying London architect), Marianne, 32 (neé von Ritter; Swedish-born architect) Siri, 9, Virgil, 7, Peter, 4.

G: Main house, first floor front: Denis deVoors, 37 (industrial chemist) and his wife Cynegonde, 35, Alaric, 13, Larissa, 11, Vivienne, 8.

H: Main House ground floor and ground floor of the Tudor remnant: Eric Brandon, 32 (children's author) and Isabella (editor on *Vogue*), Calley, 8, Ruth, 6.

I: (to the gate-lodge at the end of the drive) Terence Lanyon, 41 (economist at LSE) Hilary, 37, his wife, Maynard, 8, Diana, 6, Karl, 4, Mortimer, 3.

Sunday, 4 November 1956

The newsreel crews did not open the barn doors and switch on the Kliegs until Nye Bevan stepped forward to speak. The man carried a special aura around with him, anyway, but the sudden spotlights turned it to gold. And he knew it, too. You could tell that from the way he paused, unblinking, smiling his knowing, lopsided smile, promising the usual Welsh fireworks. He stepped forward, only a pace, but somehow it set him in perfect congruence with Landseer's two soot-blackened lions and the inky base of Nelson's Column. The previous speakers faded into shapes of grey behind him on the platform. A hush settled over the entire square, which was packed with protesters, right up the steps of the National Gallery.

'Oh, this is going to be *good*,' Eric murmured.

Nicole turned round and shushed him. 'It's not open-air theatre!' she hissed.

But Bevan proved her wrong at once. '*If* Sir Anthony Eden is sincere . . .' He paused, dropped his right shoulder, tilted his head, twinkled his eyes, and let the stress on that conditional hang in people's minds. He was talking to *his* people. 'I say *if* he is sincere . . .' Again that pause, but you could feel the sidewinder coming. He stood tall and lofted his right hand to punch the air: '. . . then he is too *stu-PID* to be prime minister!' A Biblethumper's finger poked the blow upward, raising every eye to Nelson, towering above.

The tension dissolved in one long, laughing cheer. After that it didn't really matter what Nye said by way of actual argument; in that one leap of oratory he had nailed Eden to the rock from which he would never again escape. He was, indeed, *far* too stupid to be prime minister. He and his French counterpart, Guy Mollet, had colluded with Israel to start a war against Egypt without first asking Uncle Sam's permission. And Uncle Sam – temporarily Uncle Ike – was saying no, it certainly wasn't all right and they were to stop it at once.

Of course, it didn't suit Bevan to credit the Americans with coming to the rescue – as Eric pointed out when they wound their way through the darkening streets of St Giles, back to his car. 'But I wonder what Willard's going to make of it? What do you say, Nicole? A gang of Egyptian socialists, bristling with weapons supplied by the communists, nationalize property owned by the French and British, and *America* says, "Let them keep it"! Bit of a mystery, eh?'

'Don't rise to it, darling,' Tony cautioned as they turned up St Martin's Lane.

'Oh, shut up about politics,' Isabella said. 'Did you notice how many Teddy Boys there were in the crowd?'

'You think they aren't *political*?' Eric asked her.

'Did you see the one with fur lapels near us? That was genuine astrakhan. And those were the pointiest winklepickers I ever saw. Only this week we were speculating they were on their way out. But maybe not. Perhaps they're just getting more extreme.'

'That's the thing about British political protests,' Eric said. 'There's nowhere better for checking up on the very latest trends in fashion. The Europeans can't hold a candle to us. I was looking at the Hungarian uprising on TV last night. Not a fashion note to be seen! I blame their addiction to water cannons. How about that Hungarian uprising, though? Nicole? The Russians are being just ever so slightly unneighbourly, don't you think?'

'The Hungarians were duped into rioting by the Voice of America,' she explained patiently – the standard line from Radio Moscow.

'Why?'

'Isn't it obvious? They wanted to provoke the Russians into coming to the brotherly aid of the masses—'

'So they succeeded.'

'They wanted to show the Russians up as militaristic oppressors but Britain and France spoiled it by this Suez adventure – and that's why the Americans are punishing them now. Five years of anti-Soviet scheming up the spout!'

Tony put an arm around her and gave a squeeze. 'Illuminating as all this is,' he said, 'we really ought to be discussing the possibility of a Dower House purchase. If we could make a realistic offer to the sand and gravel company, they'd have to—'

'Why is this place called Seven Dials?' Isabella asked. 'Does anyone know? Sorry, Tony. I agree – we ought to talk about that.'

'Chris and Debbie could never afford it,' Eric said. 'Even if the rest of us could cover their deposit, they couldn't afford the mortgage.'

'Maybe the Johnsons could buy their flat outright,' Nicole suggested. 'And Chris and Debbie could go on paying the same rent to them? Where did we leave your car?'

'Just the other side of Endell Street. Actually, I can short circuit all this by saying that we – the Light of My Life and I – would not be interested in buying our part of the Dower House, and if you'll just stop throwing rocks at me for a moment, I'll tell you why. I feel like a cup of coffee and a sticky bun. All that cheering-to-the-echo has left me parched and weak. Shall we go in here?'

He ducked into the small café, leaving the others to follow, a little surly until the aroma of cinnamon buns and Danish pastries hit them.

'It's all to do with Schedule A,' Eric went on when they were settled. 'Isabella could explain it much better than me but I'll do my best. If you own a house outright and live in it, the Inland Revenue considers that since you're not paying rent to anyone else, you must be paying it to yourself.'

Nicole was shocked. 'That's not fair. Suppose your family had owned the house for generations?'

Isabella shed her gloves, took out her nail polish, and began repairing the varnish on her fingernails.

Eric shook his head sadly. 'All dictionaries used by the Inland Revenue have a blue pencil through the word *fair*. But they would claim that Schedule A is *equitable*. It puts the tenant of the humblest cottage on a level footing with the duke in his palace. I can't *believe* you don't approve of this arrangement, Nicole? A spectre is haunting Europe: all men are born free but are everywhere paying rent, so to speak.'

'Well, I agree with it for a duke . . . yes. But not for ordinary people like us.'

Eric continued: 'Anyway, if it's a choice between a long-term commitment to ownership or a short-term one to a *rentier* and no financial advantage either way, that's no choice at all. But the day they abolish Schedule A, renting will be a mug's game. And on that day I'll be first in the queue to buy the Dower House.'

'He's making it all up, you know.' Isabella paddled outstretched nails randomly about her.

Eric went on: 'Terence and Hilary are of the same opinion. They won't buy until the Tories abolish Schedule A and unfairness stalks the land again.'

'There's just one teeny-tiny fly in the ointment.' Isabella decided the varnish was dry enough to let her wriggle her hands back into her gloves. 'You, my darling, are not the only clever know-all in the world. If we wait until it's abolished, a big outfit like our gravel company and their clever land agent, John Gordon, are bound to cop on that abolishing Schedule A has raised the value of every house in the land. They'll raise the asking price to us accordingly. Faint heart ne'er won fair Dower House. I need new gloves.'

'Ah,' Eric said. 'Good point.'

Nicole, who had been watching Eric's eyes stray towards some object over her left shoulder, shifted slightly to her left. Eric leaned slowly to his right and again stared at something behind her, this time over her other shoulder.

'What's the big attraction?' she asked him. 'As if I didn't know.' For she could see the woman in the looking glass behind Eric's head – a good-looking young thing sitting alone by the door.

'I know her,' he explained. 'I was just wondering if she recognized me.'

Isabella panned a languid gaze in that direction and asked, 'How d'you know her?'

'It's rather tragic,' he replied. 'She's the daughter of an Indian Army colonel, born in India, brought up by an aunt and a grandmother back here. An unhappy and rebellious childhood. The same with her brother. He's in jail at the moment for some black-market swindle—'

'How d'you know all this?' Isabella pressed him.

'But her troubles don't end there,' he went on imperturbably. 'She's in a very unhappy marriage. She's discovered that her husband has been keeping a mistress. Which' – he shrugged tolerantly – 'is nothing so dreadful these days, but he's not keeping her in some bijou flat in Maida Vale like any sensible fellow, he's keeping her in a lock-up garage in Dalston.' After a short silence he added: 'Often in chains.'

Isabella groaned. 'He's making it all up. You're making it all up, aren't you! And what d'you mean – keeping a mistress is no great shakes these days?'

'Are you?' Tony asked. 'Making it up?'

'Or even . . .' Isabella started, and then thought better of it.

Eric smiled. 'You asked me the other day why I never have and never will write grown-up fiction. I'm just proving that I could if I wanted. That was *all* fiction – but based on a germ of truth. I do, in fact, know the woman. By sight, anyway. She works in the accounts department at Cassell's. And I'm sure she has a perfectly average, respectable marriage with some equally unremarkable and blameless chap and they rent a small Victorian house in Islington and are planning their first baby for this time next year.'

'So what was the point of it all?' Isabella asked angrily.

'Quite simply this, my dear. *Both* those "scenarios", as movie people call them, are fictions. I don't actually know the woman from Adam – or Eve. I never set eyes on her before this afternoon. But if I took both scenarios to a publisher, as ideas for a modern novel – one full of outrageously improbable plot lines, the other filled with real life – which one d'you think he'd encourage me to pursue? The more outlandish the scenario, the happier he'd be. That's why I prefer to write for children – the only down-to-earth realists I know.'

'Furniture that moves about by itself and talks after midnight?' Nicole asked.

'For example!' Eric agreed.

Faith came out into the yard as soon as she saw Eric and Isabella's Lagonda return. 'It looked like a good rally,' she said as they clambered out and stretched themselves. 'We've just watched it on the news. Nye was in sparkling form.'

'He had the crowd at his feet,' Nicole assured her.

'Eden is foaming at the mouth and nibbling the Downing Street carpets,' Eric added. 'It will take an entire earldom to cure him.'

Faith laughed. 'Alex has heard that Macmillan sent a box of knives out to be sharpened this morning. So Eden might get his earldom quite soon. Interesting times!' To Tony she added: 'Did you get a chance to talk about Topic Number One?'

He glanced swiftly around at the others. 'Yes. We're all agreed that it makes sense to buy the house now – assuming the gravel company will sell. We're not sure if Chris and Debbie will be able to afford it and unless Isabella can work her magic on the Lanyons as she did on Eric, we think they'll want to continue renting.'

Faith gawped at Isabella. 'You?'

Eric threw an arm around his wife's shoulders and gave her a hasty kiss before she could dodge him. 'When it comes to high finance,' he said, 'this lady is peerless. They should give her an earldom, too.' Turning to her, he added: 'D'you want to go down to the gate lodge and twist the Lanyons round your little gloved finger – the one with the perfect nail varnish?'

And to his surprise she answered, 'Yes. Since you ask.'

Monday, 5 November 1956

The Dower House Purchase
First General Meeting - Monday 5th November 1956

There is now a clear majority in favour of canvassing the gravel company as to the possibility of a purchase of the house and five acres presently being rented. Before we do so, however, we must be clear in our own minds, and all agreed, as to how we will then divide the property into apartments. This initial meeting, to be held in the ballroom, will therefore address only the following question:

Is the present division of rooms a suitable basis for creating six discrete freeholds under one roof? If people think that some entirely different division of the house would be more appropriate, would they please bring suitably marked plans to the meeting. Sally and Marianne have some simplified dyelines of the existing house plan, omitting all signs of the current division.

Terence and Hilary have started discreet legal

inquiries, in London, not with local solicitors,
and will report on the implications.
 Any other business should be aimed at producing the
agenda for the next meeting.

(Felix and Angela, as our only two freeholders to date,
have kindly agreed to chair and minute this meeting, to
be held in the ballroom.)

- - - - - o -/|\ - o - - - - -

Cynegonde deVoors said, 'I'd like to start by saying I'm glad—'

'Me, too,' Denis deVoors put in. 'We're both agreed.'

'Of course, *dear,* I speak for both of us here. I think the division accepted by the Prentices for our apartment was a disaster. No wonder they left after three years. And—'

'Four,' Eric said.

'I beg your pardon?'

'Four. Years. Four years. They were here for four years.'

'Very well. I understand. I'm not deaf. Four years. Now I've lost the thread.'

Eric smiled. 'You were about to make a grab for *our* two principal rooms, I believe.'

'Well! I must say, I wouldn't exactly call it a *grab*. But any fair-minded person must see how impossible our situation is, because each of our rooms opens into a communal space. Every other apartment has a lockable entrance door.'

'So you—' Isabella began.

'I haven't quite finished, if you don't mind. I was *about* to say' – she turned to Eric and Isabella – 'that all the front rooms of the main house, ground floor and first floor, should be combined to make one apartment.' She settled into her (necessarily) ample skirts with a happy little sigh.

Eric grinned at Isabella and responded, 'Well! I must say that's jolly generous of you, Cynegonde – far more so than anyone here would have expected, I'm sure. But it only leaves you and Denis with two rooms. Large rooms, I grant you, but you'd need a ladder against an outside window to . . .'

Cynegonde closed her eyes wearily. 'I thought I made it clear

I was describing the realignment of *our* apartment. To compensate *you*, this ballroom and the room above would be added to your apartment, together with the cellar room below us here and *all* the cellar rooms underneath the Palmers' *and* the one under your butler's pantry. Just put in two or three spiral staircases – bob's your uncle! You give up just two rooms but you gain eight.'

Felix stepped in: 'So, Cynegonde, if Eric wants to get from his studio overlooking the backyard to here, overlooking the main lawn, he walks along their passageway, up the half-flight of stairs, through their kitchen, into the butler's pantry, down a new spiral staircase into the first storeroom, along the cellar passage and into the room below this, and up another new spiral staircase? Is that the proposal?'

Eric said, 'Between seventy and eighty paces, I reckon. Unfortunately, it's not Isabella and I who *need* the exercise.'

Cynegonde bristled. 'I walk four miles a day without even leaving our apartment. I know, because I had one of those pedi-things round my ankle for a week.'

Adam rushed in: 'Cynegonde and Denis have a point, though. Every room in their apartment does open into communal space. It's going to make it difficult to insure that unit.'

'One solution,' Willard said, 'would be to lock the glazed doors between the lobby and the main hallway – and the back door into the hallway, making it exclusive to the deVoors' apartment. How many people use the main hallway for access to the garden, anyway? We could just as easily use the back hall.'

No one, it seemed, used the great hall to get to the front drive and garden.

Marianne said, 'Couldn't we do something more imaginative? A flimsy glass door isn't going to impress the insurance company anyway. Couldn't we design a gothic sort-of screen at the head of the stairs?'

'A *pastiche*?' Tony was aghast.

'Well, what Soane did in the boudoir is a pastiche,' Sally pointed out. 'The gothic style was already dead for centuries. I like this idea – a gothic screen at the stairhead and double-glazing in the arches. It could be our gift to the old place.'

'We can hear practically every word Eric and Isabella say,' Denis said.

'And they say a *lot*,' Cynegonde added. 'Our proposal is quite logical. The attic floor stays as it is. Then—'

'That's *so* generous of you, Cynegonde,' Marianne said. 'Willard and I will be eternally grateful.'

Cynegonde did not smile. 'Your attic floor stays as-is. Then beneath it there are three vertical slices. *Logical* slices. Front for us, middle for the Brandons, and no change for the Palmers. Surely a community of architects and designers can see it's logical?'

Terence Lanyon held up a finger. 'Whatever the boundaries, each apartment will have to be valued by at least two independent surveyors. And it seems to me' – he turned to Cynegonde – 'that the grand apartment *you're* proposing to create would be worth about as much as the other five in the main house put together. So it'll be around eight to ten thousand, just for your one apartment! Is that more or less what you have in mind?'

The smile on her lips (if that's what it was) could have been drawn with a 6H pencil. 'We'd have to consider that,' she said.

Their car was a pre-war Morris Twelve with a lacework of rust for its floor. The relaxation around the room was almost palpable.

'Do we pursue the idea of a gothic screen at the stairhead?' Marianne insisted.

Felix looked all around. 'A preliminary sketch for less than a fiver?'

Murmurs of assent.

'Carried,' he said.

Angela picked up her biro and recorded the first decision.

Willard said, 'One of the reasons Marianne and I welcome this movement towards an outright purchase is that we will at long, *long* last be forced to sort out the electricity supply to each flat and – finally – put each family on its *own* meter.'

'Communal meetings will never be the same again,' Faith said.

'Double glazing in the arches round the stairwell would be a godsend,' Isabella said. 'Alaric, Larissa and Vivienne are not the *quietest* children in the world.'

Cynegonde smiled tolerantly. 'Denis and I do not believe that children should be inhibited. But I must say, Isabella, that I thought you agreed with us on that point – considering what we hear coming up through the floor and the stairwell from Calley and Ruth.'

Eric cut in: 'Debbie and Chris will be the only ones with no ground-floor rooms. They also have the smallest flat by far. But if the Wilsons gave up their spare bedroom, which has never been more than a dumping ground for Sally's expired enthusiasms—'

'I say!' Sally complained.

'A jacquard loom, never repaired? A self-playing piano that only works up to middle-C? Sundry silversmithing tools? A dismantled litho press . . .'

'All-right-all-right! Don't go on! . . . Go on.'

'. . . and if I give up my studio in return for this ballroom, then the Riley-Potters could have two ground-floor rooms directly beneath their existing flat.'

'How connected?' Sally asked.

'Christ, you're the architect. An external staircase in the inner courtyard? Fully enclosed. We'd get consent for that, surely? And it wouldn't matter that Chris's studio would be separated by a short trek across the back hall. Lord knows – I've often *wished* for such a gap.'

'Ha ha,' Isabella said.

'But *we* lose a room,' Adam pointed out. 'We'll need that for my Aged Parents one day.'

Eric conceded the point. 'On the other hand, it wouldn't take much work with a crowbar to turn the old stable nearest you into a Dangerous Structure, which could then be dismantled brick by salvaged brick and rebuilt into an old-folk's flat for your parents.'

'Sure!' Willard put in. 'And the three remaining garages are walking their last mile, too. Nobody's happy using them. I see that even the Lagonda is being parked outside these days.'

'Four homes for APs?' Faith asked – realizing that their cottage would face the geriatrics, directly across the yard.

Willard grinned. 'Or one AP apartment and one *new* dwelling to be sold to a *new* family – a tenth member of the community.'

There were dubious faces until he added: 'And split the loot equally among the rest of us?'

Alex spoke up: 'Not a word of this must leak out. If the gravel company gets wind of it, the price will rocket.'

'But where will we park our cars?' Faith asked. 'The backyard gets impossibly crowded these days.'

'There's a hundred yards of pheasant run lying idle – below

the bit we use for drying laundry. If we put in a hoggin floor and ran some current out there, we could ban all parking in the backyard.'

Felix banged the table with his sculptor's maul. 'Are we agreed on a division of the big house?'

Cynegonde returned to the fray: 'We should ask for a valuation of each room, individually.'

'Why?' The question rose on all sides.

'Isn't it obvious? We can then put apartments together this way or that way to see what's affordable and what's beyond reach.'

Chris cleared his throat awkwardly. 'Talking of being beyond reach – much as Debbie and I would welcome the two downstairs rooms – it may be all academic, anyway. She and I may be going to fight the Russians in Hungary. We were at a meeting in the Slade last Wednesday. Quite a few people are volunteering.'

'And who's going to look after Amanda and Hector?' Nicole asked.

'Maybe we won't be gone all that long.' He shrugged. 'We'll find someone. Sorry. Not on the agenda, I realize. Just thought I'd let you all know.'

'And what about valuing each room individually?' Cynegonde insisted.

'Aieee!' Willard ran his fingers through his hair. 'Where to start?'

Hilary, in what she hoped was sounding like a kindly voice, told her: 'The apartment you said you'd prefer would have four vast rooms. You could build an entire house in each of them! Do you really, seriously imagine that a room-by-room evaluation would do you any favours, pet?'

Cynegonde shrugged. 'It just seems so logical to us – three neat vertical slices – front, middle, and back.'

'Let's get *both* suggestions valued?' Isabella suggested. 'On condition that we and the deVoors can then bid for the front slice if we both think it's within our reach.'

'Carried?' Felix asked – redundantly.

'That went extraordinarily well, I thought,' Alex said to Faith as they crossed the yard to their cottage. 'What about Cynegonde, eh! Poor old Denis.'

'Never mind him – what about Chris and Debbie? Fighting

Soviet tanks in Hungary? What in God's name do they think
they're playing at?'

He laughed. 'D'you really think there's a snowball's chance in
hell that they'll even reach Dover – never mind Budapest!'

'I suppose not.' After a pause she went on: 'You seemed a bit
distracted.'

'Things on my mind.'

Once inside the cottage he made straight for the drinks
cupboard. 'I had to make a choice today that I never thought
would arise.'

'Jas-mine? Tar-quin?' Faith called out.

'She said they'd be at the Palmers'.'

'Well, I want them bathed and fed before the fireworks. You
can bath them?'

'They can bath themselves now. I can just stop them drowning
each other.' He poured a stiff one.

'For me, too,' she said. 'About this choice you've made . . .?'

He sank half the glass before responding. Then, carrying the
gin bottle, he led the way to the sitting room and slumped in
his chair. 'We got wind that the government . . . Actually, I
doubt it was the whole government – just the usual little High
Tory cabal. Anyway, we heard they were about to commandeer
the BBC, starting with overseas broadcasts from Bush House. At
dawn tomorrow. So we had a day to—'

'But why?'

'They think we're being too *neutral* over this absurd Suez
adventure. My God – we're falling over backwards to find *anything*
good to say about it at all. Comb the entire world's media –
newspapers, magazines, radio, TV – the only favourable comment
you'll find is from France and Israel. *Quelle surprise!*'

'So what was this choice you had to make?' Faith was gazing
out at the yard, trying to imagine two apartments on the far side.

Felix and Angela emerged by the back door of the main house;
Angela had her figure back again after Susan.

'You'd better sit down,' Alex warned.

Slightly alarmed, Faith obeyed. 'My-my!'

'Yes. I had to decide – finally – between being a BBC man or
a government man. This Suez lunacy brought it to a head.'

'It's made everyone bolshie. Isabella told me Eric got call-up
papers as a reservist and he just stuffed them back in the envelope

and threw in a handful of cornflakes and wrote "Return to sender" on the outside and posted it back. She's afraid he'll be arrested.'

Alex shook his head. 'He won't be. Too many like him.'

There was a knock at the door. 'Only us!' Felix called as he and Angela entered.

'Pick up a couple of glasses on your way through.'

Faith arched her eyebrows.

'It doesn't get into breast milk,' Alex said.

'Bloody Cynegonde!' Angela plonked the two glasses at Alex's elbow. 'I need this. How'm I going to minute *that* and make it sound sensible?'

'You think *you've* got it hard. Wait till you hear what I've been doing today!'

Faith was alarmed. 'Are you free to talk about it?'

'Free as a bird, love! The die is cast, for better or for worse.' To the Breits he explained: 'I was telling Faith just now that we heard the government was going to commandeer the BBC's foreign services to put out propaganda of their own. They think we're too neutral. We heard they had a bunch of SAS hiding up the street, waiting for orders to take over. So I went up to Saint Giles's Circus and bought two dozen hammers at that ironmonger's, and then I went round Bush House, distributing them to the engineers and giving them *written* warrant to smash the studio equipment and transmitters the moment the army moved in. Cheers!'

'*What!*' Faith let slip her glass but caught it again, spilling gin-and-bitters down her slacks. 'Oh, shit!'

'They'll sack you?' Angela said.

'It'll be interesting,' Alex assured her. 'I certainly won't go quietly. It all blew up because we translated Gaitskell's attack into Arabic and broadcast it on our Middle Eastern services. The Tories don't understand that this isn't nineteen thirty-nine all over again. If Ike gets re-elected tomorrow – which is pretty much a racing certainty – he'll order us and France to stop the invasion and withdraw. Then we'll be safe – at Bush House, I mean.'

'Can you be so sure?' Felix asked. 'Why should the Americans want to leave Nasser holding the canal? They've already withdrawn finance from the Nile dam at Aswan, so—'

'That's why Nasser seized the canal, of course. National pride. But suppose Britain and France go ahead and retake the canal

– what then? We can't hold it. We couldn't even hold our *peace-time* bases in Egypt. So the UN would have to make the canal an international entity with universal access. In which case, the world's eyes would turn towards Panama. How could America promote a status for Suez that they'd absolutely reject for Panama? No – better let Egypt keep it and come to some purely local agreement over access.'

'Aaah!' Angela gave a strangled scream. 'This *bloody* country! I'm sorry, pets, but it drives me to despair. Britain should really make up its mind, once and for all, if it wants to be the forty-ninth state or part of Europe.' She smiled wanly. 'I think I just want to get drunk.'

Alex waved towards the gin. 'Be our guest!'

'No, thanks, tempting though it is. We have to get ready for the fireworks. It's eight thirty on the big lawn, yes? Also, we promised Gisela we'd be back straight after the meeting – which went amazingly well, I think?'

Faith winked. 'Nothing concentrates the mind like the thought of having to part with *real* money.'

'Well – Cynegonde's not going to give up too easily, I'll tell you that.' She turned to Alex. 'I think Eric and Isabella are abso-lute *saints* to put up with *them* living right above. Apparently Denis collapsed with some kind of nervous exhaustion last week. Eric had to rush him in to Hertford General – soaked in sweat and shivering. And Cynegonde standing at the top of the stairs yelling "*Spineless!*" as Eric was helping him down. We are all so bloody *civil* to that creature!'

Felix touched her arm and murmured, 'Enough.'

Alex said, 'One thing I didn't mention – and there's a D-Notice on this so you won't read it in the papers or hear it on the air – but there have been small-scale mutinies throughout the army. They're handling it with kid gloves because . . . well, if they take a hard line, the insubordination could get a lot worse.'

Faith asked, 'What about Chris and Debbie going off to fight the Red Army, eh?'

'Hah!' Felix waved dismissively. 'The Russians will have poor old Nagy hanging from a lamp post before this ridiculous rescue party reaches Calais.' He yawned. 'Come on, *Liebchen* – Gisela's waiting to go out.'

When they had gone, Faith rose and returned to the window. 'What d'you think about a tenth apartment for the Dower House – right across the yard from us?'

'Willard's idea. I think he's right about tearing it down and rebuilding *something* on the same site, but not a tenth apartment.'

'But Willard has dangled the prospect of sharing out the profits on creating a tenth apartment. I'll bet everyone in the main house will be tempted.'

'Unless we can tempt them with something *much* bigger?' Alex grinned.

'Go on.'

'It's quite obvious the gravel company will be stopped from scarring the whole valley with gravel pits. So they might want to get the *entire* parkland off their books as well as the house and gate lodge. And wouldn't it make a fine golf course!'

Faith chuckled. '. . . which would need a *clubhouse*! But that would be very small.'

'I don't mean across the yard. That's ideal for the APs. But there are two or three hundred acres for the eighteen holes *and* the nineteenth. Food for thought, anyway. But don't breathe a *word* about this. We must get everything lined up and fireproof before making a move.'

Catherine wheels were nailed to the last two uprights of the pergola; the bonfire was built in the shallow concrete well of the dried-up pond; Terence and Willard set off the rockets on the farther side of the haha, beyond which no child was allowed; Sally and Isabella were in charge of the roman candles, which they set off in a specially trimmed area to one side of the bonfire. Adam and Tony had the fire extinguishers, in case a rocket veered off into the yew hedge around the once-formal garden. Eric, who had supervised The Tribe in the making of this year's Guy Fawkes, was in charge of the bonfire. The Tribe (twenty children aged five or over, from Adam Breit, five, to Alaric deVoors, thirteen) had half-a-dozen sparklers each, two of which they were expected to share responsibly with the younger children. The very young ones stood and watched with Cynegonde at her bedroom window, above the ballroom. Nicole and Marianne did the sausages and baked potatoes while the remaining parents supervised The Tribe with varying degrees of bossiness.

The Guy's wax-and-plastic face melted gruesomely and some hollow reeds stuffed inside his jacket gave out an eldritch shriek as they burned. Half-a-dozen rockets that Willard had brought went up within a few seconds of each other – up and up and up until they burst into glory and bathed the entire valley in a brilliant magnesium flare; the bang was delayed almost two seconds. Someone threw jumping jacks in among the throng. It delighted the children and alarmed their parents, who did not discover that Tommy Marshall was responsible – or culpable – until he had dropped the tenth and last one among them. Tommy was the bastard son of Lena-such-a-sad-case, who worked for Nicole and Tony; his father hadn't made it up Omaha Beach on D-Day.

With polite little coughs the roman candles volleyed balls of red, green and blue fire twenty feet above their heads before dying in a smoky, lazy, sparky flame no brighter than a wax candle. In between, the Catherine wheels on the pergola spat out persistence-of-vision circles of fugitive colours, served up with a drift of acrid but exciting smoke. And when the last firework had fizzed and banged and expired, there was still the bonfire to redden their cheeks and put a dazzle in their eyes as the sausages sizzled over a mini-fire of raked-out embers, and daring hands teased burned or par-baked spuds from the larger fire, and the little ones came out with Cynegonde to join in the fun at last.

'The really amazing thing,' Eric said when the festivities finally broke up, 'is that something so carefully organized could go pretty much as planned and yet still manage to be so completely chaotic.'

Later that evening, when Faith had finished reading that night's chapter of *The Monster of Widgeon Weir* to Jasmine, and Alex had finally persuaded Tarquin that the Norman archers in his toy fort were several centuries too early to have enjoyed their own Guy Fawkes night, they settled in happy exhaustion, half-numb with wine, to watch – Faith assumed – *This is Your Life*. But when she went to switch the set on, Alex said, 'There's something else . . .'

She had been going to sit on the carpet, leaning back between his knees – because no one else could massage her neck half so well; now she sat in a chair, obliquely facing him.

'Have you thought any more about Graham Ackroyd's suggestion?' he asked.

'Is this the "something else"?'

'No, but it impinges.'

'Tell me the "something else" first, then.'

'It's the Voice of America. They've at last twigged that their broadcasts carry little authority overseas precisely because it's just one long hymn of praise to democracy, motherhood and apple pie. The Voice of America is as bad as Radio Moscow. The way they tell it, Uncle Sam never puts a foot wrong. But Johnny Foreigner just yawns at all that vainglory, while he listens to *us* with respect – because we give them warts and all. So now they want to hire me as . . . they call it editorial advisor but the job is to find and hire editors who can "tell it like it is". They want to run it—'

Faith interrupted: 'Why you? There must be hundreds of Yankee journalists who can do that.'

'I hope so. Obviously they want an English "fall guy", as they call him – an Aunt Sally they can blame if the State Department decides it's not on, but they also want someone with my stature and reputation in sound broadcasting who can't be dismissed on a mere whim. They're prepared for a fight but they need a heavyweight.'

'And the stuff you can't talk about? The "Ministry of Education" in Curzon Street? Perhaps today's business with the hammers has exhausted your stock there?'

He shook his head. 'I doubt it, somehow. Chaps are pretty hacked off with Eden and the French. It was all done against our advice, you know. Heigh-ho! I really meant to ask about *you*. If I take up the VOA offer I'll be burning my bridges with ITV. So if you still harbour any dark thoughts about leaving publishing and moving into television, specifically ITV, this is the time. A month from now will be too late. Graham Ackroyd probably won't even be on speaking terms with me.'

'In other words, you've made up your mind.'

'Waal, honey, ah guess ah jess 'bout have. Question is – have you?'

She drew breath, held it, let it out hard. 'The decision couldn't have come at a worse time. The Persian book is in a kind of crisis. Baqer Rowhani is doing—'

'The Persians might cancel?'

'No — quite the reverse. More powerful courtiers than Baqer have got wind of it and want to muscle in. They're saying his ideas are *not glorious enough*! They want sixty-four more pages . . . seven-colour printing on *all* pages . . . hand-tooled leather binding with enough gold to empty Fort Knox . . . a hundred presentation copies with polished but uncut gems all over the binding. And as for *Our Promised Land* — thanks to Suez, which has kept Ben Gurion out of our hair, *that* book has finally gone into production. And the interest is phenomenal. So, just at this moment—'

'Your two babies!'

She frowned. 'Two? Oh! The *books*! Yes, so I'm *in the catbird seat*. I'm being discretely *headhunted*. You'd better start getting used to these idioms. Headhunted by Doubleday. But the question is — do I stay and make Manutius the publisher it *could* be if Fogel the Destroyer wasn't always undercutting Fogel the Creator? Or do I cut and run for the calmer maelstrom of American corporate publishing?' She chuckled. 'It would be kind of fun if we both ended up working for American outfits, eh!'

'Kind of ironic, too. There's Willard, rapidly growing more English than the English — you know he's on the committee of the Athanæum now? An honorary knighthood looms. Anyway, for you — one way or another — it's going to be publishing and not TV.'

She nodded. 'And I think I'll stay with Manutius, too. D'you know why?'

He shook his head.

'Our dear Doctor Bronowski. I'd miss Bruno *so* much in New York.'

Thursday, 15 December 1956

Eric rose to his feet; the meeting hushed. 'In Italy,' he said, 'Mussolini Always Interferes. So – *Information*: These winter Sundays are—'

'Permission to smoke, sah?' Adam (who had recognized the old army mnemonic) cried out.

'Yes – sorry, you men. Carry on smoking. *Information*: These winter Sundays are a pain in the neck, especially with The Tribe now thirty strong. *Intention*: Some of us aim to alleviate the boredom by organizing visits to the great London museums and galleries. *Method*: Willard—'

'Some of us?' Cynegonde asked. 'Who is "*some* of us"?'

'It doesn't really matter, pet,' Eric assured her. 'It's just one of those ideas that floats around until someone takes pity and adopts it.'

'It would still help to know.'

'Well, I think Felix thought of it first.'

'Me, actually,' Angela said. 'I caught myself thinking, "Let's take the children down to the river and come back without them".'

'Angela? Felix? Let's just say it was a *bright* idea. Permission to laugh. *Method*: Willard—'

'Permission to groan, sah?'

'Carry on groaning, chaps. Willard can fix a thirty-seater coach for Sunday afternoons for four pounds ten. Leaving between twelve thirty and one and returning between five thirty and six. We'll do the Tate two Sundays in a row, then the Science Museum two Sundays in a row, then the National, then the Natural History—'

'Why *two* Sundays in a row?' Cynegonde asked.

The others stared at her. Surely everyone knew that, thanks to government stinginess, most of these places opened only half their collection on alternate days.

Eric explained. 'In any case, it will do the older ones no harm to be forced to concentrate on just half the collection each time.' He turned to Faith. 'Is Bruno going to meet us there this Sunday?'

'He said he would if he could but not to wait.'

'Fine.' He glanced down his notes. '*Administration*: if we took them from the age of six upwards, it would be sixteen, leaving nine behind. So we need a crèche back here and up to half-a-dozen parents with the coach. If most but not all of The Tribe bring one friend each from school. Or ballet. Or riding school . . . wherever. One each. We should break even at three bob a head. Which is tenpence cheaper than going by train and Tube.' He was bemused a moment. '*Information, Intention, Method, Admin* . . . what the devil's that last *I* for?'

'*Inquiries*, sah!'

'Ah, yes! Thank you, sah-major. Any questions, you chaps?'

'Who will be conducting the lecture?' Cynegonde asked. 'Have you arranged anything with the gallery?'

'It's not a pedagogical occasion,' Eric assured her. 'More one of opening eyes and making discoveries – untrammelled by the prejudices of the present generation and the sheer, unutterable ignorance of those past.'

'Bruno's there!' Faith said as the coach trundled northward up Millbank and pulled to a halt outside the Tate.

'I'll park this crate in Herrick Street, sir,' Freddy Henson, the driver, said. 'Back at three thirty sharp to pick you up again.'

'Synchronize watches, everyone!' Eric called out. 'It's fourteen-oh-three. Back here at fifteen thirty hours or half past three, whichever comes first.' He stepped off the coach. 'Bruno! Good to see you. No family?'

'Lisa couldn't get away from Cheltenham. Next week it's the holidays. Judith will come if Lisa will.'

They paused at the top of the steps to watch a string of Thames barges ferrying coal upriver to Battersea – a scene from a monochrome Whistler in the mists of a December afternoon. 'Time to switch to Bronowski briquettes, d'you think?' Faith asked.

He chuckled. 'It may come to it yet – with this new Clean Air Act. Will those children be all right inside there?'

Eric shrugged. 'This is our first experiment. Willard, Marianne and Cynegonde are *in loco doctoris*, but I suppose we'd better assist. We'll mop up the bolshie ones. Talking of experiments, I'm enjoying *Science and the Common Understanding*. But Freddy Ayer isn't going to like it, I think.'

'Sooner or later he'll realize just how sterile positivism is.'

'I'm only at page sixty-one, so don't spoil it, but I hope you don't just *link* creativity in art to creativity in science.'

'As opposed to what?'

'Well, I suspect they're one and the same.'

Bruno smiled his merry-eyed, pinch-lipped smile. 'I think you'll approve, then. Tell me!' He spread his arms, barring them as they made to cross the threshold into the gallery proper, trapping them beside Rodin's *Kiss*. 'What pictures are you hoping to see today?'

Faith said, 'The Turners and the Pre-Raphaelites for me – and I always look for one to surprise me. I whizz round past all the paintings until something screams stop. Last time it was Samuel Palmer's girl standing in a landscape. Amazing! A very great man once told me that Sam Palmer's paintings are what Blake struggled to achieve all his life.'

Bruno punched her arm lightly – more of a nudge, in fact. 'And you?' He turned to Eric.

'Three I never miss. Graham Sutherland's *Entrance to a Lane*, the *Falaise Castle*—'

'The Othon Friesz,' Bruno said.

'Yep. And the Augustus John portrait of Yeats. Oh, and of course there are others. Stanley Spencer's *Self Portrait*. Henry Lamb's portrait of his wife . . . Where to stop! What about you?'

He turned about and led them in. 'Faith has pre-empted me on two of them – the Turners and the Pre-Raphaelites. They're like the Bible and Shakespeare on *Desert Island Discs*, of course. I'm hoping that Lamb's extraordinary portrait of Lytton Strachey is on view – I read that it's on loan from the Chantrey Bequest. It's the one where his legs flow like melted plastic, down from the armchair and into the carpet and the trees are straight out of a railway poster. Quite extraordinary.'

They found Cynegonde with Virgil, Rachel, Pippin, and Guy, standing before Peter Lanyon's *Porthleven* – half-map, half-painting. 'I just wish Alaric hadn't scooted off like that,' she was saying. 'We were actually *in* Porthleven last summer and we actually *met* Mister Lanyon, who is a very fine painter, though you'd hardly think so from a first glance at *this*! However, if you look more closely, something very subtle begins to happen. At first, it's just a crudely drawn map of the fishing harbour with little Cornish fishing boats bobbing around inside. But now forget all that and half-close your eyes, and just look at the whole thing. What d'you see now?'

Virgil started hesitantly: 'It's like a—'

'Hands up first, Virgil. Put your hand up before you speak. It's like a . . . what?'

'A man. This side of the harbour is like a man.'

'Splendid! Not many people ever notice that. You're very clever!'

'And a woman,' Pippin said, before remembering to put up her hand. 'The other side of the harbour is like a woman.'

'Wonderful! We've got some very clever children here today! What sort of man and woman?'

Rachel raised her hand. 'A fisherman, miss? A fisherman and his wife.'

'Oh, you are all too good! But there's no need to call me "miss". D'you see it, Guy?'

'No,' Guy said. 'And we wouldn't get many marks for a map like *that* in school.' He slipped his hand into Faith's and asked Eric, 'What are you going to see?'

'Some modern cave paintings. Want to come along?'

Cynegonde smiled above the boy's head and mouthed a silent *thank you!* As they turned to go, she added: 'By the way – the full gallery is open again, and will be from now on, the man told me. Only the British Museum is stuck with the half-and-half system now.'

'Whatever became of Riley-Potter's Hungarian adventure?' Bruno asked as they made their way to the Yeats portrait.

Faith laughed. 'He went back the following week – he and Debbie – but only five volunteers turned up. And none of the organizers. But there was some football match on the telly, so they all sat and watched that and then came home again.'

'The British are no good at revolutions,' Bruno said. 'Even the Peterloo Massacre would have been a very ordinary weekend clash on the Continent.'

The Yeats had been removed for cleaning, so they went to look at the Turners instead.

'What about the cave paintings?' Guy asked. 'Are the caves underneath us?'

'Well, it's more convenient to show them upstairs here,' Eric explained. 'But *all* these things hanging on the walls are really just cave paintings.'

Bruno raised an eyebrow. Faith sighed and said, 'Ho-hum!'

'Sure,' Eric insisted. 'I told Guy all about it last Sunday. I'm sure cave paintings started when some primitive man – slightly drunk – picked up a bit of charcoal from the fire and did a lot of scribble on a rockface. And giggled. And sobered up a bit. And said, "That's amazing! It looks a bit like a wild boar". And he tried to make it look a bit *more* like a wild boar. And that's how—'

'It couldn't possibly have been a woman who did it, could it!' Faith said.

'Of course not. They were saving themselves for the critique. It was surely a woman who came along with a handful of berries and crushed them on the drawing to colour it and said, "See! That's *much more* like a wild *bear!*" The truth about beginnings is always simple – take it from me. The man who split the atom started by cracking the nuts in his Christmas stocking.'

They stopped before Turner's *Sunrise*, the one at Norham Castle, where Marianne was shepherding Alaric, Larissa, Tommy and Jasmine. 'How often,' she said to them, 'have you woken up in the morning and looked out the window and seen just nothing but a low mist hanging over the park and maybe just a hint of the sun struggling to shine through it? And how often have you thought, *Oh, well, you can't see anything out there today?* Well – look again! Look at all you missed!'

'In the mist,' Alaric added.

They giggled. But they looked, too – for quite a long time.

'It's amazing, really,' Jasmine said at last.

'Cave painting,' Guy said knowingly, and looked to Eric for approval.

Marianne gave them a puzzled look but long experience of Eric discouraged her from pursuing the comment.

'How many paintings are hanging in this gallery?' Bruno asked the children in general.

'How many?' Alaric asked back, without bothering to count. 'I don't know. I'd estimate eighteen.'

Now Alaric counted. 'Twenty!'

'So that wasn't a bad estimate. And now you know what twenty looks like, you can make your own estimate when you get to the next gallery. And the next. Challenge yourself.'

'The Sutherland,' Eric said. 'We must see the Sutherland before we go to the Pre-Raphaelites.'

They traipsed back to the main hall, Marianne and her group in tow.

'It's vital for youngsters to get a practical grasp of numbers as early as possible,' Bruno told Eric and Faith. 'How many paintings? How many people? How big is this gallery? And so on.'

'Even if you don't know the answer?' Faith asked.

'It's not necessary. You'll stimulate them to measure the school hall, the gym, their classroom – and remember it as a sort of standard. It's important to lift the numbers off the page and stick them on real things out there.'

They were all stopped dead in their tracks by Francis Bacon's *Three Studies for Figures at the Base of a Crucifixion*.

'Oh, they've put this back up again,' Faith said. Nothing in her tone suggested she was happy to see it once more.

'Eeeurgh!' Alaric cried, at which several other children made noises of agreement.

'What d'you think, Bruno?' Faith asked.

His lips chewed at the answer before launching it: 'I'm not sure he's on the side of the angels.'

'Nor is Graham Sutherland,' Eric put in. 'Bacon has knocked him right off course. An older painter should never let a younger one share space in his studio. And look – they've hung the Colquhoun up beside it. This is the gritty corner, all right.'

'*Woman With Leaping Cat*,' Larissa read. 'Why would anyone want to paint that? She looks like a witch.'

'That's why the cat's leaping,' Alaric suggested.

Bruno peered at the date. 'Painted in nineteen forty-five!'

'You sound surprised,' Faith said.

'In nineteen forty-five British artists had been cut off from artistic developments in Europe – specifically, France – for the best part of six years. And yet . . .' He gestured at the picture. 'It's right up with the European *avant garde*. I find that most telling. It suggests that here was a movement with its own innate direction. And momentum. It did not feed off itself – or one artist off another. In the way that Sutherland has started feeding off Bacon.' He peered closely at the Colquhoun. 'When will the Tate buy its first McBryde, I wonder – talking of artists dining at each other's tables?'

'Eventually,' Alaric said, 'the whore gets tired of this and she says, "You don't need to keep on jumping at me. It hurts. We can just lie on the bed and do it the normal way". And the man says, "Hell to that! If you're gonna charge five quid, I'm gonna make a hole of my own".'

Tommy's snigger was loud enough to turn every head in that particular gallery – including Cynegonde's.

She came over to her son at once, dragging her little party in tow. 'Perhaps you will kindly share the cause of your merriment with the rest of us, Alaric?'

'All right,' he replied easily. 'A mother tells her little girl, "If you get dirt on this dress, I'll strangle you". And the little girl falls into a very muddy puddle – so her mother strangles her. That's all.'

Vivienne, Calley, and Virgil laughed; Cynegonde did not. 'That is both feeble and unfunny,' she said.

'It's a new kind of joke from America,' Alaric told her. 'They call them *sick* jokes.'

'Like at the crucifixion of Jesus,' Tommy chipped in, stretching his arms wide and horizontal. 'One of the other guys on the cross beside him turns to Jesus and says, "Hey buddy! This is some way to spend Easter, huh?"'

Cynegonde did not think it even faintly amusing but Tommy's acting was so comical that when a couple behind her laughed aloud she could not keep a straight face. 'Go on with you!' she said, turning away. 'You're dreadful – both of you.'

Ninety minutes proved the utter limit of The Tribe's aesthetic tolerance; no vote was needed to move them on to the Lyons Corner House at Charing Cross – the twenty-four-hour café on three floors. On the way out Bruno took his leave and said to Eric, 'I ran into Gombrich at the Courtauld a couple of weeks ago. He kindly gave me a draft of his inaugural lecture at the Slade, for comment. I don't think I'm free to send you the entire text but there is one sentence in it that you simply must see. You won't believe that it is, indeed, a single sentence – but it is. And it is also a perfect example of the German-speaking mind at work on the English language. I'll drop it off for you at Manutius.'

When Eric called in at Manutius the Tuesday following, what Faith called 'the sweet little dwarf' who acted as receptionist/switchboard girl (and satisfied the company's legal quota of employed cripples) handed him an envelope addressed to him in Bruno's unmistakable hand; inside it he found a typewritten slip that read:

```
It has always struck me as extraordinary that the
authorities which, by their parsimony, so starve the
British Museum of funds, thereby creating from it a
half-museum, with the one half open on Monday, the other
half on Tuesday, and the first half again on the
Wednesday, and so on, should at the same time spend so
lavishly on our defences against the 'poisonous evil'
(so called) of Marxism, little realizing that this
poison brew was, so to speak, cooked up within those
very walls and that, as so often in Nature, where the
poison lies, there also the antidote is not far to seek.
```

'Bullseye!' Eric said. 'Thank God for the Germans.'

Monday, 17 December 1956

Laboe, 13 December, 1956

Dear Felix and Angela,
    Yes, Tante Uschi and I would very much like to spend Christmas with you and the children this year. How they must have grown. Pippin seven already! And the new one, Susan – I hope she's sleeping through the night by now.
    We both continue in very good health, considering our age. Wartime starvation was probably very good for us – certainly there are many very well-fed people now in poorer health than either of us. The same with you and Angela, perhaps?

The time is so close now that I'll save our news and my opinions until we are together again. But there is something you might be able to do, meanwhile. You remember we discovered that old Billy Breit's sister Naomi, your great-aunt, married a Jew called Noam Finkel. And Billy never spoke to her again. Well, we've learned more about them since you last came to Laboe. They died in the Twenties but they had a son called Solomon, who survived the war in hiding in Berlin and now lives in Israel. His wife died in 1943, in Auschwitz (not so lucky as you two!). Solomon would be my first-cousin. And his son, Walter – who would be your second-cousin – married, in 1933 in Vienna, a Jewess called Rebekka Mandelstam. They were more far-sighted than most of us because, in 1934, she came to England to work as a translator at Reuters. Eight months later, also in 1934, Walter followed her and worked in finance until the war. After it, through his connections at Ullstein Verlag, I think, he got a place negotiating foreign rights at Odhams Press. The woman who told me this, an old school friend of Rebekka's, has lost touch, so maybe this is out of date.

Anyway, that's the background. The amazing thing is (we only heard this two weeks ago) that both are still alive and working in England. He is still at Odhams. She now works for the BBC World Service. Her old friend says they changed their name to Finch and she now spells herself Rebecca. So it's Walter and Rebecca Finch. She thinks they had three children, one of whom died. The other two – an older boy and a younger girl, would now be in their twenties. Early, mid, late? She doesn't know. Nor their names. But she does have their old address, which may still be right: 9, Oldgrove Gardens, West Hampstead (NW3). The nearest tube station is Finchley Road, she says.

Tante Uschi and I would love to meet them during our visit but they have taken such care to efface all trace of Germany in their identity that they might not welcome us out of the blue. Is it too much to ask of you – to approach them and see if they wouldn't mind our visiting them and reuniting these two strands of our family story?

If you think it is too much, please ignore this request. We'll 'screw our courage to the sticking point' and go there ourselves.

They may not even speak German still.
  Tante Uschi sends her love to you and Angela, and so do I,
  Vati
  I can send my own love – and I do!
  Tante Uschi

Felix folded his father's letter with a sigh.

'Heavy?' Angela asked.

'Premonitions.' He handed it to her.

She read it and put it back in its envelope. 'I think we Germans – and ex-Germans – are too sensitive. These Finkels or Finches are probably so British by now that Vati's scruples will just bewilder them.' When he did not reply she added: 'Would you like me to do it?'

'No! No, I'll do it, of course.'

'I could find some excuse to go down to Bush House and, come to think of it, Alex must know her.' She picked up the phone.

'Oh, don't!' Felix said.

'Alex? Angela here. Fine, thanks. Listen – do you know a woman at Bush House called Rebecca Finch? Oh, good! The thing is, Felix's father thinks she's . . . or, rather, her husband – Walter – is Felix's second cousin. He wants us to prepare the way for some kind of reunion when they come for Christmas. Could we drop over sometime this weekend and pick your brains? Are you sure? You're not in the middle of . . . OK. Very good of you. See you!' She cradled the handset. 'Come on. He's free now.'

A few minutes later they were in the cottage sitting room. 'I was in Fortnum's today,' Faith said, 'and they were selling these passion fruits, which I simply couldn't resist. Have you ever had them added to a G&T? It's *divine!*' She passed them a glass each. 'Alex says you've run down a long-lost cousin?'

'His wife is Rebecca Finch,' Alex said as the Breits settled on the sofa and sipped the passion-fruit G&T – and raised an appreciative eyebrow or two.

'Isn't it great?' Faith said. 'Who's Rebecca Finch?'

Alex replied: 'We sat next to her on deck for a while on the jaunt up the Thames to Hampton Court.'

'Ohmigod!' Faith said. 'That woman!'

'Oh dear!' Angela murmured.

'No!' Faith backtracked. 'Nothing bad. Just . . . I don't know. A bit creepy. We sat and chatted about nothing in particular – the way one does – and she she didn't say anything weird, but . . . nothing you could put your finger on . . . Except when we talked about our children – managing children and a career – I thought she'd say something about how lucky *we* are here. The way we all gain from *being* a community. But it was just a blank. I got the impression . . . *we* got the impression' – she glanced at Alex – 'that her children weren't top of her list.'

'That there wasn't *any* top or bottom of her list,' Alex put in. 'Just a Rolodex of items to be done and ticked, no matter where she started. As Faith says – it's hard to pin it down. Maybe you artistic types will have more luck. Cheers!'

Nothing ventured . . . Felix thought as he picked up the phone and asked the Hertford operator to get him the number – KILburn 4478.

'Yes? Four-four-seven-eight?' A woman's voice. She sounded perfectly English.

'Hello. Is that Mrs Finch? Mrs Rebecca Finch?'

'Who is this?'

'My name is Breit. Felix Breit. I wonder if it means anything to you, Mrs Finch?'

'The sculptor?'

'Yes.'

'I've heard of you – of course.' She was relaxing. 'In fact, I work for the BBC's overseas service, you know – and oddly enough, I subbed a piece about your show at the Whitechapel only last week. It's not about that, I hope?' A little nervous chuckle.

'No. I wish I'd heard it – I hope it was favourable?'

'Highly.'

'I was really calling to ask if my grandfather's name meant anything to you – Billy Breit, the painter?'

There was a long, sinew-tightening pause before she said, 'What d'you want, Mister Breit?'

'I won't beat about the bush,' Felix said, abandoning a pun he had half thought of making about Bush House. 'Your husband, Martin, and I are second cousins and so much of our family's history has been lost or destroyed—'

The phone went dead.

Angela came out of her studio. 'Well?'

'I'm in the book,' he said, picking up his maul and chisel. 'She can find me if she wants. I'm not going to hound the poor woman.'

Half an hour later the phone rang. 'Cousin Felix? This is your cousin, Martin. I think it's time we met.'

'I'd be delighted,' Felix told him. 'Mind you, I didn't even know you existed until a letter came from my father this morning.'

'Oh, really?' He seemed surprised.

'But you seem to have known of our kinship for some time?'

'We can talk about that when we meet. Up in town next week? Or – thinking of this petrol-rationing scare – this Wednesday? Our youngsters will be home – your second-cousins once-removed. You could meet them, too. You and your wife, of course – Angela, isn't it? I gather she and Becky both work for the BBC.'

Taking only baby Susan, then just three months old, they drove in through Hendon, Brent Cross, and down the Finchley Road to the point where combing through a maze of Victorian redbrick semi-detached mansionettes that were 'not quite Hampstead' brought them to number nine, Oldgrove Gardens – slightly posher than the rest with its pillared portico and carved-stone window reveals.

They parked outside and, since it would be lighting-up time in less than an hour, they plugged the lighting pod into the cigar-lighter socket and clamped it on the offside window.

'We've just bought one of those,' said a wiry, dark-haired man, striding towards them from the house. 'Cousin Felix – welcome! And . . . Angela? May I?'

'Of course . . . Martin.'

They shook hands all round.

'You're all right for petrol?' Martin asked.

'Yes, we stocked up last week, ahead of rationing. Tomorrow, isn't it?'

'Yep! Another fine mess that Eden got us into.'

Felix laughed. 'Well! Isn't this wonderful! To imagine that one has lost touch with almost all one's relatives, you know, and then to learn we've been living and working close enough to have passed each other many times without knowing it!'

'Do bring that poor baby in out of the cold!' Rebecca

– presumably – called from the portico, a svelte silhouette against the lighted hallway behind her.

Walter ushered them up the eight feet of a front garden path, saying, 'Isn't it ridiculous to be compelled to leave all the sidelights on in these little backwater suburban streets! The number of neighbours we have to help push-start each morning!'

'Oh, you shouldn't have!' Rebecca said as she accepted the bunch of Christmas roses the Breits had brought – 'from our own garden in Hertfordshire,' Angela explained.

'It's a very *Continental* custom – bringing flowers when you visit,' Martin remarked. 'But we notice it's catching on here, too – softening us up for the Common Market, eh!'

'And this is Wendy,' Rebecca said, 'and Harry. He's studying medicine at Saint Bart's. She's at Miss Harding's finishing school in Sloane Square.'

'Preparing for a life in the typing pool,' Wendy said, shaking hands and ignoring her mother's basilisk stare. 'What an angelic little baby! How old?'

'Born on the fourteenth of September.'

'Exactly three months tomorrow,' Walter said. 'Ninety-one days, counting both ends.'

'The accountant!' Rebecca said in a curious mixture of apology and pride.

'She's called Susan,' Felix said. 'Just losing that amazing blue colour in her eyes. We think they're going to be more turquoise than blue.'

'Enough about babies!' Angela said with theatrical weariness.

Wendy shot her a sharp glance, drew breath, opened her mouth, but said nothing; Felix noticed it, however, and – without quite knowing why – thought it significant. Their eyes met and she did that young-girl thing of nodding side to side and looking upward until her eyeballs went fleetingly white.

'Can we pop her behind the sofa?' Angela asked. 'I fed her and winded her on the way, so there's a good chance she'll drop off to sleep.'

'By all means.' Martin took one of the carrycot straps and helped Felix lower Susan into the dark well behind the sofa – where Felix spotted the latest edition of the *Wisden Cricketer's Almanac* with the Eric Ravilious woodcut on the cover.

'Oops!' Martin murmured as he retrieved it. '"Not a word to Bessie", eh!'

'Tea!' Rebecca gave a curt nod to her children, who immediately departed to the kitchen. 'Don't say anything significant while we're out there,' Wendy pleaded as they left. Rebecca raised both hands in a despairing gesture that was every bit as 'Continental' as bringing flowers when visiting. 'It's the maid's day off,' she explained.

'So much to cover,' Martin said. 'Where does one start?'

'Your father survived in hiding in the war?' Felix said. 'Like mine. We fell out – my father and I – in the thirties after my mother died in a boating accident – with old Billy Breit, in fact – so I lost touch with him. He married an old friend of theirs – Tante Uschi Schneider. We didn't make it up with each other until 'forty-seven.'

'Your father was Georg?'

'Er – George. Old Billy wanted Christian first names. Maybe that's why you're called Martin, too?'

'Well, my grandmother – Naomi Breit—'

'Old Billy's sister,' Felix said.

'Yes – though *he* was first named Solomon, you know.'

'Which is the name she gave to your father! Your grandmother was spitting in the eye of old Billy, eh?'

'I suppose so. He never spoke to her again. I never knew the old fellow died with your mother. And in a boating accident. Was she Jewish?'

'No. Lutheran – Ursula Winkler from the Taunus. Born a Lutheran but a born-again atheist by the time she met my father. He had no religion, either. Both of them reacting against fiercely Protestant upbringings.'

'Yes.' Martin pulled a face and, glancing at his wife, said, 'Something like that happened with me. I was reared very Orthodox – bar mitzvah . . . the works. But when we came to England we shed all that. Changed the name to Finch, got baptized into the Church of England. In fact, I'm a sidesman at Saint John's Wood High. On my way to becoming a deacon.'

'Though we sometimes go to the French Church in Soho Square,' Rebecca said. 'Just for the language, you know. What about you, Angela?'

She grinned. 'There's a dearth of Lutheran churches in Hertfordshire, fortunately. Actually, I'm as agnostic as Felix but without the parental baggage.'

There was a silence and then Martin said, 'We were so afraid that Germany would win the war. I think most English people were, too, at the outbreak in 'thirty-nine.'

'Was your conversion a matter of deliberate policy?'

Martin looked at Rebecca and she looked at him; eventually she broke their silence. 'In the beginning, yes. But we pretended so ardently that, well . . . the Anglican Church . . . Anglican faith . . . it's . . . how can I put it?'

'It doesn't intrude much between Monday and Saturday?' Angela suggested. 'And it has plenty of room for agnostics? In fact, I quite like going to Matins in our local church in Dormer Green. I love that old-fashioned language. "Erred and strayed like lost sheep" . . . "the devices and desires of our own hearts" . . .'

'"Make clean our hearts within us",' Rebecca murmured.

'In fact,' Martin said excitedly, 'you've just reminded me of the actual moment when I had my own Supper-at-Emmaus moment' – he pointed to a reproduction of *Christ at Emmaus* hanging above the fireplace – 'and that was from something in the Book of Common Prayer. The Second Collect for Peace. I heard the vicar say, "Defend us thy humble servants in all assaults of our enemies; that we, surely trusting in thy defence, may not fear the power of any adversaries".' He glanced at his wife. 'Did I ever tell you this?'

She shook her head, blinked, and sniffed.

'That was the moment when I said to myself, "Yes! Even if Hitler wins the war and the Nazis govern here, *this* is the faith that will protect and defend us!" The power of words, eh! Of course, Hitler knew all about that power, too.'

The rattle of the tea trolley out in the hall preceded the youngsters' return.

'What are you talking about?' Wendy asked as she backed into the room, guiding the leading end of the trolley.

When neither of her parents answered, Felix said, 'The Book of Common Prayer.'

'Oh, good!' she said. 'I was so afraid it might be something important.'

Angela glanced at Rebecca; the basilisk stare was back again. To fill the silence she asked, 'What would *you* consider important, Wendy?'

'Milk in first or milk in last?' she replied. 'Will it rain tomorrow? Shall we have a white Christmas? Lots of burning questions of the day.'

'That's enough,' Martin said quietly.

'Milk in first, please,' Angela said.

'Is genealogy important?' Felix asked Wendy. 'To you?'

'Only to get it straight and then put it to one side,' she told him as she passed Angela her tea. 'We've got most of it – mainly through stuff we read about you in the papers. But what about your father, George – there's been nothing about him.'

Martin looked across at his wife, who went on staring impassively at the fire. He said, 'We've covered that. I'll tell you both later.'

'What I didn't tell you,' Felix put in, 'was that he wrote to me last week accepting an invitation to spend Christmas with us – which *we*, Miss Wendy – living as we do in the depths of rural Hertfordshire – sincerely hope will be anything *but* white. And in that same letter he said he'd dearly love to meet all of you – so perhaps this is the moment to ask you if you'd like to join us on the eve of Christmas Eve – the twenty-third, in other words – when we hold open-house to the community. A week today. We're still European enough to think Christmas Eve is more important than Christmas Day.'

And then, naturally, Angela and he had to explain what 'the community' meant – which ended Rebecca's reverie and had the two youngsters accepting the invitation before their parents could hem and haw.

'You were in one of those concentration camps, I gather?' Harry said, handing round a plate of ham and cress sandwiches. 'Mauthausen, was it?'

'Harry!' his mother said sharply. 'Really!'

'It was in the papers, Mother.' To Angela: 'Or would you prefer cake?'

Felix glanced at Martin, who shrugged and said, 'I know – why didn't *we* get in touch with *you* since we knew you survived and could easily have found you? I suppose there's a kind of guilt in—'

'I say, Father!' Harry was now embarrassed.

'Just you be quiet,' Martin told him. 'We got out early, Rebecca and I. We didn't stay and fight when there was just the slimmest chance that fighting might have prevented . . . what happened later. We weren't refugees. We both went into good jobs. We managed to get out with a tidy sum. My father refused . . . was too proud to join us while he could. He survived the war in hiding but my mother was caught and she died in the one called Auschwitz.' He smiled apologetically at Felix and Angela. 'It might have seemed somewhat triumphalist of us to get in touch with you? No? But I can tell you this now – the moment *you* picked up the phone to get in touch with *us* – that was one of the happiest of my life. I hope our fears were misplaced – well, obviously they were – but we acted out of respect for your possible feelings.'

'In your place, I'm sure I'd have felt the same. I'm less sure, mind, that I'd have had the self-discipline to act on it. Angela was in a KL, too, you know.'

'Car-ell-two?'

'Ka-El – *Koncentrationslager*. She was in Ravensbrück.'

'Are you Jewish?' Rebecca asked in surprise.

'No. I was Political. The red triangle.' She patted her arm.

'A German – *you* fought! Jews – and *we* fled!'

'That's absurd!' Felix said.

Wendy added her voice, rounding on her mother: 'You did no more than tens of millions of British, Irish, Italians, Swedes – *and* other Germans – have done for centuries. You went to a better country for a better life. You left when the Nazis were just another party in the Weimar Republic – before Hitler was even chancellor. You did *not* flee – you just emigrated to better jobs.'

From behind the couch came straining noises, a muffled fart, and a giggle that might have been the start of some crying. 'Oh, dear!' Angela said. 'Is there somewhere I can go and change her?'

Wendy took her upstairs to the bathroom.

'What did they do with the two of you in the war?' Felix asked. 'A publisher I work for – a German Jew – got thrown into an internment camp, in a hut full of Nazi sympathizers. The British had no idea! It was only for a few weeks, mind. Then they employed his publishing skills in the propaganda war.'

'I met him then,' Rebecca said. 'Wolf Fogel? I worked at Reuters until the war and then they directed me to Bush House, where I worked on black propaganda under . . .' She hesitated.

'I wonder if I can say his name now? I suppose I can. He went out to manage radio in India and then came back to Bush House. But he's just resigned over Suez.'

'Alex Findlater,' Felix said. 'That's amazing! You'll actually meet him on Christmas Eve. He and his wife are our nearest neighbours in the community. She's Wolf Fogel's right-hand man. What a small world, eh?' He waited for her to remember the boat trip up the Thames but she obviously didn't.

Martin said, 'I had no such luck. It seems the British security people would trust a native German with information and propaganda but not with money, which is my speciality. I worked at Barings' until the outbreak, then I tried to join the Army Pay Corps but they put me in a reserved occupation proofreading telephone directories out at the printing works in Watford. Six bloody years proofreading telephone directories! But it gave me the time to study and become a chartered accountant and I picked up a lot of printing know-how on the job, so I more or less fell into the accounts and contracts department at Odhams – of which I am now head.'

'In one way,' Felix said as Angela and Wendy returned, 'I wish we had been in touch with each other earlier – I wish I'd known your father's address in Israel when I went there in nineteen fifty.'

'I wish you had, too. You might have been able to persuade him to come and live here instead. I know he's not happy there but he's too stubborn to admit it.'

'But at least the climate is good for his arthritis,' Rebecca countered. 'He'd be miserable here, too. You can't live in rat-infested cellars for five years and not . . .' Horrified, she glanced at Felix and Angela. 'Oh, my runaway tongue! I'm really sorry.'

Angela looked at Wendy, who was struggling to hide a smile. Felix laughed and said, 'You're right, Rebecca. It *is* more than humans are meant to endure – but some of us did – and have found serenity. Of a kind.'

'Give or take a nappy change or two,' Angela said grimly. 'Listen, Susan's just a bit fretful. It can't possibly be teething but she's got that flushed cheek and watery eye. I hope she's not going down with a cold. Anyway, I think we ought to start making tracks.'

'I'll have a look.' Harry became professional at once. He felt Susan's brow, furled up an eyelid, felt the pulse in her neck and said, 'I think the fire may be to blame. It depletes the oxygen and increases the CO_2 in the room – and a baby lying at floor level would be the first to feel it. I think that's all it is.'

And so, reassured, and with protestations of delight at having met at last – and yes, it was only a week before they'd all be together again – they parted.

'Ham sandwiches!' Felix said as they made their way back up West End Lane.

'Certainly nailing *their* colours to the mast.'

'And you saw that reproduction hanging over the fireplace?'

'The *Supper at Emmaus*? It's a fake, isn't it – the original, I mean? Faked by that Dutch artist who faked lots of Vermeers and sold one to Goering.'

'Yes. Han van Meegeren. They must *know* it's a fake, surely? But he pointed it out as if it were genuine – the artistic embodiment of his own conversion to Christianity. How could he *not* know it's a fake – it was in the papers for months during the trial? He's a dark horse – Martin. But I must say – as regards Rebecca – I didn't see any of that sort of creepiness Faith was talking about.'

'Well . . . Wendy was trying to tell me something when I was changing Susan. I could feel her working up to it and . . . I don't know – either not having the courage or the time? I don't know.'

'What *did* she say, then?'

Angela shrugged. 'Chatter. Nappy folding and pinning. Why milk-fed babies' shit doesn't smell as bad as grown-ups'. She asked me which was our nearest station – which didn't strike me as odd until we were back downstairs. Surely they'll come by car? He said they're OK for petrol.'

Friday, 21 December 1956

The following Friday, just after lunch, the phone rang in the Tithe Barn.

'I'll get it,' Felix called.

'Mister Breit?' A woman's voice, youngish, vaguely familiar. 'This is Wendy – Wendy Finch.'

'Of course! I thought I recognized—'

'I'm terribly sorry about this. I looked up the buses and everything. I had it all taped and then the train was late and the bus didn't wait. I'm at Hertford North. Is it far to walk?'

'Depends on your shoes, Wendy. I'll come and get you – it'll only take ten minutes or so.'

'Oh, but I didn't mean to—'

'Not to worry. I can kill two birds with one stone. One thing you *can* do is walk up the hill by the station to meet me at the top. Turn left under the bridge and immediately left again up the hill. There's an off-licence at the top, across the road. I'll meet you there.'

'Who?' Faith asked from the doorway of her sound-studio.

He shrugged and raised his hands in bewilderment. 'Wendy Finch. Obviously wants to pay us a call before they come on Sunday. I'll get the booze while I'm at it.'

She was waiting outside the off-licence, hatless, in an unfashionable burgundy-red gabardine raincoat with parachute pleats at the back. Her smile was broad when she recognized him but there was a certain tremulousness about her, too. She recovered a little while Felix stocked up with the liquor for the party – and a lot more when he said, 'You're a great help, Wendy. But,' he added as he held open the car door for her, 'I hope you don't bring bad news?'

'Oh – nothing like that, no,' she replied. 'But I'm glad you came alone because it's really you I want to talk to. I want to tell you about my mother before we all come out on Sunday.'

He started the car. 'Perhaps we'll go back the long way round, then. Fire away.'

After a tense silence, she said, 'Do I have to start at the *very* beginning or . . . I mean, did you and Mrs Breit notice anything odd about my mother last Sunday?'

'That's a bit of an awkward question, Wendy.'

'But I mean it seriously. Honestly. Did you?'

'Slightly,' Felix admitted. 'Faith, our neighbour, met your mother on a Bush House jaunt up the river and told her all about our community. Yet when we described it again last Sunday, there was no apparent recognition. That did strike us as a *bit* odd.'

Wendy said tonelessly, 'When you get to know her, it won't seem odd at all.'

They turned into Thieves Lane and started on the downhill run to Hertingfordbury. Wendy continued: 'What you've just said is only a small part of what I want to explain. It's so much bigger than that. Mother cannot cope with any deep emotions. She can cry at a novel or a weepy film, get angry with . . . well, just about anything.'

'Like dropping a copy of Wisden behind the sofa?'

Wendy laughed. 'You saw that! Yes – poor Daddy. She could sympathize with us when we banged our head or cut our knees. All the surface emotions of daily living – fine! But anything deep . . . relationships . . . there seems to be a sort of fuse, a cut-off point. And then she just freezes and goes into a sort of automatic mode. I think she's guilty about having escaped. So guilty she just . . .'

'Escapes again?' Felix suggested. 'Into herself?'

'Yes!'

They left the village and started on the long climb south of Panshanger, up to Cole Green.

'We came past all these houses on the train,' she murmured.

Felix said, 'Guilt! I thought my art was all-important. Much more important than worrying about a few Jews getting roughed up on the streets.'

'And Angela?'

He shrugged. 'Similar.'

Silence. He slowed down to take the turn.

'It's got worse with us now,' she said at last. 'So when Harry or me do something she really disapproves of, she doesn't know how to deal with it so she just clams up. She can't cut us out of her life, of course, but she just stops talking to us. It's even more than simply not talking. Way beyond not talking. She completely not *interacts*. She'll be standing by the washing machine and I'll hand her a slip or a blouse and she'll leap backwards as if she's been stung and I just have to plonk it on top of the machine and walk away. I've tried throwing my arms around her and hugging her and kissing her – and she doesn't resist, she just turns into a block of ice.' After a lengthy pause, she added: 'She and I haven't spoken much all year, in fact.'

'And what does she object to so strongly?' he asked.

'I don't want to go to that typing college. I want to go to Saint Martins or the Central. I want to do textile design.' She unbuttoned her raincoat to reveal her dress. 'I printed this myself at the Camden Town Working Men's College and—'

'Ha! Angela went there before we were married. Evening classes.'

'Yes. For me, that was a six-week freeze-out.'

The dress pattern was made up of those spiky-organic motifs that were all the rage at the Festival of Britain, five years ago. Felix wondered if someone who was that unaware of changes in fashion could ever make a career in textile design. 'I have to turn for home at this next junction,' he warned.

'I think I know why she does it,' she said. 'But it sounds crazy. *You* don't ever have . . . I mean, you don't have emotions or emotional situations that just make you freeze and when you look inside yourself, there's nothing to see? Do you have hollows inside you where there should be emotions, is what I'm getting at?'

Only someone as young as her . . .

Or as emotionally starved as her?

Or as close to her wit's end?

Dear God! I should have done a course in mine-clearance. 'No,' he said. 'And before you ask it, nor does Angela.'

'You're sure? Because she seemed pretty offhand with Susan last Sunday and I thought – oh no, *please* don't let it be like Mother!'

All Felix could do was laugh – not unkindly. 'Believe me, Wendy, when you've had four babies of your own, *you'll* be pretty blasé and offhand about the cow's tail, too.'

Her smile was like a flash of sunshine. 'That's all it is? You're sure?'

'That's all it is. And yes, I'm sure.'

'Phew! That was my biggest worry. You don't mind me asking? You're not offended, I hope?'

He risked a laugh. 'Funnily enough, Wendy, I've only known you a few hours, all told, and yet – of all the people I know in all the world – you are the very last one who would offend me by inquiries of this nature.'

'You won't tell Angela that I asked?'

'Get on with it.'

She swallowed audibly. 'It's the war. The *bloody* war. To them, art school represents anarchy. But typing school is serious business. Artists are the most disposable people – as I don't need to tell *you*. But every administration, democratic or totalitarian, needs typists. Survivability! That's Mother's only measure of value, and Daddy's, too, to a lesser extent: will it help survive another invasion or revolution in which unwanted people can just be swatted down?' She was panting now, quite hard. 'Well?'

He pulled the car over, just beyond the entrance to Panshanger airfield. 'I believe you, Wendy. But what can I or anyone else – even you and Harry – actually *do* about it? They are as they are. And at their age, d'you think—'

'Don't cut them,' she said. 'Don't drop them – please! You and Mrs Breit actually endured what—'

'Angela, please. We are kin.'

'You and Angela actually endured what they fled from and you haven't just survived, you've rebuilt your lives in a way my parents have never managed to do. I don't mean . . . I'm not asking that you and they live in each other's pockets. But just don't drop them when their caution and negativeness . . . negativity? Anyway, when it comes to the surface. Which it will. If they can see how you two have—'

'What if *they* drop *us*? What if our successful restart – such as it is – seems to accuse them and they can't face it?'

After a long, lip-chewing pause, she said, 'How successful *have* you been, then?'

'Whooo!'

'I'm sorry. Look – you can drive me back to the station now. I can't say more than I have already.'

'No – certainly not. But that's the one question no one has ever asked. Ever. Even I haven't asked it of Angela – though I have wondered sometimes. And she's never asked it of me. But perhaps it *should* be asked – especially if we are to help my cousin and his wife in the way you suggest. You can't polish glass with a hot marshmallow, as Tommy Handley once pointed out.' He pressed the starter button. 'Home! Before Angela sends out a search party.'

As they freewheeled down the rest of the hill to Poplars Green, he said, 'You see how this road runs in an almost complete semi-circle between Cole Green and here? Originally, back in Tudor times, it ran straight, but in the eighteenth century whoever was lord of the manor at Panshanger decided he didn't want it running through his private parkland so he pushed it out to the boundary and put up a wall. And the locals had to accept it because he was the lord of the manor and that was an unalterable fact of life. They just had to get on with it.'

She reached over and squeezed his arm. 'You're a very good person, Felix.'

Not for the first time – nor even for the hundredth – he wondered if late-teenage girls ever realized what effect their very presence had on men of his age. Men of any age, actually.

'What a little terrier!' Angela said when Felix came home after dropping Wendy back to Hertford North that evening.

'A cross between a terrier and a bulldog,' he replied. 'But she'll have to smarten up her fashion sense if she's going to make any headway in textile design. I told her that if she got together a portfolio, I know someone who'd show it to Miss Batty at the Central – Terence Conran's teacher. Except that Conran created himself – too much in demand even to finish his studies! Perhaps she should show her stuff to Isabella first. I'm sure she wouldn't accept my word for it that she's trailing a bit behind the times.'

'What about her other question – survival? While you were on the phone I told her you don't grow healthy plants if you keep on digging them up to inspect the roots.'

He nodded, his gaze fixed on some cattle out in the park. 'All the same . . . can't help wondering from time to time.'

'But how would you measure survival success? Commissions for sculptures? Lectures? Teaching? You pass, flying. Psychosomatic disorders? You haven't complained. Unless farting is psychosomatic. Andrew thinks it's exquisitely funny that in German you're his *Vater*!'

He cocked his thumb and fired his index finger at her.

'Seriously,' she went on. 'D'you get nightmares? Are you ever back in Mauthausen in your dreams?'

He shrugged. 'Maybe I should be? Who knows. Dreams may be a way of ab . . . ab . . . what's the word? Of cleansing the psyche. Like lancing a boil. Just about the only time it crosses my mind these days is when I see Germano at Manutius. He's getting a lot of freelance work these days. Marvellous stuff. And so he should. But we never talk about it – about those days.'

But "those days" do "cross your mind" when you see him. How? In what form? What precisely?'

'Not *Mauthausen* – not the whole camp. Or camps. Just one hut. Or one small section of the roll-call. Something like that. I see friends who died. I think of them. It's almost like a duty.'

'But no actual image? I mean, an image of an actual event?'

He closed his eyes and there was a long silence – which she did not break – before he said, 'One. Only one. My first day there. Carrying twenty-five-kilo stones up the Stairs of Death – the Stair for Angels – from the quarry up to the stonemasons. I only managed it because I counted them each time. Going up and going down again. Obsessively. And in fact, even after liberation I couldn't break the habit of counting every set of stairs I ever went up or down. "Eleven, twelve, thirteen. These of cast iron. Four, five, six. These of wood", and so on. But on that first day there was a young lad in front of me, about seventeen. Starved. Probably had TB. His shoes disintegrated on his first ascent. Made of cardboard. He only got halfway up. He fell backwards into the grass beside the steps, clutching the stone, which fell on top of him and broke his ribs. And he lay there, unconscious, with such a beautiful smile, blood oozing out of the corner of his mouth, breathing erratically, very shallow breathing. No one dared stop, of course. The guards didn't even bother to finish him off. Next time I saw him, on the way back down . . . *kaput*! But still that smile on his lips. It haunted me for the next year, that smile, because it seemed to promise that death would be such a beautiful . . . thing. You could just go on smiling, smiling. Poor little bastard.'

'But you never yielded to the seduction. What the smile seemed to promise.'

He shook his head. 'What about you?'

'I *remember* everything. At the time it was what kept me going – to remember everything so as to give evidence against them. As if I was an undercover policeman, sent back from the future. And a fat lot of good that was! Their own meticulous record-keeping hanged them anyway. But I've already told you my one memory above all others – the day Milena Jesenská died in the camp hospital – how the entire camp, Jews, gypsies, queers, Jehovah's Witnesses, politicals – everyone – felt it as a personal loss to them. That was inspiring. That a single death still had the power to move us, despite . . . everything else.'

'I've just had a thought,' he said. 'Shall we go out for a walk – just as far as the gate lodge? Are you in the middle of anything?'

'I'm *always* in the middle of *anything*,' she said as she went to fetch their duffel coats and boots, 'struggling to reach the end of *something*!'

The sky was a cloudless indigo and there was no breeze. The late December sun reached almost horizontally through the bare branches of the beeches and limes that, in summer, made a tunnel of the end of the drive; now it trapped them in a torn lacework of fine shadows. The unforgettable, unforgotten reek of fungus and wet moss filled their nostrils. Beyond the railings a cow gave a sudden explosive cough. Another cow, in another lifetime, had once done that – and covered Felix from shoulder to ankle in green diarrhoea, a serious matter when you're on the run and in hiding.

A gray squirrel took provisional fright and skittered up one of the limes. Felix put his arm around Angela's shoulder and kissed her warmly on the cheek.

'What's *that* for all of a sudden?' she asked, blushing and pleased.

'Because I can,' he told her. 'Also – look above us.'

'A squirrel?' Her gaze traversed the branch. 'Oh – that!'

'That' was a large bunch of mistletoe that several Dower House men had chickened out of harvesting for several Christmases past, what with the slenderness of the branch and the age of the lime.

'What was the thought that struck you just now – back home?'

He had to think, to replay a little of their conversation there. 'Oh! I was wondering if having survived *inside* the camps might not have advantages over having survived *outside* them. Thinking of Vati, you know? We each went on the run in almost identical ways but he escaped to safety in Sweden and I got betrayed down in Vichy. Really he ought to feel proud, but – hearing all this from Wendy about her parents – I wonder if escape is such a wonderful thing, after all?'

The muffled roar of a badly silenced motorbike drew a sonic line along the road at the bottom of the valley. Above it, on the far hillside, a light aircraft left a more visible trail of over-rich exhaust as it took off from the airfield and rose steeply over the public golf course. Angela halted and turned about. In Pagets Wood, behind them, a colony of rooks was arguing the nightly settlement of branches and decaying nests. A little more to the left the massive bulk of the Dower House, darkened by half-a-dozen lighted windows, squatted between the trees that overhung the cottage and the runaway yews of a once-clipped hedge. Toys were being packed away, televisions switched off, tea-towel turbans from the nativity play ironed, stock pots were bubbling, vegetables were peeling; in the Tithe Barn, Gisela was running an elbow-tested hot bath beneath a blanket of Matey foam – 'it cannot harm your baby's eyes'. And every flat had a secret hoard of Christmas presents and all those things that Father Christmas had yet to bring.

'I really don't want to think about it any more, darling,' she said.

Sunday, 23 December 1956

Calley, now eight, was old enough and dextrous enough to be entrusted with the drying-up after dinner – even the precious Indian Tree service, which had the coral-red colours that Faith said were almost as good as the lost red the Persians had invented by grinding up real coral. The distinction between real and . . . well, *not*-real was starting to bother her lately, sparked by her role as an Eskimo woman in the school nativity play. ('My name is Nanook. I chew the sealskins and make them soft . . .' etc.)

'Isabella?' she said, carefully but firmly grasping the meat dish that cost over three pounds.

'Yes, darling.'

'If you were an actor on the—'

'Actress.'

'Yes. If we were on the stage – two actresses – playing a mother and daughter doing the—'

'It wouldn't take much acting – we *are* mother and daughter.'

'Yes, but if we weren't . . . no! Even if we were. Let's say we're a *real-life* mother and daughter who *happen* also to be actresses and we get this part in a play where—'

'These parts – there are two of us, so it's plural.'

'Yes-yes. We get *these parts* where there's a scene where we have to do the washing up. And—'

'Are we servants? Who else is in the play? Could we have a buffoon? You know how your father hates to be left out of things.'

'I can also do a very sober and upright and profound Hanging Judge,' Eric called out from the butler's pantry, where he was trying to get Ruth off to sleep.

'*Shuttup-bothofyou!*' Calley screamed. 'All I want to know is this. If a real-life mother and daughter get hired for a play where they have to *play* a mother and daughter and if there's a scene where they have to wash up real dishes with real hot water and soap and dry them with a real drying-up cloth – then what is *acting* and what is *real*? That's all.'

'All?' Eric said in a horrified voice as he came back to the kitchen. 'All? You ask a question that would keep a parliament of the world's greatest philosophers disputing for a year and a day – and you say that's *all*?'

'I don't see the slightest difficulty,' Isabella said calmly.

'Of *course* you don't, darling,' Eric agreed.

'Actors are always doing *real* things as part of their act – they smoke cigarettes . . . scratch their heads . . . pour out drinks even though we know the drinks aren't really alcoholic—'

'Oh, don't spoil the magic!' Eric pleaded. 'What about when they kiss passionately – even though we know, because it's in all the gossip columns, that they're not even on speaking terms offstage. Is the kiss *real*? What *is* a kiss? Is it just the physical contact of two pairs of lips – as we might say that one billiard ball *kisses* another? Or does it involve . . .'

'Oh, God – he's off!' Isabella said to Calley. '*Now* see what you've started!'

'. . . the emotional impetus towards approximating those four lips as well. The philosophical distinction we like to make between the mental and the physical is no more than a matter of convenience. Because every change in our mental state must involve a physical – specifically, a chemical – change in the brain.'

'Bruno does these things so much better,' Isabella told her washing-up mop. 'Are you listening to this?' she asked Calley. 'Or just acting listening?'

'Just acting listening,' the girl replied in a stage whisper.

'Very commendable!' Eric was unperturbed. 'Most of life is just a matter of acting the expected reality – if you think about it. By the way, are you and Ruth absolutely sure you want fish fingers for dinner on Christmas Day?'

'Yes!' Calley answered eagerly. 'And peas and chips.'

'Yes!' Ruth shouted from her bunk in the butler's pantry. 'And tomato ketchup.'

'And' – Calley was determined to have the last word – 'Instant Whip for pudding, too.'

'Certainly not! Christmas pudding is not negotiable.'

'Instant Whip *and* Christmas pudding, then.'

'OK. That settles it. Isabella and I will have *filet mignon*. Or *boeuf en croûte* washed down with plenty of *Chateau Beausejour*.' He cocked an ear for a contradiction and got none.

'What made Ruth cry?' Isabella asked when Calley was changing for the Breits' Christmas-Eve-eve party.

'God,' he said.

'Yes. But specifically.'

'She said she didn't want to go to Limbo. And I asked who said she's going to Limbo? And she said Mister Burnham said it's where all people who haven't been baptized go. I couldn't say the man is talking through his hat, could I!'

'So what did you say?'

'I told her Limbo wasn't all that bad – just a teeny bit boring at times – rather like Surrey, only a lot bigger. And that seemed to satisfy her.'

'So I've got this idea for a new game,' Calley told Vivienne and Samantha at the Breits' party. 'Everything we do . . . we don't just *do* it, instead we do it *as if* we're doing it!'

'Super!' said Vivienne, who hadn't really taken it in. 'How?'

'It doesn't make sense,' Samantha objected.

'We *act* everything instead of doing it for real. When we go to school, we act *as if* we're going to school. When we do ballet on Saturdays, we don't just *do* ballet – we *act as if* we're doing ballet. See?'

'You're loopy,' Vivienne said, having cottoned on finally. 'What's the difference between doing something and acting as if you're doing it?'

'Don't you see?' Samantha tapped her temple. 'It's here. The difference is up here. I like it. I vote we resign from The Tribe and form our own club called, er . . . the As-Iffers.'

'No!' Calley insisted. 'We mustn't break up The Tribe. But the boys have their own Smoking Set—'

'Silly Joke set,' Vivienne said.

'Same thing. So we can have our own Actress Set.'

'What if any boys want to join?' Samantha asked.

Calley thought about it. 'All right – the As If Set.'

'What's that when it's at home?' Maynard flipped a salted peanut into the air and caught it in his open jaws like a dog. He turned at last to look at them.

'Were you listening?' Calley asked.

'Maybe.'

'While pretending to look at Felix's sculpture?' Samantha said.

He tossed his head awkwardly. 'Could have been doing both.'

Samantha turned to the other two girls. 'I think he's already a member – he just doesn't know it.'

'I do. We do it all the time – think of one thing and do another.'

'No!' Calley insisted. 'Do everything as if you're an actor doing it. If an actress darns a sock on the stage, she does everything right. She does really darn the sock. But she's *acting* darning a sock. She sits there doing it as if she's *really* doing it. Now d'you see? We As-Iffers are pledged to do everything *as if* we're really doing it. Now d'you see?'

Eric, who had been hovering near, said, 'Is it all right if Maynard acts *as if* he understands you?'

'Go away!' Calley shouted at him, laughing. Then she saw the point and added: 'Yes! As long as he really does understand. People can only be As-Iffers if they really are doing what they're doing *as if* they're doing it.'

'You *are* loopy!' Maynard flipped another peanut, caught it, and drifted away.

'It's not really a game for boys,' Samantha said wistfully.

'Not boys of his age,' Eric agreed as he, too, moved away.

'Your German is still perfect,' Vati told Martin Finch. 'I can understand it in your case, Frau Finch, but do you speak it at home?'

'Never!' Rebecca told him.

Martin said, 'I got terribly rusty until I went into publishing. It has advantages there, obviously. So' – he laughed as if he still hardly believed it – 'I, a native-born German, went to German evening classes! But I soon got it all back.'

'Still not spoken at home?'

Rebecca shook her head. 'We have been English since nineteen thirty-five, Cousin Georg.' After a pause she added: 'But it doesn't make us any less kinsfolk of yours, of course. Felix says you managed to hide in Denmark in the war.'

'Ah yes. Sweden, finally. Before he and I met again – we didn't get reunited until after the war, in 'forty-seven. Before that, I was afraid of meeting him again. Not only because we had some stupid quarrel back in the thirties but . . . well, we both went on the run. He was making for Switzerland and was betrayed and I made for Denmark and was . . . luckier. I felt guilty at succeeding!' He gave a dry laugh. 'And poor Felix feels guilty – a bit – maybe less and less as time goes on – but guilty that he got put on a medical experiment that saved his life. So that was a kind of escape, too – when so many of his friends died. Guilt! Do we all have to feel guilt for *something*? In our blood, perhaps?'

Rebecca was about to reply but Martin cut in: 'Actually, just look around here. I don't know about your home in . . . Laboe, isn't it? But we have a very run-of-the-mill four-storey house in West Hampstead and very nice run-of-the-mill friends. But just look around you here, and wouldn't you say that of all of us, Felix and Angela have come out on top? All these amazing friends? And this amazing community!'

Vati leaned towards her. 'Don't ever say I said so, but the one fly in the ointment for me is that awful "concrete" music Angela plays. What is it? Just noises!'

★   ★   ★

'D'you think Willard's getting more English than the English?' Faith asked. 'Three years ago I chaperoned him for a hunt with the East Herts. And now he's standing for election as master.'

'Shoes from Codner, Coombs, and Dobbie in Jermyn Street,' Marianne said. 'Shirts and ties from Turnbull and Asser nearby, suits from Anderson and Sheppard in Savile Row.' She giggled. 'I drive him mad because I go to Marks and Sparks and Aquascutum.'

'You left out the guns from Purdy.'

'That, too.'

'Oh,' Faith went on. 'Talking of South Audley Street – we've taken a ninety-nine-year lease on number forty-seven, from the Grosvenor Estate. It has the most wonderful Art Deco lift.'

'You're not moving away?' Cynegonde edged in, not quite between them.

'Sorry, dear – no! It's a bit like the Robert Street flat for the Breits – only a damn sight more expensive. We can entertain there, use it as a pied-à-terre after theatre nights and' – she lowered her voice – 'convene meetings we'd rather our present colleagues knew nothing about.'

'There's no loyalty anywhere these days,' Cynegonde said. 'Denis is talking of joining this anti-apartheid movement. I know you both approve of that but I can forgive you because you're ignorant. He's not. He grew up there. We both grew up there. We had wonderful Native servants who were really our friends. But that's all they're fit for – servants. If those Natives ever come into power the place will be wrecked, I tell you. They don't think like us. Still, it's Christmas. I mustn't—'

'How *do* they think, Cynegonde?' Marianne asked.

'I can give you a very simple example,' she replied. 'Simple but striking. How tall is Siri, now? Very tall for her age, isn't she?'

'Hybrid vigour, they call it. She's a hundred and forty-two centimetres.'

'Oh, God, how tall is that? No, don't bother, just show me – with your hand.'

Marianne held out her hand, roughly level with her breast.

'You see!' Cynegonde said excitedly. 'You hold your hand horizontally. So high! But if you were a Native, you'd hold it like this.' She stretched out her arm with the hand held vertically, thumb-up. 'No white person would do it like that. You see! It's a fundamental difference between our brains and theirs.'

Marianne had to turn away but Faith, who managed to keep a straight face, said, 'Have you tried this question on Tommy Marshall?'

'But he's not a Native – he's American, or half American.'

'He's black. Coffee-coloured, anyway.'

Cynegonde was baffled. 'But I'm not talking about skin colour. I've got no *colour* prejudice, for God's sake. I'm talking about the Bantu – Xhosa, Swazi, Zulu . . . the *native* South African. Say what you like, their minds *are* different. I'd never say inferior – just different.'

Alaric, keeping down his voice so that the other boys had to lean inward to hear him at all, said, 'So this whore eventually gets tired of it and says, "You don't have to keep taking a running jump at me. We can go over there and lie on the bed and do it gently". "Hell to that!" the man says. "If you're going to charge five quid, I'm going to make a hole of my own!"'

Their loud guffaws were quickly subdued by urgent signals from Alaric. Tony, who had been eavesdropping nearby, drifted off; he'd heard it before – before the war, indeed. He threaded his way towards Nicole, who looked somewhat beleaguered by Willard and Terence.

'And now it's martial law!' Willard was saying.

'Mass arrests,' Terence added. 'A total military clampdown. If the toiling Hungarian masses are so grateful to be rescued by the Red Army, it's a quaint way of rewarding their gratitude, don't you think?'

Nicole shot a weary glance at the ancient hammerbeams. 'If the entire proletariat rose up, there wouldn't be room for a single tank on the streets. It's obviously a much smaller element, deluded by propaganda from the Voice of America – which is now the voice of Alex Findlater – and the BBC and spurred on by *agents provocateurs* who . . . you see that woman talking with Felix's father? Her husband is Felix's second-cousin. They're German, originally, but they came here in the thirties. She works for the BBC's overseas service, pouring out propaganda into the DDR. They'll be provoking uprisings there, too – you'll see.'

'Why do Willard and Terence bother to argue with Nicole?' Isabella asked Sally. 'It's so pointless. She'll never give up her opinion and they won't budge from theirs.'

'It could have something to do with the fact that she is still the most beautiful woman out of all of us. They just like the excuse to admire her while they go through the ritual. It's harmless enough, surely?'

'Our girls want fish fingers and Instant Whip for Christmas dinner.'

'Are you going to give it them?'

'Well, it saves all that palaver with a goose – and it means Eric and I get to eat beef Wellington with Ardennes pâté. Eric's very good with pastry – but don't tell him I said so.'

'We're getting a capon from Bacon's farm. D'you know what the Swedes have for Christmas Eve? Marianne's been preparing it for days – dried fish! That's the main course – and they eat rice pud for afters.'

'Poor Willard and the children. What's Nicole doing? Christmas Day is the one day we don't invade each other's homes, come to think of it.'

'Oh, Nicole will always cook something novel rather than something traditional. She's gone all Hawaiian this year. Something with pineapple. Don't tell her but Tony asked us to save him a slice of our Christmas pud.'

'It's good – Odhams?' Fogel asked.

'Can't complain,' Martin replied. 'It's not like some literary outfits. We do good business in Europe.'

'You go there personally?' Alex asked.

'Just to make sure no one's playing silly-buggers with us. I suppose I go five or six times a year.'

'Vienna? Munich? Berlin?'

'And Hamburg – Springer's in Hamburg. But also France and Italy – actually, I suppose it's more like ten times a year.'

'Interesting. D'you go behind the Iron Curtain at all?'

Martin pulled a face. 'That's a sore question at the moment. The Russians pirate a lot of our copyright stuff and—'

'Not just yours,' Fogel put in.

'No, I agree. It's a general problem. They claim they'll pay royalties but you have to go to Russia to collect them – and you can only spend them while you're there. Which is fine if you're an author – you can live like a tsar. Shop in the stores reserved for senior party members. Dine on Beluga caviar. Drown in vodka. But what can a publisher do? Their print quality is pretty atrocious.'

Alex said, 'There are ways of getting your money out.' He passed him his card. 'I have some friends who might be able to help. Give me a buzz sometime in January.'

'I'll tell you one big fault with Americans,' Eric said to Willard. 'You not only want to succeed, you also want it to be clear to all the world that your success was entirely due to your own efforts – though if luck played a part too obvious to hide, the deity is also invoked. But, as every true-born Englishman will be careful to tell you, success comes as an *enormous* surprise. And it certainly owes absolutely *nothing* to one's own misguided efforts to bring it about. But heigh-ho! We'll just have to do our poor, miserable best to manage the whole show now that we're top dogs. Oh – and by the way, here's a list of people who are to be rounded up and shot at dawn tomorrow. That's how *we* ended up owning half the world, you know.'

Willard leaned close and said, conspiratorially, 'Are you trying to warn me, Brandon? What list? Am I on it? What have you heard?'

Eric punched his arm playfully. 'Aww – you're no fun any more!'

Willard wet a finger and chalked one-up to himself on the air. 'To be serious, Eric, old bean – and I know how much you hate that – but to be serious, I think what you've just said is no longer true. It *was* true when Marianne and I first came here. Drove me mad when guys refused to take credit for anything they achieved. Even the ads almost *apologized* for the products. "Bovril prevents that sinking feeling!" *What?* That's the *best* you can say? And "Virol – growing girls need it . . . nursing mothers need it . . ." Back home they'd tell you why *everybody's* gonna *die* unless they get a shot of this stuff. And architects! Don't tell me about architects! I'd congratulate them on this or that new building and they'd go all coy and mumble that it was a "bit of a floooke ecktualleh".'

'And now they don't?'

'Not very often. If I compliment someone now, he's more likely to say, "Well, thank you – coming from you, that's quite a compliment". True, an American would more likely say, "That was nothing. Just wait till you see our entry for the ex-why-zee competition!" But the English are getting there.'

'God – the craven, sycophantic bastards!'

Over in his corner Alaric was doing Goon imitations – principally Bluebottle and Eccles.

'I should have brought my gun,' Willard murmured to Hilary and Terence.

'You hear dreadful Goon imitations everywhere nowadays,' Terence agreed. 'But the worst I've heard in a long time was in that pub in Jermyn Street last week—'

'The Cockney Pride,' Willard said.

'Yes. We were in the public bar and they have this old mahogany and cut-glass partition between that and the saloon bar, and we heard these appalling Goon imitations coming over the top. And I got up on a chair to poke my head over and tell them to shut up – and it was *them*! In person – Sellers, Milligan, and Secombe! I almost fell off the chair. Without a microphone they sound less like Moriarty and Bloodnok and Grytpype-Thynne and Neddy Seagoon than . . . well, than Alaric over there.'

'What brought you to Jermyn Street?'

'The new Design Centre in the Haymarket, actually. One of my postgrads is researching correlations between design, product-ivity and profit. There's a theory that anything well designed from an engineering standpoint will also be aesthetically pleasing. Does that work in architecture? If a building is a good "machine for living in", will it also *look* good?'

Willard shrugged. 'Define "good"! Good for the balance sheet? Good for the health of the people who use it? Should prisoners think that their prison is "good"? I get this all the time with the civil service. They tell me they want a building that will positively encourage public access and enable the civil servants to deal with them efficiently but that's just hokum. All they really want is opulence and comfort for Senior Grade Two and above. Satisfy that and you can screw the public and blame the limited budget.'

'I know it's probably an utterly tactless and unkind thing to tell you,' Cynegonde said to Nicole, 'but the Vichy government was the salvation of France. Without them and what they managed, you'd be worse than even Italy today.'

'Go on,' Nicole said icily.

'I know it's hard to believe but just think back to before the war. France collapsed in six weeks. Six *weeks*! That was entirely because of your pre-war governments, you know – squalid, greasy coalitions of dozens of parties, all of them competing to be more corrupt than the rest. Pétain changed all that – and he was popular, wasn't he.'

Nicole nodded reluctantly. 'There were many misguided people.'

'Many fed-up people. Millions of them. Of course, the Vichy government was corrupt, too. And brutal. A disgrace. But you've got a thriving agriculture now because they stopped the peasants dividing their land into smaller and smaller estates among all the children – which freed most of those children to work in industry, which is also thriving now. And it was Vichy who put the running of the country into the hands of technocrats. Jean Bichelonne, for instance.'

'A pal of Albert Speer!' Nicole sneered. 'You should talk to Marianne about that one.'

'Not a pleasant man, of course – but your industry wouldn't be half as great as it is today without him. Even so, your people missed a trick at the end of the war when the new constitution put all that power back into parliament—'

'Have you been talking to Eric?' Nicole asked. 'This is just the sort of *au contraire* incitement he goes in for.'

Cynegonde bridled. 'I studied politics, economics and philosophy at Witwatersrand,' she said.

'Ah, well!' Nicole said – with such a forgiving smile that there was no need to add, 'that explains it.'

'The bloody carpenters and joiners,' Willard said to anyone who'd listen. 'You're not gonna believe this – they're now banning the use of pump-action screwdrivers on three of our building projects. You know the things – they also call them yankee screwdrivers?

These guys are afraid of finishing the job quicker and losing money. Trade unions? *Trade* unions? I call them Job Exporting Unions. A terrible retribution is building up out there.'

'God, if I'd known that negotiating a mortgage was so much trouble,' Adam said, 'I'd have happily stayed renting for ever.'

'You don't need to tell us,' Nicole assured him.

'Nor us,' Isabella said. 'We're looking for three thou' – which is eighty per cent – but because Eric is freelance, they're asking for complete accounts going back over three years. And that's not just, for instance, "expenditure on books and journals – X-number of pounds", it's *every* book individually listed, *every* magazine. And that's the same in every other category, too. "Office supplies"? Paper clips. Rubber bands. Pens. Magic Markers . . . it's a nightmare.'

'The same with us,' Tony agreed. 'And how likely is it they'll ever read it all?'

Adam said, 'I suppose if you put *Razzle* or *Men Only* down among "magazines", they might think you're a bit frivolous.'

'The thing is,' Isabella said, 'that if the lending limit is thirty months' income, then Eric and I between us reach the three thousand in half that time – and still they dither on and on. They seem to suspect a woman's earnings and concentrate on the man's.'

Nicole sighed. 'And there's no competition. You can't go to anyone else and shop around for a better rate because the Building Societies Association sets one rate which *all* of them have to follow.'

'Centralized direction,' Eric said, joining the huddle. 'We might as well be living in a communist state.'

Nicole bridled. '. . . where we could rent this old house for next-to-nothing from the commune.'

'Not *this* old house. This old house would be the summer dacha of some party bigwig, with tripwires in the haha and electronic bugs in every room.'

'Stick to the point!' Adam complained wearily. 'The irony is that Chris and Debbie are poor enough to qualify for a mortgage from Hertford council – and theirs is the only one that has gone sailing through!'

'The humble and meek have inherited the earth!' Eric said.

'Did the council come out and actually *look* at the flat?' Nicole asked. 'They can't have seen those murals!'

'Mortgage moans?' Sally joined the huddle. 'We're just about ready to throw in the towel. It's not just our individual finances – they want to know about fireproofing, soundproofing – all that – between individual flats.'

'Thank heavens Willard and Marianne can buy their bit out of petty cash!' Nicole said. 'Otherwise, we'd never hear the end of it.'

'They won't buy unless we first sort out the electricity, though,' Adam pointed out. 'I call it blackmail.'

'And we can't afford to sort out the wiring until we're sure of our individual mortgages,' Sally said. 'There must be a name for a situation like that – where you can't do A because of B and you can't do B because of A.'

'We called it "the oojum bird" in the army,' Eric said. 'It flew round in ever-decreasing circles until the inevitable happened. I suppose we ought to have a communal meeting?'

'Oh, God! Not until well into January – *please!*' Sally said.

'Well – Happy Christmas, one and all!'

Monday, Christmas Eve 1956

The only part of the day that didn't quite conform to the *Weihnacht* pattern was the carol service in the parish church on the afternoon of Christmas Eve. Angela would have preferred to stay in and listen to the Festival of Nine Lessons and Carols on the BBC, but Vati and Tante Uschi carried the day: Christmas was incomplete, even for four born-again atheists, without a proper service with proper music in a proper church. In all other ways, however, the Breit household had never celebrated so German a Christmas.

Felix and Angela had wondered at the number of trunks the grandparents had brought with them – but not for long. Two of them were exclusively for Christmas – Eve and Day; one held all their best clothes, the other a cornucopia of Christmas *things* – glass baubles from Thüringen for the tree, nutcrackers from the

Erzgebirge, nuts, candles, candleholders on universal joints to clip on the branches of the *Tannenbaum*, angel chimes, paper angels, a little wooden peasant who puffed his pipe with smoke from a concealed incense-cone inside him, *Pappkrippen* – small nativity scenes that packed flat but could be pulled out to form a mini-ature stage set, several *Stollen*, packets of *Lebkuchen*, a whole case of *Glühwein* . . .

'How did you persuade Customs that you weren't commercial travellers?' Angela asked as she helped them unpack.

'The man ahead of us had two shotguns and a fishing rod,' Vati said. 'They just waved us through.'

They were shocked that the children spoke so little German at home – though, largely thanks to Gisela, they understood it well enough and could speak it with an English lilt when pressed. When Gisela left to go back home until mid-January, the two grandparents took over from her with a missionary zeal. Vati – or Opa to them – read *Struwwelpeter* and *Max und Moritz*. Pippin flinched at the sight of Struwwelpeter's fingernails, though she wouldn't have minded his hair – she could have tamed that into something rather swell. But when Opa thrust the page beneath her chin and said, '*Er ist drollig, neh?*' she didn't find him in the least jocular and hid her eyes.

Andrew's favourite was the one in which the little girl plays with matches and burns to death; he didn't think it fair that Gisela would let Pippin light the fires in the house while he would have to wait until he was six which was far-far-far into next year and anything could happen to him meanwhile. Anyway, he often used matches to kindle little grass fires in the old pigsties, where everything combustible had long since been burned.

Douglas just waited until Opa reached the page where the tailor snips off the thumbs of *der Daumenlutscher* – the little boy who couldn't stop sucking his thumbs – then he cried, 'No-no-no!' and hid his head under the nearest anything, even if it was a cat.

'*Nicht no-no-no!*' Opa chided. '*Sondern nein-nein-nein!*'

'Police-Fire-Ambulance,' Pippin told him.

In the bath-before-bed, Tante Uschi – Oma to them – heard them sing through clouds of Matey foam, *Alle meine Entchen* and *Hoppe-hoppe Reiter* and a Swedish one they'd learned from Siri – *Små grodorna, små grodorna* – all about pretending to be little frogs (which involved quite a lot of splashing). Then she sang them lullabies that Felix had forgotten:

> *Kindelein zart,*
> *von guter Art,*
> *schließe die Äuglein, schlafe!*

and

> *Am Weihnachtsbaum die Lichter brennen,*
> *Wie glänzt er festlich, lieb und mild*

Felix stood outside the nursery door and tears zigzagged down his cheeks.

Vati crept up on him, saw the tears, touched one lightly as if he doubted it until he felt it, and smiled. '*Das ist – ja – gut!*' he murmured – but did not linger.

As soon as the Christmas-Eve-eve debris was cleared away – and Gisela safely on her way to the boat train – Tante Uschi set about preparing to decorate the place for a *proper* Christmas. The paper chains that Pippin had brought home from school, which had draped the Christmas Tree for the party, were now hung in swags and swathes all along the balcony; and she and Andrew were set to making more – with scissors, coloured sugar-papers, and Gloy – to drape above the doors and windows. She herself, meanwhile, began to dress the tree in proper German fashion – something to which you could sing *O Tannenbaum* without reservation – with sparkling glass ornaments and living candles, all as upright in their adjustable holders as the Prussian Guards. Felix had to haul his father off the rickety studio ladder when it was time to place the bronze *Christkindl* on the very topmost spur of the tree. 'I'm up and down this thing a hundred times a day,' he said. But as he fastened it, he paused. 'We never had a *Christkindl*, did we? I thought we had an angel – a cardboard cone with a little Meissen body and head.'

'It's from Tante Uschi's family,' he explained. 'That's how family traditions grow up – hybridization. If you come to us for Christmas next year, we'll have Pippin's paper chains, too. Richer and richer every year.'

'You could freshen the greenery on the Advent Wreath while you're gabbling away,' Tante Uschi told him. 'The purple candle is the one we light tomorrow. The other three go in order . . . you know.'

'I know. I know!'

'Did you pre-burn them – short, medium, and long – just for this one night?' Angela asked, impressed at their thoroughness.

'No, we took them off the Advent Wreath we had at home. I didn't know you can't get advent calendars in England or I'd have brought some – one for each child.'

'You can, actually,' Angela said. 'I only saw them last Thursday, in Heal's. You can get them in Heal's now – we must remember that for next year.'

'Bit by bit the Channel is shrinking,' Felix remarked.

The German proselytizing continued relentlessly through all that evening and the next day. On their way back from the carol service, walking across the frost-hard stubble, the children ran ahead and enticed the grandparents to follow closely – to help look for trapped rabbits and to show them the bestest tree. Susan slept soundly in the papoose on Felix's back.

'Do you find the words "charm offensive" flitting through your mind these days?' he asked Angela when he was sure the others were out of earshot.

'What's that?'

'It's what we're getting from the old folks. Germany-this, Germany-that. They're as subtle as Oriental carpet sellers, the pair of them.'

'I keep thinking about poor Wendy. Well, I don't know why I say *poor* Wendy. Maybe it's poor Rebecca and poor Martin. I mean – to be Jews – dedicated, faithful Jews – and then to realize that if you stay in Germany, they might kill you, just for that reason. She must have been one of the first to realize that possibility.'

'She?'

'Well, she was the one who came to England ahead of him. But then, having got here, and breathing that enormous sigh of relief . . . to wake up one morning and realize you're *still* not safe. The Channel's only twenty-two miles wide. And England is full of pacifists and the upper class is in love with the Nazis. Just imagine the shock – for a German – to discover that all the

British army songs mock the government, mock the officers, mock all authority! Not exactly reassuring if you're German. So they gave up all they'd ever believed in and became Church of Englanders, stopped speaking German – except professionally – changed their name. English chameleons, vanishing into the background. But what's going on inside their minds? What's it *doing* to their minds?'

After a silence Felix said, 'D'you know what I think must have been the worst moment? Not during the war but when the war was over – the war in Europe – and they knew they were safe – and there was no longer that pressure of fear, the fear that could say to their uneasy consciences, "Don't get all high-handed with me – at least we're safe!" When that pressure was gone, they had to face all those newsreels showing that the *Vernichtung* was not only real but was far, far worse than anything they had imagined in their worst nightmares. I mean . . . their own parents! All their family . . . *vernichtet!*'

'Did they tell you that?'

He shrugged. 'Can we doubt it? One hardly needs to ask.'

'Perhaps the only way out of that would be just to have *no* feelings about it at all. Every time you felt a twinge of conscience you'd just swat it away impatiently. It's the peace of death, or the death of part of you – but it *is* peace. Isn't that exactly what Wendy described?'

He shrugged awkwardly. 'It was a bit more than that. She begged me not to cut them out if they became part of our circle of friends. Not to cultivate them and then drop them.'

Angela laughed drily. 'I thought she *really* wanted to cajole you into helping her get into the Central!'

'If she's any good, I'll gladly do that.'

'And if she's not?'

'I'll tell her so. If she's a genuine artist, discouragement won't stop her. But she'd better hurry up – I'm off to America on the sixth.'

'The *fifth*!' Angela shrieked. 'And that's the fifth time I've told you. Where does this "sixth" come from? My God – if I wasn't here you'd be wandering around Heathrow on the sixth, wouldn't you!'

Her exasperated shriek had make the others stop and look back. They had now reached the bestest tree.

'Coming!' Felix began to trot. The children, meanwhile, got their grandparents to lift them inside the hollow trunk. Drawing alongside, he put his mouth to the crack and moaned, genuinely out of breath, *'Ach! Ich bin so müde! Ich bin so alt und so müde!'* – not quite what the youngsters were expecting. There was a stunned silence. Pippin copped on first, gave a slightly forced laugh, and asked, *'Wie alt bist du dann, alter Baum?'*

Tante Uschi was shocked. *'Wie alt sind Sie!'* she corrected. 'A four-hundred-year-old tree deserves not to have little girls calling him *du!'*

And Angela thought: thank God we escaped Germany!

After their Christmas dinner, when the children were fast asleep and the *Glühwein* that had been heating by the fire began to flow, Felix went to turn on the television but was halted halfway by Vati, who said, 'When are you coming back to Germany?'

Felix threw another log on the fire and returned to his chair. 'Not before midsummer at the earliest. I'm off to America on the . . . ah . . . *fifth*! The fifth of next month.'

Angela gave him three slow handclaps.

'I don't mean for a visit,' Vati went on. 'I mean coming back for good.'

'To Germany?'

'Well, you needn't say it like that! All those things that people said about it . . . all those things that *we* said about it – how the boy and girl fanatics of the *Hitlerjugend*, the *Arbeitsdienst*, and the BDM would never lose their faith, so democracy would never take root . . . how Adenauer was too old and Erhardt had no social conscience . . . how too much of the physical economy had been reduced to rubble . . . how we just didn't have enough manpower—'

'OK-OK!' Felix put up his hands. 'None of it has happened! We know that. But it doesn't mean that Angela and I—'

But Vati was running to a script. 'Just hear me out,' he asked. 'It isn't just that all those predictions have proved false – it's *why* they proved false, which is also why Germany will be a far better place to live than England can possibly be. The boy and girl fanatics were not *Nazi* fanatics. They went on fighting just as fiercely after Hitler shot himself and the Nazi state collapsed. They were fanatics for *Germany*. They still are, now, but as engineers, architects, lawyers, bureaucrats. And wily old Adenauer gave us a *federal* Germany, which has a division of powers that any would-be Führer will find it almost impossible to gather back into one Reich. But the biggest reason of all – in every sense of the word *big* – is *Der Dicke* himself – Ludwig Erhardt. "Don't ration anything", he said. "Rationing makes black markets and corruption". Compare that with England, where the government always seems to know what's best for everyone. We set our industry free in Germany – those people find markets and satisfy consumers better than any bureaucrat. Compare *that* with England, where they order industrialists to go to areas that are dead or dying! And we have one workers' union per industry – sixteen industrial unions for the whole of West Germany. The Ford plant in Dagenham has *forty-nine* unions – just in one plant! And our unions have seats on the boards of—'

'Vati! Please!' Felix pressed his hands to his temples. 'This has nothing to do with Angela and me! West Germany is going to be the greatest powerhouse in Europe. She will be peaceful and productive and her army will be more like boy scouts than soldiers. *Geschenkt!* Angela can speak for herself but my career is here. All my contacts—'

'Contacts! You are an international artist. My colleagues on *Spiegel* – art critics – anybody I meet in the art world – they all say Germany would love to have you back. You'd get enough commissions to keep you going for a century.'

'But that's true now! I have three possible commissions in America. I'm going there to see which two I'll have to turn down. Or postpone. I teach at the Slade. I'm on the examining board of the Royal College . . . no – listen! You should know these things. I'm on a specialist panel of the Arts Council. I'm a trustee of the Tate. I'm on the committee that supervises the standards for the art examinations of the Oxford and Cambridge joint exam board . . . it goes on and on. I turn down four or five requests a month to join something, advise some institution or corporation, contribute to this or that symposium. These are my roots now.' He looked at Angela.

'As for me . . .' She leaped in before Vati could respond. 'You've seen a bit of our life here, not just this time but on past

visits – the community, the children, *all* the children – The Tribe
as we call them – and all our friends here. How could you even
imagine we'd think of moving back to Germany?'

Vati drew breath to tell her but she plunged on: 'It's true I
could get work as easily in Germany as I can here. Even more
easily. And it could be more stimulating, too. I mean . . . with
the Darmstadt School creating a kind of music that no dictator
can ever again misappropriate as Hitler misappropriated Wagner
and Richard Strauss . . . what was I saying? Yes! With all the
exciting experiment going on there, even if it *is* much too purist
. . . also Karlheinz Stockhausen! He's going to be the greatest
composer of the next half-century. He has very interesting ideas
about music in space. Not music out there among the stars,
though it's connected, of course. Everything's connected. What
was the question again?'

'It's still about going back to Germany or staying here,' Felix
reminded her gently. 'Have some *Glühwein*.'

Only the week before Faith had told them that a perfect hostess
never offers '*more* wine.' No matter how many glasses a guest had
already consumed, a perfect hostess would only say, 'Have some
wine.' The implication of Felix's words was not lost on her.

'Oh! We'll be staying here – without a doubt. And my head
is perfectly clear. But you may refill my glass all the same.'

'You've given us the attractions of the German musical scene,'
Tante Uschi said. 'But what would be so good about England?'

'A clearer field. You see that little room at the far end? My
studio. Anyone in England who's interested in *musique concrète,*
or twelve-tone, or atonal . . . anyone who wants to play about
with the sound, change it electronically – or even *create* it electronically – they all know that *that* is the place to come. *The*
place to come. In the whole of the country, *this* is the place to
come. When I arrived in England in nineteen forty-five, even
though I'd been out of the business for three years, I knew more
about tape recording than anyone else in the country. Now, of
course, a just-finished apprentice at the BBC knows more than I
did then. But I've kept ahead. Nowadays I know more about
electronic recording than anyone else in England. And probably
as much as anyone in Germany, also. Digital electronics will be
next – and I'll be ahead there, too.' She smiled at her parents-
in-law. 'I'm sorry, my darlings! We love coming to see you. We

enjoy our visits back to Germany and we're glad everything's going so well. But this is *home* to us now. We're never going back.'

Saturday, 5 January 1957

This time the train arrived promptly at Hertford North and Wendy caught the bus that would drop her at the Gate Lodge on its way to Welwyn Garden City. As it groaned up the hill at Sele Farm and trundled along the road towards Panshanger it shook with a metallic rattle that threatened to dismantle the bus itself. She wondered if it wouldn't be safer to get off and walk. The weather outside certainly invited it – a dry, sunny morning braced with a skin-deep frost. She was now beginning to wonder if she should go through with this meeting – this unheralded visit – at all.

A townie, inside and out, she was an interloper here in a landscape that had hardly changed in a century or more. Not at home even when at home, she expected no heartfelt welcome when the bus left her in a pale cloud of petrol-reeking exhaust, staring across the road at the Dower House gate lodge.

'Can I help you? Oh! You're Felix's cousin, aren't you! We met at their drinky-poos.' Hilary was batting a doormat against the gatepost – and wondering why she had suddenly adopted the character of Isabella, who could say 'drinky-poos' just like that.

'Yes. That's right.' Wendy crossed the road. 'Second-cousin once removed. My father is his second-cousin. My great-grandfather—'

'I'm there! I'm there!' Hilary assured her. 'Have you come to see them? I think they both went into Garden City. Felix is off to America. Angela's just driving him to the station.'

'Oh.'

'Did they invite you out here today? That's very like them, I'm afraid. She'll be back any moment – unless she's gone shopping.' She tilted her head towards the lodge. 'Come in and wait if you like. I'm just about to break for a cuppa.' She turned about and faced up the drive before megaphoning her hands round her mouth. 'Chris!' she yelled. 'Tea!'

Wendy noticed, for the first time, a man standing in the middle of the park. He was wearing a stocking cap, jeans, cowboy boots, and a duffel coat. 'Oh, *that* Chris,' she said. 'Something-Potter. I met him at the drinky-poos, too.'

Hilary laughed. 'Please don't call it drinky-poos. I don't know *why* I said that. He's Chris Riley-Potter. A painter. Just a bit down on his luck at the moment – though he's managed to get a council mortgage ahead of everyone else here. Oops! Did Felix tell you we're all trying to buy the place?'

'He didn't. But I'll not breathe a word – don't worry. Won't it be super if you all own the place!'

''Lo Wendy!' Chris called out, though still a good way off. 'Is that your portfolio?'

'Yes. You can have a look if you like.' She started to follow Hilary towards the lodge.

'I'll thaw out first.' He was much nearer now. 'This frost is kinder to brass monkeys than to me.'

'Now then, now then!' Hilary chided.

'It looks good and fat.' He patted the portfolio as he drew level with Wendy on the threshold. 'Were you hoping to see Felix?'

She nodded glumly.

'Hard cheese!'

Inside, bathed in the Aga-warmth of the kitchen, they shed coats, gloves, and headgear while Hilary lifted a mewing kettle off the hob and drowned a small mountain of tea in her dull-aluminium teapot. 'You know where the biscuits are, Chris,' she said. 'I hope Mortimer's behaving himself?'

'He was when I left – playing very nicely with our two. Or with Amanda, anyway. Hector's still at the age when they play alongside other kids rather than with them.' He sat again, opened the biscuit tin, and looked at the clock. 'It'll be *Listen with Mother* right now.' He grinned at Wendy. 'Fret not! One day you'll be talking like this, too.' He sighed. 'I certainly never thought the day would come for me.'

Hilary set down the tea tray. 'Next year he'll start school – and I'll get a *bit* of my own life back. I don't think we should open Wendy's portfolio until the tea is cleared away again. I've seen dreadful things happen with Terence's papers – to say nothing about the rare books from the special-loans department.'

Wendy, who had already tugged one bow undone, tucked the

loose ends beneath the portfolio, as if leaving them visible might be too tempting.

'Were you hoping Felix would dig a hole and pull you through to the Central or somewhere?' Chris asked.

She nodded. 'It's *the* place – what with Miss Batty. Also – I've just heard this – Mervyn Peake teaches there, too. If I don't come up to scratch with textile design, I'd like to have a go at book illustration. Or cartoons. I mean *Punch*-type cartoons, not cinema.'

'Ah me!' Chris caught Hilary's eye. 'I can remember a time when that many doors were there for me to open, too. Try them all, pet. You'll still get the chance because your first two years will be foundation. You'll have a go at the lot.' He turned back to Hilary. 'The deVoors have secured a mortgage. She's asked Marianne to go ahead with the design for the gothic rood screen.'

'Rude screen?' Wendy asked.

Hilary explained.

'The Brandons want the ballroom. But the main hall, staircase, and the cellars will all remain communal.'

'Will Adam and Sally get their AP flat?' Hilary asked.

Wendy looked bewildered.

'David Copperfield?' Hilary prompted her. 'Aged Parent . . . AP? There's a plan to surreptitiously turn the garage nearest them into a dangerous structure – which it jolly nearly is already. Then we can legally take it down and reuse the bricks to build a small apartment for APs – Peter's APs in this case.'

'And Sally's none too happy about it,' Chris added.

'Golly – it must be funny living so close to each other here – everyone sharing everyone else's feelings.'

'It's just the same as any family,' Hilary said. 'Except that ours is a bit bigger.'

'Nobody shares feelings in our family,' Wendy said. 'I've been thinking about that ever since the drinky . . . the Christmas-Eve-eve party. Both my parents said it gave them a headache – which they think was because of the noise and—'

'You mean Angela's concrete music?'

'No! I like that. No – it was that they thought Felix was family and everyone else was mere acquaintance . . . acquaintances – until it dawned on them that it's not just the kids who are growing up like brothers and sisters. The grown-ups have become . . . well, family, too. Some are like just in-laws, some are like cousins, and some are . . . well – like *half*-brothers and *half*-sisters, anyway.'

Hilary and Chris exchanged glances. Chris said, 'I suppose we've just grown. Not grown *up* but grown *into* it. But you're right. I mean, before we got our council loan, everyone else was prepared to chip in and cover the loan for Debs and me.'

Hilary stared at her cup. 'I know you had no choice, but Terence is worried that someone in the council will spill the beans to John Gordon.'

'And then?'

Hilary turned to Wendy. 'He's the land agent for the sand-and-gravel company – our present landlords.'

As if it was the most obvious question in the world, Wendy said, 'Would he be pleased or sorry to get this place off his hands?'

Hilary uttered a single, astonished laugh and turned to Chris. 'Well! That's a new slant, I must say!' Then back to Wendy. 'Yes – would he be pleased or sorry? You're absolutely right. Everything hinges on that . . . I wonder?'

'I bet he'd be pleased,' Chris decided. 'Of course, he thinks we're all mad. But he *likes* us. I think he'd drop by for a chat more often if he knew we couldn't bend his ear about the lead flashing or the blocked drains and stuff.' He tipped the last of the tea down his gullet, handed the cup to Hilary with the most charming smile and, turning to Wendy with the smile undiminished, patted the table and said, 'Time for a shoofti, then.'

Biting her lower lip, she tugged at the two remaining ties and opened the portfolio.

Immediately, as if some invisible director had clicked his fingers, Chris became solemn, intent, single-minded. Without a word, without another glance at either woman, he examined each bit of artwork, each sketch, each design . . . taking it up, gazing at it, half-closing his eyes and peering at it, holding it at arm's length, and eventually laying it down on this pile or that until the port-folio was bare and the table dotted with seven or eight sorted piles.

'These for your sketches,' he said, scooping up one pile and putting it back in the folder. 'Your textile-design roughs, your drawings from life, your etchings. I'd put in all the pulls of each state if you still have them. Did you do any litho?' He looked at her for the first time since picking up the first bit of artwork. The flirt had vanished; this was serious stuff.

'I've just started,' she told him. 'They're on the same nights so I could only do one or the other. D'you think they're any good?'

'Good?' He frowned, as if he thought she was being frivolous. 'Well, of course they're *good*! You *know* they're good. They're bloody marvellous. These other ones I've left out are marvellous, too. But what I've picked out is enough. Enough to show your range.' A cunning smile parted his lips. 'But . . . tell you what – stick these others in a big envelope and leave it in. And if they say, "What's this?" look annoyed and say you never meant to bring them. I think you'll be in on a breeze, old darling.' His eyes swivelled from one woman to the other. 'And you can wish *me* luck, too. This afternoon I'm off to see the head of education at Stevenage New Town about a mural for the dining hall of one of their new schools.'

Hilary reached across, grabbed him by the wrists, and shook them in time with her words. 'Chris! That's wonderful! Have you got any sketches?'

'Not yet. It's a three-hundred-and-sixty-degree panorama going right the way round inside the room above the window tops. I'm thinking of something figurative, something Breughelish, something Stanley-Spencerish – the River Ouse from its source to the sea. Or the Great North Road, from Roman times to the present – just the portion that goes through Beds and Herts – the scenery, the houses, the trades . . . lots of ideas.'

'And you'll include details the kids won't spot – *some* details – until they've been looking at it for years!' Wendy said eagerly. 'Would he have *two* schools going?'

Chris laughed. 'Help me if you like – keep you out of mischief at weekends.'

Not daring to test his seriousness she snatched up his hand and shook it. 'It's a deal!'

A car passed by, into the grounds and up the long drive. Without turning to look, Hilary said, 'That's Angela, back from Garden City.'

Wendy rose. 'I must go.' She looked at the scattering of artwork on the table. 'These won't interest Angela. Can I leave them here and get them on my way home?'

'I'm in all day,' Hilary assured her. 'Just about every day.'

When Wendy had gone, Hilary turned to Chris and echoed scornfully: '"Keep her out of mischief at weekends". *Ha!*'

Wendy listened to Angela's tape the way a hen listens to a novel sound – head forward, cocked to one side, eyes unfocused. 'It's bea*uuuu*tiful,' she said at last.

Angela pulled a dubious face. 'Are you sure? It's not meant to be. D'you know what it is?'

She shook her head. 'But it's powerful. Final. There's a powerful finality to each separate . . . crunch, or whatever it is.'

'I made it by putting the mike inside a wellington boot and then crushing snails on different surfaces – concrete, earth, gravel, wood. And on the side of a dead badger.'

It was Wendy's turn for the dubious face. 'I wish I didn't know that.'

'Still think it's beautiful?'

'Well . . . aweful-with-an-e, you know? Awe*some*. What will you do with it?'

'Add it to the library. I'm not a composer, but my sounds library is to a modernist what a Strad or a Bechstein is to a trad composer. I have the biggest collection of clean sounds in England. In Europe, probably.'

'Clean?'

'No technical noise – hums, tweets, whistles, and stuff. But we do have a problem with hiss.' She rewound the tape and pressed *Play*. 'Hear it?'

This time the hen-stance was even more intense. 'Like a distant waterfall?'

'*Exactly* like a distant waterfall. It's called white noise. But there's a young chap who's just graduated from Stamford – worked with Ampex before that – who has some very interesting ideas about getting rid of it. I've just started corresponding with him.' Watching Wendy's response to this news she realized that 'interesting' was a relative term. 'But enough of that,' she concluded.

'If it's a library . . .' Wendy said. 'I mean – d'you give each tape a name?'

'A name and a tag. I call this one *À rebours*.'

'After the novel by Huysmans? Oh, that's good! Because the

hero – des Esseintes – blends odours to make new and unique scents, never before experienced by a human nose.'

'Yes!' Angela laughed. 'You're pretty quick on the uptake, you know.'

Wendy struggled to find something self-deprecatory that did not also sound like a rebuff.

Angela went on: 'I expect you came out here to show your portfolio to Felix?'

Wendy nodded. 'Should have phoned – I know. I showed my stuff to Chris and he thought they weren't *too* bad. Did you know he's got a commission to paint a mural all round the hall at some school in Stevenage? He said I can help if I like.'

'How . . . generous!' Angela said. 'The point I was going to make, though, was this: if you hoped Felix might use his influence to get you in at the Central—'

'I missed the application date.'

'I know.'

'Because of my parents' opposition.'

'Yes, I understand all that.' She hesitated. 'Just one thing . . .'

'What?'

'Your clothes, dear. The department is called "*Fashion* and Textiles". Forgive me for pointing this out but you are beautifully and expensively dressed for the debutante page of *Country Life* rather than for—'

'I know! I know!' She mimed the tearing-out of her hair. 'But it's my mother – *both* my parents. They'd have a fit if I went about in jeans and a fisherman's smock and a duffel coat.'

'Oh, well, I think students of fashion would be a little more inventive than *that*!'

The idea only increased the girl's glumness. 'What d'you suggest then?'

'Me? Fashion? Ha! Why ask me when Isabella Brandon of *Vogue* is less than a quarter of a mile away – or will be when they come back from their Saturday-morning shopping! Meanwhile, what d'you say to a bit of lunch? Veal-and-ham pie . . . cottage loaf and stilton . . . tomato soup . . .'

'Were you listening to Angela's tapes?' Eric asked as Wendy closed her portfolio and retied the ribbons.

'Honeybu-u-u-un!' Isabella said with some menace. 'This is about fashion – way over your head.'

'They'reabsolutelysuper!' Wendy replied swiftly, so as not to seem rude to him, before turning, all rapt attention and wide eyes, to Isabella.

'Slowly she elfed her way out of the worldly grape,' Eric told her.

'*Too* slowly for me!' Isabella said.

'Sorry . . . I don't quite—' Wendy ventured.

'Exactly,' Eric agreed. 'You see my point. That sentence bears the same relation to the English language as Angela's tapes bear to the language of music. Or – come to think of it – the relationship between the fashion advice you are about to be given and all ideas of *rational* dress.' He smiled at Isabella. 'But I'm sorry, my dear – you have pearls to cast.' At the threshold, without pausing or turning around, he murmured, 'Cultured pearls, of course.'

'He's wrong about Angela's tapes,' Wendy said as she followed Isabella into their drawing room. 'All her sounds are natural. Real sounds. Not created in some box of electronic tricks. But when you hear them coming at you out of a really super set of loud-speakers . . . wow! Or headphones. I mean, it's a new world exploding inside your head. A familiar world but also new. A familiar world *remade* anew.'

Isabella turned and stared at her, much to Wendy's discomfort. 'D'you *write* much?' she asked. 'I mean, as well as draw and paint and things?'

'Why?'

'Just now you said something like "a familiar world that's also new" and then corrected it to "a familiar world remade anew" – just like a journalist honing an article to bring out the precise meaning you want. I'm doing it all the time, of course – so I wondered. Do you?'

'Write?' Wendy shrugged. 'Only my diary.' She bit her lip in parody. 'Full of dark and shallow secrets!'

Isabella waved at a chair. 'Just sit there a mo and read those magazines . . . or . . . whatever. I must make a phone call.'

Half a minute later the phone at Wendy's elbow went *ping*! She realized that Isabella must be using an extension, probably in Eric's studio. Before she could stop herself, she lifted the handset and – aghast at her action – put it to her ear, simultaneously covering the mouthpiece with her free hand. Scarcely daring to breathe, she listened.

Ringing tone.

Then: 'Condé Nast publications.'

Then Isabella: 'Good afternoon, Joy. Is Jocasta Innes there this afternoon? I know they were having to—'

'No. They finished up before lunch, Mrs Brandon. I could patch you through to her at home if she's there?'

'Yes, please – she's moved recently and I don't have her new number here.'

The new number was already ringing.

'Jocasta Innes.'

'Jo! Isabella. Sorry. Saturday and all that . . . but—'

'We finished the recast if that's what—'

'No – not that. Joy told me that. Splendid work. But listen – this is about that trainee position. Shut up, Eric.'

'What about it?'

'Do we have anyone yet, because – I'm taking a huge leap in the dark here – but I think I may have found someone. Nineteen years old. Good family. Conservative dresser. Hopes to get in at the Central under Miss Batty. Draws very well – interesting style – interesting—'

'You've seen her work?'

'Yes, she brought her folio here to show Felix Breit – she's his cousin, by the way. I've seen it, too, and I'm quite impressed. But more than that – Eric! I'll hit you – more than that, much-much more, is her use of language. I've noticed her self-editing several times – and it's always for the better. I would vote we give her a try. She's at a loose end until next year's intake. Anyway, how are you fixed for Monday? Shall I invite her—'

'Monday I'm tied up with the printer.'

'Ooh – kinky! Tuesday?'

'Tuesday morning's fine.'

'Sooper! Enjoy the rest of your weekend – kiss-kiss!'

'You, too, Bel!'

Click!

Wendy, with her heart still trying to leap out of her ribcage, hoped she had managed to drop the handset in perfect synchrony

with Isabella; she scrabbled frantically for a magazine, opened it
without looking at it, and turned a welcoming smile on the
doorway through which – as her footsteps presaged – Isabella
would arrive at any moment.

Isabella began speaking even before she reached the door: 'Your
other great attribute, Wendy – which I didn't mention to dear
Jocasta – is that you have absolutely no scruples about eavesdropping on other people's conversations.' She stood in the doorway,
smiling radiantly.

Wendy burst into tears. 'I don't know what made me do that,'
she sobbed. 'I just . . . it just . . . oh, I'm so ashamed. So
ashamed!'

Isabella, who had meanwhile crossed the room, startled her
out of it by plucking the magazine from her grasp and then
returning it to her the right way round. 'You do still have a few
rough edges,' she said calmly. 'But you're not in the least ashamed.
You did exactly what I would have done in your shoes. The
truth is, my dear, you are a *journalist*. You don't know it yet –
and I'm sure you don't believe it. But – as you heard: we're
offering you a year as a trainee at Condé Nast in order for you
to find out.'

'Internship!' Eric said as he joined them. 'That's what the Yanks
call it. We must ask Willard – is the recipient of an internship
an *intern* or an *internee?*'

Thursday, 24 January 1957

British telephones nag Brrr–Brrr / Brrr–Brrr / *Come-onnn!* In
America they trill Trilililililll . . . . . . Trilililililll . . . . . . *Take
your time* . . .

Felix took his time; if they rang off – sorry, hung up – it
couldn't have been important. *He* was important. Here, anyway.

Actually, he just wished he was home again at the Tithe Barn.
His business here in Manhattan was concluded satisfactorily (finan-
cially, anyway). He had made new friends, seen a lot of interesting
work (and even more rubbish – but that was true everywhere),
and he now understood the art/commerce nexus here a whole

lot better. But his left hand itched for a welding rod and his right longed for the weight and balance of an acetylene torch. Indeed, now that that astonishing girl in Scribner's had wised him up to the virtues of argon-shielded arc welding, he was almost desperate to get back.

Only his reunion with his uncle, Tony Bright, now delayed him.

Trilililililll . . . they . . . he . . . she . . . did not hang up.

'Breit,' he said at last.

'What?' asked a scandalized female voice – which then laughed a laugh that could only be Faith's. '*Breit?* You've been around Fogel too long. Well, how's New York treating you, *Breit?*'

'Not bad. You sound very close – this is a good line.'

'If I opened my window and you opened yours, we could both ring off. I'm here – at the Elysée – one floor above you. In fact, I think I'm right on top of you.'

'It wouldn't be the first time,' he said.

'Now then! Are you at a loose end this evening – or shall I rephrase that? Anyway, shall we meet downstairs in the Monkey Bar? Ten minutes?'

The pianist was tinkling melodies from Li'l Abner, Mr Wonderful, and Happy Hunting – all the recent Broadway hits and turkeys; the smoke was . . . well, not too thick, nor was the chatter too loud. Felix sat alone, cradling and sipping an almond daiquiri, and waiting – in that mellow, amber, Monkey Bar *Stimmung*, which creeps over one's spirit like a balm. He could not help wondering why Faith had mentioned nothing of her visit when back at the Dower House. And did Angela know of it? Surely she would have called him?

Faith was great company – he couldn't deny it. And she'd called on Doubleday so often that Manhattan must be like a second home to her by now. Americans were splendid hosts but their invitations were all to restaurants, theatres, concerts, clubs; you'd get a rare glimpse of their homes at crowded cocktail parties but the entertainment he really craved – watching the kids being read to or sung to sleep and then settling down in carpet slippers with a beer in the hand for a mindless hour or two of shallow opinion-swapping and easy reminiscence and mildly astringent gossip – that never occurred to them. But those were the very things that helped you into a new society and finally let you belong.

So – bless you, Faith!

And yet . . .

'Faith!' He rose, bear-like, almost upsetting the table.

They kissed the air beside each other's ears. 'I'll have what you're having,' she said, sitting down and smoothing her skirt.

Felix nodded. The waiter had heard.

'I saw the About Town piece in the *New Yorker*,' she said. 'You're a hit.'

He shrugged.

'No? You're not a hit?'

'There's something about it that makes me uneasy, Faith.'

'Like?'

He glanced awkwardly around. 'Maybe not talk about it here. Have you eaten? I've been told of a good Italian restaurant down on Fiftieth Street, near the Waldorf-Astoria. Think we could walk that far?'

'Lovely.' Her eyes quartered the room, raptorial and sharp. No one she knew.

'D'you always stay here?' he asked.

She turned her full attention on him at last. 'You're worried about Angela!'

'And you're not worried about Alex?'

She shook her head as people do when they wonder how to explain something simple to the simple-minded. 'We both know there aren't going to be any shenanigans, Felix. You and I lived together once upon a time, and we parted best of friends, you to Angela, me to Alex. The End! No slice-off-a-cut-cake that wouldn't be missed. Anyway, the opportunities for that sort of thing are far riper back home at the Dower House than they are here. That's why everybody's so careful, of course.'

'Are they?'

'Oh, yes. I see the way you husbands look at Nicole from time to time – and don't deny it, darling. You'd all be much less worthwhile if you didn't. And she is gorgeous. But I'll bet none of you has even made a pass at her. Not even Adam.'

'Especially not Adam.'

'Quite.' The waiter brought her cocktail. She insisted on giving

him her room number. 'Let's talk about something more interesting. For instance – why did you pick the Elysée?'

He leaned forward. 'Alex recommended it. Margot Fonteyn
always stays here, he said. And the Queen of Denmark. Or maybe
it's Sweden.'

'Did he!' she said coldly.

'You didn't know?'

'I knew you were in New York, of course, but I didn't know
where. I was going to ask at Moma. I only discovered you were
here when I checked in this morning and overheard a valet ask a
chambermaid which room you were in.' She chewed gently at
her bottom lip. 'It's not Alex's usual sense of humour.'

'Assuming it's a joke at all.'

'Oh, well, bugger him, eh!' She laughed. 'I can easily bounce
it back on him! Ah, listen! This is *Oh Happy Day* from Li'l Abner.
Great Johnny Mercer. We might catch it this week – I think it's
still on at the Saint James's. My treat.' She downed the rest of her
cocktail in one. 'Let's go – I'm starving.'

Outside, scarved, gloved, hatted, and buttoned against a knifing
cross-town wind that made the eyes water, they set out to walk
four blocks south and two blocks west to Casa Ciccio on 50th.
She grabbed his arm hard and hugged herself tight against him.
'Isn't this nice!' she said. 'Manhattan can be so lonely. Haven't
you been lonely since you came?'

'There have been a fair number of openings, vernissages, cock-
tails and food-in-the-hand.'

'And firm commissions? If you want me back as your agent I
can easily—'

'No!' He laughed. 'Sorry – I didn't mean it to sound like that.
No, I've actually turned down one commission and—'

'Is that what you didn't want to talk about back there?'

'No. I'll tell you about that over dinner. All this steam coming
up out of the pavements! I thought it was a movie cliché but it's
real.' They walked through a wind-devil of steam. 'Surreal,' he
added.

'I dreamed about the Dower House last night on the plane,'
she said.

'"Last night I dreamed I went back to Manderley"!'

'Don't, Felix! I'm convinced that the minute we own it, the
place will go on fire and burn down.' As they turned down

Madison Avenue she added: 'I think everyone now has enough finance to buy in. Tony and Nicole got the nod last Tuesday. Oh! God – I nearly forgot. Your cousin Wendy!'

'She came, hoping to see me, just after I left to catch my flight. I have talked with Angela since, you know.'

'Yes, but has she told you about Isabella's offer?'

'Offer of what?'

A derelict lurched at them from the unlighted doorway of a store; before he could open his mouth, Felix thrust a five-dollar bill into his hand and pushed him gently back into the dark.

Faith stared at him in amazement.

'What?' he asked, clamping her arm and hurrying onward.

'What you just did. I was in Soho one evening last autumn, in Meard Street. I'd just come out of the Macabre – you know, coffee served on coffins – and I saw a tramp rifling through a rubbish bin, and then one of the Messina brothers – I'm sure it was Alfredo – came out of one of their brothels there, saw the tramp, yanked his hand out of the bin, clamped the lid down, and thrust a fiver into the guy's pocket. And walked on. Just like that – just like you back there.'

'What would you have done – kicked him in the balls?'

'At the very least I'd have told him to be sure to spend it on liquor and the Numbers.'

Felix chuckled. 'He and I had that conversation last night. The Macabre, eh? All cobwebs and skeletons. And there's Nicole – always goes to the Partisan when she's in town and—'

'The Partisan?'

'Grainy portraits of Trotsky . . . Castro. In Carlyle Street. How do we all live so amicably in one community?'

'What's *your* favourite Soho watering hole?'

'The French pub, of course. Or – if you're asking about an actual club – the Mandrake. There's a woman there – always propping up the bar, clutching a sneezy little pekingese to her ample bosom – and actually "she" is a man!'

She shivered. 'God, it's cold. Is it much farther?'

He showed her where its marquee projected over the sidewalk.

Out of the blue, she said, 'Didn't you once tell me you have an uncle who lives over here? Near Princeton? Changed his name to B, r, i, g, h, t?'

'Did I?'

'On my first visit to the Dower House, when you collected me in the pony and trap.'

'Well . . . childhood memories!'

She sighed with irritation. 'That isn't exactly what I was asking, Felix, dear.'

'I know.' He sighed, too. 'I'm going to see him this weekend.' Then, brightening, he asked, 'Would you like to come along? It's only an hour or so by train – from wonderful-wonderful Penn Station. We could spend an hour wandering round there before we catch the train.' To her silence he added: 'Or have you other plans?'

They passed from the Siberia of Manhattan to the Mediterranean warmth of the Casa Ciccio. Felix held out his hand to the maître d', an Italian from Central Casting. The man shook it warmly enough but still blocked their way, uttering apologies and protestations of extreme grief.

Felix presented his card and said, 'I'm a nephew of Tony Bright. This is my good friend Signora Findlater.'

'Pleeeease!' With balletic grace the man stepped aside and wafted them towards a table at the very centre of the restaurant. His attitude, as two other waiters scurried to join them and fussed them into their seats, was that they had been reserving this table for God – who would now have to take the halfpenny seat. 'Is a stoopendous week for your family, Signor Breit – Signora Findlater – and please – your meal tonight is on the house. Absolutely!'

'Are you getting the picture?' Felix asked when they were left alone with the menus – his with the mouth-watering words and the prices, hers with just the words. All around them they could sense the sort of discreet curiosity diners show when someone of note enters a restaurant and is put in the catbird seat.

'The national dish of America,' she said, running her eyes down the columns, 'is menus. Nothing could possibly live up to these descriptions. Am I getting the picture? I hope not but I suspect I am.'

'Uncle Tony came out of jail yesterday – his seventieth birthday.' His voice was flat. 'I used to say I met him *once* – when I was four – because . . . well, that's what my mother always told me to say. But we saw quite a lot of Uncle Anton over here during the Great War. He was dabbling in petty crime even then – what they call "victimless" crime. Like gambling, insurance fraud, prostitution . . . stuff. When he was with us this Christmas, Vati said Tony moved into big crime during Prohibition. He never stepped on the Italians' toes and they . . . well, I imagine they must have found him useful. The police never caught him. The IRS never caught him. The FBI never nailed him.'

'So how did he end up in jail?'

'He . . . "took the rap" as they call it, for someone else. Someone bigger. A loyalty test, probably. But now they owe him one. He did a seven-year stretch.' He chuckled drily. 'A meal for two on the house doesn't even scratch the surface of that debt.'

'What were you doing over here in the Great War? I was only two-and-a-bit when it ended. Good God, Felix – we lived together for the best part of three years and there's still so much we don't know about each other.'

He grinned. 'I'll bet, even so, that you know more about me than you do about Alex!'

Iced water and breadsticks appeared between them.

She stared at him levelly for what seemed much longer than the actual five seconds. 'I'll leave that pending, if I may. Tell me why you were over here in nineteen fourteen.'

'My father thought the war would be over by Christmas – but possibly not in Germany's favour. He thought it best for Mutti and me to be here, out of harm's way. When America entered the war, Tony had to take us into his household to keep us out of internment. We went back to Germany in nineteen nineteen when I was seven but Mutti and I kept up our English until she died.'

She ordered a selection of oysters and smaller shellfish followed by *pollo alla boscaiolla*; he – *calamari* followed by *saltimbocca alla romana*. And, to help it down, a dry, white Cortese di Gavi from the south-east of Piemonte.

Luigi, the maître d', smirked as if the choice was especially apt.

'Was that what you didn't want to talk about back at the hotel?' Faith asked.

'No. Oh, no – this family stuff is trivial in comparison.'

'Wow!'

He cleared his mouth of breadstick before he went on. 'It's one of my commissions. My best paid, too – a sculpture to be hung on the side of a building on First Avenue, right opposite the new UN building. In the low forties. Something over two-hundred-thousand dollars.'

'Wow again!'

'Yes, but! The theme is . . . well, it should be the *Vernichtung* in general. But this fee is being put up by an exclusively Jewish organization here in New York called Shoah Zwei-und-Vierzig – you understand?'

'I'm beginning to.'

'No, I mean . . . well, obviously you do. 'Forty-two – the Wannsee meeting – all that . . . baggage. But it's much more complex even than that. I sketched an idea for a tall, conical structure, a truncated cone, symbolizing a chimney. I'll do it in welded steel sheet, in low-relief, but we'll probably ship it in pieces and cast it in bronze over here. And there will be tortured humanoid forms scattered at random all over the side of the building, sparse at the edges but getting more populated nearer the chimney symbol. And some of them will be melting into the chimney . . . some almost completely swallowed by it.'

'That sounds very powerful, Felix. Is there a difficulty?'

'Two. They want a scattering of metal things at the top of the chimney, representing smoke – not just any random metal shape but Stars of David of all sizes. Small enough to read as smoke particles from the distance but large enough to be revealed for what they are, close-up. I asked, "What about the Gypsies, homo-sexuals, politicals, Jehova's Witnesses – hundreds of thousands of them?" They said, "We are a Jewish organization. We represent millions".'

'Which is true!'

'I said, "What about the Christians – Catholics and Lutherans – who were annihilated for hiding Jews?" Same answer – don't qualify our message with awkward bits of minor history. Can I – in all honour – go along with that? It's actually a variation of the problems I met in Israel. They say, "This is the land promised us by God". You say, "But by all the processes that define the ownership of countries – conquest, settlement, intermarriage, law, taxation, purchase, et cetera – the Arabs have owned it ever since Roman times". They say, "True but irrelevant. This is the land promised us by God". Fogel says, "Ve are all prostitoots now" – but am I?'

'You said there are two difficulties.'

'Yes – the other one is me. One of the Shoah people, Joe Greenbaum – charming man – a psychiatrist – told me they have commissioned me not only as a sculptor but also as a Jew and as a survivor of the camps – the Shoah, as they call the *Vernichtung*. It means a mighty and appalling wind in Hebrew. A hot wind, I suppose, given the geography. And again I have to ask, "Can I accept this commission under such false pretences?" – especially knowing my own ambivalent descent and former opinions.'

Faith slipped the last of her oysters, a Cuddyhunk from British Columbia, between perfect teeth and closed her eyes to savour the Pacific. 'And what do you answer?'

'Help!' He shrugged. 'Something not far short of a quarter-million bucks weighs heavy in one pan of the scales. What do you think?'

She gathered her thoughts for a moment. 'I had lunch with an editor at Doubleday today and we got talking about the difference between writing and speaking – public speaking. And I suggested that most good writers make lousy public speakers because they assemble words at a different pace. James Joyce agonized over one single sentence for a whole day. "Perfumes of all him embrace; with hungered flesh obscurely he mutely craves to adore". Something like that. Anyway, she told me she has an author – an excellent prose stylist – who falls flat on his face every time he's asked to speak in public. He knows it – and still he accepts the invitations. She once asked him why, and he said, "It's their fault for asking me. I've never claimed to be a speaker but if I'm what they want, then I'm what they'll get!" How's about that?'

After a pause, Felix said, 'Yes, it helps.'

A man at a neighbouring table leaned towards them. 'Limeys, huh?' he guessed. 'Louie Parioli. You got connections here?' He did not introduce the lady with him.

Felix followed suit. 'Felix Breit. I've never been here before. My uncle recommended it.'

'Bright? Tony Bright? Your uncle? You must be one proud man, Felix. Tony Bright has given new definition to the concept of loyalty. He's not coming here with you? Joining you, maybe?'

'We live in London. I haven't seen Uncle Tony since before the war.'

'Oh, and lately it wasn't possible – I know!' He laughed.

'But we're going down to Pennington to meet up again this Saturday.'

'From the pen to Pennington, huh!' Again that bronchitic laugh.

'Aren't we?' Felix looked at Faith.

She nodded.

Sunday, 28 January 1957

Hotel Elysée

60 EAST 54TH STREET

NEW YORK, N.Y. 10022

TELEPHONE PLAZA 3-1066

. CABLE ADDRESS:

ELLEESAY, NEW YORK

Sunday, Jan 28th

Dearest, dearest, Darling Alex,

Well, I should be all nicely snuggled up with Felix, downstairs in the Monkey Bar, getting pleasantly woozy on daiquiris, and instead here I am, all alone in my room, writing to you. But wait till I tell you! I know I should have called you on Saturday but Felix seduced me into accompanying him on what promised to be a rather painful, or at least awkward, visit to his long-lost, or long-unvisited, Uncle Tony out in the New Jersey sticks. I had to go, just to offer moral support to the poor chap who is, after all, one of my dearest and closest friends. And yours, too, I trust? He really was in quite a tizz – understandable, since Uncle Tony had just finished a seven-year stretch in Sing-Sing.

Anyway, we left the Elysée good and early, hugging each other indecently close – it is so unbelievably bitterly cold here in Manhattan just now – and sauntered down to Penn Station, laughing and reminiscing about all the good times we've had together, him and me, and arriving still with the best part of an hour to spare. Which was deliberate, because Penn Station is one of the architectural gems of the entire Western World. In fact, I intend to talk Doubleday into doing a large-format photographic celebration of its glories. It would sell, I'm sure. Most New Yorkers I talk to say it's unthinkable that it will ever be destroyed to make way for a less grand but more obviously commercial space, but I'm not so sure. It's a superb monument to the city's past glory – and nothing can make it a more likely candidate for demolition than that. If you think of the Crystal Palace butting against the Baths of Caracalla in Rome, you have a fairly accurate portrait of the place.

So we wandered around, arm in arm, marvelling at details that Felix was seeing for the first time and that I had half forgotten. He has a wonderful eye for structure – not just how things are put together but why they chose to do it that way. I hope I can remember it all when I talk to Doubleday, otherwise he'll just jolly well have to stay on in New York and help me – not that I'd mind that, anyway!

The train ride down to Hamilton was unremarkable. ~~Felix suggested we~~ From there we took a taxi out to Pennington, which is where Uncle Tony now lives – in fact, where he lives it up, which I suppose anyone whose who's done 7 yrs in jail is entitled to do. He actually came out last Wednesday, which, by happy coincidence was his 70th birthday, and the party has been going ever since. Pennington's a sweet little village with lots of historic houses, some even older than the Dower House except for Chris and Debbie's Tudor bit – one crossroads and several minor roads that peter out in forest and arable farmland. And this is the unlikely retirement village for the most unlikely relative Felix is ever likely to have.

He's a little dynamo of a man, quite unlike Vati Breit, you'd never believe they were brothers. And, of course, he's on top of the world at the moment, after the past seven years. But it's not just the joys of freedom, it's the fact that he ~~accepted~~ agreed to plead guilty on behalf of someone very high up in the 'family' that controls almost all criminal activity in one fairly large part of Manhattan. And not just criminal activity but even some trade unions (or labor unions, they call them), which they pervert for criminal ends, of course. It's a hangover from the days of Prohibition but it's so embedded now, with even the police caught up in the corruption, that it carries on by its own momentum.

We had quite a discussion about it during one of the quieter moments. I asked him what would happen if they legalized gambling and prostitution, just as they were forced to legalize drinking after Prohibition. 'Get outta here!' he yelled at me. 'Those are our two worst nightmares.' They make hundreds of millions of dollars a year out of breaking the law — 'That's how we can afford the best cops and judges that money can buy,' he said.

All through the afternoon people with Italian names and complexions kept dropping by to congratulate him, have a drink, and reminisce about the great exploits they've undertaken in the dear dead days, and in between there were his friends and neighbours, all very middle class and respectable, delighted to see him home again — and all mixing well with the other lot. Felix said that Tony's presence in the neighbourhood is better protection against petty crime than half-a-dozen round-the-clock police patrols. No small-time crook is going to risk an increase in police surveillance and other activity anywhere near someone as 'well connected' as Tony.

There is an undeniable fascination about people 'connected' to big crime organizations. Back home in London those two Irish-Jewish-Gypsy twins we met at the Delphi club are well on the way. Remember how one of them boasted to you that they were the last prisoners ever to have been held in the Tower of London? They fascinated Willard, I know — and he has an amazing instinct for people who are on the up-and-up but haven't yet made it. Anyway, you'll be able to judge Tony Bright for yourself because Felix has invited him to the Tithe Barn next June, around the time of our midsummer party. Though getting a visa will be difficult!

As for my own work here — no particular hitches. Agreement on the Jung book is sticky, because people here — or some people in publishing, anyway — feel that his explanations for endorsing *Mein Kampff* and his other accommodations to Nazism have left him too tainted to be commercial. That's what they say, anyway. For myself, I think it just 'sticks in their craw' to OK the project just yet; we'll just have to find a popular Jung book by another author that's doing very nicely for another publisher — and then they'll be asking for 2nd galleys and final layouts by next week please. They're very pleased with the 'birds' book but still can't decide on whether it's to be Birds of the World or The World of Birds. One day I must try for a job with a publisher where such thorny conundrums (conundra?) can occupy an entire day.

Only the Penn Station book remains to be discussed (I haven't even broached it yet). There wouldn't be much sale in Europe but if we could get John Betjeman to do a book for us on great Victorian railway stations, we could cannibalize some of the Penn Station material for it. And it would work, too. Felix says the glass roof *at York is the obvious inspiration for the one here. York / New York — it's too neat to overlook. It's not one we would publish ourselves but we could 'package' it — in Fogel's latest commercialese — for Macdonald or Routledge . . . people who do a lot of 'Londiniana'.*

I'll put it to Elaine tomorrow, go shopping on Tuesday, catch a show with Felix on Wednesday, fly home on Thursday — which will leave just a day for arguing and recriminations with Fogel. If this gets there before me (and I earnestly hope it does) give lots of hugs and kisses to Jasmine and Tarquin from me — and keep a few for yourself.

Undying Love,
Faith

PS — Next time you recommend my favourite NY hotel to anyone, TELL ME TOO!

Sunday, 3 February 1957

Hilary tapped a varnished fingernail on the coffee table and said chirpily, 'Call the meeting to order.' She shuffled some papers. 'Two items on the agenda — one, the next step towards the Dower House purchase and two, what to do about the formal garden.'

Cynegonde, treading over Hilary's last syllables, said, 'Could we amend that to read: what to do about the garden in general. Denis and I think—'

'I'll put that to the vote,' Hilary said.

'But you don't know our reasons.'

'Oh, yes we do — and if the chair can express an opinion — which I know I can't — I happen to agree with you. We can't discuss the formal garden in isolation. What we need is a policy for the whole garden.'

'A Full-Blooded Planning Strategy, if you ask me,' Eric added eagerly. 'Properly costed and phased, with clearly defined staging points and—'

Cynegonde and Isabella both rounded on him simultaneously, each using the word 'serious'.

'It's going to be one of those,' Terence murmured to Willard. 'Shall us slope off for a crafty pint?'

'It's really a question of what sort of garden we *all* want,' Nicole said. 'Nobody has the time to create another Hidcote here. And anyway—'

'What is a hid coat, please?' Angela asked.

'A show garden,' Adam explained. 'Like the one at Knebworth. Or Luton Hoo.'

Nicole continued: 'We need a garden that can be let run away with itself for a few months but can also be brought back to some sort of orderliness without too much difficulty.'

'Not a Versailles,' Sally said.

Willard cut in: 'But the *chaos* – the utterly impenetrable jungle that's inside what we still call the *formal* garden – surely no one wants that? Sally – did you try to get inside there since last Saturday? Faith? Angela?'

The two other women looked at Faith, who replied, 'We all three had a go and you're right. We hacked a sort of path to the middle – found two rusty old bikes and an enamel basin as well – and there *is* a very fine ornamental cherry in the middle there. And we decided that if we could restore that square just to grass, like the lawn – not bother with any formal knot-garden sort of stuff or topiary – it would be a lovely sheltered area, especially on a windy day.'

'We could put up a simple pavilion there,' Marianne suggested. 'Shelter even in the rain.'

'Have a barbecue pit,' Willard added.

'At home we call it *braaivleis*,' Cynegonde said.

'Spelled how?' Eric held a poised pencil but she ignored him.

'There's another wilderness – between the back of the house and the line of Tasmanian pines,' Alex pointed out. 'A quarter of an acre?'

'It was once the first hard courts for tennis in Hertfordshire,' Eric added.

'Hey!' Willard's eyes gleamed. 'D'you think we could? I was champeen with the old racket in our division of AMGOT.'

Felix gave a despairing laugh. 'We can't even find time to finish off reglazing the old greenhouse by Rosy Primrose. Another half-finished, half-abandoned job. Now we're hoping to resurrect a couple of long-gone tennis courts!'

'We can finish reglazing it tomorrow,' Willard assured him.
'Well – next weekend, then.'

'We?'

'That's anyone who wants to help. Alex – you'd like to thrash
me at tennis, right? Sally? I'll bet you wield a mean racket.'

'One tennis court and one for badminton,' Nicole suggested.

'And The Tribe?' Eric asked. 'We just give them the old heave-
ho? That quarter-acre is Treasure Island, Spitzbergen, the Secret
Garden, and Pitcairn all rolled into one for them.'

'Dear God!' Tony cried. 'Adam and I design houses with
gardens measuring fifty-by-twelve yards and people manage to fit
in a vegetable plot, a pond, a lawn with a little summerhouse,
swings, slides, a Wendy house . . . And here are we, unable to
fit stuff into five acres!'

'Did you know that J. M. Barrie actually *invented* the name
Wendy?' Eric began.

'Nothing-to-do-with-the-gaaar-dens!' Isabella intoned, looking
sharply at Hilary.

Wendy, who was spending the weekend with Felix and Angela,
said, 'I didn't know that!'

'Perhaps the best thing,' Terence said, 'would be to investigate
a couple of square yards of the wilderness where this hard court
used to be. Then we'd have some idea how easy it would be to
resurrect.'

'I know where we can lay hands on a manual soil-corer,'
Adam offered. 'We can just drill straight down through whatever's there.'

'Great!' Willard beamed all round. 'The skills and resources we
command between us!'

'I have a suggestion,' Tony said. 'That we make the south-east
corner of the five acres our formal area – not too formal – but
it should extend from the lawns, the pergola, the resurrected
formal garden – details to be decided after everyone's had a shufti
at what's there now – and the bit of the front drive that's nearest
to the house. A couple of suggestions, actually. That's one. The
second is that we leave the Tribal lands to be decided after we
know what's there and how easy or difficult it would be vis-à-vis
the tennis/badminton courts. The Tribe already have the run of
the pigsties and those old stables or cowsheds or whatever they
were at the end. And we *could* now consider letting them do

what they like in the western side of the walled garden – which none of us has done anything with.'

'But we won't be able to see what they get up to in there,' Nicole objected. 'Behind that high wall.'

'If you think about it, *chérie*,' Tony told her, 'how many people can see even half of the five acres now? Only the Johnsons, and even then only if they happen to be at one of their windows. The Tribe is almost always out of sight of everybody else.'

'They're getting old enough now that we couldn't stop them if we tried,' Faith said.

'I could stop Alaric doing anything at any time,' Cynegonde assured them.

Everyone looked at her in amazement but no one disabused her.

'It'll be a triumph if we manage to keep them *somewhere* inside the five acres,' Adam said.

'Anyway . . .' Tony insisted. 'My final point. May I suggest that we reconvene in about two weeks' time – earlier or later if there's a breakthrough on the house-purchase front – and meanwhile we should go around the garden in smaller groups, not always the same group – mixing each time – and discuss ideas and possibilities at places where we can actually point to this bit and that bit and so begin to work towards a joint consensus?'

'Could you just say that again?' Hilary asked. 'Only I have to write it down.'

Eric leaped in: 'Proposed that smaller ad hoc groups examine various suggestions on-site and report back at the next meeting.'

For once everyone looked at him with gratitude.

'Is that what I said?' Tony asked – to be answered by several hasty cries of 'Yes!'

'Carried?'

Even Cynegonde's hand went up – and stayed up. 'I remember last spring we had all those rawfies come out from Hertford and Garden City to pick bluebells—'

'Out of order!' Hilary said sharply. 'Raise it in Any Other Business. We must now turn to the main item for discussion – the purchase. Adam?'

Adam opened a blue foolscap folder, dug down three or four pages, and began: 'Tony, Nicole, Sally, and I – being the architects to the refurbishment of the Dower House – met with the chairman

and the property director of the gravel company – Sir Hector
O'Dowd and John Willoughby. We wasted the first fifteen to
twenty minutes while they pretended to be disinterested in selling
and we—'

'*Un*interested!' Faith and Eric spoke simultaneously.

Adam looked baffled, shrugged, and continued: '. . . as if they
were uninterested in selling and we maintained our position that
we would not be interested in anything close to the market price
– while hinting that we could be persuaded, for a consideration,
to accept a clause barring us from lodging a protest if they wanted
to extract sand and gravel from the park.'

'Is that wise?' Alex asked.

'We think it's safe. They'll get permission for Panshanger because
the house is a roofless ruin – and that's hundreds of acres of
green-belt land. They'd never get permission to extend up the
valley, not in our lifetimes, not in our children's lifetimes. But
they're such bloody optimists, these people, and they think they
have the county in the palm of their hands. So, of course, they
think such a clause would be worth quite a discount on the sale
price. Penny on the drum – I think we'll be able to get the whole
place for ten thou.' Twelve at the most, but we're aiming for ten.'

There were whistles of surprised approval.

Alex said, 'They do understand that you're not actually negotiating the price – you're just—'

'They do, indeed,' Tony assured him. 'Our line is that we need
a rough figure so that we can go ahead and plan the proper division of the property into apartments. Soundproofing, rewiring,
fire-resistance . . . blah-blah-blah. Because there's no point our
even starting on detailed drawings if the price is over our heads,
anyway.'

'It's been a great help,' Nicole added, 'to be able to say we
have to refer this back to our finance committee and their advisers.
They know we've got a professor of economics who sits on many
government boards.'

Terence gave an elaborately mocking-bow.

'And an architect who's preferred bidder in God knows how
many London boroughs—'

'And other British cities.' Willard did the boxing-champ thing.
'Just today we're notified of expansions in Cumbernauld north
of Highway A80.'

'Not that the Hertford Sand and Gravel do all that much business up in Bonny Scotland,' Eric said.

'Aha! But Sir Hector is also chairman of the Balloch and Dullatur Sand and Gravel Company. By tomorrow he'll know who's going to be specifying what up there. Oh, I love this United Kingdom. I love its . . . small-worldliness!'

'So – dear friends and neighbours,' Sally said. 'We believe it's safe to start on detailed drawings for the builder, showing the changes we'll need to satisfy the mortgage companies that we have workable, independent apartments here.'

'One thing?' Debbie said hesitantly, looking immediately to Chris.

'Yes,' he said. 'We've had a bit of luck one way and another, Debs and me, and we think we could afford to build a staircase down into the garden immediately outside our . . . the room with all the feet.'

'But,' Adam objected, 'we'll be doing you a Leonardo-at-Fontainebleau staircase in the inner courtyard.'

'Yeah, but we'd like to walk straight down into the garden, see?'

'You'll be able to do that, too. We're planning to knock an archway through the curtain wall between us and the Palmers. It'll let the evening sun into that courtyard – you'll have your own little Italian piazza there.'

It took a moment or two for the previous idyll to be replaced by this more splendid vision. Then it was, 'Cheers, mate! You're the architect!'

Sally persisted. 'Are all agreed that we start, then?' Hearing Cynegonde draw breath, she added: 'Speak now if you have the slightest reservation. We can always start off the purchase with those who are agreed and fit in the doubters later.'

No one actually looked directly at Cynegonde but they all heard her breathe out again.

'*Nem con*, egad!' Eric said to Hilary. 'A first, surely!' Later he told Wendy, 'You're not alone as a literary creation. Pamela is another name invented by a writer – Samuel Richardson. Pamela and Clarissa. I think a novel should be banned unless the author donates one new name – male or female – to the language. But I'm sure no one invented Cynegonde. I think it would be impossible to invent Cynegonde, don't you?'

At that moment the lady herself was crying out over the

hubbub of a meeting breaking up: 'I would still like to raise the question of the bluebell wood.'

'It's not part of the five acres,' Hilary said, on her way to bring in the eats and drinks.

'But it attracts all those frightful people out from the towns – *and* they go back with armfuls of bluebells – *and* the way they pick them leaves the bulbs vulnerable to fungus infestation. I've seen it.'

There was a baffled silence. '*We* have no power to stop them,' Alex said. 'That's up to the gravel company.'

'*They're* not going to spare workers to protect the woods – not even to put up some barbed wire.'

The discussion unwound for several minutes as more and more fanciful schemes were batted into the long grass. Eventually it was Wendy who spoke: 'May I suggest . . .?' And into the surprised silence she went on: 'You could just put up a notice—'

'Trespassers will be prosecuted?' Felix asked. 'Nobody believes that. And who's to catch them?'

'No. A notice saying something like: "You are now entering the Dower House Snake Sanctuary. Please do not annoy the snakes. They are harmless if you do not provoke them". I'm sure *I* wouldn't risk my dipping my hand down among the undergrowth after reading that.'

Wednesday, 1 May 1957

It took a joint meeting of five different building societies and banks to establish the criteria under which they would agree to mortgage individual apartments in such a mixture of joint and several ownerships. And there was a further complication in that the Breits wanted to throw their quarter-acre of garden into the communal five acres and join the non-profit Dower House Community.

'We don't see that our situation is any different from a city block of flats,' Willard said. 'There you have individual ownership of the flats but communal ownership of—'

'Communal *use*,' said the Hatfield & Harpenden Building

Society. 'Usually the ground leaseholders or a management company will *own* the communal areas.'

'So . . . if our community incorporates itself as a management company . . .?'

'How will you stop someone selling their flat but keeping the shares in the management company?' asked the London & Home Counties Building Society.

'And,' said the Church of Wales, 'some of your flats will be valued at double or even treble what others are worth – how will that equate with equal voting rights?'

'Uncertainties like these make any loan more risky, you see,' concluded Burdett's Bank.

The arguments and qualifications rolled onward for the best part of half an hour before Eric judged it time to say, 'Didn't I see recently that Burdett's Bank – last month, I think this was – you granted a "joint-and-several" mortgage to the Earl of Wishart and his daughter and her brother-in-law to buy a hunting and fishing estate in Scotland?'

All eyes turned to the Burdett representative, who, after a bit of bluster, finally hit upon: 'Ah! Yes, but they were a *family!*'

'But – please do correct me if I'm wrong – the earl has the main house except for one wing owned by his daughter. And the brother-in-law has a substantial cottage within the estate. And you gave each of them a mortgage on their own bits of brick-and-mortar. And you further granted their management company, comprising the three of them, a separate mortgage on the land and shooting and fishing rights? So isn't our case vastly less complex in that we just want the bricks-and-mortar bit of the same arrangement?'

Later, when the financial wizards had departed and everyone had the loans they wanted, Eric added: 'I could see the man just itching to say, "Yes, but the Earl of Wishart is an *earl,* dammit! And you're just commoners". What enormous social progress we have made!'

Terence laughed. 'And immediately after that, when the banker caved in and the others thought he might offer to mortgage the lot and scoop up all their business . . . how they piled in with offers of their own!'

'They always intended to give us what we wanted,' Faith said. 'They just hoped to exploit our unusual circumstances to screw us.'

'I think that's immoral,' Debbie said.

'It's just capitalism,' Nicole told her.

'Sure,' Willard agreed. 'In any decent society, this place would be a country club for senior party members and the Tithe Barn would be where they could buy things at discount prices – all the stuff the proles never get to see.'

Isabella, who had fled the meeting as soon as it broke up, returned in triumph with the latest *Debrett*. 'There's no such person as the Earl of Wishart,' she said, handing the opened book with a so-there flourish to Eric.

He took the book from her and snapped it shut without looking. 'All life's a gamble,' he explained.

Sunday, 19 May 1957

The Dower House Community Association

Matters arising from the meeting of May 17th 1957

The following is the agreed final division of the Dower House and cottage relative to the total purchase price of £14,500:
Apartment 1 (Isabella and Eric Brandon) £2,500
Apartment 2 (Cynegonde and Denis deVoors) £1,250
Apartment 3 (Nicole and Tony Palmer) £2,100
Apartment 4 (Sally and Adam Wilson) £2,100
Apartment 5 (Debbie and Chris Riley-Potter) £950
Apartment 6 (Marianne and Willard Johnson) £1,750
Apartment 7 (Faith and Alex Findlater) £2,100
Apartment 8 (Hilary and Terence Lanyon) £2,150
(This leaves a contingency fund of £350)

The DHCA will be a legal entity, the owner of all the Dower House property excluding the apartments listed above and, later, the Tithe Barn. The Articles of Association of the DHCA will be drawn up by Symonds and Willet of Welwyn Garden City to incorporate the following:

1. The membership of the association will be limited to the owners of Apartments 1 to 8 plus the owners of Apartment 9 (the Tithe Barn – Angela and Felix Breit) after the conveyance of their grounds to the Association. A quorum will comprise ten members from at least six apartments.
2. All members will have an equal voice and a spouse may speak and vote for an absent spouse at any meeting. The votes are the perquisite of the apartment and are merely exercised, not inalienably owned, by the occupier(s).
3. Apartments 7 and 8 will pay their own municipal rates and water rates. For the main house, these rates will be divided equally among Apartments 1 to 6. (Families are responsible for their own electricity bills, now that we have all-new wiring and separate meters at last.)
4. A communal fund will be established to pay for structural and fire insurance on all buildings and drains, structural repairs, garden improvement and maintenance including insurance of communal tools and machinery, general public liability, and any other expenditure approved by a quorate meeting. Individuals will be responsible for insuring the contents of their own apartments and public liabilities incurred by them off the premises.
5. The chairmanship will rotate for each meeting, and run in order of apartment numbers, though people may swap turns to accommodate holidays, illness, etc.
6. A treasurer will volunteer or be appointed, elected, or co-opted for each financial year, to coincide with the tax year.
7. All the grounds and the long drive will be held in common but individuals may work private vegetable plots in the walled garden and particular flower beds or borders by common consent; they may also claim particular sections of the drying area in the old pheasant run.
8. The Association will not organize such routine matters as rotas for cleaning the communal spaces,

mowing the lawns, weeding the borders, maintaining
the dustbin area, etc., unless informal arrangements among members reach a breakdown.
9. Changes to these articles may be made at any time
by unanimous vote or at the AGM by a 66 per cent
majority with at least 6 families in agreement.

'So it's all sweetness and light from now on,' Eric said as he and
Isabella returned to their apartment.

'What about car parking and the garages?' she asked.

'Well . . . their days are numbered. Aren't we hoping that a
few gentle taps with sledgehammers will make them hazardous
enough to tear down and rebuild as an AP flat and a tenth
apartment?'

'Tenth apartment? I didn't hear that.'

'Well, it's a good thing one of us uses the earwax remover.'

'Love and peace, please,' said Calley, not lifting her head from
her book.

Isabella said, 'I don't like the idea of a tenth apartment. What
do Faith and Alex think? They'd be looking straight at it across
the yard – and the newcomers would be looking right into their
windows.'

'In other words, darling, revenge would be pretty instantaneous.
The point is it would only cost a thousand or so to build and
Sally reckons we could sell it for four or maybe five. So four-
hundred-plus to each existing family would be a nice sort of
Christmas present next year.'

'Ah!' She slipped the paper into the Dower House box file.
'Who shall we put in there?'

'You mean whom shall we propose?'

She bit her lip. 'I'm sure Chris will want to propose that awful
Terry Garlick. He's been let out of prison and Chris keeps talking
about what a reformed character he is. As if being a croupier in
an aristocratic gambling club in Berkeley Square was the pinnacle
of respectability!'

'That's not the problem. The problem is that no one else would
vote for him and then Chris would mope about the place for
weeks. Remember when we voted for the deVoors and he wanted
that artist who sucked paint in his mouth and spat it out again
on the canvas? He was inconsolable for weeks.'

'But *he* died – cobalt poisoning or something. I thought that was why poor Chris was inconsolable.'

'That, too, yes.'

'And we only let the deVoors in . . .' She glanced towards Calley and finished: '. . . because they were the best at the time.'

'Cynegonde has a heart of gold,' Calley said.

Eric agreed. 'Gold is the heaviest of all metals except uranium – and the least capable of reacting with any other element or compound. You have an ear for the *mot juste,* darling one!'

Calley still did not lift her eyes from the page.

Willard stood at the bedroom window, arms spread wide, hands resting on the sashes. Marianne put down her comb and went to him. Wrapping her arms around his chest, she sank her head between his shoulder blades and murmured, 'Ours at last!'

'Mm,' he grunted, straightening up and shaking her off.

She took a step back. 'Something rankling you?'

'Riling me, honey. The word is riling.'

She returned to the dressing table and started to plait her hair in the two pigtails that she would eventually coil above and behind each ear. 'For instance?'

'When I came back to Hamburg in 'forty-seven . . .'

Her fingers froze. He saw it and paused. After a brief, tense silence, she said, 'I don't think we should start this conversation. Not when we're due to go out in' – she checked the clock – 'fifty-six minutes.' When he said nothing, she added: 'And you haven't shaved yet.'

'So you do know what's riling me.'

'Of course,' she said calmly.

'What d'you mean – of course?'

She took a deep breath. 'I really don't understand why you've chosen this moment to pick this fight. The Stevenage contract is *so* important to you – to both of us. And don't tell me you can't just park this rankling-riling business and play the charmer with me – you'll certainly need to play the charmer with the planning committee this evening.'

'How d'you know it's going to be a fight? Has it *got* to be a fight?'

'Go. And. Shave.'

'But—'

'Please! I've just reached a tricky bit. Just go!'

Sandra poked her head round the door. 'I'm giving them scrambled egg and fish fingers and instant whip,' she said. 'And salad.'

'And yourself?'

'There's still some cold beef. And I defrosted the apple tart.'

'Good. We shouldn't be too late, but if they've all gone down and Nicole will listen out for them, you and Lena can go off to your evening class. They should be gone down before then.'

Willard fumed in silence all the way to Stevenage but he did, indeed, manage to show his considerable charm over dinner with the new town's planning-committee chairman and his closest political colleagues – just as Marianne managed to charm their wives. Watching her at work, Willard was once again reminded of what an asset she was – especially here in England. Those immaculate plaits! She had the regal bearing of a Swedish aristocrat, with all the easy grace that went with it; and he could see these middle-class wives responding, almost unawares.

It was a far more careful and congenial Willard who slipped behind the wheel for the journey home.

'Are you sure you ought to be driving, honey?' she asked primly.

He was surprised. 'I hardly touched a drop.'

'I was thinking more of the conversation I know you're itching to start, now the dinner's over and done with. I think the contract's as good as signed, don't you?'

'Sure.' He slipped into gear and pulled smoothly away. 'As for the other thing – the *conversation* – well, I guess "riled" was not quite the word. "Puzzled" is more like it. Put out at being left out.'

She laughed and squeezed his arm. 'D'you really think that if I *had* told you about my father's allowance that time in Hamburg – d'you think you'd have agreed with me about not touching it?'

He slowed down and finally pulled in to a lay-by. 'Allowance?' he asked. "What allowance?"

'When Hermann Treite came to me with his scheme to *buy* East German dissidents from the GDR, I used an old allowance from my father to finance it. Isn't that what's riling you?'

'But I've never heard of your father's . . . this *allowance*. What is it? I thought you were using part of the *inheritance* for that – the bit you put aside for the Von Ritter Trust – all that workers' welfare stuff.'

For a long while she just stared at the road ahead – at the darkness, the occasional car, a woman walking by the light of a torch. He did not press her. Indeed, he now had a lot more to think about, even before she started to explain.

At length, she said, 'While I was working for Albert Speer, Pappa sent me an allowance of five thousand Swedish crowns a month. He wanted the daughter of the house of von Ritter to sparkle in what passed for the *haute monde* among those Nazis – those vulgar street fighters and career men. And their wives – oh, God, their *wives*! I hardly ever touched the money – only enough to live *my* way. So I left them in a foreign-currency account, in *svenska kronor*, with the Hamburger Sparkasse and only turned them into Reichsmarks as the need arose. After I read the Wannsee transcript, I used even less – enough to maintain my position so that I could go on passing other stuff to Hermann Treite.'

'Did he know of this back then?'

'Pappa?'

'No. Treite.'

'Yes, he knew. Not how much. But I told him if he ever was in a jam, I could help – but it was tainted money in my eyes – *Blutgeld*. And then, after the war, when I stayed with him and Biggi for a while and he kept telling me to use it.' She laughed coldly. 'He's happy enough now that I didn't!'

'And you – sketching quick portraits in the streets. In Sankt Pauli! My God! And you had . . . *how* much stashed away in Swedish crowns?' Another thought struck him. 'That's why you didn't have to exchange Reichsmarks for Deutschemarks at the changeover!'

'Clicketty-click, Willard!'

The woman with the torch stopped beside the car, rapped on the window and called out, 'Everything all right, then?'

He wound the window down. 'Fine,' he said. 'We just came from a meeting and we're trying to remember all the names while they're still fresh.'

'I've got ninety-seven sheep,' she said. 'And I know the name of every one of them.'

'But do *they* know?' he asked.

'They come if I call them, each to its own name.'

'That's mighty impressive, ma'am. Say, can we give you a lift? We're in no hurry to get home.'

She pointed to a dim light across the field. 'Thanks, but it's not worth it.'

The moment the window was wound up again he turned and spoke as if there had been no interruption: 'We could have gained a year on ourselves! When we came to England . . . all that time we put in, doing up the place, building our office.'

'Don't you think we needed it, Willard? Don't you think *you* needed it?'

He started the car again and nosed out into the highway. 'I don't know what you mean.'

'We needed the best part of that year together. We needed the delay to you starting up in business so that history did not repeat itself. Our history. It didn't hold you back one single day. And you can truthfully say *you* did it all. All thanks to my silence! *You* did it *all*.'

He stared moodily at the road as it unwound out of the darkness towards them.

She nudged him gently. 'You still think you wish you'd known, right? Let me tell you – you know everything except yourself, my dear.'

'So what about the money I *thought* you were promising Treite – your father's legacy?'

'*You* don't need it, either. It's there in trust for Siri and Virgil and Peter if ever they do. And if your wonderful Tory government has abolished free university places, it will take care of that, too. And they can have their share when they've proved they could actually manage without it – like you and your GI grant.' After a moment's hesitation she added: 'I'll admit I've been wrong – very wrong – in one respect.'

'Oh?'

'We should have had this conversation years ago.'

'You didn't say how much it was. Or is now, rather.'

'And you can't work it out? Sixty-thousand *kronor* a year for eight years? Take away maybe two . . . two-and-a-half thousand each year? Four per cent interest? When I changed it into

Deutschemarks the rate was about five *kronor* to four DM. And it has sat there, untouched, at around four per cent ever since – another nine and a half years . . . clicketty-click?'

His knuckles strained against the mesh of his driving gloves. 'Seven . . . seven-and-a-half million?' he guessed at length. 'That's if it stayed in *kronor*.'

'Not bad. It was about five-and-a-quarter million *kronor* when I made the exchange to DM. Now it's just fifty-thousand-odd short of six million DM. We are going to buy a lot of East Germans' freedom with that!'

Willard gave a low whistle, reminiscent of a falling bomb. 'A million pounds sterling! A *million*! We could have bought the entire Dower House out of petty cash and *given* everyone their parts. Jeez – all that *fuss!*'

She chuckled. 'OK – let's say I change my mind. Sorry, Hermann – I'm giving it to Willard instead. What will you do?'

'Do? With a million quid? I'd buy – I mean, it's pretty obvious the gravel company knows it's restricted to quarrying the old Panshanger estate. So I'd buy up all the land I could this side of the road, right up to the church and as far towards Queen Hoo as I could afford. And if I couldn't buy, I'd cut the landowners in on the deal. And I'd build the best private eighteen-hole golf course in the Home Counties and the best nineteenth hole in England. But – hey! – not a word about this to *anyone*. I want it all hogtied and swaddled before going public.'

I'd cut the landowners in on the deal. That one sentence revealed to Marianne that this was no spur-of-the-moment dream. Were the holes and hazards already anchored in the landscapes of his mind? Which member of the House of Lords was pencilled in as club chairman?

'Tempted?' he said.

She laughed and punched him in the ribs, half in jest, half in real aggression. 'Damn right I'm tempted – and damn *you!*' Her pulse must be over a hundred.

'Anyway,' he said casually, 'Treite may not need your money after all.'

She turned to him sharply. 'Did he tell you that?'

'No, but when Hermann was visiting the Breits that weekend, Alex invited him to go to church with him and—'

'Alex? Church?'

'Yes, well, that's not the only uncharacteristic thing. There was no service that Sunday – no Matins, anyway – because they'd all swanned off to Saint Albans. Alex said he "forgot" but it gave him the best part of an hour for a solo chat with Treite. So you see, honey – this thing is already far and away bigger than your measly million quid.' He paused briefly before adding: 'Welcome though I'm sure it is. And once all this secret funding is secured, the Von Ritter guarantee could lapse. But you'd have the kudos – and the personal satisfaction – for starting one of the most worthwhile ventures of the Cold War. And you'd still have everything you have now. Intact. Ready to buy us a golf course.'

Saturday, 8 June 1957

Adam opened his pocketknife and dug the tip of the blade into the mortar high up on the back wall of the first garage. 'Lime mortar,' he called down. 'We're in luck.'

'But we can't simply scrape away the mortar,' Sally said. 'That's just too obvious.'

'We've got to make it look at if it rotted away,' Tony said. 'That whole wall is too dry.'

Adam jumped down. 'If we collected all the buckets, we could form a human chain between here and the tap in the yard.'

'You boys – out!' Marianne said.

Alaric did not budge. 'D'you remember the old stirrup pump that used to be in the air-raid shelter?' he said.

'What about it?' Tony asked.

'I know where it is.'

'How did you know it used to be in the old air-raid shelter?' Adam said.

''Cos that's where it was when I borrowed it.'

'Go and get it!'

'If . . . I mean, can me and the others do the pumping?'

Glance by glance the adults consulted. 'The moment anyone gets "accidentally" soaked . . .' Marianne threatened.

The boys didn't wait to hear; they ran outside and legged it in the direction of the old pigsties.

'Little buggers,' she murmured. 'I'm going for my oilskins.'

'I think we have to construct a *scenario* here,' Eric said. 'If we go outside and just remove a slate or two and take out the hooks so as to leave the gutter swinging, we'd sort of reverse-explain the wet wall that Alaric and chums are about to create.'

Willard, as he joined the demolition squad, said, 'Why don't we just "accidentally" fell the lime tree diagonally across all three garages?'

'How?' Adam asked. 'Wouldn't it look just a bit obvious?'

'Not really. We could wedge it out at waist height to make sure it falls that way and then cut a different wedge at ground level to make it look as if we had really intended it to fall that way but were beaten by a sudden gust of wind from the south-east.'

They all went round to the back of the garage and looked at it.

'It's rather a beautiful tree,' Nicole said.

'Yeah – well, you don't park your car under it in the summer. It sheds some sticky treacle like Niagara pours water. Anyway, it's too close to Adam's and Sally's.'

Nicole said, 'Has anybody tried just *asking* the county planners if we can demolish the garages and rebuild?'

In the ensuing silence the boys came running back with the wartime stirrup pump and a couple of fire buckets, still showing traces of red and of the word FIRE. 'It's got a leak but we plugged it with bubblegum,' Andrew said.

'The wall is yours,' Tony assured them. 'Get it as wet as you like. We're thinking of another plan.'

'What?'

'That tree.' He mimed its fall across the roof.

'Oh, yeah! Hot stuff!' The stirrup pump and bucket were cast aside at once. 'When?'

'Well, not now – that's for sure.'

'Why not just ask permission?' Nicole insisted. 'We already don't dare use the building to garage our cars. That inspection pit is a death trap. All the rafters have woodworm and beetle holes. The ridge tiles leak in lots of places. Why wouldn't they let us take it down? Preserve the bricks, preserve the slates, and rebuild?'

'Because,' Willard said patiently, 'they might insist we rebuild them *as garages.*'

'We should just say we can't accept garages there, because of the danger to the children. It's twenty-five now. Plus two with Susan and Tommy. And the backyard is their playground. Would they put parking spaces all along the edge of a school playground?'

'Quite a point, Willard,' Tony said loyally.

'Hey kids!' Willard turned to them. 'Pick up that stuff and go make all the mess you want in there.'

'And don't fall in the inspection pit!' Nicole added.

Sally turned to her husband. 'A modest little domestic dwelling in salvaged brick plus associated outbuildings? Sounds like the perfect wee job for the Palmer-Wilson partnership. There's nothing in it to call for the genius that Marianne and I lavish on *our* commissions.'

Wednesday, 3 October 1962

Wendy let herself into the Breits' Robert Street flat, slammed the door behind her, leaned against it, closed her eyes, and gave out a sigh of relief.

'Don't be alarmed!' a voice cried from somewhere on the first floor. 'It's only me.' Faith appeared at the stairhead and started to descend. 'They're electrifying the old hydraulic lift in South Audley Street and there's the dust of centuries everywhere. Not in our apartment, fortunately, but everywhere else.'

'Fine.' Wendy started for the kitchen. 'Have you eaten?'

'Well . . . I didn't like to presume.'

'Come on. Let's see what we've got.'

'Felix, let me have the key. I have an early flight to Paris tomorrow.'

Wendy put on the kitchen light; the cat leaped down guiltily from the draining board and looked up with pleading eyes.

'Did I forget your milk?' Wendy opened the fridge, took out a half-pint bottle of gold-top and filled the cat's bowl. The cat sniffed it and walked out of the kitchen, tail erect.

'So-o-o like my daughter,' Faith murmured. 'Alex's daughter, anyway.'

'Oh, Jasmine's OK. Weren't you like that at fifteen? Well, we have leeks, we have bacon lardans . . . and butter. I can do a fry-up in no time. And there's some white plonk.' She extracted a bottle of Liebfraumilch, three-quarters full. 'You could pour some of that now.'

She stripped the leeks and cut them into inch lengths, which she then sliced in half so that they fell apart.

'Quite an evening, was it?' Faith asked as she handed Wendy her wine.

'Oh – I was a guest of the bloody BBC. You were so right not to join them!'

'Is that what you're thinking of doing?'

'No!' She put a quarter-inch of water in the frying pan, turned the gas up full, tipped in the fragments of leek, and cut knobs of butter on top.

Faith switched on the cooker-hood light and extractor.

'Oh . . . yeah . . . thanks.' Wendy sighed. 'I'm not really with it tonight.'

'What were you doing at the Beeb? Are they buying your TV rights?'

A dry laugh was the answer to that. 'No such luck. They must be running short of ideas, though, because they circulated all the London publishers – the fiction houses, anyway – saying they were holding open-house for new young novelists who might be interested in working for television. At least I got a sherry and some biscuits.'

'So you were down at the TV Centre. Isn't it just perfect!'

Wendy stirred the leeks vigorously, leaning back to avoid the clouds of steam. 'In what way?'

'You haven't heard Eric's joke? He told Willard it's a perfect match of form and function. You set off purposefully along any corridor and you march past innumerable doors bearing impor-tant names, household names, and grey eminences you've never heard of . . . and yet you always end up precisely where you started.'

Wendy laughed. 'That's bang on! It's certainly what happened tonight.'

The water was all boiled off by now and the parboiled leeks began to sauté in the butter. Wendy tipped in the bacon and stirred the lardans evenly into the mess of leeks.

'Was Grace Wyndham Goldie there?' Faith asked.

'To name but one! They were *all* there – Donald Baverstock, Stuart Hood, the one they call Five-Finger Exercise – i.e. Huw Wheldon. And there was a fiery Welshman who had difficulty controlling his saliva. And they all stood up in turn and *orated* about their *passion* for television and their utter-utter determination to encourage new talent to feed into—'

'– which is why you were there?'

'I was there because Tom Maschler volunteered me. There must have been about a dozen and a half of us first-time novelists. This is almost done.'

Faith reached into a wall cupboard for a couple of plates, saying, 'I'll run some hot water over these.' Over the pop of the geyser and the quiet roar that followed, she added: 'You're his new star, I suppose. England's answer to Françoise Sagan. I've read all your reviews. Cape's first Angry Young *Woman!*'

Wendy chuckled. 'I don't know about that. Though I was pretty angry about tonight's circus. An utter waste of time.' She turned off the gas and pulled the sautéed mass into a heap. 'This tastes a lot better than it looks,' she promised.

Faith set the plates on the table and refilled the wine glasses. 'They were fishing for ideas, of course. Don't be tempted to send in anything directly – only through your agent. Did Eric tell you what happened with David Mercer and the great Huw Wheldon?'

Wendy blew a forkful cool and popped it in her mouth. 'Mmh-mmh.' She shook her head.

Between bites – and compliments on a dish that did, indeed, taste far better than it looked – Faith told how Mercer, on hearing that Wheldon was planning a new programme called *Monitor*, wrote in with some ideas for the launch edition, all to do with Paris. He'd just spent a year in Paris writing a novel – so he knew them all. That was before he started writing for television. Anyway, it whetted Wheldon's appetite enough to invite Mercer to a lunch at the Athenæum. And Mercer gave him the works – who to see, what they were doing, the latest pecking order among writers, poets, philosophers, painters . . . the lot. And Wheldon said fine, call me next week. And then it was don't call me, I'll call you. And then . . . silence. 'And when the first programme went out, *quelle surprise!* – it was

David Mercer's scenario down to the last scribbler, dauber, and existentialist. So don't trust any of those buggers with a new idea!' She scraped the last morsel of bacon from her plate and savoured it. 'That was delicious, darling. Your talents are limitless.'

They carried the rest of the wine through into the sitting room and turned on the TV. The programme was . . . *Monitor*! Wendy looked at Faith, who shrugged; she turned it off again and watched the dot fade. 'Wheldon's bloody good at what he does, though,' she conceded.

'I mustn't keep you up,' Faith said. 'You looked all-in when you came in from the street.'

'Oh!' Wendy sat down, cross-legged on the carpet. 'That was actually nothing to do with the Beeb. It was on the Central Line coming back from White City. The man opposite me was reading the *Star* and the headline was about this missile hooha in Cuba and I just sat there thinking, *If they dropped it now, there's a good chance I might actually survive! Oh, God, please don't let me survive . . . please don't let me survive!* And when I came up to the street again, at Warren Street, and they hadn't dropped The Bomb, I just felt so relieved! But sort-of depressed-relieved. If you know what I mean.'

Faith laughed grimly. 'Well, we'd better crack open another bottle or neither of us will get much sleep tonight.'

When she returned, she asked, 'What would be so awful about surviving The Bomb?'

'In a world populated by Swiss businessmen, Harold Macmillan and his cabinet, and the forces of law and order? The *new* law and the *new* order? Thanks very much! I'd look for the nearest bare bodkin.'

Sunday, 4 November 1962

Cynegonde opened her bedroom window and shouted, 'Not there, you idiots! On the front steps – between the pillars.'

'We already did that,' Denis told her. 'This yew hedge gives a . . .' His voice trailed off as the window came crashing down and

Cynegonde vanished. 'Now we start all over again,' he said to
Alaric. 'I don't know why we bothered.'

Cynegonde appeared in the portico and yelled, 'Over here.'

Father and son trotted to obey.

'Your handkerchief,' she said as soon as they drew near.

Denis handed it over and she immediately bent and burnished
the already mirror-like gleam on her son's best boots. Alaric lifted
them up in turn and presented the soles for her inspection. They,
too, were polished to a black-mirror finish and the metal studs
gleamed.

'What's that for?' she asked. 'Stand properly.'

'That's how I get made stick-man when I'm rostered for guard
duty. I stay in the guardroom while the nignogs go out on patrol.
Clean handkerchief, clean fingernails – I even bull the inside of
my belt.'

'Stand still!' She started picking imaginary lint off his uniform.

'Aren't you pleased that I'm the pick of the bunch?'

'I never wanted you to go into the army in the first place.
And why you had to pick the *Service* Corps—'

'The *Royal Army* Service Corps, if you don't mind. And we're
a *cavalry* regiment, I'll have you know. But now it's done, aren't
you pleased I'm the pick of the bunch?'

'I'd be disappointed if you weren't. Now – stand between these
two pillars, take off your left glove, hold it in your right hand
along with your stick—'

'Cane. It's called a cane.'

'—and peel back your left sleeve with one finger so as to look
at your watch. Lean forward and put one leg back as if you're
walking. You're a busy man – going between one important
meeting and the next. Are you ready, Denis?'

'It's going to look terribly fake,' he warned.

'Not as fake as it feels,' Alaric said.

'Shut up both of you and just take the picture.'

For the next ten minutes she was Alfred Hitchcock and David
Lean to Alaric's star performance as God's latest gift to the
British army, all against the background of Soane's classical
portico, which could well be mistaken for part of the Royal
Military Academy at Sandhurst or even Buckingham Palace.
'Now!' she said, satisfied at last, 'the family will see how an
officer *ought* to look.'

'I'm not an officer yet,' Alaric pointed out. 'Just an officer cadet.'

'You'll be a general, believe me, by the time your father manages to print these off and we get them home to South Africa. Anyway, the regimental sergeant major has to call you sir.'

'No he doesn't – he has to call me *su-u-uur!* The first time he did it I thought there was a feral dog somewhere near. And he was actually on the far side of the parade ground.'

Released into the wild at last, Alaric sauntered round to the south side of the house where he sat and sunned himself on the top steps of the short flight that led up to the ballroom – now Eric's studio. He lit up a precious C to C. His Uncle Pendragon, who had folk memories of starvation in the Boer War, sent him regular parcels from South Africa, filled with biltong, dried locust beans and bananas, and packets of the Cape-to-Cairo brand (also known as Cough to Coffin).

'Boo!' His sister Larissa and Jasmine sprang out from Eric's studio.

'Now who could that be?' he drawled, not looking round.

'My darling bro!' Larissa bent over, flung her arms around him from behind, and pouted her lips to lay a quantity of saliva behind his ear.

Jasmine, watching, thought it might be quite nice to do that – flinging the arms, not the saliva part.

Alaric menaced his sister's bare arms with the glowing tip of his cigarette.

'How's army life?' Jasmine asked offhandedly.

'Pretty good so far.' He patted the stone step beside him and she took up the invitation at once, with an only partly conscious sashay of her hips.

'Tell her about being Church of England,' Larissa giggled as she stepped daintily past them and tripped down to stand on the path.

'Really?' Jasmine said, fascinated.

He gritted his teeth. 'Of course I'm not. But you never put yourself down as atheist or agnostic for church parade on Sundays, because they all get sent to the cookhouse to peel spuds. I thought of saying Parsee but they have so many *worthy oriental gentlemen* in the British army that Aldershot can probably put up a regular church even for that lot. So I said C of E – that's all.' He grinned down at Jasmine. 'How's school, young 'un? Done your O-levels yet?'

'This coming year. I think I'll do all right.'

'She'll get A-A-A all the way,' Larissa said. 'She's at the Blue Coat School.'

'Are you really an atheist?' Jasmine asked him. 'Or an agnostic?'

'Atheist, of course. Aren't you?'

'I don't know. Don't you think there must be *something?*'

'Out there?' He blew a smoke ring that lingered a second or two on the gentle breeze before turning chaotic. 'Entropy,' he said. 'If there is a God, he's running down. It's one of the laws *he* made up so he can't grumble if time's arrow is prodding him in the back.'

Larissa stood and faced them. 'I'm not going to listen to another lecture on Logic.' She turned and sauntered away, still allowing her friend time for a change of mind.

'Logic?' Jasmine prompted.

He sighed and stubbed out his dog end and put it away inside the matchbox. 'Let's just leave it, eh? People can't be argued into belief and they can't be argued out if it. Tell us what's been happening since I left.'

'They still don't know what to build where they knocked down the garages – beside that one AP apartment Sally and Adam are building for his dad. And Calley's going to be a poetess. She's my bestest friend . . . since . . .'

'Since what?'

'Oh, nothing. Do you shoot guns?'

He showed her the crossed rifles on his left sleeve. 'That's a marksman's badge. I get an extra shilling a week thanks to that. What sort of poetry?'

'It doesn't rhyme but you can tell it isn't just prose. "My world's a window. Looking in, / You'll see a limbo unbaptised / And stuffy as all Surrey on the finest day. / 'Escape!' you say – still looking in? / Well here I come – Now you look out!"'

Alaric laughed. 'Not bad!'

'She always likes a twist at the end. I wish I could write like her.'

'What are you good at, then?'

'Organizing things. Making lists.'

'I thought Maynard was good at that.'

'He *was*. But he's fourteen now. Turning silly. Do you have to peel potatoes?'

'Not on Sundays – I told you. Oh, God – those kitchens! They keep the Light Programme running over the loudspeakers all day. If I hear *Stranger on the Shore* just one more time . . .!'

'Diana wants to be a mechanic when she's grown up. She got the lawnmower going again when Chris broke it. He's banned from driving it now. He can only rake. D'you think the community's changing or is it just we're noticing different things because of growing up?'

He sucked at a tooth. 'It's bound to change,' he said judiciously.

The sash window behind them screeched up and Eric stepped out. 'Couldn't help overhearing,' he said. 'D'you think it's changed since we each bought our own apartments here?'

Ruth followed him out, paintbrush still in hand. 'You shouldn't butt in on other conversations,' she said.

Eric winked at Alaric and said, 'I can't think *where* she gets it from.'

'All the communal bits are a lot better cared for,' Ruth continued.

'That's from the same horse's mouth,' Eric told the other two.

'But it's true!' Jasmine insisted. 'Sometimes you just didn't want to go into the back hall when it was certain people's turn to clean it.'

'No names, no pack drill,' Alaric said.

Ruth went back to her painting.

Larissa returned, now with Siri in tow. Jasmine moved closer to Alaric – as if making room for Ruth to sit down. Or for Eric to pass. Or something. Siri always seemed quite indifferent to Alaric but you never knew.

Alaric ignored them. 'So!' He hung a friendly arm around Jasmine's shoulders. 'How's The Tribe? Who's in, who's out?'

Paying the two elder girls the tribute of avoidance, she replied, 'Well, it's sort of . . . *pfft!* You've gone. Betty's at Sussex doing PPE. Sam's an apprentice at that satellite-dish place in Cornwall – they were both here at the midsummer party. Charley's something in the film industry. In Soho. I don't know about Hannah Prentice.'

'She's doing *au pair* work in Germany,' Larissa said. But Jasmine was already continuing: 'Tommy's working in Welwyn Department Store but he makes more with his rock band on Saturdays.'

'Nuts in May – they still going? I thought they broke up.'

'Different line-up. Tommy re-formed them last month. They're groovy.'

'So I guess Larissa is now the eldest.' He looked his sister in the eye and added: 'Pity the poor Tribe!'

'Ha-ha!' she sneered, but again Jasmine was unstoppable: 'And I'm next – me, Theo, Samantha, and Andrew.'

Siri spoke, bringing Jasmine to a halt. 'But it's not the same. It's never been the same since we stopped walking to school over the fields. Especially with you, Eric. The young ones still do, of course. Tarquin and Andrew, Constance . . . Susan was the last. There are no children at home in the daytime now. But even when we *are* all here, the boys are more into football, model aircraft and stuff and we're more into horses and Saturday hops and stuff. When are you going back, Alaric?'

'Tonight. Aldershot – Mons Barracks, Aldershot. Six weeks from now I'll either be preparing for a commission or I'll have been quietly smuggled out by the back door and posted somewhere as a clerk.'

She gave a theatrical shiver. 'Doesn't that scare you?'

'Not much. The nignogs who fail as potential officers usually get sent as clerks to some cushy place – NATO HQ in Fontainebleau, FARELF HQ in Singapore . . . all sorts of places.'

'Cripes!' Jasmine cried. 'I think I'd fail on purpose. Tskoh! Boys are lucky!'

'There's lots of good careers for girls in the modern army, you know. I'll put in a good word for you when the time comes. But what are you really going to do?'

She made a diffident, weaving sort of movement of her head and almost whispered, 'Music. But I don't want to be a player . . . more sort of academic or . . .'

'Or what?'

She hoped she wasn't as red as she felt. 'I don't suppose I'd ever be good enough for it but the sort of music Angela works with. She gets some fantastic people visiting her and the things they can do with different sounds. It's like music from Mars or somewhere. Really, I'd like to do that – even though I *know* I'd be no good.'

'Aaaagh! Ten years from now I'll be sitting in the Festival Hall and you'll be taking a bow from the royal box and all the tape-recorder operators on the stage will be giving you a standing ovation and I'll nudge my neighbour and whisper, "I've known her since she was about six!" You'll see!' He stood up and stretched. 'Gotta go, young'un. Duty calls. Officer cadets are not allowed to travel in uniform because nobody knows whether to salute us or not. It confuses the peasants – which is bad for morale.'

She watched him do a Fred Astaire down the steps in his gleaming best boots and his knife-edge trousers. Larissa sneered: '*I'll* salute you, Alaric!'

He glanced back at her and laughed as he gave her an ironic salute.

'Will you write to me?' Jasmine called out before she could have second thoughts.

'Only if you'll settle it to music.' He turned the corner, stamping left-right-left-right on the gravel of the front drive.

'*Set* it to music!'

'I'll take that as a promise.'

She didn't want to kiss him or cuddle him or anything soppy but she did quite like being with him.

Larissa said to her, 'I hope you know what you're doing, young'un.'

'I hope you realize what *Alaric's* doing,' Siri added. 'Trying to use *you* to make *me* jealous – fat chance!'

Jasmine rose to her feet and, catching Eric's eye, said, 'Well?'

'Everyone should have something hidden in their teenage years that will make them cringe with embarrassment when they come of age. I know I ha . . . *ooofh!*'

She cut him short with a hard, sideswipe punch to his stomach, using the heel of her hand. 'I don't want to hear about it!' she shouted as she cleared the steps in one leap and stormed away.

Tuesday, 4 December 1962

Alex opened up their new R-TYPE Bentley as they crested the hill on Watford Way and the pincushion of Hendon's lights spread itself out before them. Four-and-a-half litres of cylinder volume gave quite a satisfactory kick in the back as they headed for the Great North Road and home. 'It feels like snow,' he said.

'Mmmm,' Faith replied.

'Your mood is . . . uffish?' he asked.

She stretched her arms and leaned into the soft grey hide of her seat. 'I think I'm facing the law of unintended consequences.'

'At Manutius? Or with Doubleday?'

'Manutius. You know I've been gently forcing an expansion of our output – the Junior Knowledge Series, the Adult Series, the Science Paperback Series – which I expanded into producing library hardbacks last spring – the Life Enhancement Series, et cetera, et cetera. And then there was our move into Golden Square, all the time taking on more staff—'

'To tie Fogel down in details and plans – yep! Isn't it working?'

'Too well, you might say. Remember when we met Peter Glemser at the *World Atlas* launch and he told us Reader's Digest Books had started hiring from Fleet Street?'

'And Fogel said they stole the world-atlas idea from him?'

'Well . . . that's Fogel's version. He should have kept his mouth shut. Anyway, we also started hiring subs from Fleet Street because, say what you like, they do understand deadlines and they can shape text to any given requirements in next to no time. But we overlooked one small matter.'

'The bloody unions?' he suggested.

She leaned forward to see his face better. 'You knew?'

They were nearing the Northway roundabout. Two cars moved aside to give them priority – one of the perks of driving a Bentley.

'You knew?' she repeated once they were past the speed limit on Barnet Way and he could really step on it.

'You're not alone,' he assured her. 'I remember when we had an ITN team out doing an interview with one of the print unions – at the *Sunday Times* in Grays Inn Road, in fact. In the old days at the Beeb we'd have sent Slim Hewitt and Trevor Philpott to do the interview – a two-man team. But the unions in commercial TV have never allowed that sort of efficiency. So there was our man asking questions about overmanning and their union shop steward just listened with a grin while he counted *our* team. And then he said, "I see you've sent along thirteen people to do this interview. An hour ago, the BBC managed it with four". Egg-on-face time for us. But I bet they're still getting away with murder. D'you know, they had an entire phantom shift at the *Sunday Times* – people who were rostered but who never turned up except on payday. And the management knew all about it but couldn't stop it because to lose an edition – just one edition – would have cost far more.'

'Oh, God – you're just adding to my nightmares,' she moaned. 'We hired Colum O'Donnell and Peter Wiles, both from the *Mirror*, and they're both bloody good at their jobs – unfortunately. And now they've gone ahead and organized a chapel of the NUJ at Manutius. It turns out that—'

'But you're not *journalists*. You're *book* editors and designers.'

'They simply redefine *journalist*. You can see what the NUJ is up to. With the expansion of traditional book publishing into mass-market areas, and books that are first published in magazine-style instalments, they can see a chance to bump up their membership – and subscriptions, of course. What other union could represent editors and designers in publishing?'

They slowed down briefly for Bignells Corner.

'But didn't you say that ever since Roy and the other American executives moved in, Manutius has been paying salaries well *above* the market? What's in it for your people to make them want to join a union?'

She threw up her hands in resignation. 'I don't know. I don't get it. The childish glamour of having a card saying PRESS in big, bold letters? Insurance? Just wishy-washy left-wing sentiment – solidarity with the brothers? The union is being all sweetness and light at the moment, but once they're entrenched . . .'

'What? What harm can they *actually* do?'

'I don't know – but I don't want to wait until something or other gets sprung on us. Fogel is furious, of course – and itching to find some way to blame me. But at least I'm ahead of things so far. I have my informants.'

The green mercury glow over Hatfield haloed the more distant sodium yellow over Garden City – a cowslip patch in the sky. 'What worries me,' she said, 'is that I didn't *foresee* it. Yet now that it's happened, it's so bleedin' obvious.' There was a brief silence, in which he decided to say nothing. 'This is the nightmare. Fogel doesn't see it. To him the union is nothing more than a brake on his own freedom of action. But I think it threatens our very survival. Somewhere out there is a clever designer and an ambitious editor – perhaps they already do freelance work for us – or for *Digest* or Paul Hamlyn. They're watching us and they're thinking, "I could do that – better and cheaper". And they'll be the must-see-must-grab at next year's Frankfurt and we'll all be saying, "Why the hell didn't *we* think of that?" Is it the fate of *all* organizations, Alex? Maybe I should have kept Manutius just as it was – small, anarchic, fun, nimble . . . and destined to die when Fogel retires.'

'You left out the word *successful*,' he said. 'The problem with all *successful* small organizations is that they can't stay small. Only one-man bands can do that.'

The combined lights of the two neighbouring towns were a kind of spiritual fulcrum of their daily journey to and from the Dower House – the point where the balance between 'London' and 'home' would tip. So, as they snaked their way down the wooded hill at Digswell, just before turning right on the B1000, it hardly seemed like a change of subject when Faith said, 'What about Jasmine, then? Should we be worried by all this hero worship of Alaric?'

He did not answer at once but in the end her silence forced him to say, 'Your guess is probably a lot better than mine. Teenage girls and their emotions are an utter enigma to me. What was it? "An enigma wrapped inside . . .?" Something. What were you like at that age?'

'Rebellious, of course. But I was at boarding school – a restrictive, *con*strictive, *pro*scriptive, claustrophobic . . . Jasmine has no excuses like that. I wonder if it's fair to ask Angela? She has the best relationship with the girl these days.'

The forty soaring arches of the Welwyn Viaduct loomed black-on-black ahead, a darker shade against the distant glow of Hertford. A slow goods train traversing it, way up high, painted billows of smoke and steam in a lurid red underglow from the firebox.

'But,' he asked, 'it wouldn't actually *come* to anything, I mean – this pash for Alaric? Would it?'

'You mean might it lead to a quiet visit to Harley Street?'

'Well – one has to face such possibilities. I know she's only fifteen-and-a-half but I'm not thinking so much of *now*. She'll reach the age of consent next July – only seven months away. D'you mind my asking . . . when you first . . . I mean, how old were you when . . . you know.'

She laughed. 'I was sixteen. With the gardener's boy. But I only wanted to see how things fitted together and what it felt like. I made him withdraw after . . . well, ten, fifteen seconds. And I finished him off by hand. Yuk!'

The car gave a little lurch to the right, instantly corrected. 'Well! I say! I didn't actually mean—'

'He was happy enough,' she added, stroking his arm. 'I can show you. Do we have time before we get home?'

'No!' He laughed and elbowed her hand away.

'I think he feels *flattered* by Jasmine's interest but he doesn't take it seriously. Didn't your cousins hero worship you when you were a rowing blue for Cambridge and you fenced for Britain in the Berlin Olympics? What d'you think he'll end up doing?'

'Anything. It's not impossible he'll go back to South Africa. Take up the fight against *Apartheid*.'

'Ha! Cynegonde *would* be pleased!' she said.

'Cynegonde's mad. She thinks there should be two *equal* South Africas – one black, one white – both equally prosperous – competing in friendly rivalry but never mixing. Alaric stopped arguing with her ages ago.'

As they turned into the long drive, the first flakes of snow began to fall.

Saturday, 15 December 1962

The Dower-House Owners Association Extraordinary General Meeting – Saturday 15 Dec

This meeting has been called by at least five families who believe that we cannot allow the indecision surrounding the remaining area of the former garages to

continue into 1963. This is the last weekend in the
year when everyone will be present, so the meeting will
be held in the Tithe Barn at 8 o'clock. A decision on
the remaining building site beside the Wilsons' AP flat
is the only item on the agenda (please!). Faith

By ten past eight there was a quorum. Snow was melting on a
dozen pairs of wellington boots or galoshes, shucked off inside
the door, and feet (encased in hairy Lapp moccasins in reindeer
hide, in white goatskin slippers from Greece, in simple seaboot
stockings, in grand old English carpet slippers) luxuriated in the
heat that rose from beneath the Breits' new Junker floor.

'Are the Lanyons coming, does anyone know?' Felix asked. 'It
concerns them least of all, but—'

'Except they'll share in any profit,' Cynegonde said.

'That should be our least consideration tonight,' Adam told
her.

'It's all right for you – you've got your grandfather ensconced—'

'My father, actually. And we *bought* the AP apartment – if you
recall.'

'Yes, but the way property prices have risen—'

'Please!' Faith interrupted. 'This gets us nowhere. What about
the Riley-Potters?'

'Marty Wilde is playing in Saint Albans tonight,' Eric said.
'Don't count on them.'

Isabella added: 'Debbie told me she didn't mind if it was a
new four-bed unit or this other idea—'

'*Other* idea?' Cynegonde again. 'We weren't told about this,
were we, Denis? What other idea? Why can't we just vote for
building a four-bed apartment and have done?'

'Because the *other* idea is to fit three two-bed apartments beside
Jim Wilson's, which we could use for other people's APs or for
guests – because it was bad enough when we had to separate the
boys from the girls, but now – I don't know about you all – the
girls want rooms of their own, too. Not in *our* case, obviously,
but several people have told me that.'

Felix agreed: 'The boys don't mind so much. But what about
Larissa and Vivienne?'

Cynegonde clearly had difficulty imagining that her two girls
might have – much less express – a choice in such a matter. 'I

thought this meeting was all going to be *so* easy,' was all she said.

'Well, what do other people think?' Faith asked. 'How many of us would put in for an AP apartment like Jim Wilson's, if we built them? Not me for one, I can promise you. Nor Alex.'

Tony said, 'I don't think *my* mother would come.'

Nicole thought the cultural shock would be too great for any of hers.

Willard agreed 'on behalf of' his old folks.

Eric thought that his parents would welcome such a facility – 'not now but in a few years.' Isabella, surprisingly, agreed.

'How would they get on?' Marianne could not help asking.

'The same as me and Isabella,' Eric assured her. 'Like a house on fire. But our insurance should cover that.'

'Very funny!' Isabella said.

Terence and Hilary arrived at that moment, brushing off snow and stamping their feet. 'We had to walk,' he announced. 'It's very deep. You'd better call Reeve to come up with his Fordson or none of you'll get out on Monday.'

'Unh-unh!' Willard raised both hands in a familiar blessing. 'I liberated a snow-skeeter from one of the sites for the weekend. It's not much bigger than the Atco but it would clear the whole Canadian-Pacific line in a day – guaranteed. I'll have it clear before breakfast tomorrow.'

Marianne said her mother was well settled in Gothenberg.

Terence said his mother would probably have a room in the gate lodge.

Hilary said wild horses wouldn't move her mother ten yards, never mind a hundred miles.

Nobody mentioned the Riley-Potters because they all knew he wanted a place for Terry Garlick and whatever shady lady he was going with at the time. But when the idea of rooms for guests was canvassed, almost all were in favour. Then everyone turned to Cynegonde, who said, 'I still think a new apartment would be best, don't we, Denis?'

'It's what *we* would prefer,' he agreed. 'But people are clearly in favour of the guest rooms. Will we get planning permission, though?'

'Ah!' Cynegonde's eyes lit up. 'Yes! Well said! Will we?'

'That's the next hurdle,' Faith admitted. 'We need plans to lay before the good people at County Hall. And because we are a majority—'

'Shouldn't we vote before that is assumed?' Cynegonde snapped.

'If you'll just let me finish the proposition . . .? I'd like to propose that the cost be borne only by those who favour the plan to create guest rooms there; but if *those* plans are rejected, *then* the costs of designing and submitting plans for a single apartment will be borne by our community fund. For which, let me add, a special levy will be required.'

'Seconded,' said several voices.

It was carried *nem con.*

'*Glühwein!*' Angela said. 'Almost non-alcoholic, and *Lebkuchen.*'

Suddenly Cynegonde's voice soared over all: 'I want to bring everyone's attention to the mystery of the crop-dusting plane that flew back and forth over the field beyond the Tasmanian pines last Tuesday.'

It was intriguing enough to stifle any objection.

'I'm not doing this as part of the communal meeting, so you needn't minute it, Faith, dear – but most of you were away last Tuesday morning when a crop duster began spraying that field. I thought it was odd, because all the potatoes were already harvested and it was left fallow. So I went to see what was up. I thought it might be spraying toxic stuff for snails or creepy-crawlies – which could kill birds who might eat the corpses. And the other funny thing was that it didn't *behave* like a crop duster. It would make one pass over the field and then go off in a big-big circuit – from Panshanger to Tewin Water and up towards Dormer Green—'

'Could you trim the fat a little, dear?' Willard said. 'For some of us the day's work is just beginning.'

But she was imperturbable. 'It did a big circuit up towards Queen Hoo, down over Lambdell Wood, and then it would turn and make another pass over the field. And then do the circuit again, maybe not quite so big. Then another pass over the field to dump another few hundred gallons of God-knows-what before he went off for yet another—'

'OK!' Willard interrupted again. 'What you saw was a crop-sprayer pilot who was full of *joie de vivre* and had himself a little fun just flying around. Do we really have to—'

'Then why was he spraying nothing more toxic than *water?*' she asked triumphantly.

A stunned – or puzzled – silence fell.

'How can you possibly know that?' Willard asked.

'Because there was a plastic fertilizer bag at the edge of the field and I shook it dry while he was off on one of his grand circuits and laid it back down and later I collected . . .' She turned to her husband, who said, 'Two hundred and fifty mil.'

'Yes,' she said. 'That much. A cupful. And I gave it to Denis and he took it in to the lab and analyzed it and it was . . .?'

'Water,' Denis confirmed. 'With faint traces of Mecoprop, which is a systemic insecticide sprayed on young, growing crops.'

She turned on Willard and said, 'That was some crop-sprayer!'

He shrugged. 'OK, it was a trainee crop-sprayer pilot with badly washed-out tanks practising. They've got to learn somewhere, don't you think?'

'What did you make of that story of Cynegonde's?' Alex asked Faith when they were back in the cottage.

'If it's true, it's a mystery,' she said. 'Maybe, as Willard said, he was a trainee crop-sprayer, which is why he only used water. But still he must have asked permission from the Reeves to use their field. We should ask them. Of course, Cynegonde's certain it's something sinister!'

'What if she's right?' he asked.

'Come on – pull the other one!'

'I'm serious.'

'But why?'

'What did you think of Willard's behaviour?'

'He was bored,' she said. 'So was I.'

'But did you notice *when* he butted in and tried to stop her?'

She tried to think back, but her memory was not sharp enough. 'OK – tell me when?' She turned to the drinks cabinet and uncorked the brandy.

'I was watching him – it always pays to watch Willard, not just listen to him – and he was quite calm when she was describing each pass over the field but he turned pretty agitated when she described those circuits the plane kept making.'

'Well!' She laughed as she handed him his drink. 'You didn't observe all that without also coming to some conclusion.'

'The crop-spraying was a blind. I think Willard may know

very well what that plane was really doing last Tuesday. But if he hadn't kept trying to deflect Cynegonde, I might have suspected it was one of these speculators looking for landfill sites. Or sand-and-gravel possibilities. But why would a plane go round and round over the same ground – in ever-decreasing circles?'

She shrugged.

'It was meant to be a dumb question,' he told her.

'To take photographs?'

'And that's a not-so-dumb answer! It would be easy enough to hide a recce camera among all the paraphernalia for crop spraying. So, anyway, let's assume I'm right in my suspicions – why would Willard be party to a scheme for a plane to take clandestine photographs of the countryside – of just three- or four-hundred acres of the countryside hereabouts? To bring it right home: Why would *I*, too, be highly interested in acquiring those very same pictures?'

'Oh-my-God!' she said as the penny dropped at last. 'You're not suggesting—'

'I am,' he said.

'Are you going to challenge Willard or what?'

He thought it over before replying. 'I'd prefer him to have to come to us. Does Fogel still own Cartographic Associates?'

Tuesday, 12 February 1963

Roy Garden was making one of his interventions – the sort that sounds as if it's moving the agenda forward but is, in fact, merely summarizing the position so far. Fogel, who seemed to be listening intently, was studying each member of the board in turn. The fog of ambiguities in which he thrived was now not helping much. All these people owed him their jobs – in theory. In practice . . . well, that's where the ambiguities came in.

Roy himself, styled Editor-in-chief, was actually the man who could cut off the flow of dollars from Manhattan to Golden Square. A word from him and Manutius would be back in what Eric Brandon called the Singledays – the years before Doubleday turned into Daddy Bigbucks.

And then there was Faith, who would fight to the death for
the interests of Manutius – unless it threatened her own career.
She, too, had the ear of people at Doubleday; in fact, she now
had more sway with them than he himself. Letting her make so
many trips on Manutius's behalf had been a mistake.

Too late now.

And what of Ronald ('Please don't call me Ron') Tweed –
the other American? Logic should put him in bed with Roy.
But they were both members of that lone-hunter species called
'editors'. Roy was a Doubleday man from birth; but Tweed had
cut his teeth under the great Harold Ross, founder-editor of
The New Yorker. Ross always said, 'Editing is the same thing as
arguing with writers – same thing exactly'. Arguing was in the
blood of anyone who learned the trade at his knee. Whichever
way Roy jumped, Tweed might simply choose to argue the
opposite. Until now it had worked well, preventing any band-
wagon from steamrolling the company into dubious projects.
But Tweed was idiosyncratic enough to argue against Roy *and*
yet vote with him when the chips went down.

'And so,' Roy was saying, 'we already have two projects in
trouble.' He turned to Tweed. 'And now, what about our *History
of English Literature*?'

Fogel interrupted. 'The Persian dynasty book is still going well.'

Roy waved a hand at him – something he had never done
before. 'We'll come to that, Wolf. But it's already factored in.' He
turned again to Tweed. 'Have Lord Snow and Pamela Hansford-
Johnson agreed to our proposal?'

But it's already factored in? *But*? Why the *but* – the most
menacing word in the language?

Tweed cleared his throat awkwardly. 'I may have soured things
slightly there. Not permanently, I hope, but a letter of apology
may just make things worse.'

'What happened?' Roy was icily calm.

'We were at the *Mermaid* the other night to see the Noël
Coward revival and I noticed Sir Charles and Lady Snow across
the foyer. I thought they were still in Connecticut. Anyway, I
went over to them and I swear I meant to say: "Welcome back.
How was Wesleyan College?" And so forth. But I just opened
my mouth and heard myself saying to her – kind of joshing, you
know – I said: "*You're* getting fat!" And her jaw just dropped a

mile and she said, "What do you mean – I'm getting fat?"' He glanced around the meeting, nodding reassurance as he added: 'But she is, too, getting fat.'

Several people laughed – not because it was so surprising but because it was so *un*surprising. He concluded, 'I guess *I* presumed our friendship is closer than *they* presume. Or they didn't acquire our New England humour over there. But the money's good and they *do* want it. They can't disguise that. I'm sure we can assume they're on board.'

'Sargent is keen on the project.' Faith smiled warmly at Fogel. 'He admires both of them greatly – and he's had good reports from Wesleyan College. They made themselves well known in America.'

Everyone already knew this, of course. Fogel wondered why she was making such a point of it – as if *he* needed support here. Dammit – this was still *his* company.

'The Bronowski project?' Roy asked.

'Regrets,' said Frederick Ruane, Fogel's gopher.

'What?' Fogel jumped.

'Yep! I called him just before this meeting. I didn't get a chance to tell anybody yet. He'd love to do it . . . feels desolated to cry off, but his TV commitments alone make it impossible to—'

'But that's exactly why we want him,' Fogel complained. 'If we offer him more?'

'We can't afford it, Wolf,' Roy said. 'That's what this is all about.'

A year ago Fogel would have slapped him down; but that was a year ago. 'Norman McKenzie must be able to find us someone at Sussex to do all the donkey work – the way we did with Bertrand Russell.'

'I don't think Bruno would be happy with that,' Faith said. 'Some people never were prostitoots!'

'Penguin has turned down the Science Paperbacks Series,' said Michael Arkwright, the editor concerned. 'Pevsner looked at it and said, "If we wanted to publish shit, we've got plenty of people who could make it in-house". Maxwell also said no thanks. I think we have to admit that our attempt to marry copyright-free text from Russia with a library of illustrations from Italy is not going to work.'

'Why did Maxwell say no?' Fogel asked.

'Because the Russians will also give away the same text to him for peanuts. They just want their authors published in the West. And he won't pay you royalties on the Italian archive because you beat him to the deal.'

'Why have we got two more editors working on the series – apart from you?' Roy asked. 'It should be a simple marry-cut-and-paste job.'

'Because the translations the Russians are providing are shit. We have to rewrite every paragraph . . . every word. We should keep the layouts we've got, and the pics – because everybody likes them – and commission our own text to fill the spaces in between. It's what we usually do. We'll salvage more than eighty per cent of the costs for an extra twenty-five per cent on the budget.'

There was a brief silence – somehow ominous – while Roy scribbled his notes. Then, with a crisp 'Thanks to all!' he lifted his sheaf of papers, patted them to a neat bundle, and popped it into a blue folder. 'We'll consider everything you've said most carefully.'

The slaves went back to their desks, leaving the room to the overlords. Fogel lit a new cigar. Symbolically, Roy shucked his jacket off. This looked like turning into an all-ticket bout.

'We must now consider our response to the National Union of Journalists.' Roy thrust the blue folder into his briefcase and drew out a red one. 'They haven't exactly got us by the short-and-curlies, as I heard O'Donnell boast, but we can't simply brush them off.' Faith caught his eye. 'You want to say something?'

'Just this,' she replied. 'We're treating the NUJ as *the* problem, but—'

'You think they're not?' Fogel asked.

'No, Wolf, I think they're a symptom of the problem. The real problem is that we have a workforce of highly talented people here but they have no—'

'A *flexible* workforce,' Fogel insisted, because he knew what was coming.

'Flexibility was fine when we were back in Rathbone Mews – the exciting, pioneer days. But what happens now? Designer-X works on adult book-X. He does a good job. It all goes off to press. We have a party. Next day he's working on a new Science Paperback or Junior Knowledge book.'

'Flexible!' Fogel said.

'From our point of view – sure. But from his? No structure. No *career* structure. No coherent vision of his future beyond an annual chat with you, me, Roy, Ronald. We *have to* change that. And what about that recent shemozzle in which our warm-hearted Americans hired a sub-editor on a salary of a thousand while the editor for whom he was working – hired by us miserly English – was still on eight hundred?'

'Old stuff!' Roy complained. 'Cut to the coda.'

'The answer's plain. Each series should be produced by its own department and everybody in that department should be able to see the way to progress. We lost Edwin to the *Sunday Times,* Bruce now has his own design studio, Nick has gone to Rainbird, Arthur has gone freelance, Germano is joining Penguin, Romek will only work freelance for us . . . These were all bloody good people, Wolf. And maybe we couldn't have held on to all of them, but if – during the heady days of our expansion – if we'd had a structure with clearly defined careers, I'm sure we could have kept most. Instead . . . *of course* the NUJ seems to offer something that we're not providing.'

'The NUJ provides a *career* structure?' Fogel asked. 'Are you seriously saying—'

'Of course not! But they do provide *a* structure – the only one our people can see. One can't blame them for taking it up. I know you hate hearing this, Wolf, but there's a point where flexibility turns into anarchy. And we've passed it.'

Fogel chomped on his cigar while he mastered his anger. The ingratitude of that woman!

Roy leaped into the silence: 'And it shows in the balance sheet, Wolf. Last year we could have pulled the irons out of the fire—'

'And another *rabbit out of the hat*,' Tweed said.

'Exactly so.' Roy was imperturbable. 'But this union stuff has really ruffled the feathers over there. Unions in Manhattan means the Mob but *European* unions mean Commies. If Joe McCarthy were still alive, they'd be shivering—'

'*In their boots*,' Tweed suggested.

'I know all this!' Fogel shouted. 'I have Sargent in my ear until the air-conditioning goes off for the night in Manhattan—'

'In short,' Roy continued imperturbably, 'Manutius is currently higher on the Doubleday radar than is comfortable. And our tradition of pulling rabbits out of the hat is wearing thin.'

'What rabbits?' Fogel asked.

'Like signing up Jung and Ben Gurion.' He paused before adding: 'And Nikita Krushchev?'

There was a sudden frisson around the table.

'We have?' asked an incredulous Tweed.

Roy looked directly at Fogel. 'It would be a good move, Wolf. Not his memoirs – Doubleday would like those for itself – but the companion volume with the broad, historical sweep. It should be like the Ben Gurion book – except about Russia, of course, giving the rationale behind the USSR . . . where it went wrong under Stalin . . . the new ethos he pioneered . . .'

'The *other side of the coin*,' Tweed offered.

'Precisely. And you're the best publisher in England to get it out of him, Wolf. Heck – you're the best in the *world*.'

Fogel mashed out his cigar and immediately lit another. The drift of the meeting seemed to be turning in his favour; so, of course, he distrusted it. 'Go on,' he said warily.

'Faith is right about the need for reorganization. But it goes deeper than that – or, to be precise – it needs to go higher. To us. Here's an idea off the top of my head. Let's just run it up the flagpole.'

'And we'll *see if anyone salutes it*.' Tweed nodded earnestly all round.

'Faith has described our amorphous structure well but we, too, overlap considerably in function. Of course, we *need* to do that to some extent. Our business is so international that most of us spend far more time abroad than executives in comparable positions in traditional British publishers – and certainly more than in *any* American house . . .'

'And blah-blah-blah! He went on like that for *hours*,' Faith told Alex on their regular evening drive home. 'Tweed even ran out of clichés to tease him with.'

'D'you think Fogel has a chance with Krushchev?' he asked.

'One can never tell with the Russians. Even at this moment he may be languishing in the cell where they flung Beria, facing the same sort of hollow charges.'

'I don't want to pour cold water on the thing but whatever Krushchev gives you won't be worth much. Even at the height of his power, he'll still make sure his text is approved by everyone who might conceivably harbour secret ambitions. He'd make sure they could never use it against him in any show trial.'

Faith smiled. 'That's not the point, darling. The point is that it gets Fogel doing what he's good at – and loves doing. And it leaves me and Roy to reorganize Manutius into becoming a proper publisher with really good prospects for spectacular growth.'

'You and Roy? Or Roy and you?'

She laughed. 'Need you ask? And aren't you glad you work in that paradise of sweetness and harmony known as Voice of America?'

At the turn-off to the B1000 the usual transformation happened: London moved out to the edge as the Dower House came into view (or would have come into view if this weren't February). 'Any movement on the golfing front?' she asked. 'It's almost two weeks since you got the landscape model from Cartographic Associates.'

'I was coming to that. D'you mind not hunting this Saturday? I thought of inviting some of the fellows out for a look.'

'Can they come up with the spondulicks – that's the point?'

'Yes and no.'

'Oh?'

'Well, knowing what sort of weight Willard carries in the world where petty cash starts in the millions, I don't relish a fight – even if we were sure of winning. I'd prefer us to join forces.'

'But – also knowing Willard as we do – that idea has to come from him.'

He grinned. 'Which is why I'm setting up the meeting for this Saturday. Word will get to him and he'll come knocking at our door. I just hope it's not one of those "best-laid plans".'

Wednesday, 13 February 1963

'De bad feelin' 'twix' Brer Fox en Mr Dog start right dar, en hits bin agwine on twel now ey ain't git in smellin' distuns er one er n'er widout dey's a row.'

And so ended the first chapter. Willard snapped the book shut and said, 'Waaal . . . yo' t'ink we gwine stick wid it, son? Dis am yo' heritage, too.'

Virgil yawned and stretched out in the bed, already thinking of the two creamy thighs and the red-rosette garters that would ease him off to sleep in the traditional way for a fourteen-year-old boy. 'Ef'n *yew* read it, paw,' he said. 'Me? Ah jess stumble and fall right dar.' He touched a finger at the top of the binding.

Willard kissed his own fingertips, touched the boy's forehead, and rose to go.

'Willard?' Virgil asked in his normal voice. 'Is it easy to build a model?'

'Sure. You just buy the kit and follow the instructions and—'

'No. A model of *places*.'

'Oh – like an architectural model. We do it all the time – you've seen them. Good night now.'

'Yes, but a model of a place, not a building – like a model of all the fields and woods and roads and stuff round here.'

Willard's hand fell from the doorjamb. 'Around here?'

'Yes. From the valley up to beyond Bluebell Wood.'

He came back and stood by the bedside. 'Have you actually *seen* one like that?'

The boy stared out of the window. 'I just wondered if it would be easy to make.'

'But what put the idea into your head? You have seen one, haven't you.'

Virgil swallowed heavily. 'I promised. It's a secret.'

His father laughed. 'Oh! You mean the one over at the Findlaters! Did they show it to you? They told me it was top secret.'

'Jasmine showed me. She made me swear not to tell anyone.'

'Well, your secret's safe with me, son. And – to answer your question – yes, it's not at all difficult. As a matter of fact, I have one pretty much like the one you saw over there in the cottage. I'll bring it home tomorrow.' He reached out a hand. 'Sand in the right eye? No – you're too old for that.'

Virgil grinned shyly. 'You can do it if you want.'

So Willard did: 'Sand in the right eye . . . sand in the left eye . . . shed a little tear . . . here's mud in your eye!'

Out in the kitchen, he said to Marianne, 'Well, hot diggety dog! I jess *knew'd* it!'

'Is that unusual?' she asked.

'Alex and Faith – I knew it. Remember when Cynegonde went on and on and on about that crop-spraying plane?'

Marianne chuckled. 'And you tried to shut her up!'

'Yes – bi-i-ig mistake. I could see Alex looking at me – click-etty-click – but I never thought he'd—' He broke off and paced up and down, thinking.

Marianne completed the train: 'Never thought he'd guess what you're planning here?'

Willard murmured: 'But . . . a scale model already? He can't have got that far into . . . it's barely two months. *And* they went away for Christmas.' He turned to Marianne. 'They must have been working on it for longer than that. Of course! That's why he picked up on me! I'll bet he had his old buddies make a stereo survey – from the air.' He slapped his thigh. 'Honey! We've got to move!'

'From here?'

'No! *Our* project.'

Siri drifted into the kitchen and picked up a stick of celery.

'You can't still be hungry!' Marianne said.

'No, I heard you talking. I haven't finished my homework. But are you talking about the Findlaters' golf course?'

Her parents exchanged glances. 'Golf course?' Willard said.

'Tarquin told me. Faith and Alex are tired of the municipal course at Garden City. They want to dot a few holes around here. In the parkland. Just for themselves.'

'Oh!' Willard relaxed. 'That's OK then – just for themselves. Go back to your homework, honey-chile. Call if you want me to give it the once-over.'

''Kay.' She drifted out again.

Willard shut the door. 'You believe that,' he murmured, 'and I have an ocean-front property in Iowa that might interest you.'

'It could be true, though.' Marianne carried the salad to the table.

'Honey – if the kids overheard *us* talking about the project by its proper name, what would *we* tell them? "Oh, it's just a few holes in the parkland for our own amusement". But we wouldn't go making a complete scale model just for that.'

'If you're so sure, why don't you just go over and ask them? And offer to join forces while you're about it?'

He drew breath to pour scorn on the idea . . . and then let it out again.

'It would be very divisive otherwise,' Marianne added. Then, 'You know – all this has come about through the kids. D'you think they might be a better channel of communication?'

'Now let's be quite certain about this, Jasmine,' Alex said. '*Exactly* what *did* Siri say?' He wished it wasn't February, and dark, and raining. It would be so much easier if they were out strolling in the woods, with the sun filtering through the bare branches – or anywhere where silences would not seem so portentous. 'Take your time.'

'Well . . .' She was so hesitant. 'She did ask me not to say a word.'

'Not a word to Faith and me? Or to anyone?'

'It was more like "Don't tell anyone but guess what I heard!".'

'No swearing you to secrecy? Cross your heart and hope to die? That sort of thing?'

'No. Nothing like that.'

'So maybe what she meant was, "Don't let this get back to Marianne and Willard" or "Don't blab it out to the whole community"?'

She shrugged. 'Could be.'

'So if we promise not to breathe a word *to them* – cross our hearts and hope to die – you could tell us? You know, it could be very important to all our futures.'

'Hunh? But how?'

Time to plunge. 'Well, I'll let you into a secret, darling – and you *can* tell Siri this, if you like. The fact is . . . Well, you've seen the model we had made of the countryside around here? Faith and I are trying to raise the capital to lay out a golf course on that land. We told Tarquin it was just a few practice holes, but in fact it's a proper eighteen-hole course.'

Her reaction, though minuscule, told him all he really needed to know. He was proud that she had masked it so well. He continued: 'But we suspect that Willard and Marianne also—'

'Yes!' she almost shrieked with relief. 'That's what Siri told me. She said she and Virgil heard them talking about building a golf course.'

'Did they say where?'

'I don't know.' She stumbled to a halt.

'Sorry!' He kicked himself. 'Go on.'

'And Willard said they have the capital but there are one or two . . . somethings . . .'

'Details?'

'No. People who put money in.'

'Subscribers?'

'Yes! One or two subscribers he'd rather do without. And he said he wondered if you and Faith also had the same idea.' She stared at him, every muscle rigid.

Things were falling into place. 'Well!' he said, fixing a steady gaze upon her. 'I wonder what could have given Willard that idea?'

'Me!' She burst into tears and sprang out of her chair to throw her arms around him. 'I showed our model to Virgil. I'm s o r r e e e!'

He hugged her tight. 'Darling-darling Jazzy! You've probably done our family the greatest service *ever!* Truly! By the rule book it was wrong but there are times when we all have to break the rules – and this was certainly one of them!'

As quick as she had been to cry, she was even quicker to revive. 'Really?' She followed up with a disgusting, salt-laden sniff.

'Really and truly.'

'Why?' She drew away from him and accepted his offer of a handkerchief while he explained.

Later, at lights-out, he assured her she could go ahead and tell Virgil or Siri everything. 'But,' he added, 'pretend you think you're not supposed to tell them. Don't make them swear on their lives or anything like that – just say "don't tell anyone" the way she said it to you.'

'Why?' Jasmine was mystified.

'Because you've proved yourself *our* heroine, so don't you think they deserve the chance to be their family's heroes, too?'

'Why did you say that?' Faith asked him when they were downstairs again. 'Isn't that a risk?'

He held his thumb and fingers a hairsbreadth apart. 'Willard will appreciate he's not the only one who can retreat gracefully. And talking of spilling the beans – the town is buzzing with rumours that Jack Profumo has been sharing a totty with a KGB man from the Russian Embassy!'

'Jeeeesus! Is it true?'

'No one's doubting that – the only question is who's going to dare break it first. It's not going to be a comfortable time for my old friends – it's beginning to look as if Philby was the Third Man after all. The Americans are going to love us!'

Two days later, just before breakfast, Willard phoned the cottage to beg a lift into town.

'He *says* Marianne's taking his car in for service,' Alex added with a wink as he passed the news on.

Jasmine winked back.

'What's all this?' Tarquin asked with the whine reserved for younger-children-feeling-excluded.

'It would take too long to explain now,' Faith assured him, 'but your sister will tell you all about it after school today – promise.'

Thursday, 4 April 1963

Marianne listened to the footsteps on the stair. 'Felix!' she said. 'Two to one.'

'No takers,' Sally said.

'Ten to one.'

'Not even at a hundred to one. I'll bet *you* he's been driven out.'

'No takers,' Marianne replied. 'Hallo, Felix – we were just talking about you. Driven out?'

'Oh!' He sank heavily into a chair. 'I did need a break.'

'We could hear it from here,' Marianne said. 'It almost sounded like real music this time.'

'Oh, it is. This fellow spent years with Stockhausen. Devised the notation for *Carré*. And the great man actually trusted him to work out the entire composition plan. He's quite an influence in *avant garde* music in England. So bit by bit they recognize what Angela can do for them.'

'Her library.'

'And with what she can do to manipulate sound

itself – electronically. She's an official advisor to the Radiophonic Workshop now, back at the Beeb, you know. She deserves it, too. She really has tried.'

'Yes,' Sally agreed. 'Trying is a word I, too, associate with her music.'

He laughed. 'I can't disagree. You either like it or . . .'

'. . . or take refuge among friends,' Sally concluded. 'Welcome.'

'Are you designing the clubhouse? Can I look?' He rose again and ambled towards Marianne's board.

'It's only a "basic-requirement" design,' she warned. 'The final details will depend on where we ultimately locate it. That's all still in limbo.'

'Oh, God! I never want to live through another communal meeting like that! I can see the Lanyons' point of view, mind. It would be an unacceptable intrusion on their amenity in the gate lodge. Why are Willard and Alex so against moving it to the far side and bringing the traffic in from the Dormer Green road?'

'Because they want a lo-o-ong first hole.' Indulgently she added: 'Because they're men.'

'But they could put the first hole right at the—'

'Stop!' and 'Cease and desist!' the two women shouted. Sally added: 'The last thing we need is yet another designer! They both think they're good enough to design this course themselves – and they're not. They really ought to get in a pro. But they can't do that if they can't even tell him where the clubhouse is going to be.'

Felix began to take in the layouts on Marianne's drafting table. 'Those are pretty big rooms,' he commented. 'Or am I getting the scale wrong?'

The two women exchanged glances. 'I guess it's not a state secret,' Marianne said. 'But they think the place should be more than *just* a golf course and clubhouse.'

'A *lot* more!' Sally said heavily.

'Considering the location – not too far from the London end of the motorway – and only a mile or so from the Great North Road – this is going to be an ideal location for business people from the Midlands and the industrial North to come south and hold meetings with, er, *counterparts* in London.'

'Bankers,' Sally said. 'City men.'

'Also a good place to hold conferences or strategic meetings with overseas associates – being near to so many airports as well. So the clubhouse will be—'

'. . . where – get this now, Felix, because this is the nub of it – it'll be where, if you're the chairman of a mining company and you want to suggest an *arrangement* with your opposite number at a smelter, something that will make life a lot easier for both of you. You can discuss it in the healthy Hertfordshire air where those inquisitive folks from the Board of Trade won't be able to overhear you. That's what it's really about.'

'And you don't agree?' Felix asked her.

'I don't have the luxury of agreeing or disagreeing but I think it's going to change our community in ways we can't even guess.'

Felix walked over to the window and stepped out upon the balcony. 'No,' he said as he returned. 'You can't see it from here – that small field beyond the walled garden. It's big enough for what's on your boards – plus parking. Quite generous parking. And it would be out of sight.'

The two women looked at each other. 'What's *wrong* with me?' Sally said. 'That's where I lunge Copenhagen – why didn't I think of it?'

'If we straightened out that corner . . .' Marianne mused. 'The county would love us for that. We could even widen the road all the way to the village – put in our new drainage as we go. They couldn't refuse.' She turned to Felix. 'You're a genius, man! I suspect that sculptors have a different feeling for landscape than the rest of us – a sort of tactile, *embracing* feeling.'

Sally was making a hasty sketch on a spare dyeline of the golf-course map. 'It's perfect,' she said. 'God – those two men are going to feel sick they never thought of it themselves. We can run a track through the edge of Bluebell Wood, parallel with the road, and then put the first tee in the park the other side of the short drive. A child could surely lay out a par-five from there.'

Marianne, still looking anxiously at Felix, said, 'Are you going to change your mind about becoming a golfer now – now that you've broken our logjam? You'll be the club hero.'

He came out of his reverie and smiled. 'No – to me golf will always be a way of ruining a perfectly good stroll. Anyway, I probably haven't got the right colour socks. Now can I ask you a question? Is your money – I mean the Von Ritter Fund – behind this scheme?'

Marianne laughed. 'You've become more English than the English, Felix. In Sweden you'd have no need to ask such a question at all – you'd just drop by the town hall and look it up.'

'Eh?'

'Sure. Everybody's annual tax declaration is displayed in the town hall for everybody else to see. So of course I'll answer. My family fund guaranteed Hermann Treite's scheme for East German escapees in order to get it off the ground, but it was never actually needed. Nowadays it's American, West German, French . . . *Western* money that funds that particular operation. And the same thing happened here, with the golf course. Skandinaviska Banken, holding our fund in Sweden, guaranteed the loan in London that got us off the ground. But so many businesses and City people have now bought into the scheme – especially since Alex joined forces with us – that, again, the guarantee was never invoked. I don't know how Alex has fingers in so many pies – he's only got ten. But the sober truth is that banks will lend you *anything* as long as you can prove to them that you don't actually need it.'

Tuesday, 7 May 1963

Angela had been making wine since 1961 but it was not until just before Christmas 1962 that she made her Great Discovery, which transformed her from a maker of quite drinkable plonk into an œnologist, or whatever it was Eric had said. Actually, it was Felix who started the business. It all happened one evening when she was changing the water in the bubble traps that stop wild yeasts from contaminating the fermentation jars. Felix took one of them out of her hands and sniffed it. Then he sniffed it harder. And then turned to her with the light of revelation in his eyes.

'What?' she asked.

He took a tentative sip. 'You try it,' he said.

'Not on your nellie!'

'Well, I think it has all those flavours you've been struggling to get in your wine.'

'This isn't some trick?'

'It's what Denis deVoors calls the higher esters and stuff.'

From then on, with the help of some lab equipment from Denis, she made sure that "the higher esters and stuff" condensed and fell back into the wine before they could add a pointless enrichment to the bubble-trap.

That was six months ago. Now, on an unseasonably raw and blustery day in May, she was standing at the kitchen sink, preparing to start her fourth fermentation batch since Christmas. She was also pitying the surveying team struggling with the wind and the showers out there in the parkland, round about where the first tee would be sited.

'That poor trio,' she said to Felix. 'They obviously didn't expect this weather. I'm going to take them some coffee.'

She took the last of the saffron cake, too, which they had brought back from Cornwall at Easter. They were different, these surveyors, from the ones who had surveyed the plot she and Felix had bought with the Tithe Barn. For one thing, this team included a woman! Indeed, she seemed to be the boss, for it was she who bent over the theodolite and signalled the man with a dish-on-a-pole to move this way and that, while the other man wrote down whatever she called out. They were packing to move on as Angela drew near.

'I've brought you some coffee and cake,' she called out. 'This weather is so miserable, I felt quite guilty all snug indoors.'

They blew on their fingernails, stamped their feet, accepted the goodies, and blessed her. But she was fascinated by their equipment, which was all dials, buttons, knobs and other controls. 'Does it make any sounds?' she asked.

'No – it's a mekometer.' The woman's accent immediately identified her as a foreigner.

Angela looked up at her – and froze.

She knew *this* woman very well.

It was two decades since they last met but she would remember the circumstances until the day she died. And if this woman had had her way, that day would have been two decades ago.

She was in such a panic that her entire body just locked; her face registered no emotion; her eyes did not go large, nor did she blink. And fortunately her mental faculties returned before the use of her muscles – another trick she had learned two decades

ago. She snatched a handkerchief from her pocket and pretended
to nip the non-existent sneeze in the bud.

'Bless you!' said ss-*Aufseherin* Irmgard Heugel, formerly of
Ravensbrück *Koncentrationslager*. 'You should get back in the
warm.'

Angela, now fully in charge of herself again, stood rigid, handkerchief at the ready once more, while she mimed the dwindling
possibility of another sneeze . . . finally relaxing into a smile. 'My
husband's a sculptor,' she explained, patting her duffel coat. 'Dust
in everything.'

'Your husband,' said one of the men. 'Would that be Felix
Breit?'

Angela nodded. Her pulse was steadying.

'I go past his political-prisoner sculpture at the corner of Clissold
Park every day,' the man said as he reached out his hand. 'Jim
Corbett.'

They introduced themselves all round. The other man was Frank
Hulme. And Irmgard Heugel was now 'Inge Dobson'. When she
took off her glove to shake hands, Angela saw that she wore a
wedding ring on her right hand, as in Germany. She managed the
handshake without flinching. In fact, she was surprised at how
numb she felt. The world wasn't reeling, just . . . airless . . . blank.
There was an imperative to keep everything normal.

She turned back to Corbett. 'The *Unknown Political Prisoner*,'
she said. 'Who do you think it is? What sort of person do you
think of when you see that sculpture every day?'

He gave an awkward shrug. 'Could be anyone.'

'But for *you* – is it anyone in *particular*? My husband wants to
know how effective it is.'

'Well, I suppose – down the years, like – I've thought of
Makarios, Kenyatta, other Africans . . . well, Ghandi, of course.'

'Radek?' Frank Hulme suggested lightly. 'Pyatakov? Bukharin?
Zinov'yev?'

'All right, all right, you two!' 'Inge' chided, adding with a grin
for Angela, 'See what you've started! Drink up, lads. This one's
a par-five!'

They swigged the coffee and made cement of the cake with
it, handing her back the thermos and Melamine mugs with grateful
noises and a great deal of rubbing of hands. Moments after Angela
started homeward, she began to doubt her identification of Irmgard

Heugel. When she returned, Felix sensed at once that something had happened. She told him everything.

'While she was there,' Angela said, 'I had no doubts. The voice, every little gesture, the way she stands even – everything. Everything about her screams "ss-*Aufseherin* Heugel"! And yet there was no sign that she knew I had rumbled her. She was "Inge Dobson" to perfection.'

'And you can be sure?' he asked. 'It's been what . . . nineteen years?'

'Oh, I can be sure! *Die Heugel* was one of only two camp personnel there who had actually known me in the ss days – when I was one of *them*. They were especially vicious to me. Heugel was ex-BDM, like most of them, and her mother had the Hitler cross. Together they denounced her father and he died in Dachau. She even boasted about it to me – as if to say, "That's how a *loyal* German behaves! A loyal German does not make secret tapes of her superiors and tell lies about it for weeks". They were all under orders to keep me alive. I was not to have a quick and easy death. But she steered as close to that line as possible. So believe me – I know every little gesture. I learned to pick her voice out if she was fifty yards away down a crowded corridor.'

He took her in his arms and held her tight. She was as tense as a tempered leaf spring – hard, rigid, not a shiver. 'What d'you want to do about it?'

'I want to go for a walk. I want to walk till I'm numb, till I'm as cold outside as I feel inside. But I can't go out because *she's* there.'

He glanced through the kitchen window. 'They're just going over the brow of the hill.'

'It's not just the horror of meeting her, it's . . . at least the air we breathe inside here is ours. Oh, Felix!' Her voice broke. 'Felix! Felix!'

'Yes. Sshhh!'

'I'm being punished, aren't I! For thinking we were free at last. Ever since Christmas, I've . . . I mean, it was only this last Christmas that I really felt free. And now this!' She broke from him and yelled up at the dark between the rafters: 'Haven't you done enough!'

She hurled herself back in Felix's arms and buried her face in his chest once more.

'Shall we drop everything and go to a movie?' he suggested.

'There's *The Brain that Wouldn't Die* at the . . . no. Perhaps not. *Carry on Cabby* then?'

She kept her face pressed to his shirt and just shook her head.

'A show, then? What's on in the West End. We can ask the Johnsons to—'

'No!' She drew away from him at last. 'I just want to go to bed.'

'Oh.' He released her. 'OK. You have a nice hot bath and I'll go up and put your blanket on.'

'With you,' she added.

'Ah. I'm not sure that's what it's intended for.'

'*Fuck what it's intended for* – it's what I want.'

They did not come back downstairs until just before teatime, when the children were due home from school. 'Feeling better now?' Felix asked as they negotiated the stairs.

She laughed.

'Well!' he said. 'I didn't think it was *that* funny.'

'Sorry.' She patted his hand on the banister rail. 'I was thinking of a joke Alaric told Andrew on his last leave. About what men of different nationalities say after having sex. The German says, "Dot voss goot – now vee eat, ja?" And the American says, "Gee, that was great . . . er – what d'you say your name was, honey?" And I can't remember all of them but the English gentleman says, "Are you feeling better now, darling?"' She took his hand as they reached the bottom of the stairs. 'So you now qualify as an English gentleman!'

There was a knock at the door; her hand suddenly gripped his like a pipe wrench. 'No! Please, no!' she murmured.

Felix ran to the door, opened it and said at once, 'Please, go away!'

'No!' Angela shouted as she ran to join him.

There was a moment's silence as they faced each other again. '*Ich hab' gewußt Sie erkannten mich,*' she began . . .

'We speak only English here,' Felix snapped.

'*Sie!*' Angela cried. 'Now you call me *Sie!*'

'I knew you had recognized me. I just came to say that I will arrange for a replacement. It may not be possible before Friday but I'll do my best to keep out of sight until then.' She turned and walked away. After a few paces she spun on her heels and added: 'I'm . . . so sorry.'

★   ★   ★

Next day Angela fiddled with her tape library – and fiddled. And fiddled. Until, around eleven, she put on her coat and gumboots and set out for a walk. Seeing her on her way to the door, Felix rested his mallet and said, 'You're not going to . . .?'

'Not going to what?' She posed like someone caught in O'Grady Says.

'Do anything rash?'

'I don't know,' she replied. 'But I can't just leave things as they are.'

'Why not? It seems to me the most sensible—'

'Because it's then just meaningless. Accidental. Random—'

'But that's what it is! Exactly what it is! Don't for God's sake give it *meaning* now!'

She thought about it but said, 'No. That's just too bleak.' She opened the door and stepped outside.

'You're playing with fire!' he called after her, but the door was already slammed shut.

He gave her five minutes and then followed.

She found the three surveyors down by the river. The woman saw her from a good way off but continued with their work until Angela came to a halt, standing where a hedge divided the parkland from the former water-meadow. Then she set the two men to some sort of fill-in work while she turned and made her way towards Angela.

'Are you going to denounce me to them?' she asked as she drew close.

'What?' The question took Angela aback. 'No!'

'It hadn't even crossed your mind, had it. Maybe you're beginning to understand why I had such a particular dislike of you.'

This was a million miles from all the possible openings to any discussion they might have. Angela was marooned in the resulting silence.

'I should have hanged – I know,' the woman said. 'Along with the others.'

'Völkenrath,' Angela said. 'Schwarzhübe. Bosel. Bormann. Closius. Irma Grese. Marschall. Salvequart. Schreiter. And Zimmer, Emma Zimmer – the Bunker guard.'

'I knew you'd remember them. Us. I'd forgotten Salvequart – Vera

Salvequart, the Capo. They hanged her, too. And yes, my name should be in that list also. I don't know why the British court . . .

'Eight years,' Angela said.

'Yes. And I served only six. For three of them I nurtured my hatred for you – not just you – all of you. And the British. And the Germans who let the Führer die, who stabbed the Fatherland through the heart. I was going to come out and re-create the Nazi party and . . . *ach!*' She gave up. '*You* were in the ss, too. Surely you remember those feelings? My cell was next to Völkenrath's. As they led her away she shouted out for me to hear: *Laß die Flamme nicht sterben!*'

Angela stirred uncomfortably. 'What changed?'

'Not God. I didn't find God. Not permanently. There was no road to Damascus . . . look, can we walk around a bit? I'm feeling shivery.'

'You don't want me looking you in the face.'

She nodded. 'That, too. What changed was that I became dependent on the prison – the routine of the prison. If a meal was five minutes late, I'd get in a fury. Or even if it was early! Yes, I could be starving – not literally. Not like . . . you. But I could be hungry. It made no difference. If the meal was early, I'd fly into a rage. I needed an ironfast routine, you see, to . . . to . . . I can't find the words. But d'you understand?'

'Go on.'

'In the end I realized that the prison routine was all that was left of the routine of . . . the *other* prison. The camp.'

'Ravensbrück.'

She made a shivery sort of noise that contained the syllable yes.

'So? You're not making much sense, *Aufseherin* Heugel.'

'Oh? I think I am. We are that kind which cannot be left empty. You, too. I sat in my cell, day after day, week after week, and I remade the camp—'

'Ravensbrück – say its name.'

'I remade . . . Ravensbrück. Völkenrath would have accused me of letting the flame die, but she no longer frightened me.'

'You? Scared of her?'

'Everyone was scared of her. But now she was . . . away. Out of it. And the fire *was* out. And I must coldly face . . . face what we did there. What I did there. Especially to you – the ss traitor. I did it all again. And again. Without . . .' She tapped her breast. 'Without righteousness this time. The priest said take it all and offer it to God before you go mad.'

'Absolution?'

'Well! Certainly no absolution. It was a new fire burning in me – a different fire. A cold fire.'

She fell to silence, leaving Angela to wonder if that was it. 'And then?' she asked.

'Then they released me. Time served. And so even that flame died. And here I am. I work. I'm married. I have two children. I will do my best by them and my husband. But . . .' She ran out of words at last.

Angela, feeling numb and not knowing quite what to say, said, 'Your children?'

What about this woman's children? Why mention them? Just go.

The woman was offering her a small two-by-two photograph of a pair of bored-looking children. A handsome, curly-headed boy of about six and a good-looking, slightly older girl.

'Not the easiest age,' Angela said. And then, to her own amazement, added: 'We have four.'

She took a grip on herself, passed the photo back – and then held out her hand.

The other, horrified, took a step back, saying, 'Oh . . . no!'

'Yes!' Angela insisted. 'I never want to see you again – that's true. But this is how we have to part.'

'Why?'

'I don't know. It just is.' She threw her shoulders back and tossed her head. 'Anyway, *Aufseherin* – I don't have to explain myself to you any more. Just do it – and go!'

With the faintest ghost of a smile – a wan, woebegone smile – the woman obeyed: '*Jawohl!*'

When Angela was halfway home she found Felix, waiting for her.

'Playing with fire!' she said. 'There *was* no fire.'

Wednesday, 15 May 1963

Only eight children now threaded their way across the fields to and from school – two Lanyons – Karl and Mortimer – two Breits – Douglas and Susan, two Riley-Potters – Amanda and Hector, Peter, the youngest of the three Johnsons, and Constance, the third and last of the Palmers. But the pattern did not change. The boys formed one loose group to discuss football, dinosaurs, catapults and boomerangs, and how lousy their teachers were; the girls usually went on ahead, eager to get to ponies or My Little Pony (or Tressie – her hair grows! – or Barbie), discussing who did what or shouldn't have done what at school that day – and how lousy their teachers were.

So they were the first to meet the lost-looking man and two children about their own age, making their way up the path towards the village. 'I don't suppose you've seen three people in yellow oilskins, carrying a tripod about the place, have you?' he asked Debbie, who was in the thick of the sprawling crocodile, trying to keep it vaguely bunched together.

Karl pointed down the valley, where a belt of trees masked a view of the water-meadow beyond. 'They were down there, this morning.'

'I saw them up near the haha at lunchtime,' Debbie added.

His two children stood and stared at the eight Dower House children, who stared back at them.

Peter Johnson took the initiative, stepping toward the girl with an outstretched hand. 'Hello. I'm Peter Johnson. We all live in that big house beyond the coppice there. Would you like to come and see it – you and your brother?'

Nodding and biting her lip, she shook his hand and glanced up at her father, who said, 'That's jolly friendly of you, Peter. We've been hearing a lot about that house this week. My wife is in charge of the surveying team. We really came out here to collect her for a fish-and-chip supper in Hertford. But if I've got to traipse all over the two-hundred-and-fifty acres to find her . . . well . . . would it be an awful imposition?'

Debbie just laughed and waved a hand over the mob. 'We won't even notice the addition,' she said. 'I'm Debbie Riley-Potter, by the way.'

'Billy Dobson.' They shook hands. 'And these are Margaret and Francis.' He leaned over them. 'D'you two want to go with these people up to the big house and play with them until I find Mummy?'

'Ye-es!' they chorused.

There was excitement among The Tribe, too.

'But if you find her first, don't spoil the surprise, eh? I want to be the one to tell her.' He set off ahead of them for the bottom of the field, where he could skirt the coppice all the way down to the water-meadow without trampling any of the crop. Fifty acres of ripening winter wheat soon swallowed him up.

'Have you won the pools, then?' Debbie asked as the children resumed their homeward ramble.

'No,' Margaret replied. 'He's . . . ow!' She slapped her brother's hand away. 'That hurt.'

'Daddy said not to tell,' he reminded her.

'He said not to tell Mummy. We can tell these people.' She turned back to Debbie. 'He's just been made headmaster of the Ebenezer Howard School in Garden City and it's to be a surprise for Mummy. She doesn't even know he applied for it.'

'Because he didn't think he'd get it,' Peter added.

'You didn't need to tell them that,' his sister said crossly. 'He's going to start in September.'

'Well, good for him, anyway!' Debbie said. 'That's the best school for miles. A lot of The Tribe have gone there. In fact, some of them are there still.'

Margaret frowned quizzically at the word *Tribe*.

'This shower.' Debbie wafted a hand over the children. 'We've had thirty or more children from the big house walking this path to the village school – these are the tail-enders.'

'The cream-of-the-cream!' Karl insisted.

'Mister Perch,' Peter Johnson added, 'says we're the best the Dower House has ever sent him.'

Debbie leaned towards Margaret and said in a loud stage whisper, 'Mister Perch says that to *every* final year.'

'But he says it's *true* this year.'

Debbie merely winked.

Before they reached the felled trunks that spanned the waterlogged ditch, the girls had claimed Margaret and the boys had absorbed Peter. There was so much to show the two of them on the way that their father had had time to find their mother (saving the good news for later) and arrange to pick her up near the haha. He was then in time to meet The Tribe as they emerged from the coppice.

He knew from the way the children eyed him that his secret had been shared among them. He stared at them fiercely and said, in the voice of a sergeant major: 'If any of you breathes a word of this before I've had the right moment to tell my wife, I'll pull your arms out by the roots . . .' But he fell to an astonished silence as they chanted in unison: '. . . and beat you round the head with the soggy end!'

'How do you lot come to know that?' he asked above their laughter.

'It's what Eric always says,' they answered.

'Eric who? An army man? Was he in the war?'

'Eric Brandon,' Debbie told him. 'He must have been.'

'Good heavens!' the man exclaimed. 'Old Eric Brandon? Good heavens! Are any of you lot his children?'

'You'll meet them at the Ebenezer Howard. Ruth, his youngest, or young*er* daughter started there last autumn. And Calley—'

'Well, well, well! Is he here now? At home, I mean?'

'I'll show you.' Debbie led Dobson round to the big lawn, leaving the children to take Margaret and Peter under their wings. 'He uses the old ballroom as his studio,' she explained. 'You obviously knew him – if he's the same one.'

Dobson laughed. 'There's only one Eric Brandon! We were in the same mob – the Education Corps. He got posted into Intelligence, I stayed in Education. Worked with the Germans over denazifying the schools, the curriculum, the textbooks . . . the staff. He had it cushy, I can tell you.'

'Here we are. I've never heard him say a word about what he did in the war.'

But that did not stop her from trotting up the steps and calling out: 'Eric – it's Judgement Day! All those fancy tales you've told us about the war are coming home to roost!'

Eric dropped his watercolour brush, turned, and ambled – and then ran – to the window. 'Dobson?' he said. 'Is it you?' He lifted the sash and bowed his way out to rise and shake the man's hand. 'It *is* you! I haven't aged a bit – but *you* have. Dreadfully!'

Dobson roared with laughter and turned to Debbie. 'Told you!'
She left them, saying, 'Call me when there's blood spilt.'

'How did you track me down?' Eric asked. 'Obviously I didn't
pay Corporal Carnell enough to "lose" my forwarding papers.
Come on inside – it's just a humble cottage but to me it's home.'

Dobson hesitated. 'Actually, my wife thinks I'm on my way
to bring the car round to the front. She's in charge of the survey
team for this golf course of yours.'

'Not mine.'

'Well, anyway, I ought to go and let her know that I'm obviously *not*—'

'I'll go with you. I'll just get my jacket.' He retrieved it from
the back of his chair. On his return to the window he said, 'You
must stay to dinner. Your wife, too, if she's house-trained.'

Dobson explained that he'd just landed a plum job and they
were off to celebrate. Eric did not waver: 'Then you must *all*
stay to dinner. You can't just pop back into our lives and vamoose
to some fish-and-chip emporium.'

'I . . . I really don't think we can impose like that. At such
short notice.'

'Nonsense! The cook will take care of it – she's an absolute
marvel.'

'I say! You do rather live in style, Brandon. A cook, eh!'

'Yes. The only slight drawback with her is she has this part-
time job editing *Vogue* but she'll be home in an hour or so.' He
dodged a punch on the arm. 'Actually, there's a bloody marvellous
fish-and-chip shop in Hertford. We could nip in there and bring
a feast back here. Come on – where did you last spot the
memsahib?'

They sauntered off across the big lawn towards the haha.
'Memsahib is just about the last thing you could call my Inge—'

'Oh, God – you married a bloody foreigner, too, eh? Half my
neighbours here did the same – and the other half *are* bloody
foreigners.' He stopped and turned to point at windows in the
house. 'Swedish. French. South African. And the two people who
live over there—'

'I know. Felix Breit, the sculptor, and his wife – the composer.
I gather they're both concentration camp survivors. Inge did a
lot of work, helping people like that, before she met me.'

'But you soon put a stop to all that nonsense, eh?'

They resumed their stroll.

'She's an absolutely fantastic organizer,' Dobson said. 'She's going to be invaluable in this new job of mine. I didn't tell you where it is, did I. We're going to be near-neighbours.'

The two Riley-Potter children, Amanda, ten, and Hector, nine, took the two Dobsons in tow. After an awestruck moment in the sitting room, drowned by Chris's *Feet* mural on the floor, walls, and ceiling, they scampered to their bedrooms, first to the wigwam where Hector and his two most trusted braves would sleep with their senses tuned for the slightest rustle of a leaf and from which he was nightly carried like a log, to wake up, unsurprised, in his regular bed. And then to the impromptu Wendy House where Amanda slept with a giant doll called *Too Small*.

'You've got *How to Catch a Pink Elephant*!' Margaret, nine, said, running her eye along Amanda's bookshelves. 'That's my favourite.'

'Signed especially for me by the author!' Amanda pulled it out and pointed to Eric's signature and dedication: *To Mandy – oops! Amanda! With oodles of love – Eric Brandon.* 'I don't like it when people call me Mandy,' she explained. 'He did that for a joke. He's always joking. He's the one who said he'd beat us round the head with the soggy end.'

'My dad's pal from the war. I wasn't born then.'

'Me nor.'

'You call your mummy Debbie.'

'Everyone here calls their mummy and daddy by their real names. We've got nine mummies and daddies here so it wouldn't work.'

'Gosh! Francis and me'd just giggle if we called them Billy and Inge.' She giggled even at the thought of it.

'I've got lots of his books.' She waved at the shelves. 'He does books on history and engineering and the Antarctic and stuff, too. His wife's Isabella. They argue all the time but they never really *quarrel* – you know? Not actually quarrel.'

'Like brothers and sisters, a bit.' Margaret turned to Francis. 'You two might as well push off.'

Amanda told Hector, 'Take him over to the Tithe Barn, let him listen to Angela's fart tapes.'

The two boys flew off, crying, 'Yeeeeaaaah!'

She turned to Margaret, who was rigid with shock. 'It's not

real farting – just done with radio valves and things but it's jolly realistic. Boys love it, of course. I got *From Me to You* last Saturday. Shall we play it?'

'Fab!' Margaret agreed. 'I got *How Do You Do It?* for my birthday but I don't think they're as good as The Beatles. Are you *allowed* to say fart?'

'Not to my Nana and Granddad. Nor shit, either.'

'Got any clay, Felix?' Hector asked nonchalantly as he and Francis invaded the Tithe Barn.

Felix let his mawl and chisel drop to his sides as a sort of gymnastic apology. 'I'm waiting for a delivery this very—'

'Liar!' Angela shouted from her studio. Then, spying Susan, watching from her bedroom door above, she added: 'D'you want to come down and join the modelling class, darling?'

'Give me five minutes,' she replied importantly.

'Where did Douglas go? I haven't heard a squeak out of him.'

'He's up in the Johnson's making a plastic model of some historic old steam engine with Peter.'

Felix laid down his tools with a sigh and led the two invaders over to the modelling area. 'But you stay over here and you put these aprons on. I've got chips of limestone flying around out there. I don't mind either of you getting blinded by them but the one thing I don't want is if they get into my clay. Understand? Now what d'you want to make?'

'Elephants,' Francis said. 'Like in that book.'

'Eric's book,' Hector explained.

'Ah! Eric!' Hope kindled. 'Would you like to *meet* him?' he asked Francis, smiling his most encouraging smile.

'He's gone off with my dad,' Francis said. 'They were in the war together.'

'OK!' Felix sighed again. 'You already know how to make an armature, don't you, Hector. I'll make one for . . . Francis?' He quickly bent some old coat-hanger wire into the head, spine, and limbs of a generic quadruped. 'African or Indian?' he asked.

'What's the difference?'

'African ones slope down more towards their back end.'

'African,' Francis decided.

'You make decisions quickly, young man.' Raising his voice, he added: 'I hope it's contagious.'

'I'm not going to rush to a decision!' Angela called out.

'Mummy doesn't like people who dither,' Francis explained.

'And how about your father?'

'He's going to be headmaster of the . . . something to do with a knees school in a garden or a city.'

'Welwyn Garden City?' Felix suggested. 'The Ebeneezer Howard School?'

'Gosh! It almost looks like an elephant already. Hector – look at my elephant!'

Hector dumped Francis's ration of clay on the modelling table. 'Felix can bend wire into the shape of running water – that's what Chris says.'

'Only when he wants a favour!' Angela called out.

'Off you go, then.' Felix left them to it and wandered over to Angela's studio. 'Charming little fellow,' he said. 'Francis.'

She switched off the tape. 'Four minutes, thirty-three seconds,' she said. 'If his father really is going to be head at the Ebenezer Howard, *and* is an old army chum of Eric's . . . actually, can you *imagine* Eric having an old army chum? It seems so unlikely. He never talks about the war.'

'What of it, anyway?'

'Well, it can't do any harm to make friends. Pippin and Andrew both being there. Douglas and Susan, too, soon enough – it's all to the good to be in the same social circle. Don't you see?'

The two boys were talking away like a pair of drunken auctioneers – mostly about all the different ways they would kill an elephant if they met one in the African jungle.

'All I'm saying is it can't do any harm. That's all. Next time we give a party, we'll invite them.' She jerked a thumb towards the modelling area. 'Especially if theirs and ours get on as well as this!'

Felix went back to his carving and Angela – he presumed – to yet more minutes of tape-recorded silence. And both listened to the two young boys with half an ear – listening to thoughts and words that, in an adult, would indicate a deranged mind but which, on their tongues and in their falsetto made an elusive, antic sense.

At last their juvenile stamina gave out and Hector said, 'We can put wet flannelette over them and come back tomorrow or sometime. Like this.' Then: 'Angela! Can we listen to those tapes?'

'Ah, well, I'm afraid my tape deck . . .' she began in a deeply apologetic tone, only to be cut short by a cry of 'Liar!' from Felix.

'Oh, I suppose you must!' she said wearily. 'Come on, then – the sooner we start, the sooner . . . oh, hello, you must be . . .' Her voice trailed off.

'What?' asked a puzzled Francis. He turned to Hector, who just shrugged.

Angela appeared, framed in her studio doorway, and said to Felix, 'Did you know about this?'

'What?'

Margaret and Amanda burst in through the front door and stood there, panting heavily. Margaret called out to her brother as he emerged from the studio, 'Daddy says you're to come over with me to the big house.'

'Come and see I'm making an elephant,' he said, already heading for the modelling area.

'No – now!' she said. 'They've got fish and chips going cold.'

Angela walked across to her for a closer look. Margaret, slightly unnerved by this, reached out and clasped Amanda's hand. Realizing she was embarrassing the girl, Angela tried to reassure her, saying, 'Your mother showed me your photograph the other day – yours and Francis's.' She turned to Felix to make sure he took her meaning, but Margaret's reply would have done that, anyway. 'She's surveying all around here for the golf course. That's why we came to find her 'cos she doesn't know about Daddy and being the new headmaster.'

'And,' Francis added, 'we're having fish and chips to celebrate.'

'. . . which is why you've got to come over with me *now*!' his sister shouted.

'But we just wanted to listen to—'

'Susan! Will you come down here this minute!' Angela shouted up to the rafters.

After a brief, frozen silence, the girl emerged on to the balcony. 'What?'

'Don't you *what* me, young lady! Come down here and put on the fart tape for these boys.'

Margaret started to protest but Angela said, 'Don't worry. I'll make everything right with your father . . . your parents. I just have to talk to Felix a moment. This is something very important.' With a jerk of her thumb, she indicated the kitchen.

'What now?' she asked when the door was closed behind them. 'What do we do?'

'I don't know. The possibility of a meeting was always—'

'Well, of course we didn't *prepare* for it. Especially not in England. Especially not in the heart of the countryside. And not' – she raised both arms in a gesture of hopelessness – 'with an English husband who's going to be our children's headmaster.'

'And two very nice children of her own. I know.'

'I'll bet she hasn't told him – her husband.'

'And just think—'

'I know!' She exhaled sharply and slumped. 'I can't do it – can I. It'd be wrong.'

'Could you say that *she* ruined *your* life?'

She shook her head, thought it over, looked into his eyes. 'That's the key question, isn't it – did she ruin my life?'

'And the answer?'

'And the answer is – I didn't let her.' She gave another hopeless shrug and said wanly, 'And I'm not going to let her do it now, either.'

'You're going to expose her?'

'No!' She almost shouted it. 'The opposite! I'm going to—' And then she laughed. 'Show her the opposite, I suppose. Show her she *didn't* ruin my life. Rub her nose in it! Come on! We'll all go over there with them.'

'We?'

'Oh, yes – you've got to be part of it, too.' When he still hesitated, she said, 'I need you.'

'*Che sera sera!*'

She elbowed him and then took his hand. 'Not *quite* as nonchalant as that!'

The juvenile laughter at the endless loop of electronic farts was getting just a little forced – and the protests were mere tokens when Angela switched off the machine. 'Come on,' she said. 'We're all going over. They're at the Brandons', I suppose? Is your mother there, too?'

'No. She's waiting the other side of that ditch.'

'The haha?'

Margaret frowned. 'Is that really its name?'

'Yes. Why's she waiting there? Did she say?'

'Because her boots are all muddy. We're going to collect her at—' Her voice trailed off because Angela had already turned to go, pausing only at the door to hurry them all along.

Felix caught up with her at the carriage sweep in front of the portico, where he gripped her by the shoulder and hauled her to a stop. 'Have you really thought this through?' he asked.

'No . . . yes! Something in me must have been thinking because it all suddenly fell into place. It was only waiting for someone to ask "did she ruin my life?"' She darted him a quick kiss. 'Clever you.'

He stared deep into each of her eyes in turn. 'I wish you'd just find enough time to let me in on it.'

'I could denounce her and ruin her marriage – maybe – and wreck the lives of those two children. Will that make me free? Anyway, she's seen us. I'm going to talk to her now. You?'

He turned towards the house. 'I'll stall them till you've done.' Ascending the steps, he gave Inge Dobson a wave.

Angela laughed as she set off for the haha. 'It's catching, eh!'

The woman turned to go. Angela called out, 'Stay right there.' And when she arrived at the rim of the haha, she reached down a helping hand, saying, 'If you put one foot on that stopped-off bit of pipe it makes it easy.'

'Please, don't?' The woman held her ground.

'Don't what?'

'Tell everyone. Please! This would be your perfect moment.'

'I've met your children,' Angela said. 'They're super kids.'

'Eh?'

'And your husband's an old army pal of our friend Eric Brandon.'

Inge, bewildered, shook her head.

'I can't expose you without ruining their lives, too. But this is the important thing, Inge – even if you were all alone in the world, what would it prove if I ruined your life? It would prove you still had the power to harm me – that I still feared you and so would feel I must . . . what's the word? *Vernichten.* Eliminate you. But I don't fear you. And you have *no* power to harm me. So, *Inge – Mrs Dobson*' – she smiled again and stretched forth her hand – 'come up and meet the Brandons – meet all of us.'

The woman turned her back on the house, and on Angela, and gave one long howl of anguish that must have been heard down on the valley floor.

Angela leaped down and ran the few yards that separated them. With some force she turned Inge to her and held her tight, despite her struggles. An extraordinary god-like exultation filled her, which she vaguely knew had some long, tenuous connection with the thousands of humiliations this woman had once heaped on her . . . no, not exactly on *her* but on someone who had once been her. And that was an important difference. *The* important difference.

At last the crisis was over and Inge straightened up again and took out a handkerchief and said, 'I must look a fright.'

'Not these days,' Angela assured her.

She gasped – and then broke into a laugh. 'You're incredible!'

'Don't say any more just yet.' Angela took her arm and turned her towards the clapper gate, some fifty yards away at the western end of the haha. 'I'm not going to lie for you,' she said. 'But I'm not going to tell anyone else the truth.'

'You don't know the truth.'

'Well, I'm not going to tell the bit of it that I *do* know. And what's this bit I don't?'

Inge said nothing.

'My God – is it worse?' Angela asked.

She shook her head. 'I know it wasn't enough but it was all I could do.'

Passing through the clapper gate seemed to unlock her tongue. 'My father died in the war – as I said.'

'In Dachau.'

'Yes. And my mother died while I was in prison. In fact . . .' She paused.

'What?'

'No – it's too complicated. She didn't die poor – just leave it at that. She was shot. In the black-market wars in Frankfurt-am-Main. So, when I came out of prison I had some money, quite a lot. I always told people it was on the Irish Sweepstake. And so I bought a house and I made a refuge for people broken down by . . . the KLs. Not just Ravensbrück – any of them. *Gott im Himmel!* I never realized there were so many. And their own countries didn't want them back. Do you know Cornwall?'

Angela linked arms with her again as they regained the lawn. 'We were there at Easter. Why?'

'Ha! We were in Marazion then, too. We always rent one of those old railway carriages that they've turned into holiday homes.'

The Breits had driven past those same carriages more times than Angela could remember. But she said nothing; in fact, it meant nothing right now.

'Anyway,' Inge went on, 'there's a legend down there about some saint who was given a punishment to bale out a big pool – a huge pool – with a whelk shell.'

'The Loe. The pool is called The Loe.'

'Low! Yes, that's just how I felt with my one little house. So many victims . . . one little house – like a lake and a whelk shell.'

They came to a halt, quite close to the portico. 'You should have told me this the other day,' Angela said.

'And you would have listened? You wouldn't have thought I was just fishing for . . . would you even have believed me?'

Angela gave a wan little smile and released her arm. 'Let's go inside. The Brandons do have some very good sherry.'

At the front door she paused and wafted a hand for Inge to enter first. '*Wilkommen!*' she said. '*Du.*'

Wednesday, 12 June 1963

Eric sifted among the papers on his desk, found what he was looking for and passed it over to Jasmine. 'I had it typeset to please her,' he said. 'And how about you? Do you feel somewhat crowded out by your two highly gifted parents?'

Jasmine read:

Diogenes Requests

Behold! On every flyleaf in every book . . . it's always there:
Your name, Father dear – as if the book were yours!
A Cruiser Commander's Standing Orders
A History of the Concrete Roofing Tile

Wild Rabbits Throughout History
Our Weather Records since 1587.
You cannot possibly own such books.
Do you not see it, Dad: they own you!
For the nonce, that is . . . just for the now.
And what of them, I ask, in years to come?
I own that they, in their turn, will own me, too.
But where on every flyleaf in every book on all my shelves
Have you left room for me to write my name as large as yours?

Calley Brandon (aet. 14¾), 1963

'Not really,' she said, passing it back. 'Calley's clever. Pippin says they always used to read her poems out when she was at the Bluecoats. Who's Diogenes?'

'The Greek philosopher who asked Alexander the Great to move aside because he was blocking the sun.'

'Ah – I see.' She sat down and faced him. 'Did you always know what you were going to be when you grew up? When you were . . . sixteen?'

He pushed his typewriter aside. 'Well! If Calley looks set to be a poetess, you're a dead cert for a trial barrister, Jasmine. All right . . . all right! I'm going to answer you.' He rubbed his hands and leaned forward with a grin. 'I was going to hunt whales – because they paid enough in three months to last the rest of the year. During which . . . ah! *That* was the problem – the other nine months. Time for the *real* me. Which was a blank. An empty man. A man of straw.'

'Did you really catch whales?'

'No. Hitler put the kibosh on all that. But it turned out that the British army was desperate for empty men – because we're the only ones who can make two-plus-two equal twenty-two. We can take a hint and turn it into a conspiracy. But when I got demobbed I realized I needed a crash course in reality, so I started writing books for children. And that's how most people get launched on their careers. I don't seem to be reassuring you?'

She pulled a face. 'I can't see anything on the horizon. It's all just . . . blank.'

'Excellent!' He dry-soaped his hands. 'Oh, I do envy you that blank. Pity me – eyeless in Gaza and at the wheel with slaves.'

Her smile was mirthless.

'Something will happen,' he assured her. 'On a package holiday to Turkey you'll fall in love with a Roman mosaic floor. And twenty years on you'll be presenting a TV documentary on *The Other Roman Empire*, trotting all over the Middle East, the most glamorous thing on the screen! Or you'll argue about God with Alaric and grow up to become the scourge of all those armchair atheists whose thinking is just skin-deep. Like broken china – these things happen.' He tapped her forehead. 'Just stay open for business.'

His gaze released her. She stared past him, out into the parkland. 'What about a book on all this, Eric? For kids who are starting to wonder . . . you know.'

'Maybe. But it's good that *young people* these days are thinking about such fundamental things. First and last things. The war – or rather the fact that we *survived* the war – has made us all irretrievably frivolous. The great Bernard Levin says that my generation's political motto is *Après moi les feet wet.*'

'You *should* write a book about it.'

'No.' He pulled a face. 'My books have so much colour printing in them these days that the British book market isn't big enough to pay back the costs. So we need the American market, too – and this sort of talk doesn't go down too well over there. They're still a very young nation and – as you know better than I – the young can still find room for illusions of all kinds.' He put Calley's poem back on top of the pile. 'And tell me – what d'you think of my old friend Dobbin? Oops – shouldn't have let that slip. That's what we called him in the Education Corps. He used to put us all to shame not just by the amount of work he managed to get through but by his amazing thoroughness. But he's not going to be your headmaster, is he – so you can say what you like.'

'I don't know him much but I like Mrs Dobson. She explained to me how you can use triangles to put everything in the world down on a map. D'you know that Alex and Willard are buying two-hundred-and-fifty acres but will actually have more, maybe two hundred and sixty, because when they're writing down the areas on the map they ignore hills and valleys and pretend it's all flat and down at sea level?'

'Yes, I often think it's hard on mountain countries like Switzerland and Tibet. If you wanted to paint them all one colour, you'd probably have to buy twice as many buckets of paint as you think you'd need. Hmmm. Maybe there's a children's story in that. What else does Mrs Dobbin do?'

'She let me make one measurement – two hundred and sixty-one point seven three.'

'Ah! So when Sally and Marianne find that the clubhouse doesn't quite fit, we'll know who to blame!'

She pouted and dug him with her elbow as she rose to go. Then, peering over his shoulder at the work on his desk, she said, 'What's *that*?'

'It's going to be a story called *Blackie – the Albino Polar Bear.*'

She gave him a pitying look and made for the door.

'It's not for your age group,' he called after her. Then, to himself: 'An eight-year-old will understand the logic perfectly.'

Tuesday, 16 July 1963

12.7.1963

My dear Felix and Angela!

You asked Hermann Treite to find out whether what Irmgard Heugel said about her work after her release from prison was true. I don't know why you didn't ask me – with all my contacts at Spiegel it was very easy. Anyway, Der Hermann realized it and asked me to take over. A week – that's all it needed. You needn't think I'm past it. Even if I stumbleover typing, sometimes. There, I did it again. I feed this ungrateful machine gallons of oil. Anyway –

Die Heugel's mother was a hundred per cent Nazi, the kind you cannot argue with at all. There was a big cell of them in Fft-am-Main, all involved in the black market after the collapse. She was killed in gang warfare in 1951. IH could have been paroled for the funeral but declined. But she inherited DM750.000 – from black-market dealing, of course, but that could not be proved. Her dossier says she had a conversion to Catholicism before her release.

Many people like her claimed that sort of thing,
to be sure, only to revert once they're were free
to mix again with their old comrades. But it seems
to be true in her case. She used the money to buy a
large, partly derelict house near Schwalbach-am-
Taunus, just north of Fft, restored it, and
replanted the gardens, large gardens, to their
pre-war state. The picture I enclose was taken by
the Fft stringer. You owe him - or me, actually - a
bottle of good whiskey. She renamed the place <u>Das
Haus Milenas</u> but no one could tell our stringer why.

When the house was converted, in 1953, she
started taking in former KL inmates in 1953. We kid
ourselves if we think the Vernichtung ended with
the war. You two were lucky. Tens of thousands were
not. You had skills that were wanted in England.
Outside Germany, anyway. But most countries, East
and West, the East especially, still do not want to
take back such 'war-damaged goods'. Only the UN and
people like the reformed Irmgard Heugel helped
them. She made arrangements to change her name to
Ingeborg Schneider but never put it into practice,
though she was widely known as 'Inge'. She dyed her
hair black and had lost a lot of weight in prison
so she was well established there before someone
recognized her. After that she made no secret of
her former life as SS-Aufseherin.

She met and married William (Billy) Dobson shortly
after her release. He was working for the German
government, advising on textbooks to replace those
used in the Nazi era - apparently he did something
similar when he was attached to AMGOT in 'forty-six.
Then, in 1956, she suffered some kind of nervous
collapse, handed the house and almost all the
remaining funds over to the Catholics and went with
her husband back to England. I can't say whether he
knew of her history in the SS but as she made no
secret of it after she was recognized, it must have
been spoken about among the residents. And he speaks
fluent German. Assume he knows it now, I'd say.

That's all we've been able to discover about
her. Digging deeper into her past - the father's
death in Dachau - the mother's activities in the
black market - will require more than a bottle of
good Irish but it's possible if you want.

And so to the family. Mutti Uschi's arthritis is
a little worse than at Christmas, I'm sorry to
say. She practically lives on aspirin, which can't
be good for her stomach. The doctors keep talking
of the disease 'burning itself out' but no sign of
that. I soldier on, a little more stooped each
month, a little more reluctant to test the strength
of my back each morning. But we hold jolly parties
where we can all talk about our fascinating defects
and symptoms. At least we're enjoying a good
summer. (So far.)

I've read young Wendy's novel at last. I don't
know why I was so reluctant to start. Afraid she
would shatter my illusions about her, most likely.
Anyway, it's very good. The critics were right for
once to heap their praise on it. I haven't heard
from Martin and Rebecca, yet, what they think of
it. Have you? Maybe they are still in shock!

My own biography of Billy Breit is languishing
in limbo. I think I have traced all his pictures
that survived the two wars. His realistic and
heroic style is greatly in vogue in the Soviet
sphere but not his anti-Semitic beliefs
(officially), so the ones in that half of Europe
are hidden in gallery vaults and getting them
photographed for my biography is a matter for
delicate 'negotiation' - where your funds come in
very useful. Also, of course, Treite's intimate
knowledge of the many devious ways to make sure
that hard currencies fall into the right hands over
there when you want particular results.

People sneer at the sentimentality in his
paintings but he was no worse than Mengs or
Vernet or Zuccarelli. And you can't say that even
Fragonard and Watteau are devoid of

sentimentality. So I think his time will come again.

Are you coming to us this Christmas, have you decided yet? Even if you can't make it, what about the children? Now that Pippin is fourteen, she must be old enough to look after the other three on the ferry? If you put them on at Lowestoft, we can meet them at Bremen, and it will be quite an adventure for them. Think about it anyway.

Yr loving Vati

What he's saying is he doesn't mind if you don't come as long as we can have the grandchildren to ourselves for a while! - Tante Uschi

Wednesday, 28 August 1963

Sally had drawn the outlines of the new clubhouse on a small sheet of Kodatrace. She laid it on the bare site plan and said, 'Here?'

Marianne left her board and came over. 'Too close to the road,' she said.

'But that will give a bigger parking area and more room for landscaping.'

'It will also cast a shadow over the road on frosty mornings and slow down the thaw. The highways people will reject it.'

'Ah! Yes.' She moved the outline farther south. 'Good thing we have a Scandinavian on the team. How about here?'

'In Sweden, frost pockets like that would be electrically thawed, anyway.'

'How about here?' Sally repeated.

'On the other hand, I presume we'll be electrically thawing our own forecourt, so it wouldn't cost much more to extend it to the shadowed area on the public road. Then we could put the clubhouse right against the boundary and have no dead ground. Let's do a costing of both and see what we gain.'

'Meanwhile, how close can we put it to the boundary if we don't thaw the public highway?'

'Well, they have to accept the shadow of the existing hedge, so get the sunrise trajectory for December and put the clubhouse just far enough to stop its shadow spilling over the hedge top. The data are all in that handy architects' tables book we got from Alcan.'

'Are we going to go with Alcan for the lights and glazing? Sandy was on to us again last week.'

'Alcan's the fallback. Willard's cooking up a possible deal with Pechiney.'

'In metric? Oh, please God, no!'

Marianne laughed. 'I can't *wait* until we go over to metric. But meanwhile the French will prostitute themselves in feet and inches for a profit. The deal would include several of Willard's stack-a-prole high-rises up in Cumbernauld, too. We're just the afterthought.'

There was a knock at the far door but before they could say 'come in,' Nicole shouted, 'Only me!' and walked up the passage. 'What d'you think of these?' she asked, offering a plate of small coconut cakes, the size of petits fours.

Still warm, they dissolved deliciously on the tongue.

'Vanilla?' Sally guessed.

'Just the faintest trace of cinnamon? Or is it allspice? What gives locust beans their flavour?'

'Whatever it is,' Sally added, 'it's a winner. Is this for the Calor Gas competition next month?'

Nicole nodded. 'One of them. You really think it's a winner?'

The other two laughed. 'You don't need us to tell you that,' Sally said.

'You should open a cookery school,' Marianne added. 'Cordon Nicole – something like that.'

Nicole drew breath to speak, but then hesitated.

'What?' Sally helped herself to another sample. 'Just want to make sure my first reaction was right.'

'In that case,' Marianne said, 'me, too.'

'I was thinking,' Nicole said. 'This Country Club/Golf Club place – are they planning on sort-of English-hotel food or . . .' The sneer left her voice on the 'or' but she let the alternative hang.

Sally shrugged. 'It's not for us to say but I'll bet neither Willard nor Alex has given it the slightest thought. Why? Are you suggesting *you* could turn it into a gourmet heaven?'

Marianne said, 'Wow! The vista that opens up suddenly!' Then, more soberly, 'But I know what Willard will say.'

'What?'

'Nothing against the excellence of the cuisine – he wouldn't dare – but what about cost control? Orders for white Piedmont truffles and so on?'

Nicole grinned. 'And would an American man dare lecture a Normandy Protestant Frenchwoman on thrift? And as for truffles – give me two hundred grams of sunflower seeds and I'll give you a white-truffle flavour that would deceive ninety-nine per cent of the diners. Not a Bib inspector, of course, but a hundred per cent of English people. I'll show him *thrift!*'

'Bib inspector?' Sally asked.

'The Michelin Man – Bibendum. Our tiny restaurant in Honfleur had one star. A little bigger – a little more choice on the menu – and it would have been two. And who was the *maîtresse de cuisine?*'

Marianne looked at Sally. 'What now?'

Sally turned to Nicole. 'I was thinking. Back around nineteen fifty, when Adam and I first got the idea to pull out of the new-towns schemes and go private with you and Tony, we asked both of you over to dinner. D'you remember two catering students, from Hatfield? They'll have found places long ago, of course. But that was quite a good meal they put up. Willard would be less likely to oppose the idea if you had a whole team lined up – graduates from the college there. All living locally. Don't need staff accommodation. That'd show who's thinking of thrift – even as early as this!'

'Oh – I've got it!' Marianne laughed. 'Get Willard to fund a scholarship there – The Willard A Johnson Catering Scholarship. There'll be no problem then.'

'That's one thing I've always admired about you,' Sally said. 'Your fanatical loyalty to your man.'

'He loves that sort of thing. I'm doing him a favour. You'll see. Can we polish off these coconut things, Nicole?'

Fifteen seconds of ecstatic silence, broken only by ambrosial munching, followed before Nicole said, 'What would we do for information without our children! Apparently Jasmine told Constance that her father and Willard are thinking of allowing members of the Dower House community and their guests to eat at . . . what was the word? Con . . . con-something rates?'

'Concessionary rates?' Sally suggested. 'But why?' She turned to Marianne. 'Has Willard said anything?'

'Does Willard ever say anything until it's gone past the point of no return? But I'll bet I know what it's all about. The Riley-Potters and the deVoors are not too happy with the siting of the clubhouse. Too close to the Dower House for their liking. They'd rather put it at either end of the course. Cynegonde is saying she thinks it ought to be as close to Dormer Green as possible. Right on that big bend in the road.'

'Well,' Sally said. 'It would make the sewerage and waste drainage a lot simpler.'

'Don't even think it! The designers want that slope for the tricky ninth – where the men get separated from the boys. I'll bet Willard and Alex are banking on Cynegonde falling silent when she hears that the Dower House community will have discounted rates in the restaurant.'

'Well, the Riley-Potters will certainly leap at it,' Nicole said.

'But that will only make Cynegonde dig her heels in firmer,' Sally pointed out.

'Interesting times ahead!' Marianne sang.

Nicole retrieved her empty dish but, in pirouetting round to leave, knocked over a photograph on the mantelpiece with her ponytail. She caught it before it fell to the hearth and set it upright again – a photo of Siri when she was just a few days old.

'Oh, yes,' Marianne said. 'I put that there to remind me to change it. She had one taken in Harrods for her birthday last month – poster-size, of course, but it came with a six by four that will fit that frame.'

Nicole was still staring at the baby image. 'Sixteen years,' she said. 'Where has the time gone!'

There was a brief silence before Marianne said, 'You remember that night?'

Nicole grinned. 'I'll say!'

'Me, too. I didn't really feel I belonged here until then.'

'What?' Sally was surprised. 'Just having a baby—'

'No.' Marianne went on looking at Nicole. 'It wasn't "just having a baby", was it.'

'Ah,' Nicole said.

Marianne pressed her. 'I've often thought about it . . . often wondered.'

Nicole put down her dish and gave a slightly guilty laugh. 'It was Felix and Angela.'

'They told you?'

'They didn't mean to. They didn't know I was there – in the walled garden, the morning after our first midsummer party . . . when you and Angela—'

'I remember.'

'You and Angela what?' Sally asked.

'It's a long story – and a long time ago.'

'I wonder if Angela thinks that?' Nicole said.

'How did she and Felix tell you without meaning to?' Marianne insisted.

'Oh, that. I went out to pick some herbs in the walled garden. And you remember how thick the . . . *consoude* was then?'

'Comfrey.'

'Yes. And I remembered as a little girl lying in a great bed of it behind my uncle's garden in Honfleur. So I lay down in it and . . .' She snored. 'And voices woke me up but I stayed hidden because they might think I hid on purpose. And it was Felix and Angela. And I didn't understand most of it but I heard enough to know you risked your life against the Nazis in the war. Then, of course, I was ashamed of the way I'd treated you. So I tried to help with the baby. With Siri. Must I explain more?'

Marianne shook her head.

'All because you went out hunting for herbs!' Sally said.

Nicole nodded. 'You see a lot, I can tell you.' A memory struck her suddenly. 'Like Angela and this Mrs Dobson. I'm sure they know each other from some time before. Lena saw Angela carry out some hot coffee to them when they started the survey and I was out looking for Saint George's mushrooms that next morning, down in the valley, and I saw Angela come down to her and at first it looked like they were arguing. But then they shook hands, so they probably weren't. But Felix came down and watched them from a distance, as if he was worried for her. So I'm sure they'd all met each other before, somewhere.'

Sally chuckled. 'Maybe she's an old flame of Felix's. And Angela went down to warn her off!'

Nicole nodded. 'I wondered that, too – especially that day her husband discovered Eric lives here. She wouldn't come near the house until Angela went down and practically dragged her into the Brandons' flat – and I wasn't gathering herbs then, before you ask. I was painting the glazing bars on our bedroom window. The one overlooking the lawn.'

'And come to think of it – Felix *has* been a bit down in the dumps lately.'

'No. That's because Georges Braque just died. He was one of the artists who signed a petition for Felix's release after his first arrest.'

'Oh, yeah? That's what *he* says!'

'An old flame of Felix's, eh!' Marianne giggled. 'Even *more* interesting times ahead!'

Tuesday, 10 September 1963

Eric was returning from the village, pondering (as one does) his advice to Jasmine, when a movement on the path up ahead startled him from his reverie.

Calley?

Yes, it was his daughter all right – standing stock still and alone. He came to a halt and watched her for a while. Two microscopic gametes, one from him and a larger one from Isabella, had produced . . . all that! Rising fifteen but already slipping away from them, half-launched, half-inaccessible.

What *was* she doing there, rooted to the earth, eyes wide open, not moving a muscle?

'I can see you,' she called out. 'I saw you the moment you climbed over the stile into the field.' She maintained her pose and did not turn her head towards him; her words alone acknowledged his presence.

'You don't sound too pleased,' he challenged.

She gave up and, flopping into a more habitual pose, called out, 'Come on up! I'm sure I'm interfering with some important errand or thought.'

He broke into a trot and, drawing near, replied, 'That suspicion is mutual. My errand was to the post office. My thoughts were plucked from the usual ragbag. How about you?'

She linked arms with him and they walked home side by side. 'I was over in the wood the other day,' she began, 'and I suddenly realized that everything I could see was *living*! One stone – sticking out of the side of the ditch spoiled it. But then I thought, *No!* I couldn't see them but even that stone was covered in a film of bacteria, the transparent mycelia of yet undiscovered fungi . . . pollen spores. So *everything* I could see – give or take the limitations of my eyesight – everything was alive.'

'Including you.'

She hugged his arm briefly to her and said, 'Bingo! You know that feeling, too!'

'Yes. Plus the fact that—'

'No! Let me tell you my . . . my—'

'Epiphany.'

'Yes! My epiphany was that I was the only living thing there capable of comprehending it all. A fox or a badger or a squirrel – they could *look* at it – they could even see things that I would miss – but they wouldn't comprehend the *whole* of it. From bacteria and mycelia and spores right up to the tallest-tallest tree. But then I wondered if that made me *more* like I'm part of it or does it separate me off? So that's what I was trying to discover when you came along.'

'And I stopped you reaching a conclusion?'

She sighed. 'Not really. I had just got around to thinking the only way to find out was to write a poem about it.'

They emerged into the field, where John Reeves was halfway through his autumn ploughing. He reached the end of the furrow – or the three furrows he dug with each traverse of the field – flipped the plough, and started back towards them.

They watched him for a while in silence, and then Eric said, 'How's the *paid* work coming along?'

'Huh?'

'Well . . . the hope-to-be-paid work.' When she still did not twig, he said, 'The song lyrics for Tommy!'

She snatched her arm away from his and set off home, turning only to say (putting on an American accent – and not just any old American accent but a pretty good imitation of Thelma Ritter): 'Aw, gee, thanks, Paw – you sure know how to light up the day fer a goil!'

'Nuts in May . . . Nuts in May . . .' Calley repeated the name of Tommy's band over and over again.

> *H̲ere we go g̲athering ṉuts in M̲a̲y . . .*

Four beats.

> *The c̲urfew t̲olls the Kn̲ell of p̲arting d̲a̲y . . .*

Five beats. Iambic pentameter? Better, anyway. Five beats. I want
a strong iambic pentameter, please, O Muse.

> *The st̲ain of t̲ea̲rs that w̲ill not w̲ash aw̲a̲y.*

Bingo! That's my target, then. Something like . . .

> *My pillow where the nights are washed away*
> *Is stained with tears that will not wash away*

No!

> *The pillow where my nights are cried away*

Still no. Still two 'away's.

> *My pillow where each night I cry till day etc . . .*

Good enough for a marker. Leave it at that and find the beginning. There was a nice juxtaposition of 'climate' and 'weather' I
thought of last night . . .

> *Yours was the greater strength, mine the tether.*
> *You my very climate, you were all my weather.*

Tether doesn't belong. We're into meteorology now. What does
strength do?

> *Yours was the strength that held my life together.*
> *You were my climate, you were all my weather.*

Stick with the metaphor or counter it?

> *But you left me . . .*

No. Too abrupt. Stick with the metaphor.

> *You were the sun that filled my days with light.*

Something-something-something all is night?

> *Now you've left me here and all is endless night.*

No. Stress on weak syllables – and one too many, anyway.

> *You've left me in a hell of endless night.*

No. I need that 'now'.

> *Now I'm in this hell of endless night.*
> *My pillow where each night . . .*

No – can't have two nights.

> *My pillow where I beg you 'One more day!'*
> *Is stained with tears that will not wash away.*

How's it looking?

> *Yours was the strength that held my life together.*
> *You were my climate, you were all my weather.*
> *You were the sun that filled my days with light.*
> *Now I'm in this hell of endless night.*
> *My pillow where I beg you 'One more day!'*
> *Is stained with tears that will not wash away.*

Pop song? Schmooze? Ballad? Never mind. Tommy will work something out. It might be fun to play it *against* the poetry with a really loud headache beat and that bias-something synthetic music maker of Angela's, and Tommy singing with a gravelly lower-class London accent?

The very thought of it made her giggle.

It shouldn't have much of a melody, not like a ballad. Just keep it within five notes and hammer them hard. Five discords. That would be a new sound, for sure.

Except the chorus could be like with a cinema organ warbling on a few angelic chords, like on the religious shows on Luxembourg when they're appealing for money.

> *Oh my baby! Oh my darling love!*

No! Not pentameters for the chorus. Four beats:

> *Oh my baby! Oh my baby!*
> *Baby, baby, baby, baby!*
> *Oh my darling love!*

He could sing it in canon with the band. Not like *Frère Jacques* where they come in after every fourth beat. Just the one beat: *Oh my oh my oh my* . . . and so on. And sustain the *dah* of *darling* until they all catch up. No – just keep repeating *love love love* . . . until they all catch up. That's better.

Second verse. Less nostalgia. More punch.

> *But still I've got my pride and this I'll say*
> *You'll never ever make me rue the day*
> *I loved you – when I gave you all I've got.*

And then?

> *And you my darling took the bleeding lot.*

You can't say that!

But why not? She's going to be a killer in the third verse, remember. Maybe a bit of bleeding now would sort of pave the way? And you could sort of turn it with:

> *This bleeding heart that you once made so gay*
> *Is stained with tears that will not wash away.*

Yeah? Well . . . we can work on it.

Chorus.

The last verse flowed without revision.

Don't hold your breath. I'll not stay down for long.
Just hold your tongue 'cos you have done me wrong.
Your eyes that stole my heart away from me
Are soon enough to learn their destiny.
Those eyes will 'Love me! Love me! Love me!' pray
And bleed with tears that I'll not wash away.

She read it through several times and changed not a comma. Here and there she improvised snatches of a possible melody – though that would be for Tommy to add if he thought he could make something of it – up-tempo on the first five lines of each verse then stretch it to double on each last line.

She laughed out loud at the sweetness of revenge in the final verse, and at the thought that she, who had never loved with such intensity as that – and would certainly never pine so wetly, no matter how passionate her love had been – could even so find the passion to express it. She slept on it for twenty-four hours and then showed it to her father.

He, too, read it several times and then looked up at her with a frown.

'What?' she asked.

'Are you happy with it?' he asked.

She shrugged awkwardly.

'Are you?'

'No,' she sighed. 'But I can't see where to start to make it better.'

'I was afraid of that.' He rose and searched for a book on his shelves. 'Yes!' he said, returning with the autobiography of Benjamin Robert Haydon. 'You should read this. Powerful stuff. He was a very competent history painter. *Christ's Entry into Jerusalem. The Resurrection of Lazarus. King Alfred*, et cetera. Ah, yes – here it is.' He passed the book to her, his finger on a particular line.

'I roughed in the head of Christ and stood back amazed,' she read. 'What about it?'

'It's the authentic voice of the runner-up, the *silver* medallist, the *almost*-great artist. And so – darling one – if you can write as fluently as this at fifteen and not stand back amazed, I have a dreadful foreboding that you may one day be a truly first-rate poetess. And I'm sorry to be the bearer of such woeful tidings, but there's absolutely nothing you or I can do about it.'

Monday, 14 October 1963

'This old crate is showing her age,' Alex said as he and Faith set off down the long drive that Monday morning. 'There's a two-door James Young version going for a thousand down near Barnstaple. They only made six – two are in America, one's in India, one's a write-off. Only two left in England.'

'Mmmm,' Faith said.

'I thought we might motor down there some weekend and have a quick shufti at it. Maybe give it a spin. It's the four-point-six litre engine and a two-door aluminium body, so she should have more poke than this beast.'

'Mmmm,' Faith said.

'These responses lack something of your usual sparkle, my dear?'

'Sorry!' She took a deep breath and made some random, animated movements. 'Today's the day. Time for a showdown. I've been agonizing over it all weekend. Should I leave it until later in the week – so that Fogel has the weekend to face the facts? Or should I do it now and stay close by him all week and not let him off the hook, so that by the weekend he'll know – absolutely *know* – there is no other way.'

'And then?'

'Once he accepts . . .' She fell silent again.

'What then?'

'Well, that's the problem. I remember that time before Doubleday came in – when it looked as if we were going down the plughole. It was awful. He was utterly unreachable. And now, with this total reorganization, he's going to lose it again – or actually, it's going to *seem* to him that he's losing it, this time for good.'

'You imply that it won't be a real loss?'

'I don't know. Everything connected with Fogel always ends up being a paradox. When he first started on these international co-productions – just before I joined Manutius – we were wildly successful. And wildly talked about. The publishing world sat at his feet. But the graybeards said Manutius was too small. How many books can a handful of editors and designers produce in a year? Yet Fogel went on having one exciting idea after another. Exciting and – in the long run – money-making. But we hadn't the capital for the long run. That was when Doubleday raised the umbrella – and John Sargent and the others were wise enough to let Fogel have his head. But, inevitably, the same thing has happened all over again. And this time they're *not* willing to fund an endless expansion. But if we mark time, Fogel dies.'

'Not literally? You don't mean—'

'No. He'll go on being the genius he always has been, but it will just build up as pressure inside him – and he'll become unbearable. What he ought to do is take time out . . . stand back from the daily minutiae and create the framework for a new way to operate inside the restrictions . . . *no!*' She screwed her eyes tight. 'I mustn't say *restrictions* or he'll stop listening. Framework? No, I already used that.'

'Architecture?'

'Brilliant!' She punched his arm – and almost put them off the A1 roundabout and on the grass verge. 'A new way to operate inside the *architecture* provided by Doubleday.'

But no sooner had she said it than she slumped again. 'Won't work,' she murmured.

'You're sure? How d'you know?'

Now that they were on the main highway he opened the throttle and the newly fallen leaves were spinning in two vortices behind them; watching it in the wing mirror, Faith recalled a scene in Wendy's novel, *Edged in Stone* – the nameless heroine being collected from the railway station by her uncle in a pre-war Rolls-Royce for a golden autumnal drive through the Cotswolds to her family home . . . watching the leaves spin like that behind her. Wendy managed to imply that dead things – ideas, dreams, hopes – could revive and form themselves into something vivid, and lively, and organized. But these vortices, here on the busy A1, were soon mashed against the radiators and mudguards of the cars behind, sucked underneath and lost to sight.

'How d'you know it won't work?' he prompted her again.

'Because what I'm doing is trying to find a way for Fogel to run a *small* outfit inside the much larger outfit his own genius has created.'

'Well, hang on! He didn't create it single-handed. He couldn't have done it without you.'

'I know – but, don't you see? That only makes it worse. I followed the logic of what he was doing. I followed *him* with a mop and a bucket! He may have clinched the final deal with Doubleday but I'm the one who set it up. And they only signed on condition that I continued to look after the nuts and bolts. That's when Abnorman Crowley quit and went back home, remember?'

'How do others manage?' Alex asked. 'Reader's Digest Books, for instance. They're a lot bigger than Manutius. Is it impossible for you to grow that big?'

'Oh! Digest!' She spoke as if the name itself trumpeted the end of the world as we know it. 'They're not on our planet at all. They do dull and worthy books and they do them absolutely brilliantly. You look at them and you simply have to own them. I met Peter Glemser in Paris – about this time last year – and he described a project that he'd dearly love to do but I could hear in his tone of voice that Digest would probably never do it – or if they did, they'd suck all the goodness out of it and serve it up as a standard Digest product.'

'Wasn't he taking a risk – telling you?'

She laughed. 'Maybe he was feeling guilty about nicking Fogel's idea for a new kind of world atlas? But no – seriously, that was Fogel's fault for blabbing about it on the plane back from New York. But Glemser spilled the beans to me because he knew it's the sort of thing Manutius would never touch – because to Fogel it would seem like going back to the beginning again with *Forward!* and *Illustrated Britain*. Glemser's idea was to publish a bi-monthly hard-cover magazine called *British Heritage*. A hundred and twenty-eight pages, no ads, full colour throughout – the British equivalent of *American Heritage*, in fact. But this is the point – I asked him if his people were producing a sales dummy and he said no – the last thing he wanted was something that looked as if Digest Books had produced it. He had a vision of something much more romantic in his mind's eye – but he's a marketing genius, not an editor or a designer. He knows what he wants only *after* he's seen it.'

'So . . . it's stymied?'

'I don't think so. I put him on to Eric and I think they're cooking up something between them. But Eric – being Eric – is putting heart and soul into it and saying, at the same time, that it'll never see the light of day.' After a pause she said, 'Why are we talking about this? Oh, yes – because I haven't the faintest idea how I'm going to handle Fogel this week. This week of weeks.'

Fogel put down the phone and stared at Faith with his big, bloodhound eyes.

'Savorelli is playing golf?' she guessed.

'They *say* he is all day at the printers. And they *say* Sargent is all day at the golf course – or will be when New York wakes up. And Lavayssière is at some book expo in Rouen – they *say*. Hah!'

'Beastly bad luck, Wolf,' she said.

'Hah!' he repeated.

'There's no point in trying to phone Sargent, you know. Of course he won't be out playing golf but would you prefer his secretary to say he's not willing to talk to you until you have studied his letter, considered the proposals . . . talked with everyone here and above all talked with me?'

'Yes, you!' he replied. 'This is *you*, isn't it.' He picked up Sargent's letter and tore it in half. 'I'll talk with *him*, not you. I'll talk with him about *me* – not some arrangement cooked up behind my back by you.' He snatched the half-smoked cigar from his mouth and stabbed at the torn-up letter, leaving it scarred with ash.

She stared at him, unmoved.

'Well?' he challenged.

'Didn't you see it's – or it *was* – an Ozalid? I have another one here.' She drew it from her folder and laid it on his desk. 'And I can go on making copies until you're prepared to be sensible and constructive.'

'*Du liebe Zeit!*' He rose to his feet, trembling all over. She thought he might vault his desk and attack her. 'I made you! You knew *nothing*! I taught you everything you know.'

'In a negative way, that's true. Sit down or you'll get a nosebleed.'

'Negative?' he shouted. 'Negative?'

'Yes, Wolf. The reason we're in this bind today is that we are the perfect team. You create wonderful, inspired, new ventures, or vehicles – whatever you want to call them. But you can't create the organization to back them up – to carry them through. But that's all right. You don't need to – because you've got me. That's what I do. And I learned it . . . not *from* you but certainly *through* you.'

'Preposterous!' he said. But he resumed his seat and relit the remnant of his cigar.

'You think so? Just reach behind you – no! Without looking. Just reach over your shoulder and touch a book. Any book – at random.'

He fixed her with a baleful stare but did as she asked. Or commanded.

'OK. You've touched the *History* volume of the Encyclopedia Series. Let's talk about that. The idea for the whole series was yours. Allen Lane was sceptical and bowed out. Max Parrish – very reluctantly – cut himself in, but only because *you* proposed it. The general feeling in the trade was – not for the first time – that Fogel had bitten off much more than he could possibly chew. What? A management team of *three*, an editorial team of *four*, two designers and two assistants, one picture researcher? To launch *a ten-volume series* covering the whole field of modern knowledge?'

'It was more than that.'

'Not to start with. It was clearly madness. But you bulldozed it through. You got Barry, Huxley, Fisher, and Bronowski as the consultant editorial board. And for the *History* volume you got Alan Bullock as subject-consultant – and you spotted him before he was even on TV. But who recruited Cottie Burland? Peter Cadogan, the Robsons, Anthony Michaelis . . . Eric Uphill? This isn't a criticism of you. Nor is it a hunt for compliments on my part. You did what you're brilliant at doing and I did what I learned to do in working *for* you. You didn't teach me – but you didn't need to. Once you staked out the territory, I knew how to fill it. And by the time we finished that Encyclopedia Series we had four editorial teams – plus two more for the adult books – the Shah and the Ben Gurion – and . . . well, you know the story. We've now got eight editorial teams, eight design teams, ten freelance picture researchers. Sixty-plus people! Not counting semi-permanent freelances like Eric Brandon. But we're still trying to run it the way we ran things back in the beginning – with everything being decided at one impossibly crowded board meeting each week. And it doesn't work, Wolf. You—'

'It does work,' he insisted. 'Every week I meet everybody who is creating something for Manutius. Everybody. It's an octopus with a pulse in each arm – and I got my finger on all those pulses. You want to stuff layers of . . . of . . . of cotton wool between me and them. Three managers report to two. Those two report to one – which is you. And you report to me. So every day I work among strangers. You say our board meeting is chaos. But I see the fear in this editor's eyes when he knows his report is next. When his turn comes, he gives a wonderful rosy story. But I have already seen the truth. Maybe not in his eyes but how he doodles . . . fidgets . . . wets his lips. How do I see all this through your cotton wool?'

'You don't – but you don't need to. You need—'

'I do. I need to feel the pulse.'

'And while you're doing that, the budgets are being broken. Every single project is running over-budget – for instance. I could go on.'

'But we always make good profits in the end.'

'In the end – yes. But we have to wait. Sometimes years – and a fat profit in the fifth year is very slim when amortized over all five. You *know* all this Fogel but you just won't face it. The Americans were happy – well, not *very* happy – but they went along with our long-cycle kind of publishing when the outlay was peanuts in their terms. But that's no longer the case. And I should warn you – they're not even convinced that *any* kind of reorganization here can produce the sort of returns they are now demanding of us. You have made us too big for them to overlook. Listen – we can beat about the bush all day. And you can dream of cutting loose from Doubleday and sailing off into the sunset with some kind of alliance between us and Sansoni and Larousse . . . but they'll take one look at our organization – our *lack of* organization – and they'll say exactly the same thing as Doubleday: Manutius is a one-man outfit and if anything happens to you, it will all just disintegrate.'

'You don't fool me, Mrs Findlater,' he said sourly. 'If anything happens to me – *you* can take over Manutius and turn out Reader's Digest-type books. I know this because I can see you want a Digest-type structure here.'

'OK, Fogel, if we're descending to that level, I have more important things to do. If you call John Sargent at five, our time, he'll tell you the same and then maybe you'll see it's not just some absurd ambition on my part. And perhaps tomorrow—'

'Because you will call him before me this afternoon and tell him what to say!'

'Oh, yes! The head honcho at Doubleday now takes orders from me! You really are—'

'He listens to you. I've seen it. He talks and his eyes flicker to you every other sentence. He . . . *ach, du liebe Zeit!*'

'Oh, God – now your nose is bleeding! I warned you! No! Lean back! Head over the . . . that's right. Look at your shirt. Where are the tissues? *Joyce!*'

His secretary burst into the room.

'Tissues!' Faith shouted. And, to her departing back, she added: 'And bring a clean shirt.'

When the tissues arrived, she started to staunch the blood and a new worry took over. 'My God, Wolf – you're running a fever. You can't possibly go to the Royal Court tonight.'

'It will all be gone by then,' he insisted.

'And that's what he's done,' she told Alex on the drive home that evening. 'Gone to see his friend Alfred Marks in *Mr Biedermann and the Fire Raisers*. The stamina of that man is just phenomenal. He's not healthy. He doesn't even attempt to look after himself. And yet I've seen him looking as if he's at death's door just a second or two before he straightens up, stands tall, and sweeps into a negotiation in which he wipes the floor with the other party.'

They halted at the tailback on the Brent Cross flyover. 'When-oh-when are they going to complete the M1 into London?' Alex muttered. 'This is absurd – *every* evening. It's that amazing stamina which has made it possible for him to resist this inevitable change for so long, of course. That and his monstrous will to win – to sweep the floor with the rest of you.'

Faith sighed. 'Inevitable? I wonder. It's true that if we try to continue without a fundamental reorganization, we'll probably collapse. But even if we reorganize successfully, leaving Fogel free to get on with the creative side . . .' She relapsed into silence, which Alex did not break. She started again on a new tack. 'He feels he absolutely needs to be in touch with *everything* that's going on with *every* title, *every* week. In the same breath he'll admit it's impossible but he won't even consider the first steps towards a more rational structure. So if we do it – go over his head and do it – will we be taking away that stimulus, which he says he needs?

Will he turn into an extinct volcano and so the firm will collapse, anyway? Are we doomed in either direction?'

'Well, one way the collapse is certain. The other way it's merely possible. That's the only sensible way to take. And Fogel is a survivor. He'll adapt to the inevitable – and, yes – it *is* inevitable.' When she made no reply he said, 'Is that it?'

'I keep thinking about his sneer that if I took over, Manutius would start turning out Reader's Digest-type books. There was an awful truth in it because – you know why? Because Manutius has grown into the sort of big organization that can no longer create the inspired sort of books we made at the beginning. I daren't tell Wolf this but I'm damn sure that somewhere in England – possibly in a disused warehouse in south London, that sort of place – there's an editor and a designer and a few other bods who are dreaming up the next big sensation for Frankfurt – and it won't look anything like what we're doing. Or what anyone else is doing, either.'

'Such as?'

'Ha! If only I knew! Something we'd say is preposterous. Something Digest would market-test for a year and then abandon. Off the top of my head – aimed at *consumers*. Still a big buzz-word. Something to do with everyday life. Coping with everyday situations. Pregnancy. Debt. Moving house. Collecting dolls. First aid. Bicycle maintenance. Hobbies. All using an eye-catching comic-strip format and full colour. Sixty-four pages. Less than five shillings each. I'm not even running this up the flagpole, as dear Abnorman used to say, but it would be as far-out as that. And if it took off, the whole elephantine herd of Maxwell, Hamlyn, Rainbird, and us would flock to bring out a me-too series at *next* year's Frankfurt. But we wouldn't have invented it.'

'You don't have to invent something to make a lot of money at it. Rolls and Royce never invented a thing. They just took the best examples of engineering of their day and said, "Can you make it twice as thick and double up on the number of bolts holding it together?" We're going to do very nicely out of our golf-club adventure – and golf was probably invented by some early ape man whacking a baboon's skull across the African plain with the thigh-bone of a zebra.'

She knew well that when Alex's mind drifted towards golf, all hope of a wide-ranging discussion fled. 'I might just have a word with Eric about this crazy publishing idea,' she said, 'It's by no means certain that Doubleday will stand up to Fogel. And if they cave in, I couldn't possibly stay.'

That brought him up sharp. 'But if you go, the firm will surely collapse.'

'They might even welcome that – hoping to invite me back to pick up the pieces and go into direct competition with Digest Books. Slick, sumptuous, market-tested books. Books that make money from Year One. They'd be sooo much happier with that.'

'And you'd agree to do it?'

She reached across and squeezed his hand on the wheel. 'I think I'll have a word with Eric – come what may.'

Saturday, 23 November 1963

Marianne, who had been glancing out of the window every few minutes, said, 'That's Willard's Cadillac coming up the drive. Just look at that cream-puff suspension. I hate that car.'

'I'll be off, then.' Sally packed up her things in some haste.

'Oh – there's honestly no need for—'

'I think there is. This must be an awful day to be an American. It even kept *me* awake last night.' At the door she paused. 'There was a man on the wireless this morning telling Jack de Manio that everyone in the world will remember exactly where they were and what they were doing when they first heard the news.' She smiled wanly. 'It's true, too. I was standing on the kitchen chair nailing up a short piece of matchboarding. I almost fell off. Listen – if you want to take Willard out tonight . . . Siri can look after herself, I suppose. But if you'd like to park Virgil and Peter on us, feel free.'

Marianne blew her a kiss. Going out with Willard tonight might not be such a bad idea. There was that new restaurant, Chez Max, on the way to St Albans – allegedly 'gourmet' (though God knows what that meant in this land of one-meat-with-with). Probably booked out on a Saturday, anyway. Willard was going about pretending not to be upset . . . no, that wasn't exactly true. He *was* upset because otherwise he'd have gone out cubbing today; instead he went into town, just to prove it wasn't going to interfere with his work. He must be parking the car by now.

She drifted across to Siri's room. 'If Willard and I went out tonight, would you be OK here on your own?' she asked. 'What are you up to, anyway?'

Siri held the book up for her mother to read the title while she herself went on with the text: *The Revolution in Physics* by Max Ernst. 'It's not the latest stuff but it's the most lucid explanation I've come across – and it doesn't shirk the maths.'

Marianne raked the ceiling with her eyes. 'I'm so glad to hear that, darling, but are you going to shirk the answer to my question?'

'Oh! No – fine.'

'And Sally's offered to keep an eye on the boys.'

Siri looked up for the first time. 'I can do that. If they go down there with Theo, they'll just spend the whole evening telling smutty jokes.'

'But it's Saturday – and if that's what they want to—'

'Virgil has to finish that Spanish galleon if he stands the slightest chance of entering it for the Modelling Club prize.'

'Oh, darling!' Marianne smiled at her solemnity. 'We've never pushed any of you – you know how Willard feels.'

'Well, Willard's not always right. Some people need pushing – especially Virgil. And Peter has to hand in those sketches for the nativity play scenery by Monday, so it won't do him any harm. Eric says he can go down there and use his materials. Virgil can take his modelling stuff down there, too, actually.'

They heard Willard's cry from the front door: 'Honey!'

'He sounds cheerful, anyway,' Marianne said as she left.

Even so, Siri beat her to it with Willard's carpet slippers.

Willard went in ahead of Marianne – a Continental custom to which she had schooled him. He bore down on the maître d' – Max himself – with hand outstretched. 'Willard A Johnson and my wife, Marianne. Max, is it? You have a table for two, I hope?'

Unlike most head waiters or patrons in England, Max showed no surprise as he shook hands with them. 'You are in luck, Mister Johnson, Mrs Johnson,' he said with a slight bow. 'We have a cancellation. Several, in fact.' As he led them to a table for two in an alcove he added that it was understandable, almost as if he were chiding them.

Every table had a single rose, dyed black.

'Are we insensitive or what?' Willard asked as Max left them with the wine list and two menus – his with prices, hers without. 'Maybe we Americans are more used to ending our presidencies this way. He's not the first.'

Marianne was scanning the menu and peeking across at his. 'It's not exactly cheap.'

He lost himself in the main courses for a while:

```
La Bourride - 15s/6d
Rognons en pyjama - 15s/-
Poussin en cocotte - 17s/6d
Sole au fromage - 17s/6d
Pigonneau au choux - 17s/6d
Côte d'agneau en cuirasse - 17s/6d
Entrecôte bearnaise OR au poivre - 17s/6d
```

'It had better be good,' he said. 'What's "*bourride*"?'

'Fishy. Like a bouillabaisse but with no tarragon. And the "pyjamas" are the suet that you normally cut off the kidneys, but if you bake it in a very hot oven it goes wonderfully crisp. You shouldn't be eating that.'

'Cocotte? Always sounds kind-of interesting.'

'It just means a fireproof dish.'

'Well – that's another description of the same lady, I guess.' He laughed.

Several diners glanced disapprovingly in their direction.

'Ooops!' he murmured. 'What are you having?'

A waiter materialized, it seemed out of the air.

'The lemon spinach soup and the sole *au fromage*,' she said.

'And I'll have the oyster chowder and the *entrecôte* – rare. Just light a match and walk round it three times.'

'Bleu . . .' the man murmured as he wrote. 'And the wine, monsieur?'

Willard looked at Marianne. 'They have a half-bottle of *Clos du Chêne Marchand*.'

She nodded. His choice in wines had always been superior to hers.

'And – wow! You have a Château Canon *grand cru*! Nineteen forty-six. No half-bottles, I guess?'

The man dipped his head apologetically.

'I don't mind that with the fish,' she said.

'Well, we can't pass it up. What we don't drink we'll take away. Meanwhile, we could use some water.' When the waiter had gone, he added: 'That's one thing I still miss. In America, before you even sit down, they put a jug of water on the table. I'll insist on it at the Club.'

'Does this jog your memory about Nicole's offer?' she asked.

'Yeah, I've been thinking about that. It's tempting, but it complicates things. I mean, look at this place. It came from nowhere. This was a field last spring – and look at it now. And this is after "several cancellations"! The British are beginning to trickle back from their Continental holidays full of new attitudes to food. So I've been thinking we might have *two* dining rooms – one for the members and one for a regular restaurant open to the public, about this size. People have cars now. Location doesn't . . . Anyway, a members' dining room on its own wouldn't always give Nicole the scope she wants. Most of the members are going to ask for meat-and-veg kind of meals and jolly old English puddings. Stone's Chop House. Wheeler's George-and-Dragon menus. She swears she can cook those things better than any English cook but I don't believe in fairies, either. It'll be roast beef and fenugreek. But if she was the head chef – in charge of the whole kitchen and serving up a menu like this – no, even better than this – with a good English cook solely responsible for the members' dining room. D'you see?'

'There's room,' she said, thinking of the floor plans. 'And if the county will agree to our de-icing their road electrically, we'll be able to accommodate up to three dozen more cars, too. I think Nicole will leap at this idea.'

The waiter brought her soup and his chowder – and a glass pitcher of water floating with ice cubes and lemon slices.

'Orrefors!' Marianne said. 'We have one like this – *had* one like this – at home. The members would be at liberty to eat in the public dining room?' Really she wanted to know how deeply he had gone into the idea.

'Sure. Off the menu. They wouldn't need to decamp physically to the other dining room.'

She might have known it. This one was already past the point of no return. 'How's your chowder? This lemon-spinach soup is superb. No wonder they're usually booked solid on Saturdays.'

'Oh . . . yeah. That,' he said ruefully. 'I've *also* been thinking

– thank God he chose Johnson for Veep – a southerner. He had all the best ideas but he didn't have much clout with Congress. The shock is going to be deep, wide and deep, and if anyone can rally them and push through everything that's stalled, it's LBJ. Let's hope so, anyway – otherwise . . .'

'Otherwise?'

'*Après nous le déluge!*'

Tuesday, 3 December 1963

Angela left Inge in the kitchen while she went back to the studio for a moment. 'I'm sorry, Cornelius,' she said. 'It's just something I have to . . . I can't really . . . are you familiar enough with the set up to do a trial run on your own?'

'Possibly,' he replied. 'You could listen back afterwards and make suggestions.'

'It's not the same, though, is it. It won't be white hot then.'

He shrugged.

'I'll be as quick as I can. Only . . . I don't know.' Still in a daze – and heavy with foreboding – she returned to Inge in the kitchen.

Inge began at once: 'I said I wouldn't disturb you if it was—'

'Of course you disturbed me, pet! The *sight* of you disturbed me.' She took the roses off the table and went to the sink. 'And there was no need for these – we're not on the Continent now!'

As a joke it fell flat. 'That's where I should be,' Inge said.

'What rubbish!' Some obscure instinct made Angela break the rule and revert to German, in which they both spoke from then on.

'I'm disturbing your work. I'm sorry,' Inge said.

'It's probably a good thing,' Angela lied. 'That young man is a brilliant young English composer named Cornelius Cardew. Are you into modern music?'

She shook her head.

'Well, then – the name won't mean anything to you. Not yet. But take it from me, he will one day outshine Benjamin Britten, Walton, even Elgar in the English pantheon. I'm probably doing him a favour by not being there – much as I . . . well, never mind that now. Something is pretty obviously worrying you.'

Inge stared at the tabletop, doodled circles round a knot with her finger.

'Ach – what a hostess I am!' Angela exclaimed. 'Coffee!' She moved the kettle to the hottest part of the hob and it went from mewing to the rumble-before-boiling at once. She fished the rest of the paraphernalia out of the cupboard. 'Black? Cream? Milk?'

Inge raised her head and stared at her – as if she had heard a sound and was now trying to locate its source. 'Can you remember one good thing I did in . . . in Ravensbrück?' she asked. 'Just one?' She shook her head in vexation. 'No! First, I must know – why did they sentence you? Strip your ss membership and send you to Ravensbrück?'

Angela frowned. 'Surely you read my file? "For failing to disclose an illegal recording of an important occasion of state". They carefully omitted Heydrich's name, of course. And – to be quite brutally honest – I can't remember one good thing you did in the KL. But there was that earlier time when we were both on duty in Giesebrechtstrasse and I illegally recorded Heydrich screwing the arse off Irma. And you looked the other way when I popped it in my briefcase.'

'Yes,' Inge said vaguely. 'I never understood why they hadn't called me for your trial. As you say – I was there when you did it. I *saw* you.'

'*What?*' Angela had to rerun her mental tape of Inge's words. '*You* were at the Wannsee Villa that day? I don't—'

'No! In Kitty's in Giesebrechtstrasse.'

Mechanically, Angela poured the near-boiling water into the filter. 'You think *that's* what . . . that *that* was my crime? Dear God!'

'It wasn't?'

Angela scraped the grounds off the walls of the filter and poured in more hot water. '*Gott in Himmel!* You really thought my crime was that recording in Kitty's?'

'No! I knew *that* was too petty. I just wondered if they simply used it so as to smuggle you in as a spy among the inmates.'

The hair bristled on Angela's neck. 'So when we met again last May, you thought it possible that I was a loyal ss officer who had got away with it?'

'Yes,' she whispered. 'Or no. I didn't know—'

'But why, in the KL, were you so . . . [and here she was briefly catapulted back into English] so fucking *vicious* to me?'

sizes, I did ease up

'Well, I couldn't be sure. And I thought they'd warn me if I was overdoing it – but if I wasn't, I thought it would *help* you.'

'*Du liebe Zeit!*'

'Besides, I did ease up a bit when I saw Völkenrath treating you more gently.'

'Less viciously.'

'OK. So what was your crime, really, then? In their eyes, I mean?'

Angela stared at her, first in one eye, then the other – as if, deep within them, or between them, she might discern something beyond this ignorance. 'Hang on a mo,' she said at last. 'Just wait here – I'll go and get it – my crime. My *real* crime!'

'Oh, no!' Felix said when he returned that evening. 'Have you gone crazy?' He wandered round and round his sculpture, as if it would drive him mad to stand still.

'It's all right,' Angela assured him.

'How can you know? How can you *possibly* know? Everyone agreed it would be "all right" for Marianne's father to read it.'

'You didn't see the look on Inge's face as she read it. And even more when she finished.'

'What look?'

'And not just her look. It was what she said. She said, "The twentieth of January, nineteen forty-*two*". And then she said, "And all those experiments all over Poland in nineteen forty-*one*". And then, "All those party high-ups – *all* agreeing to it!"'

After a pause he said, 'That's it?'

'I think it struck her for the first time how *organized* it all was. She was part of it but she had no idea of its sheer size – no idea of how *small* a part she played.'

'Nor did we,' he reminded her.

'But when we did learn about it – after the war – we thought *they* must have known – everyone in the ss. But obviously an ss-*Aufseherin* was at the very bottom of the heap. Inge had no comprehension – until she read the transcript today – how organized, how carefully planned – how *long* planned the *Vernichtung* was. And how approved-of by the whole party and state apparatus. And how universally they applied it throughout Europe. I don't know what sort of denazification or de-indoctrination they carried out on them in prison, but it did nothing to prepare her for reading my transcript today. Anyway, she came here very agitated and she left much calmer.'

'Marianne's father was very calm, too – that night – but he was dead before dawn.'

'His was the calm of a man whose mind is made up. Hers is the calm of a conscience eased – just a little.'

'I hope you're right.'

'You'll see.'

Later that evening, she said, 'Inge wasn't being utterly naïve. They used to take me out of the KL, one night every month. You can just imagine the suspicions—'

'You never told me that.'

After some hesitation, she said, 'There's lots we've never told each other – nor ever wanted to tell each other. It was just a way of adding to my humiliation.'

'And *were* the other women suspicious?'

'No. The communists knew what I'd done. They knew the ss were doing it for their own sport. Eichmann had commanded that I should not be allowed to die, so—'

'Why?'

'I think he suspected I'd made that written transcript as well as the tape, and he wanted it. He wanted to destroy it, of course. So that . . .' Her voice petered out.

'What? So that what?'

'Here's another thing I never said before. Those evenings when they smuggled me out to the ss officers' mess – they were a circus of humiliation. They made me drink toasts to the Führer in brandy from the kitchen, brandy that had been destroyed with pepper—'

'Adulterated.'

'Adulterated with pepper. And they . . .' She hesitated.

'They beat you?' he guessed.

'No! Never anything physical. Nothing crude. Very refined humiliation.'

'Did they . . . you don't have to answer this, but—'

'Not *that* either. But the thing I was going to tell you . . . I almost blurted it out that time – our first time in Hamburg, in Jacob's restaurant with Hermann Treite and Birgit, when we were discussing the so-called "official" protocol of the Wannsee conference. My final night in the officers' mess was different. Two ss-*Aufseherinne* came with me and they dressed me up in my old uniform. Not a word spoken. And of course I didn't give them the satisfaction of asking questions I knew they'd never answer. Anyway, they left me alone in the room and I was wondering if I'd get shot if I jumped out of the window and – in walked ss-*Obersturmbannführer* Adolf Eichmann! This was towards the end of nineteen forty-four. Of course, we had no idea how close the Wehrmacht was to defeat. Wishful thinking among us had put them that close since nineteen forty-three, so I wouldn't have believed it, anyway. But he offered me a deal – my freedom in return for every transcript I had made of the Wannsee recording.'

Felix laughed – and punched the air. 'So *that* was when they were planning to plant the sanitized protocol in the files and cover it with that forged letter. They *had to* get their hands on any genuine copy and destroy it! He kept you alive, thinking that a couple of years in Ravensbrück would soften you up for a deal!' He stared at her in surprise. 'But why didn't you say all this that night in Jacob's? It confirms all our suspicions.'

'Say *all* this?' she echoed. 'The monthly visits out of the camp to an ss officers' mess? You forget, my darling – Germany was full of people who had the most innocent and plausible explanations for the most appalling things they'd done. But there it is – Eichmann just sat there and watched two of his Gestapo colleagues go to work on me until he was satisfied I was telling the truth and then they left me alone after that. And the two ss women came in and mopped up the blood and took me back to the camp. And, *Gott sei dank*! No more monthly free passes to the officers' mess! Lucky old me!'

He folded her into a bear hug. 'Lucky for Pippin. Lucky for Andrew. Lucky for Douglas. Lucky for Susan. And lucky also for one ex-*Aufseherin*!'

Wednesday, 11 December 1963

Alex's voice answered the doorphone; Wendy had hoped it would be Faith's. For a moment she hesitated, half-inclined to simply walk away. Breeding won. 'It's me, Alex – Wendy Finch. Is Faith home?'

'She won't be long. D'you want to come up and wait?' He buzzed the doorkeep. 'D'you know your way?'

'Yes. I was here last month.'

The lift, still an elegantly Parisian birdcage in an art-and-craftily pierced shaft of wrought iron, rose smoothly and with a gentle hum – a hum that began and ended with a quickly muted shriek; the old hydraulics, by contrast, had been quite silent. Alex was a half-silhouette, framed in their doorway on the third-floor landing.

'I always feel this is a piece of theatrical apparatus,' she told him, still caged. 'And I should step out to wild applause and perform some high-kicking dance.'

'Oh . . . feel free!' He emerged on the landing and held one hand aloft, as if preparing for some Astaire-and-Rogers routine. 'You sounded a bit down-in-the-dumps over the doorphone.'

'Well . . .' she said lightly, accepting the offer of his hand and doing a coquettish twirl. 'I feel a lot better now – kind sir.'

'Tea?' he asked when they were in the apartment.

Her eye strayed towards the drinks cupboard.

'I'll join you,' he said. 'Sun's over the yardarm. A Manhattan? Screwball? Advocaat?'

'Advocaat and lemonade – if you have any.'

'Snowball,' he said. 'The lemonade's in the fridge. I have ice.'

She fetched it and then stood at the window, staring down into South Audley Street while he mixed their drinks – a Manhattan for himself. It was late into the twilight and the girls were already taking up their pitches. Tap-tap-tapping on the paving as each likely mark passed by.

'Is it something private?' he asked as he handed her the Snowball. 'D'you want me to make myself scarce when Faith arrives?'

'Oh, no! Thank you. No – nothing like that. I'm just feeling a bit . . . yoooeeurgh. I tried Robert Street but no one's there.'

'So we're second best.' He smiled provocatively.

She poked him, one-fingered. 'No! But being with Felix and Angela would have kept it in the family. Cheers!'

'Cheers! Kept what in the family?'

She sat down on the couch; he took the chair opposite. 'David Mercer told me he has a couple of novels stuck in a drawer.'

'We should keep *that* in the family?'

'No!' She laughed. 'I was just thinking aloud – for comfort.

The thing is, Cape has rejected my second novel, *Leftover Hand*. So now I'm their first *ex*-Angry Young Woman.'

'Oh, I say – that *is* hard luck. What does your agent suggest?'

'Peter Jantzen Trunks, as Eric calls him. He rather agrees with Tom Maschler – I can't say he didn't warn me this might happen. The days when editors would nurse a new author along have gone forever. Peggy Ramsay told David not even to bother with his manuscripts – just treat them as apprenticeship pieces – purging his system of Wyndham Lewis.'

He cleared his throat delicately. 'You do know that Manutius doesn't publish fiction – except, as I always like to point out, from Persia and Israel.'

She shrugged, trying to suggest it was all *ça-ne-fait-rien*. 'Maybe I'm just a one-book novelist – and with a *roman à clef* at that.'

'Was it . . . really? I mean . . . did you actually *experience* all that?'

She tipped her head to one side, diffidently. 'At second hand. Gossip I picked up from other girls when I was at *Vogue*.'

'Ah.'

She grinned. 'You sound disappointed.'

'Not at all. Not at all. And are you a one-play playwright, too? Sorry to sound so brutal.'

'No – that's the compensation. *Tokens of Loss* is doing well. And, thanks to an intro from David, I saw Graeme Macdonald at the Television Centre last week. He said he'd be interested in something for *The Wednesday Play* "slot" as they call it. And Joan Littlewood asked me to think of her with my next. If that's going to be my métier, I should move to Peggy – if she'll have me.'

'Wonderful! So – the *jardin* that you *faut cultiver* has quite a big sunny border.'

The lift challenged with its muted opening shriek.

'That'll be Faith,' he said, rising to pour her a G&T. 'And she sounds angry.'

Wendy laughed. 'How can you tell?'

'It must be something to do with the way she punches the third-floor button. This is your last chance if you want me to make myself scarce? I could do with a shower.'

'No – please don't. Actually, I'd welcome your advice, too.'

Faith's key grated in the lock; she started speaking even as the door swung ajar: 'Bloody Fogel!'

Alex winked at Wendy as his lips ostentatiously mimed the words in synch.

'That man will never . . . oh! Hallo, Wendy – how nice to see you!' She dropped her handbag and took her glass from Alex with a kiss for thanks. 'To what do we owe the honour?'

'I was telling Alex,' Wendy said. 'Cape has said no to *Leftover Hand*.'

'But *Tokens of Loss* is getting good houses,' Alex added. 'And there are feelers from the Beeb and Theatre Workshop.'

'Wonderful!' Faith toasted her and took a gulp. 'Oh! I needed that! Your Guardian Muse is obviously steering you in the right direction.'

'Also – she wants our advice,' he added. 'Wendy, not the Muse. But I didn't get to hear what about.'

'Eric Brandon,' she said.

'Oh!' they answered in unison.

'The thing is, writing plays is not like writing a novel. I find I can't play-write solidly, day after day, the way I can with a novel. Maybe I should now say "the way I once *could* with a novel".'

'And you asked *Eric* for *advice*?' Faith asked, as if she could hardly believe it.

'Well, he seems to keep so many irons in the fire all the time . . . I just wondered.'

'And did he . . . I hesitate to ask this in case the answer's "yes" – did he offer any crumbs?'

'He said writing a novel is just "masturbating with the alphabet" and I'm well off out of it.'

The other two exchanged puzzled glances. 'Something sensible for a change,' Faith remarked. 'I hope he left it at that?'

'He also said Isabella makes up the universe as she goes along – but it's just as random as the real universe. And she gets panicked when the two don't synchronize. He, on the other hand, has always accepted the randomness of the real universe, so he never panics at all. He implied I could choose between the two approaches.'

'And do you?' Alex asked.

'I *fall* between them,' she said. 'I wish I had Isabella's faith that I could create my own randomness but really I know Eric's idea is right.'

'No actual advice, then,' Faith said, relieved.

'Well . . .'

'Oh, no!'

'He did say that if I were at a loose end I could put in a day or so each week on this long-running *Reader's Digest* project for him. He's got as far as specifying that each issue must have some one-off features that simply stagger or amuse or fascinate – balanced by other, continuing features that make readers say, "Now I simply *have to* buy the next issue to find out what happens".'

Faith turned to Alex and said, 'They actually pay good money for bright ideas like that!'

Wendy bridled. 'No! They pay good money for concrete ideas to fill that category. I think you're annoyed because he's not spending all his time on *your* scheme.'

Faith surrendered with her hands. 'Tell us – what ideas?'

'I can't divulge that!' she protested – and then relented slightly. 'Well . . . perhaps the one he's suggested I could handle. Because that's what I'd like your advice about. The working title is *The Thousand-Year Diary of Everyman* and the idea is to have well-scattered excerpts from imaginary diaries, decade by decade, from the Norman Conquest to the present day. A master-mason on Durham Cathedral. A surveyor on the *Domesday Book*. A warrender on a royal estate. The saddler who made codpieces for Henry the Eighth. A coffee-house keeper at the time of the South-Sea Bubble. A second-rate portrait painter who's got a grudge against Hogarth . . . et cetera. It would be the history of the *folk* rather than of the Establishment.'

'There's that word again!' Alex complained. 'Suddenly everyone's talking about "the Establishment"! The only people who believe an Establishment truly exists are those beyond the pale of power.'

Wendy was about to argue that that was actually the whole point when a wink from Faith silenced her, especially when she followed it with the question: 'Does Eric think you're the girl to write this epic diary?'

'Well, he's read *Edged in Stone* – obviously – and he's seen *Tokens* a couple of times, bless him. And he thinks I'm enough of a prose-chameleon to try my hand at it. And the money's good – one day a week, three thousand words, twenty-five quid and all the coffee I can drink.'

'And you're holding back?' Faith asked.

'For what?' Alex added.

'Well – working with Eric. What's it like?'

'Sprinting in treacle?' Alex suggested.

'Catching a hare on open stubble,' Faith added.

'Seriously, though?' Wendy said. 'He's got all the research material out there at the Dower House. I've never seen such a hoard. Thousands of books. He actually has one – privately printed by some megalomaniac naval officer – called *A Cruiser Commander's Orders*! You see – I could come out the night before, stay at the Tithe Barn, gut a couple of books like that for my bedtime reading, and spend the next day turning out a couple of fifteen-hundred-word entries in these fictitious diaries. *And* squirrel twenty-five quid away in the bank.'

'Can I refresh that Snowball?' Alex asked.

'He means – you don't really need our advice, do you!' Faith said. 'You and Eric will hit it off very well, I think – as long as you never say yes when you'd rather say no. And,' she added hastily, 'I'm not talking about the obvious context for a warning like that. I'm talking about your work. He can be a bit of a steamroller when the mood takes him.'

'And he might just try it on from the word go,' Alex added, handing her the refilled glass.

Saturday, 14 December 1963

'This,' said Nicole, laying the menu in front of Willard and Marianne, Alex and Faith, 'is a typical day menu of English . . . er . . . *cooking* as served in the members' restaurant. It is what they would get in, for instance, Stone's Chop House in Panton Street. The *table d'hôte* would be selected from it – plus a few items made up from yesterday's surplus. If you would make copies of it and hand one to each of your committee members asking them to order whatever they'd like, I will serve you all a meal based on those orders three days – not counting weekends – after you give me back the completed orders.'

'Fair enough,' Willard said.

'For thirteen weeks,' she continued, 'it's a different menu each week – all à la carte. Then a new set of thirteen. Four times a year. Spring, summer, autumn, winter. So never two weeks in the year the same menu.'

'Oh! I *love* it!' Willard said when they had all scanned several pages of choices '*The Four Seasons* – there's our name!'

Marianne cleared her throat. 'May I remind people that it's not even on the drawing board as yet—'

'Of course not, honey!' Willard told her. 'We didn't know what to plan *for*. We didn't know *this*!' He brandished the menus as a Roman general might have brandished some exceptional trophy of war. 'But now we *do* know, we could be looking at finished drawings by this time tomorrow? No?'

'Not to pour cold water,' Alex said, 'you shouldn't count on too much patronage from our golf club members. Our northern friends are the salt of the earth but they're always going to prefer a good plateful of spotted dick and custard over a delicate dish of *le sorbet de fraises*.'

'Ah!' Faith put in. 'But when Denry Machin of Machin and Ackroyd entertains Henri Monsou of Syndicat Monsou to stitch up a secret Anglo-French cartel—'

'Stitch-up? Cartel?' Willard mimed a sudden migraine. 'These words should never pass our lips, people! Trade unions are cartels.

Trade unions stitch up . . . tie up . . . bind up . . . *chain* up every decent employer in Europe. Trade unions are the—'

'Honey!' Marianne interrupted. 'We know this by heart.'

'It just gets worse every week, though. Now they're moaning about cutbacks and job losses in heavy industry – but who's *exporting* those jobs? The Top-Saggers, Bottom-knockers, and Card Setting Machine Tenters Society or whatever cute, archaic names they give themselves! OK-OK. Here endeth the lesson. But please understand this – if our golfing members just happen to make up a foursome of English-American-French-German golfers who just happen to have some clout in industries of mutual interest. And if they work on a few sensible defensive measures together out of earshot of Big Brother, don't let's hear anybody using emotive words like "stitch-up" or "cartel". 'Kay?' He nodded once at each of the others and added: 'Am I right, Alex?'

'Entirely, old boy,' Alex agreed.

'So where were we? Oh, yeah – the French and the Germans have excellent ways of protecting their businesses and the Machins and Ackroyds of not-so-merrie-England might find themselves learning quite a lot to their advantage over a dish of *le poulet gratin au Savoyard*.' Seeing Nicole's expression, he held up his hands in mock surrender. 'Sorry, old dear, but the Top-Saggers and Bottom-Knockers won't be giving *The Four Seasons* much patronage – not until a retired chairman of the TUC – let's call him Lord Vincent Woodcock – can sit on his terrace and gaze out over a couple of thousand socialist acres.'

Alex chuckled. 'That could happen sooner than you think, Willard.'

'Don't raise my hopes,' he replied grimly.

'And what *would* you grumble about then?' Marianne asked sweetly.

He made a pistol of his fist and shot her – and then turned once more to Nicole. 'Listen!' he said. 'All joshing apart, there is serious money to be made here *and*' – he pointed directly at her – 'a serious career to be built. We – all of us in the Dower House community – know what a fabulously great cook you are. And once *you* get in that *cuisine* of ours, Nicole, the world will know it, too. But . . .'

'But what?'

'No. Forget it. One hurdle at a time.'

'What about holidays?' Faith asked.

'None!' Nicole was emphatic. 'Not for all the first year. After that . . . maybe. This I have waited for since the end of the war. Nearly twenty years. I will make the reputation, *then* maybe a holiday. Lena can be my assistant. After a year she can be a good deputy.'

Later that evening, Faith called on Willard and Marianne – to ask outright what he had backed off saying to Nicole at their meeting.

'Oh, it was a tad premature,' he said lightly.

'Look, Willard – don't hold back . . . because we may be thinking along similar lines.'

He conceded the possibility with a nod. 'Tell me more. Then I'll tell you if you're right.'

Faith said, 'The Four Seasons would get off to a much better start if Nicole *already had* a reputation – a public reputation, I mean. More than just a housewife who won that Calor Gas competition.'

'You're thinking books?' he asked. 'Could you get one out in under a year? I didn't think that was possible.'

'I was thinking of television. She's photogenic – France's answer to Fanny Craddock. Alex has all the pull you could want with ITV. A series of eight programmes? With a spin-off book . . . hard cover . . . mouth-watering pictures. I mean, those thirty-two page, grainy, monochrome, stapled booklets the Beeb puts out to accompany Fanny Craddock's programmes are such a wasted opportunity. If you're thinking along these lines, we should coordinate.'

'Would Manutius do books like that?' Marianne asked.

Faith grinned. 'This is strictly *entre nous* – very strictly *entre nous* – for the moment. I'm leaving Manutius.'

'No!'

'Dear God!'

'It's not a sinking ship but I think it could be a vastly bigger ship if it were only run in a different way. I'll take a golden handshake – amicably, I hope – and I'll be starting my own publishing house. Don't drop a single heartbeat, Marianne, I'm not fishing for capital! No fiction, no poetry, no textbooks, no general non-fiction trade books. I'll be doing the sort of books that Manutius does

– illustrated, integrated, general knowledge but with an entirely different look and texture. Pictures of Nicole's ingredients, for instance, will look like – say – onions just spilled on the page, fading out to a white page all round and with text that walks around it. Nothing in square blocks and grids. Very loose, exciting, informal—'

'Sold already!' Willard cried. 'Have you said anything to Nicole?'

Faith shook her head. 'I didn't want to say anything to her until I could be sure we – you two and us – we were thinking on similar lines. I mean, we want to launch *The Four Seasons* with a bang – right?'

He nodded. 'We want people to come looking for *Cuisine Nicole*! Not *Cordon Bleu*, nor *Cordon Rouge*. We want her up there with Escoffier and that guy from the Ritz who's always talking to Jack de Manio . . . Trompetto. A TV series and a book tie-in would surely help. But let's see if the fish bite before we ask Nicole, eh?'

Sunday, 15 December 1963

Isabella found Calley sitting cross-legged on her bed, staring vacantly into the darkest corner of the room. 'Well, here's a limbo unbaptised!' she said. 'I can understand why you don't want the light on. Even Eric was tidier than this!'

Calley made a half-hearted attempt to scoop some of the peanut shells off her sheets and on to the carpet. 'You always say that about Eric but whenever you ask him to put his hands on any document, he can always—'

'It is period pains?' her mother asked.

'I don't get period pains. That's Ruth.'

'I'm all right.' Ruth's voice came out of the shadows.

Isabella could just make out the pale smudge of her face. 'Why are you both sitting here in the dark?'

'Because of the ineffable sadness of being,' Calley told her – without emphasis or feeling, as if she had said, "Because the fuse has blown," which was, in fact, the truth – though not the explanation. Calley had been right first time.

'Oh. Well, if that's all it is . . .' Isabella turned to go, having trod this fruitless path too many times before.

'Nuts in May didn't want my ballad,' Calley said. 'Too poetic. They want stuff you can shout three inches away from someone else's face – that's what they said. They're changing their name to Chain Gang, too.'

'Did you get an example?'

'How about:

> *Don't you bovva me*
> *Don't you bovva me*
> *Don't you bovva me*
> *Less you wanna die?!*

And they've got a new drummer who can't even keep time with an electronic-beat machine that Angela built for them.'

Ruth added: 'And everything's about violence or death. Or both.'

'You could do lyrics like that in your sleep, couldn't you?'

'That's my greatest fear!' Calley told her. 'After seeing them just practising.'

'Well, you can either come and do some ironing or you can stay here and tidy up this room.'

'She's written a poem about me,' Ruth complained.

'It's not about you. It's about Ruth in the Bible. How could it be about you? You're not . . .' A new thought struck her. 'Unless you think you're a changeling! Yes! If you think you're a changeling, then it could be about you!' She laughed.

'Shall I be umpire?' Isabella offered. 'I'll read it and then decide if it could be about Ruth – our Ruth. Have you got it here?'

'She tore it up,' Calley said. 'But it doesn't matter because I know it by heart. It's quite short.' And without a pause she began: 'It's called "Becoming Ruthless", and it goes like this:

> *I shall take my place humbly in your house.*
> *Your ways shall be my ways . . .*
> *Your word my command.*
> *Lovingly I will take your children to me.*
> *I will so faithfully obey you your people will say,*
> *'She is most becoming.'*
> *I shall become your house . . . your ways . . . you.*

I shall take your place humbly in your house.
Lovingly I shall take your children in your house.
And then my ways shall be your ways,
My word your command,
Naomi.'

Isabella sat herself down at the foot of Calley's bed. 'It's nothing to do with you, Ruth,' she said into the dark. 'But you know that already, I'm sure.' Then, to Calley: 'It's very cynical, darling. What put such ideas into your head?'

'RE,' she replied. 'So-called "religious education". D'you know, the law says they've *got* to do it. We've *got to* have religion stuffed down our throats every week. But there's only one teacher across the whole of our year who actually believes in God. So all the others just do Bible stories and treat it as literature study – which I don't mind. I love the King James English. But they were going on and on about Ruth being so good and submissive and I thought, *Oh, yeah! I'll bet!* So then I wrote that. And you can see how they don't give a hoot for really religious RE because they said it was good even though it contradicts the Bible. And then they got Miss Hotchkiss to type it out on their new IBM golfball machine which does proportional spacing and they put it up on the school noticeboard.'

'Has Eric seen it? What did he say?'

'Good. He said it was good. And then he asked me if I was disappointed that no one got annoyed with me for turning the Bible story on its head.'

'Typical! And were you?'

'What? Disappointed? Yes, I was – a bit – though I didn't realize it until he asked. But what really annoys me is the system that forces teachers to pretend they're teaching us religion when really it's got nothing to do with it. It's the *system* that's wrong.'

'Down with the system!' Ruth cried from out of the dark.

'Down with the system!' Calley echoed.

Isabella rose to go. 'There are your next lyrics for . . . what's their new name? Chain Gang?' At the door, where the light fell upon her and they could not mistake her firmness, she added: 'One to help with the ironing – one to stay here and tidy up.' After a single pace she turned and added: 'With the light *on!*'

'The fuse has blown!' They called back in unison.

'Your father will have it mended in a jiffy. There'll be no Christmas for either of you if the place looks like this!'

Wednesday, 18 December 1963

The phone rang. Felix, who was reading *Blackie the Albino Polar Bear* to Susan, shouted, 'Can someone get that?'

'I'll have to, won't I!' Angela said crossly.

But Pippin beat her to it. 'Oh, hello, Wendy. How's your mother off for bacon? . . . No – it's just a saying . . . No – *nothing* to do with them being Jewish. I didn't even know . . . OK, well . . . just keep your hair on . . . Yes and the same to you . . . with brass knobs on!' She put the handset down and left it squawking angrily while she went to tell her mother. She opened the recording studio door and said over her shoulder as she walked away again: 'It's Wendy and she's in a tizz about something.'

'Wendy!' Angela said brightly. 'Happy Christmas – if it's not too early? What can we do for you?'

'Well!' Wendy was calm again. 'That's better than "How's your mother off for bacon?" – why "bacon"? People usually say "How's your mother off for dripping?" *Anyway*, it doesn't matter. This is about something much more serious. Tell me – you know your children's headmaster in Welwyn Garden City – someone Dobson. Did you give his wife some book to read? About the extermination of the Jews?'

After a pause, Angela said, 'Well, not exactly a book, but something in that line. Why?'

'Because her daughter, Margaret, is in some sort of gifted-children programme. She was in the North London branch and stayed a member when they moved out to Garden City. And my mother got to know Inge Dobson through that. And after their meeting last Tuesday she asked my mother if they could have a talk. And they went to a coffee house in Golders Green. And . . . actually, I think it'd be better if you called Mummy about it. I'm surprised she hasn't already called you.'

'Well, of course I'll call her. Can't you tell me more?'

'Nothing useful, I think. It's about whatever you lent her. And their conversation left my mother quite worried. That's really all I know.'

'Well, of course I'll call her right away. Are we going to see you this side of Christmas? We're having our usual Christmas-Eve-eve party.'

'Oh . . . I'd love to but we're desperately trying to get in more rehearsals before the whole world shuts down on Christmas Day.'

'Oh, well, good luck with all that. I'm under a similar pressure here. But' – she added hastily, in case it sounded like a rebuke – 'I'll call your mother right this minute.'

She cradled the handset, but before she found *Finch* in their personal phone list the phone rang. She took a chance: 'Rebecca?'

'Yes. Angela? How did you know?'

'I've just been talking with Wendy. What's all this about Inge Dobson? Has she been pestering you?'

'Ah! Well . . . no. I wish Wendy hadn't . . . I wasn't intending to talk about it on the phone, actually. I was wondering if we could meet?'

'Only if you can make it out here. I've got a ferocious deadline for some . . . it's a modern sort of Christmas Oratorio. Very tricky time signatures. We couldn't go somewhere quiet when you come to our party on the twenty-third?'

There was a pause before Rebecca said, 'That might be . . . I think you should see her before that.'

'It's about something I gave her to read – I know. Verbatim minutes of a Nazi meeting about the extermination—'

'I know. She told me she'd been a wardress in one of those camps – the camp where you were imprisoned. Is that true?'

'Well, it's a long story. Just tell me what's got you so worried? D'you think I should see her? The thing is – when she returned that document to me, she was right as rain. Pretty solemn, of course, but I thought it would ease her conscience a bit if she realized what a teeny-tiny cog she'd been in such a vast machine. Anyway?'

'Yes . . . anyway. I wouldn't describe her as "right as rain" now. She told me about the work she did after she finished her prison sentence, and she said, "I thought I had washed out as much of the stain as *could* be washed out but now I must start again". Words to that effect . . . Hello?'

'Yes. I'm thinking. I suppose I'd better go and see her.'

'Soon?'

'Right away.'

'Call me back if there's anything, Angela. I'm not very good at emotional crises. I don't think I was any help to her at all.'

Angela ran upstairs, two at a time, and said to Felix, 'It sounds as if I'd better get over to the Dobsons'.'

'Inge?'

She nodded. 'You might have been right. I hope it's just a storm in a teacup.'

'Can't it wait until we've eaten? You had a very skimpy lunch.'

She shook her head. 'I couldn't eat now – not feeling like this. I'll take an apple. Some fruit.'

She resisted the temptation to speed into the town; it was a short month for the police to reach their targets and she didn't want to help them. The Dobsons' house on Bessemer Avenue was dark. She knocked . . . she rang . . . and was just heading round to the back door when a neighbour came out and said, 'If you're wanting the Dobsons, dear, they're both up at the QE TWO. I've got the young 'uns with me if it's about them.'

'The hospital?' Angela felt suddenly numb. 'Are they . . . is she . . . I mean . . .'

The woman was guarded. 'They'll tell you up there, pet. He went with her in the ambulance. They'll tell you up there. I got to go in now – sorry.'

It was visiting time and the hospital car park was almost full. She had a long, fretful walk to the reception desk. There she learned that Mrs Dobson was out of A&E and in an isolation ward – a single room – on the second floor. She tried to find out what had happened but the receptionist would only say that she could go up to the second floor and ask the sister there if Inge was able to see visitors.

At the first-floor landing Angela almost turned and retraced her steps; her imagination was filling her with suggestions that were probably far worse than what might actually have happened. The silence, punctuated by almost subliminal humming and muted institutional noises, the shiny linoleum whose polish only exaggerated the minuscule imperfections in the concrete on which it was spread, the metallic lighting that could have been designed to provoke insomnia – all depressed her spirit still further.

She waylaid a nurse out in the corridor – a short, plump,

busy-busy woman who radiated confidence even if her untidy
hair did not exactly inspire it. 'I was wondering about Mrs Dobson
. . .' Angela began.

'Are you a relative?'

'A friend.' Ridiculously she added: 'We were in the war together'
– a phrase one still heard several times a week.

The sister looked at her askance and for one awful moment
Angela feared that they knew what Inge had done during the
war. 'I'm also German,' she added.

The other relaxed and said, 'She's out of danger, but as for
visitors . . . I'm not so sure that she's—'

'Well, I wouldn't want to disturb her, of course. But their
neighbour told me her husband is here? We're friends. Perhaps I
could have a word with him? Tell him it's Angela Breit.'

Half a minute later the sister returned with Billy Dobson, who
had no smile for her. 'I wish you hadn't shown her that transcript,'
he said.

'Well, so do I – now. But listen, Billy – she begged me at the
time. And even when she returned it she said she could now see
what a really tiny part she had played in the overall—'

'She said that?'

'Maybe not in those exact words but . . . yes, it's what she
implied. Can I see her? What exactly happened?'

'She's asleep.' He looked up and down the corridor. 'They say
there's a sort of day room along there somewhere. I'd really like to
know more about . . .' He left the rest hanging as he led the way.

'About her response?' Angela asked.

'That. But the rest, too – everything else. Everything you're
willing to tell me, anyway.'

Two men in dressing gowns were sitting in semi-darkness,
smoking and watching television. 'Perhaps we'll just walk around?'
Dobson suggested.

'Did she tell you much about that transcript?' Angela asked.

'As much as I could stand. They were all *educated men*! Doktor
this and Doktor that! It's impossible to credit . . . you know – the
inheritors of Goethe and Beethoven and Thomas Mann – impossible. How did one man's criminal psychosis infect so many?'

'Including . . .' Angela tilted her head back towards the room
where Inge lay sleeping. 'Have you not talked about it?'

He did not immediately answer. 'You must understand that

when I met her she was at the opposite end of the scale from . . . you know.'

'From being an ss-*Aufseherin* – yes. Have you talked about *that* time? Has she?'

He stared at her with an expression half-baffled, half-wounded.

'It's the only way to make sense of all this,' Angela insisted.

Accidentally or on purpose, he drifted a little apart from her as they sauntered towards the dimmer end of the corridor. 'What about you?' he asked. 'Were you infected with that ideology?'

Angela shrugged. 'I did nothing to oppose it – until it was too late. Much too late.'

He did not seem satisfied. She went on: 'Heydrich, the ss chief, had a string quartet and I used to record them on tape. When the war started he inducted me into the ss as a technician – as their chief tape-recording technician. I was not political. If my father hadn't been one of the top technicians at UFA, and if he hadn't taught me almost all he knew, I'd have been . . . what? A typist? A factory worker?'

This part of the corridor was constricted with parked wheel-chairs and trolleys; no lights shone under the doors. They turned and retraced their steps.

'I'm trying to understand,' he said. 'When she first told me about meeting you again, she spoke of you as some kind of saintly character who had managed to forgive the unforgivable. She didn't go into the details but she said she was as cruel to you as it was possible to be without actually causing your death. But—'

'If she had—'

'No – let me finish this . . . this . . .'

They were passing her door again. He popped his head in and returned, saying, 'Still fast asleep. But I was saying – after a while, towards the autumn, she . . . well, she didn't mention it much, but she seemed to be hinting that there was some kind of collusion between you and the camp authorities.'

Angela sighed heavily. 'That I was still a true believer – ss-*Unterscharführerin* Wirth, working undercover as a spy in the camp. And she saw it as her duty to—'

'And you weren't?'

'Listen, Billy – I really don't think there's much to be gained . . .' Her voice trailed off when she saw how much he hung upon

her answer. 'No, I wasn't. And Inge didn't believe it at the time
– trust me! This is some . . . what's the word?'

'Gloss?'

'Yes – some gloss she's put on it since.'

'But she seems to believe it now.'

'Well – at the risk of playing amateur psychologist – I think
maybe she *needs* to believe it?'

'How?' They had reached the stairhead. 'Shall we go down
and see if the cafeteria's still open?'

She shook her head. 'They were closing down when I arrived.
Typical – it's visiting time so let's shut the cafeteria in case people
want to use it! Could it be that she purged herself – or *thought*
she had purged herself of all that past, suffered her punishment,
seen the light . . . devoted herself to helping victims to the point
– I gather – where she had a nervous collapse—'

'How do you know all this? Has she been talking to you?'

It would have been so easy to leave him with that impression
without actually committing to the lie but she refused. 'Felix's
father works for *Der Spiegel*. It was child's play to discover. Germany
believes in records! And filing clerks! Anyway, she's recovering
from her collapse when she meets you. She marries, starts a family,
comes to England – *escapes* her past in England. But then *kaboom*!
– Prisoner three-four-one-seven offers her a cup of coffee. Maybe
it was an occasional topic of conversation among the ss-*Aufseherinne*
– "Could three-four-one-seven be a planted spy? Why is she
taken out of the camp every month?" and so on. Poor Inge can't
deny her treatment of me – so she has rationalized it away: we
were both on the same side after all! She has expiated all her
other cruelties but there's no need to expiate the ones she visited
on me.' For the first time she gripped his arm and gave it a little
squeeze as she continued. 'I don't really believe it either, Billy.
Nor do I think it helps to speculate. The fact is she faced her
past once when her future was nothing but bleak. Now she has
you and two adorable children, and everything to live for. She'll
face it again, and she'll conquer it like last time.' It was not so
easy to add: 'And if I can help in any way, I will.'

'She lay in the bath and opened a vein,' Angela told Felix that
night as they lay in bed. 'Not very competently. An artery would
have been another matter. Oh . . . *bugger* her!'

'It will never be over,' Felix said. 'We were wrong to ever think it would. Even if we live into old-old age and lose our marbles, *something* – some old poison will spew up again in our muddled brains and we won't even know what it is. Just that it's vaguely familiar.'

'I don't owe her any . . . not respect . . . *consideration*! I don't owe her any consideration at all – do I? All the way back home I was saying "Good riddance! Wish she'd done a better job of it! Let her stew in her own juice!" But it was like two voices inside me – or one voice saying those things and something else, a much deeper urge, was just rebelling. Like saying *no-no-no-no!* without using actual words. I can't abandon her. D'you think I can just abandon her? Maybe it would be a sort of therapy for *me*? To help her? But maybe that would be the last straw for her. Push her over the edge. But could that be exactly what my innermost vengeful self actually wants? Be so sweet and forgiving and kind that she finally can't bear it any longer and . . . does a proper job of it next time? How can we ever know why we really do things?'

Monday, 6 April 1964

The Breits got off the bus in Marazion; they were early enough to enjoy a walk along the beach. The tide was out, exposing a temptingly high-and-dry causeway to St Michael's Mount; but there was no time for that today.

'Hermit crabs! Hermit crabs!' Susan yelled, glancing slyly at Douglas, for The Unnatural History of Hermit Crabs was really *his* subject – for the duration of this holiday, anyway. He was convinced that, contrary to what all the books said, the hermit crab *ate* its way into the shell, killing ever-so-slowly the poor wee mollusc that built it – heh-heh! (And Eric Brandon had encouraged him in this delusion because he was having a fight with Collins' children's books editors over the degree of gruesomeness they would allow to warp the minds of their young readers and he maintained that nothing the most twisted adult brain could devise would come within spitting distance – or vomiting, farting, peeing, and shitting distance, either – of the mental processes of the average eight-year-old.)

'You can go hunting them with Margaret and Francis,' Angela said. 'Come on, now.'

'But the rock pools are all *that* way.' Douglas pointed behind them.

'Yes, all *that* way,' Susan said.

'Stop copying *me*.'

'You mean stop copying *you*!'

'We are observed,' Felix said, waving at Billy Dobson, who had come out of their railway coach and was standing on the little balcony by the door. 'She'll be fussing over paper doilies and tut-tutting at their Melamine coffee mugs.'

'And we may be thankful for *that*!' Angela murmured as she took his arm.

'These old railway coaches!' Inge said by way of welcome. 'If you don't keep them spic and span it's like a whirlwind went through them.'

'Are you *apologizing* for neatness?' Felix asked as he kissed each cheek.

'Only because she knows what the Tithe Barn is usually like!' Angela said as she, too, gave the Continental greeting and handed over the obligatory bouquet.

'It's nothing like that!' Inge said crossly. 'Oh, these are lovely. Thank you so much.'

'But you know what I mean! Come on, Inge – relax! It's a holiday. Our brats want to go off and explore those rock pools beyond the causeway. Would Francis and Margaret like to go with them?'

'I've done them some lemonade.'

'After that.'

Inge looked at Billy, who nodded. 'OK,' she said.

The children guzzled their drinks, using them to make cement of their saffron cake, and then piled outside to run back along the beach to where the world grew much more interesting.

The tension remained behind them.

'So how is it now, Inge?' Felix said at once.

Billy answered. 'Up and down. One just doesn't know whether to keep on testing the waters or . . .' He shrugged.

'Or leave well alone,' Angela said. 'If only it would heal as well as your wrist there.' She reached across the table and turned the scars face up; they were hardly apparent. 'It's amazing. Are you going to say anything? *Schtummkopf!*' By now they all knew it had been just a cry for the sort of help that, in the end, must be discovered within.

'Every day in every way I'm getting better and better and better,' Inge intoned, holding finger and thumb just millimetres apart.

After that there was silence.

'More coffee, anyone?' Billy asked.

Inge looked at Angela. 'I'd like to go for a walk. I've done a sort of smörgåsbord lunch – à la Marianne. How are they, by the way?'

'Cock-a-hoop,' Felix said.

'And, thanks to an absolutely first-class survey,' Angela added, 'the design of the golf course went like a dream. They have outline permission and another couple of months should take them all the way through to full consent on the detailed plans. Let's go and see if any of our children look like drowning.'

'We'll follow you, if that's all right?' Billy said. 'I'd rather like Felix's opinion of some drawings of Margaret's.'

Inge waited outside on the beach while Angela fought the guilty sensation that she was using the lavatory while the train was in a station. When she joined her on the shingle, Inge pointed to the Mount and asked, 'Have you ever been over there?'

'No.' Angela sighed. 'We're dreadful tourists. Never been to Land's End. Never been to the Lizard. Never been to St Michael's Mount. Of course, we've been to St Ives more times than I can count – and Lamorna, and Newlyn, and Mousehole . . . all the artists' places. There was a time when we thought of moving down here for good.'

'But . . .?' They started to stroll.

'But the pull of the Dower House is too strong. I wonder if any of us is ever going to leave – except in an urn. It may be different when the children are gone. They *make* the place. What were you thinking just before I came out – staring out to sea?'

Inge took some time to answer and then said, 'You'll scream.'

'It won't matter out here. I'll make it sound like a seagull. So tell me – all.'

'Bless me, father – or mother – for I have sinned!'

Angela was astonished. 'Are you still a Catholic?'

Inge wrinkled her nose. 'I was when it helped. No – I was remembering our honeymoon. And a particular bottle of champagne. Billy and I honeymooned on the North Coast.'

'Baltic or North Sea? The Breits have a holiday home at Laboe.'

'Wangerooge on the North Sea. And Billy said this was the moment to put the past to rest and think only of the future – which was easy for me because I already suspected I was carrying Margaret. Well – a baby, anyway – you know what I mean.'

'Only too well, my dear! Go on. You sound as if there was some ceremony.'

'Of course. There had to be. I wrote a confession. All the things I confessed for my trial plus all the things I was too ashamed to confess. Billy had no illusions. Anyway, we put it in the champagne bottle we finished on our honeymoon night, and corked it again, and put the wire cage back, and then threw it in the sea. I don't know about the currents in the Channel but I was wondering just now if it ever washed up here and if someone opened it, maybe, thinking it was a cry for help from someone on a desert island or something.'

'And is that what it was?'

'No! It was hope! It was the most hopeful time, the most hopeful thing.'

'Ah! So it definitely worked back then. Are you not tempted to try it again?'

It took a long while for Inge to say, 'No.'

'That's pretty definite.' Angela stopped to take off her sandals and shake out some coarse sand. There were large tar-and-sand balls down by the water line. Tankers were supposed to flush out their tanks into a special facility in Falmouth but many did not bother.

'It was easy for me to accept forgiveness from myself when all the people I had wronged were just shadows in my mind.'

'You want more than shadows, then? I think that can be arranged.'

That evening, back at their B&B in Breage, Angela borrowed a typewriter and started typing without any heading or preliminary explanation:

Whenever they put me in solitary confinement in the
Bunker, IH personally disrupted my feeding so that

sometimes I'd have three disgusting meals in a day and
sometimes nothing for three days. We were kept in total
darkness but she would shine a torch into my face and
increase my punishment if I blinked.

IH would hit me across the face with her leatherbound
cane if I dared to look her in the eye. At other times
she would do the same if I failed to look her in the
eye.

When I had to sweep the path outside the HQ, which was
more than half a kilometre all round, IH would stand
close and hit my arms if I did not keep up an
absolutely unvarying rhythm, never resting. And when I
had to weed the flowerbeds outside the HQ, IH would not
let me either kneel or stand but I must work bent
double all the afternoon.

IH would seek me out - me out of thousands - when we
had roll calls in the small hours of the morning and
she'd find some fault and make me stand there, alone,
until dawn, while she retired to a nearby office and
kept a rifle trained on me, ready to shoot me if I did
not stand rigidly to attention. This was no matter if
it rained or snowed or was many degrees below zero.

The litany went on for several pages, ending:

In short, I cannot think of any one occasion on which
our paths crossed when IH did not do her best to make
my life even more miserable than it was.

She showed it to Felix, who said, 'I hope you know what
you're doing.'

'I'm sure of it,' she replied. 'I know I said the same when I
let her read the Wannsee thing, but that was just pussyfooting
around, as Willard calls it.'

'Well, you certainly can't say the same for this!'

'You can take me in to Helston tomorrow afternoon, where
I'll buy a bottle of champagne and then catch the bus to Marazion.

And we'll drink it to the last drop and put these papers inside and cork it down and put the wire cage back and she can throw it as far out to sea as she can.'

'And you're going to make her read it first?'

'Every last syllable. Just *saying* I forgive her doesn't mean a thing. Writing this out has cost me – emotionally . . .' Her voice trailed off. 'Actually, it didn't. I kept thinking, *You ought to be more upset by remembering all this* – but I wasn't. Still, I won't tell her that. I'll tell her I sweated blood and so it had jolly well better work.'

The following evening, Angela produced her 'Ravensbrück memoir' and poured out the first glass of champagne all round.

'*Prosit!*' They drained the glasses in one and, while Billy poured the refills, Inge, with a shaking hand, laid the sheets of typescript flat upon the table.

'What's this?' she asked, pointing to some greeny-brown smears at the foot of the final page. 'Shit? Are you trying to—'

'Smell it,' Angela told her.

Still Inge hesitated.

'It's not shit.'

Gingerly Inge did as she was told. One sniff was enough. Her whole body went rigid. '*Ach – meine Güte!*' she whispered.

'What?' Billy asked.

'Crushed geranium leaves.' Angela did not take her eyes off Inge, who was now locked, frozen, her eyes closed.

'Why?' Billy took the paper from his wife's nerveless fingers and sniffed. '*Eurgh!*'

'Tell him,' Angela said.

'It's the smell of Ravensbrück.' A whisper would have been louder.

'Of every concentration camp,' Angela said.

He sniffed again. 'And of DP camps, too. Good God!' He frowned at Angela. 'You're being very hard.'

'How else can we exorcize everything? It must be everything.'

She nodded to Inge, who bunched the papers again, laid them down and read in silence, rigid but for the moving of her lips.

'Aloud,' Angela said. 'The idea is – from me to the paper, from the paper to you, from you to the air – to the four winds – and *pffft!*'

Billy drew breath sharply. Angela caught his eye and nodded.

Inge read awhile longer in silence and then turned to Angela, who, once again, nodded, almost aggressively. 'From the beginning.'

Inge started speaking in a firm voice but she could not sustain it: 'Whenever they put me in solitary confinement in the Bunker, Irmgard Heugel personally disrupted my feeding . . .' Her voice cracked and the tears were flowing down her cheeks by the time she reached: 'Irmgard Heugel would seek me out – me out of thousands . . .' but still she ploughed doggedly on.

When she turned to the second page, Angela moved the first, face up, to where it would catch the tears as they fell. Inge made no further attempt to wipe them away or sniff them down. Angela experienced the strangest mixture of joy and compassion as she watched her old tormentor undergo – no, under*take* – this ordeal. And pride, too, as a teacher might feel when a dullard turns into a star pupil. In a way it was something of a counterpart to her own lack of emotion when she had compiled this same list yesterday. No power on earth, other than Inge's need, could have obliged her to revisit those memories and write them down; but now she realized that she herself had needed it no less – to discover how dead it was.

By the time the recitation finished, both women were in tears and every page had mutant, many-legged spiders where the typewriter ink had dissolved and run. Billy pressed the refilled glasses into their hands and said, 'Oblivion!'

'Oblivion!' They echoed the toast – and swiftly downed the refill, too. Then, more light-headed than tipsy, they rose and hugged one another in a tight threesome. 'Thank you!' Inge whispered.

'You think I didn't need it, too?' Angela murmured. 'Now roll up the paper and stuff it inside the bottle.'

They forced the cork back in and caged it in wire once more. And then went immediately out to the beach.

'I must be the one to throw it in,' Angela insisted. Inge started to protest but Angela cut her short. 'Who threw the last champagne bottle? That one at Wangerooge?'

'Me, of course,' Inge said.

'There you are, then – that's why it has to be me. I'm getting rid of . . . all that stuff, too.'

Billy passed her the bottle and, without any preliminaries, she hurled it as far out to sea as she could manage. In the dark its tumbling form flashed with random reflections of the distant street lighting and the ruby glow of the curtained carriage windows – seen, unseen, seen, unseen – like an airplane flashing high in the night sky. Its impact on the water made a brief, pale smudge and the sort of deeply throttled splash that a perfect dive creates.

Angela laughed. The other two looked at her askance. 'Sorry!' she said. 'I was just thinking, "I know how to re-create that sound exactly".' She flung her arms around Inge and hugged her hard, murmuring, '*Endlich ist es vorbei, Du!* We give each other the rest of our lives. And I'll tell you something Felix's father wrote to us. You know he works for *Spiegel*?'

'Billy told me.'

'Ah, so you know all about that – how we heard about your work in Frankfurt. He said the *Vernichtung* did not end with the Liberation. He said Felix and I were the lucky ones because we had skills that people wanted. But there were people so badly scarred by the KLs that *nobody* wanted them back, not their governments, not even their own families in some cases. But *Das Haus Milenas* always had a place for them. Now you go back inside and get drunk. Don't worry about me – I'll just collect my bag and coat and find a taxi in Marazion.'

But the moment they were back inside, Francis began fretting and Inge went to settle him. Billy took advantage of her absence to say, 'You really are some kind of saint, you know.'

'Oh . . .!' an embarrassed Angela began.

'No. Really. I had no idea. Well . . . I had *some* idea, of course, because Inge told me. But to hear it from *your* side . . .'

'The "nation of Goethe, Schiller, and so on". It's very comforting to think of a "them" and an "us" in all this but the distinction doesn't hold. Felix once said to me that he sometimes felt – when watching or even suffering the brutality of the guards – that he could so easily have been one of them.'

'Good Lord! What*ever* gave him that notion?'

'The exultation he felt when death carried off another prisoner and left him alive. We all felt that – ashamed of it, of course, but we felt it. To understand it, you had to live through the long, slow, insidious process of indoctrination, fear, discipline, and conformity that perverted millions – and not just in Germany. I was *on* that path. I could very well have ended up as a colleague of Inge's in

Ravensbrück if my eyes hadn't been opened by recording that conference.' He started to speak but she bulldozed over him. 'And even those party high-ups – even they – knew they were doing wrong. That's why Heydrich insisted on there being no protocol – and why he had all the notes gathered up and destroyed. And it's why they concocted a much more innocuous false protocol later, when they realized they were going to lose the war.'

'I didn't know about that.'

'Yeah, it worked, too. The allies now treat it as the official protocol. I gave them a copy of mine but they claimed they lost it and they're not interested in . . . Oh, well, that doesn't matter now. The main thing for you and me is not to think of Inge as someone who was *especially* wicked and has since been *saved*. It's far closer to the truth to say, "There but for the grace of God – or the accidents of history, time, and place – go you and I." We'll learn nothing if we imagine we could never, ever become like that. The people who ban Jews from golf clubs have already taken the first step – and so have those who won't let rooms to coloured or Irish, or who won't employ cripples or who make disparaging remarks about nancy boys, or object to gypsies camping down the road.' She looked earnestly into his eyes. 'You don't believe me?'

He chuckled. 'No – I was thinking – we all make jokes about the Irish. And the Scots. And, of course, the Welsh.'

'But jokes are a way of taking a backward step from persecuting them – not going forward towards doing it. There was a cabaret artist in Berlin, back in the thirties, who used to bring a little donkey on the stage and ask the audience if they thought he – the donkey – looked too Jewish to be allowed to perform. The Blackshirts beat him up because they knew very well what he was subverting with his jokes. No. Jokes are different.'

He sighed. 'OK, Angela, I now think you're even more of a saint than I thought you were before. But we'll leave it at that.'

'Please!'

Saturday, 2 May 1964

Eric gave Angela the sort of once-over she had not experienced since her initial recruitment board at the BBC. She shifted uncomfortably and said, 'You'll surely recognize me next time we meet.'

'Sorry!' He gave a short, embarrassed laugh. 'I was just wondering . . . well, I know you can keep a secret, but do you want to be burdened with one? A secret to do with Faith and me.'

'Romantic or commercial?'

'Oh, good God – commercial! The thing is . . . Faith and I would like to commission a piece from you.'

'Music? I'm not a—'

'No. An article. You know I've been working on a new concept for Reader's Digest Books for the past God-knows-how-long. Well, Peter Glemser – the chief cook and bottle-washer – has decided not to go ahead with his original concept, which was for a two-monthly hardback magazine titled *British Heritage*. I've been doing research and dummies and things for it, and it's helped him understand that magazines and books don't really mix. So . . .'

'But *Reader's Digest is* a magazine, surely?'

'Sure. But it's quite separate from the Books division – they're in different buildings at opposite ends of Berkeley Square and they cross over the road if there's a danger of meeting. Anyway – he's taking about half the stuff I've done for them and he's going to incorporate it into a book project called *Heritage of Britain*. And, being a true gentleman – as rare as hen's teeth in publishing – he's allowing me to make use of the remainder. But that's not the secret. The secret is really Faith's – but she knows I'm asking you this. And she approves. I mean, enthusiastically. She wants to join with me in launching *British Heritage* as a six-times-a-year hardcover magazine . . . a hundred and twenty-eight pages, full colour throughout, with up to thirty-two pages of advertising. Ironically enough – that's the identical formula to the magazine that started Fogel on the road to fame and fortune! Nothing new under the sun – which, in a way, is our main theme, as you'll see. But there's a big difference between our *British Heritage* and Fogel's old *Forward!* magazine of blessed memory. We want to bring out the first edition timed for the Christmas market. And we want to bundle it up with one of these new "Compact Cassettes" from Philips – have you seen them?'

Angela was now bolt upright, and leaning forward. 'Tell me more.'

'You see, we don't . . . that is, we want to distance ourselves as far as possible from the Digest Books project. They'll be all Shakespeare, and great houses, and historic battlefields, and . . . traditions. We want to tie in *what's happening today* with all that past stuff. What is it about Liverpool that produced the Beatles? Could they possibly have come from somewhere like Dorchester? Why not? And shocking fashions. Isabella tells me skirts will be getting shorter next year – maybe even slightly *above* the knee. So she's going to do a tour of the fashion-and-textiles departments of all the big London art colleges, where the new, outrageous ideas get born.'

Angela was astounded. 'Isabella and you – *cooperating*?'

'Ha-ha! The thing I'd like to suggest to you – and this is where the compact cassette comes in – is to do a piece that links modern music – British modern music – all that plink-and-bang stuff – with . . . well, you tell me! Dowland? Jeremiah Clarke? A shepherd piping away on some croft in the Hebrides?'

'*Plink and bang*?' Angela was outraged.

Eric grinned. 'I merely quote the prejudice you'll have to overcome in most of our readers. We're determined to show that all this revolutionary stuff people talk about nowadays – the Mini-Cooper, *The Avengers*, Mods and Rockers, kitchen-sink drama, Aldermaston Marches, Spies for Peace, CND . . . everything we like to think is hot from the oven. We want to show that it has roots, preferably deep roots, somewhere in our past. Talking of Aldermaston – are you and Felix going this year?'

She shrugged. 'No plans. Maybe not.'

'OK. So, Angela my pet, with a brief as vague as that, d'you think you could come up with something on plink and . . . I mean, on your wonderful *modern* British music and tie it back in to a native British tradition? The tapes will last thirty minutes each side. So you could have one whole side – half an hour – for the illustrations. We'll do a piece on dialect on the other side.'

Angela cleared her throat delicately.

'Ah, yes. Four thousand words at ninepence a word? A hundred and fifty quid? That's amazingly generous by the standards of—'

'You're on!'

'And we'll be equally generous over the cassette – but make a wishing list first and we'll see what it involves in the way of copyright, fees, permissions . . . blahblah. And remember – this is hush-hush for the moment. Shall we crack open a tin of Nescafé and drink to it?'

Still in something of a daze, Angela left the Brandons' by the door into the back hall – where she met Marianne bringing home the week's shopping. 'Coffee?' she said.

Angela lowered her voice. 'I've just said no to Eric's offer of instant but I wouldn't mind some of the real stuff. Let me help you with those.'

'There's two more bags in the car – now you know why I offered.'

On the way upstairs, Angela asked, 'Are you going on the Aldermaston March this year?'

Marianne sighed. 'I'm getting too old to sleep on lilos in barns, you know. I reckon I've done my bit. Of course, Willard will think he's worn me down at last. But who cares?'

Later, with the shopping sorted and put away, and a hot mug of the real Java in their hands, the two women went out to the balcony, where a balmy May sun was trapped.

'What's the latest from Machiavelli Towers?' Marianne asked.

'Eric? Oh, he's interested in these new Compact Cassettes that Philips is bringing out. They've got recording tape down to about five millimetres without much loss of quality – a bit of white noise but lots of people are working on that.'

'*White* noise? No – don't bother.' She glanced at Angela – and then looked at her with more attention. 'Something troubling you?'

'Why d'you ask?' Angela hadn't meant the question to sound so peremptory; she forced a little smile. 'I mean—'

'It's just . . . I've noticed a couple of times since you came

back from Cornwall . . . Look! If that B and B we recommended
didn't live up to—'

'No! Oh, God – nothing like that! Didn't I say how much
we—'

'Well, there's *something*. You have seemed a bit edgy.'

'Oh! I didn't think it showed all that much.' She sipped her
coffee and gasped with satisfaction – too demonstratively.

'Everything's all right, I suppose?' Marianne persisted. 'You and
. . . you know . . . Felix?'

'Oh, yes. Well, I mean, the number of times in a week when
I could cheerfully murder him hasn't gone *up*.'

Marianne chuckled but this time had the nous to stay quiet.

'Something has happened, though,' Angela said at last.

'Down in Cornwall? Or since?'

'Down there.' After a pause, she added: 'Did you know that
the Dobsons were down there, too? They always rent one of
those converted railway carriages at Easter.'

'And you met them?'

'With a vengeance! Or, rather, *not* with a vengeance, come to
think of it. I actually went over to Machiavelli Towers, as you
call it, to speak with Eric about it – but I'm not sure that even
he would really understand.'

'*Even* he?'

'Well . . . he does listen to women more than most men we
know – don't you think?'

Marianne laughed. 'Would Isabella agree?'

'Oh, don't be fooled by that – he listens to *her* all right – her
most of all. But anyway—'

'You got talking about those cassettes instead.'

'That – yes.' Angela took another welcome gulp and wondered
how to broach the subject – or even whether to broach it.

'So it's something to do with the Dobsons?' Marianne prompted.
'Inge Dobson?'

Angela stared at her in surprise.

Marianne took a deep breath and plunged in: 'Was she ever
. . . I mean . . . were she and Felix ever . . . um . . .'

'Ever what?'

'Before the war, perhaps?'

'You mean *lovers*?' Angela was incredulous. 'What on earth
could have—'

Marianne, all apologies, jumped in: 'Thank heavens! I didn't think it would be that – except . . . you remember the day Billy and Eric were reunited, here at the Dower House? Well, Inge stayed out in the park – just down there. And you went out to her and . . . you know . . .' she finished lamely.

'You saw us?'

The answer was just a mumble: 'Nicole did.'

'And she told you.' Angela started laughing. 'And together you jumped to—'

'And Sally!'

'*Um Gottes Willen!* So by now the whole community believes that Inge and Felix are ex-lovers! Aieee!'

'Obviously they're not!' Marianne gave an embarrassed laugh. 'But Nicole also saw you go out, down to the river, and make some kind of peace offering – and she says Felix came after you and hid in the hedge to watch.'

Angela picked up her mug and drained it. 'More?' she asked. 'If I'm to explain it all, I'm going to need it.'

She was halfway through the refill before she even started her explanation, but then she told Marianne exactly what sort of relationship there had been between herself and Inge, leaving out nothing except the chapter-and-verse details of how bestial the former ss-*Aufseherin* had been to her. She finished by describing the exorcism they had gone through down in Marazion.

Marianne, who had listened, hardly daring to breathe, hardly blinking her eyes, murmured, 'The way you tell it. I mean, it sounds as if you also needed some . . . whatever you call it. Release?'

'Catharsis? Yes. What d'you think of Billy Dobson?'

'Billy?'

'No – I didn't really mean to ask that.' She closed her eyes and shook her head. 'OK, then – what *do* you think of him?'

Marianne gave a slightly baffled laugh. 'Not very often, I must say. He's all right, I suppose. A very good headmaster – probably the best our children have ever—'

'No. As a man.'

'Well – quite good looking. Dresses neatly. The aftershave is a bit overpowering sometimes . . . I don't know. Why, anyway?'

Angela shrugged.

'So what do *you* think of him?' Marianne felt compelled to ask.

'The thing is . . .' Angela hesitated. 'The thing is . . . well, it goes back to being in Ravensbrück. Writing down all the things we were going to exorcize out of Inge.'

'Yes! Didn't it make you want to kill her? I think you're some kind of saint.'

'Oh – don't *you* start! It didn't fill me with rage and it didn't stir up all the hatred I once felt for her, for Inge. No – not Inge . . . *Irmgard. Die Heugel.* But I'll tell you what it did do to me. When you're in a camp like that . . . I mean, you can't wash properly, you've got no hair, your fingernails are cracked and never properly clean, you're bony and gawky and you shrink even from yourself, and your periods stop, and your mouth is . . . oh, it's just *all* awful. So you're not just fighting for every crust of stale bread, you're fighting all that self-loathing, too. Fighting to keep alive a dim, distant memory that you were once an attractive young woman who turned men's heads in the street. You keep spitting into the wind, assuring yourself that *that* young thing is still there inside you, under all that grime and drabness.' She tripped over a reluctant little laugh. 'And yet . . . and yet . . .'

'What?'

'Something I'd forgotten. Once, when they issued new prison uniforms, some of us went and drew out our allowance of useless sanitary towels and used them to make shoulder pads. So we weren't past all caring.' For a moment she was lost in a reverie. 'But the strange thing is – when we were liberated, I found I didn't want to revive that . . . the former me, after all. They offered us wigs – good ones, too – until our own hair grew back, but I turned it down. I could guess where the hair came from. But I wouldn't wear make-up, either. I fattened up – back to normal – of course, but I wore dungarees and workmen's calico shirts.'

'You were scared. Is that why you never tried to find me? I've never quite wanted to ask, but—'

'No – honestly. It never occurred to me that you'd stay on in Germany. That first winter, when they were still wanting to punish us! All of us. Collectively.' She shuddered. 'Why *did* you stay? You could have gone back to Sweden without even letting your parents know.'

'Three little words.' Marianne smiled and spread her hands, palms up. 'I. Met. Willard. I know he left me again but I knew he'd be coming back. But when did you give up dungarees and calico shirts?'

'In order to work at the BBC – but it was all superficial. I didn't feel *wanted* again until . . . well, until Felix.'

Marianne smiled again. 'I remember you telling me – the rose he held against your cheek and he said you were still the winner.'

Angela nodded but her smile soon faded. 'Only this time, this Easter, when all those old feelings came back . . . I mean – isn't that just *so* ironic! All that time in the camp I'd be fighting to reassure myself that an attractive *me* was hidden away inside, and all the time after Felix helped me revive her, that disgusting KL . . . drab . . . *creature* was surviving somewhere inside me. Unsuspecting. I mean, unsuspect*ed*.'

A shiver ran down Marianne, from her neck to the small of her back. 'Why did you ask about Billy Dobson – *as a man?*'

'He said what you said – that I must be some kind of saint. But his eyes said a lot more than that. You can tell, can't you. We can tell. When I went to the QE TWO that night, we had a long chat, Billy and me, about her and . . . *stuff*. But I remember gripping his arm at one point to shake some sense into him. And his reaction! Wow! You'd say it was a hundred volts. But I didn't think much about it until last month, down in Marazion.'

Marianne let out her pent-up breath in a long, wheezy whistle. 'What a situation! Has he made any open sort of move?'

Angela stared at the lead flashing with which the little balcony floor was lined. You could still see Marianne's very feminine silhouette traced there in last summer's suntan oil. 'It's not him I worry about, Marianne. Why am I *doing this* to myself? I still love Felix as passionately as I ever did or ever could. But why can I not stop my mind returning to Billy – the way he looks at me . . . the things he says. He has some interesting ideas about music, in fact. But am I fighting that KL-creature still living inside me, who just wants to triumph over her old tormentor? Because Inge loves her Billy every bit as much as I love my Felix.'

'And does Billy love her?'

'Of course he does. But he's a man.'

Marianne rose and, spreading her hands over the broad stone that capped the semicircular balustrade, leaned out and peered anxiously down. Then, relaxed again, she turned and half-sat on the stonework, saying, 'I keep forgetting that Eric likes to sit outside on the ballroom steps when the sun's out – and I'm sure anything said up here carries down as clear as a bell. But as for you, Fräulein Wirth, you've simply got to give way to Mrs Breit. You're dumb and uncaring. She's smart – but vulnerable. You must—'

'It's not that easy,' Angela interrupted her. 'I mean, the easiest thing would be to cut my contacts with both of them down to just whatever was completely unavoidable. But Inge would see that as rejection. Then we'd be back where this started. What we did down there at Marazion this Easter has committed both of us to a friendship that must run the normal course of all friendships. You don't need words to cement a commitment of that kind – it's far deeper than words.'

A short while later, as she was on the point of leaving, she said, 'As for this absurd idea that Felix and Inge were . . . you know – before the war . . .'

'Yes?'

'Maybe it would be best just to leave it simmering quietly? We can't possibly replace it with the truth.'

Tuesday, 16 June 1964

It finally happened in – of all places – Fiesole. Faith had prepared the way for a highly profitable deal with the Florentine publishing house of Sansoni and Fogel had come over to dot the i's and cross the t's before adding his opulent flourish to the bottom of the contract. There had been a last-minute hitch – a misunderstanding about gross and net receipts. It took ten minutes for Faith to iron out, during which Fogel chose to sit outside in the room – indeed, in the very chair – from which Lorenzo di Medici had once granted his patronage and dispatched his assassins. Fogel enjoyed the irony but still did not like being kept waiting. So when they sent a mere secretary out to tell him all was now ready, he looked around to find some excuse for requiting this indignity.

'Who's that?' he asked, peering at someone who appeared to

be correcting proofs in an alcove at the far end of the enormous banqueting hall. He took several sideways steps and peered again. 'Brandon!' he cried and, grinning the sort of grin that Machiavelli himself (and perhaps in this very chamber, too) would have delighted to see, he marched down the length of that long, long table, opening his arms as if to a long-lost relation. 'Dear fellow! What do you do here? Is it something for Manutius?'

'No – it's a gourmet cookbook,' Eric replied. 'Much too frivolous for you.' He made no effort to cover the papers – in which, he could see, Fogel was mightily interested. He even turned two or three sheets round – big, unwieldy colour proofs, not galleys. 'It's a co-production between Rainbird and Sansoni. These are the first colour proofs from Mondadori. I was in Verona yesterday.' He did not explain that he'd brought them to show to Faith and he prepared a lie in case Fogel asked.

But Fogel had already lost interest. 'I was a publisher already at school,' he said, sitting down beside Eric.

Faith emerged from the meeting. 'They're waiting, Wolf,' she called.

He waved her to silence and continued. 'Communist material. Ernst Fischer, Christian Broda – all wrote for me, just a schoolboy. People think I was so smart I saw what Hitler would do to the Jews even long before the *Anschluss*. Not *zo*. I saw what Dolfuss has done to the communists. *Zat's* when I left. Anyway, there were as many anti-Semites in London as in Vienna back then. But already I knew one thing about printing – you can print a million colours from only four! Some young men—'

'Wolf – they're waiting for you.'

He didn't even hesitate. '—put pictures of Betty Grable, Claudette Colbert on their walls. Me? I had tint-and-shade charts from gravure, litho, letterpress. Everywhere! Yellow, cyan, magenta and black – making a million of colours. And I see . . . it's like Hiroshima . . . I see if we put *language* on a separate black plate – a fifth printing plate – *boom!* Every publisher in the world can share the cost of printing the other four plates. The English printing of three thousand copies is now three hundred thousand maybe! Not five shillings each book (it's nineteen-thirties prices) but five pennies! The Red Sea has parted and we're in the Promised Land finally! Except it's an annoying Second World War is blocking my way.'

Faith joined them. 'Fogel! It's a fascinating tale but I'm sure

Sansoni already understands it doesn't pay to keep you waiting. Can't you hear them – rending their garments and gnashing their teeth?'

He smiled triumphantly and turned to go. 'I give you the rest at lunch,' he promised over his shoulder. To Faith he added: 'You can stay here. I have enough ink in my pen.'

'Wow!' Eric said when he had gone. 'That's some mood he's in.'

'He's building up to something. It's like an electric storm building in the air. Can't you just feel it? He'll fight like a demon to secure a contract but the moment it's signed it feels to him like prison bars. Now he has to perform according to this clause and that clause. He has to deliver. No more room for wriggling. This lunch is not going to be a picnic, trust me!'

'Well, I'll be here when you get back – if you need a shoulder to weep on.'

'Ha! You're invited, too. You heard him. But thanks for the offer. And you won't just be a spectator, either. Those dishes look scrumptious. I bet even Nicole will be pleased.'

'Won't Savorelli and Gentile and the others be there?'

'Where?'

'At lunch.'

'No! That's this evening. Lunch will be just the three of us. At the Terrazo on the Piazzale Michelangelo, I hope. There's a fabulous view over the whole of Florence, which will be some compensation. There's a bit of an overall blue cast on that one.'

Eric scribbled *blu-/giallo+* beside the image.

But when it came to lunchtime, the Piazzale Michelangelo was out. Fogel, as always, had other ideas. The minute they were in the taxi he gave the driver the address of a farmhouse in the village of Fiesole, some four miles to the north-west, past Bernard Berenson's Villa di Tati – and even closer to the Villa Medici. A Medici theme of intrigue and ambition now seemed to hang over the day.

The farmhouse had a small room, too small to be called a dining room though that was its purpose; but it also had three rough tables outside, in the shade of a line of lemon trees at the edge of the terrace, and Fogel led them directly to the central one of these. There were no other patrons.

Immediately below them, over the wall, they could peer down into the dark-upon-dark of a citrus grove, almost lost in a deep pool of shade. From that rich floor the valley rose through levels of increasing poverty – through an abandoned olive grove where the drab-coloured trees had grown wild and rangy, on up through a labyrinth of tamarisk scrub and goat maquis, until it arrived at a bare scree of sun-bleached rock where no green showed at all. The early afternoon sun fell aslant this wilderness, making a kaleidoscope of jagged shadows and shouting highlights – a bleached Cézanne. Somewhere in that confusion a shepherd (or a modern composer?) was playing his pipes – a non-stop dirge on five notes whose every combination was purest melancholy.

The same rays filtered through the lemon trees and spangled the three of them where they sat. 'It's good here, out of the city,' Fogel said. The table was pallid from the sun and scored with the years of rain and frost. The lady of the house came out and spread an ample white cloth upon it, making the sunspots shapeshift and dance; she chatted with them easily for a while and Fogel was charming to her – much too charming for the comfort of those who knew him well. There was no menu, just pasta dishes, goat's cheese with a slightly leavened home-made bread, olives and the local Chianti Rufina.

'So,' he said to Eric, as if no time had intervened, 'I spent the war learning about colour printing. Working for the Minister of Information, getting always a bit bigger allocation than I need. And, when I can, I start *Illustrated Britain* – all we are fighting to preserve – and *Forward: the New Britain and Her Future Empire* – patriotism. And all with more than half the pages in full colour.'

'Wolf!' Faith interrupted. 'Now that we are such wonderful friends of the Sansoni publishing house, we came this far out of Florence in order to discuss this contract as far from their spies as possible. What are we—'

'It's time enough!' He waved her objections aside. 'Brandon must understand how a publishing house like ours can survive. So then I put my first feelers out to *retail* publishers. Manutius is wholesale – a cash-and-carry service to national houses all round the world. Now I must learn to work with retail publishers. I gave Allen Lane the idea for the first Penguins *in colour*! *King* Penguins. He signs a contract for twelve books – thinking they will not be a big success and he can cancel. But they are! A big-*big* success and now he is tied in to a contract where this *interloper* . . . this not-an-English-gentleman . . . this Viennese *Jew* – will make big profit. And he will be blamed for it. And so then I hear that at the Athanaeum – where I cannot be a member – and at the Garrick – where also I cannot be a member – and every book launch where I am not invited – I hear he complains about this *Jew* who has chained him to a rock and is bleeding him of millions. So I go to his office and I walk past his secretary when she says I can't go in. And I tear his contract into four pieces and throw it before him, and I say, "Now, Lane, it's no contract between us. You are free! Free to do no more and no less than what any English gentleman would do to keep his word!" But I shout it! I shout it so every little person outside his office can hear. So I know – *and he knows* – the story will go all about London. And so – clever Mister Brandon – what lesson do you learn from my tale, eh?'

'That a torn-up contract and a loud voice are more valuable than an intact contract that is spoken about in hints and whispers?'

Fogel laughed heartily. 'It's true! You remember this and you're OK.'

'If ever I go independent *as a publisher*. But – as you know – I'm just a hack. Which means I'm independent already.'

Fogel stopped laughing.

The tension was eased by the excellence of the food, each dish requiring – indeed, compelling – a connoisseur-like devotion to tasting, savouring, and signalling a divine satisfaction to the patron's wife before she would relax and retire back to her kitchen in triumph. Over the cheese and olives Eric drew a dummy book from his briefcase – a volume bound in plain white boards and filled with 128 blank pages, designed to show potential customers the actual binding, size, weight and quality of the final product. Faith stiffened in alarm – this was, after all, the dummy for Nicole's cookbook. But Eric was unperturbed. 'Test for you, Wolf,' he said.

Fogel glanced at the dummy. 'What print run?' he asked.

Faith leaned back, out of Wolf's field of view, and shook her head with vigorous but tiny oscillations. She did not relax until Eric went on: 'Not that sort of test. The question is – what exactly *is* this?' He gave the dummy a shake, as if it might make a noise, a clue of some kind.

Fogel frowned. 'A dummy,' he said.

'Deeper,' Eric urged.

'Tabloid size. Cartridge paper. Saddle-stitched . . . what?'

'Deeper.'

'Don't just keep saying "deeper"! What you want?'

'Think Kant – Immanuel Kant.'

'Oh, Eric – give it a rest!' Faith said.

Fogel, still bewildered, turned to her. 'What is Immanuel Kant to do here?'

Eric answered: '*The Critique of Pure Reason – Kritik der reinen Vernuft.*' When Fogel still looked bewildered, he added: '*Das Ding an sich* – the thing in itself.' He shook the dummy book again. 'This is *das Buch an sich* – the platonic-ideal book. The *ur*-Book. The book stripped of all particularities. The book that is potentially *any* book. The book—'

'OK-OK!' Fogel waved him to silence and lit one of his big, celebratory cigars. But *that* Silence – *die Stille an sich* – was unknown to Eric, who went on: 'It's going to be my next book. I'll publish it myself. Exactly like this. Just think of the advantages, Fogel! No author, no designer, no royalties, no typesetting, no permissions, suitable for all ages, three to a hundred and three. Just a slip-cover round it saying *The Book of Your Dreams – here they can all come true.* My only problem? The price point. Production costs are one shilling a copy for a run between five and ten thousand. So . . . five shillings? Are your dreams *worth* five shillings, Wolf? Are Faith's? Are mine?'

Fogel stared at him with his big, blue, baby eyes. He rose to his feet and his skin, normally the pale colour of a light tan only slightly assisted by chemicals, darkened and purpled. He looked at the cigar in his hand as if he wondered how it got there; and then, plunging it smack into the middle of the goat cheese and mashing its tip to tiny, brittle shards, he exploded at last.

'You are so clever – both of you! You think I know nothing! I know all! Your plans . . . Peter Glemser . . . he . . . because of . . . never mind. I know! You think I'm too far removed from . . . that I don't know the half of what goes on in Manutius. I know all. *All!* Treachery? I know *all* treachery!' He turned on Faith. 'You are sacked. You are no longer with Manutius!'

Faith reached out and touched his bare arm. 'Wolf! Remember—'

'No! This time is different. This time I mean it.'

'Of course you do. At least sit down again.'

But he extracted himself awkwardly from between the bench and the table and began walking away, turning with every other step to add a few more words, so that he spun round and round like a Dervish in treacle to deliver each disjointed taunt. 'I can manage . . . treachery goes back years . . . one word from me to Sansoni is worth ten from you . . . I mean a hundred.' And so on.

Meanwhile Faith was saying, over this drip-feed of contumely: 'But I intend to resign anyway, Wolf! You know very well that I could so easily mount a boardroom takeover – and with enthusiasm and gratitude from Doubleday, let me assure you – but I can't do it.' She beat her breastbone hard with the tips of her fingers. 'I can't do it. You started Manutius and you should have the privilege of killing it off – *or* taking it on to even greater glory. With your genius – which no one disputes – you may possibly ignore *all* the traditional wisdom in the publishing world and pull off yet another Fogel coup. You know that I think your chances this time are zero but I cannot deny you the opportunity to pull it off. So you have *not* sacked me – and no one here heard those words, because if they ever leak out in London, just think what it will do to your reputation.'

That halted him at last. He sat down on – or rather sank upon – the bench at the next table. 'What does that mean?' he asked.

'D'you honestly think people don't know how many times I've pulled your irons out of the fire? D'you think Blondin could tell just *any* old Tom, Dick, or Harry to set up the tightrope for him to walk across Niagara? Gentile and Savorelli – ask them if you dare – they *know* how much blood was spilled, how much sweat was poured, before you could walk in today and whip out your fountain pen. Tell them you're thinking of firing me and watch their faces! No, Wolf – everywhere in public we part with smiles of mutual admiration and goodwill. And everyone who asks me how I think Manutius will go on without me, I'll tell them I have left you the best team in the whole publishing world.' She patted the bench beside her. 'And that's what we must discuss now.'

'Why?' He was surly . . . truculent, but his fury had abated.

'Because tonight we'll tell Gentile he's the first to know. And tomorrow they will know it from New York to Tokyo!' She turned to Eric. 'Have you got a pencil?'

He whipped out his HB clutch pencil and offered it.

'No, honey-chile.' She winked. 'You just take that dummy and piss off somewhere and use it as a sketch book, there's a good boy.'

Envoi – 1968

Thursday, 4 July 1968

Dear Alaric,

Since you find my handwriting so arachnoid, I'm
doing this on Eric's old portable whichsticks and
leaps at every chance it gets. and don't you dare
complain that it looks impersonal. I think the sort
of risks you are having to take down that coal
mine are completely criminal. Not even earplugs!
And why couldn't they have blown air in faster to
sweep away all that dust? Still, I envy you the
money you're making. You'll live the life of Riley
in London next half. (Oh, sorry, you call it
'term', don't you. Like you're still at school.)
I'm glad to hear you've stopped sinking and will
start drifting next week - but thank heavens you
weren't writing that from the deck of a whaler!

Nothing much continues tohappen here. Calley and
me are still working 5 days/week at <u>Chez Nicole</u>
and the tips are good. I'm sure a lot of the
conversations we overherearar concern illegal acts
- pricing agreements and market sharing. Alex says
if it didn't happen here, it would happen somewhere
else but it seems to me we just make it so easy
for them.

On the other two days me and Calley help Eric
with his film for the Land Commission, explianing
the five different ways the government can charge
Net Development Levy on private land when they
develop it. It was supposed to be a project for
the students but there was the Hornsey sit-in put
paid to that. And poor Eric, who's only supposed
to do two days a week there and only agreed to
that because he could use it to kidnap talented

students for employing them after college, he's
left holding the baby, working weekends and nights
to get it finished. It's good for Calley and I
though because we're learning a lot about synching
animation to soundtrack (to 1/24 of a second!) and
A-and-B neg-roll cutting which is far more
fascinating than it sounds. Faith is not very happy
that The Partridge Press is losing so much of his
time. But it would be far worse in the autumn of
course.

Also, poor Eric's in a bit /a state because his
old army chum /of Billy Dobson - his wife Inge
died last week. She took up flying in the spring
and last Tuesday her plane crashed in the old
Panshanger estate, fortunately in a gravel pit
after working hours so no one else was hurt. It
was her first solo flight, too.We all went to the
funeral on Saturday with lots of people from the
school as well, of course. It was at the
crematorium near Watford. Very creepy when you hear
that click and a hum and the coffin starts to
slide, and the little curtain parts just in time.
The ones I feel sorry for are poor Margaret and
Francis, only about 11 or 12 and losing their
mother at that age. Right at the end, just before
the coffin vanished for good, Margaret ran forward
and put something on top of the coffin which then
vanished before anyone could see what it really
was. I don't know if any of us asked her. I
certainly didn't.

There are whisperings which I don't know if I
should put them in black and white but anyway
you'll hear them when you come home. People are
saying, quietly, that it wasn't a complete
accident. The most scurreilous thing I've heard is
that someone said she was Felix's 'bit' in Germany
before the war. And there are also whispers that
she was the one who denounced Angela to the
Gestapo in the war. But Angela has been so
friendly with her, going out and hugging her, which

we all saw that day Billy and Eric met up again.
All the same, one can't help wondering why Inge
wasn't going to join in until Angela went out and
did that. Something made her stop out, and being
Felix's lover once upon a time would fit that,
wouldn't it.

It's odd to think that our parentoids ever had
passions and crushes and fallings-out and
heartbreaks. We believe that's our priviledge,
don't you think? Oh, and talking of the agonies of
love (as cynically reflected in verse and song) you
may inform Tommy that Calley sent a few lyrics to
Marty Wilde (you remember that Ricki and what was
his older sister's name? Anyway, they both go to
Tewin school and Ricki has a hit single with
'Hertfordshire Rock' and 'I am an astronaut' on the
flip side) and he, Marty Wilde, says they're not
bad and he's coming to see her when he's finished
this tour and they can maybe fix up something. So
Tommy can put that in his pipe and smoke it! He
has spurned tomorrow's ace lyricist, so there! Kim!
That's her name. They're in the school's new
swimming pool every chance they get. Kids today –
they don't know how rugged and deprived it was in
our time, do they!

That's all just about for today. Let me know how
well/ill the drifting goes. It sounds much less
strenuous to be working horizontally against a
rockface than vertically against something under
your ~~feet~~ boots. And Calley and I just love the
sound of <u>air legs</u> – you couldn't nick a couple of
pairs for us, I suppose?

Kiss-kiss
Jasmine

P.S. . . . no. Forget it.
P.P.S. Tee-hee!

Thursday, 15 August 1968

'Oh, no! Please – no!' Angela caught a glimpse of the Dobson children running down the short drive. Two minutes later came the noise she had dreaded: a knock at the door – a knock she had come to know only too well ever since the plane crash.

She forced a smile to her lips and lifted the latch. 'Billy! How good to see you! Do come in.'

'I'm not intruding?' The man was a wreck. There were rings beneath his eyes and he hesitated over every movement. 'I hoped to see Eric, but there's no one in.' Vacant-eyed, he gazed over her shoulder. Not looking for Felix. 'The whole place wide open but no one in.'

'We do tend not to lock doors here.' She resigned herself to it and stepped aside.

'You're off to Wales, I know,' he said as he drifted in. 'I'm sure you're packing or something.'

'The Forest of Dean, actually.' She led the way to the kitchen. 'Felix and the brats are already there. Except Pippin. She's gone off with Jasmine and Calley and Alaric to some weekend rave where Tommy's new group is performing. The Sinkers and Drifters. She'll come on under her own steam or she might be waiting for me in Tewkesbury. That's what kids today call a firm arrangement.'

He wasn't listening. Why was she telling him all this trivia, anyway? 'Trouble?' she asked, sliding a mewing kettle on to the hottest plate of the range.

'My staff.' He flopped down at the table and rested his head in both hands. 'Salt of the earth.'

'Or would you prefer lemonade? Hot day like this.'

'Oh . . . er . . . whatever you're having. Tea. I find it more cooling than soft drinks.'

She heated the pot. 'If you've come to discuss musical theory,' she said lightly, 'this is not the absolute best of—'

'No! No – nothing like that.' He managed a smile.

He was quite attractive when he smiled.

'I came to ask a favour. An *enormous* favour. But perhaps, as you say, it's not the best—'

'Ask on – I can only say no.' She tipped a good heap of biscuits out on a wooden platter.

'The thing is my deputy . . . well, all the senior staff, really . . . they've ganged up on me and insisted they can organize everything for next term without any help from me. And I'd be no help anyway, the way I am. So the long and the short is that I'm to take the rest of the hols completely off and not turn up until the first day of term.'

She put two mugs – the Bernard Leach seconds – on the table and fetched the milk from the fridge. 'You and the children would be welcome to join us in the Forest. We've rented an enormous house in Coleford. Just outside, actually. There's tons of room.' She faltered when she saw tears in his eyes. 'Oh . . . Billy!' She reached across the table and squeezed his arm. 'I'm so sorry. I miss her, too, you know – dreadfully.'

'I know. I know.' Briefly he clutched at her hand. His was cold.

She went on: 'It was only after she died that I realized—'

'D'you think it was deliberate?' he asked suddenly.

Her hand flew off his arm, as if it had given her an electric shock; she put it back at once and squeezed again.

He persisted: 'Did she mean to do it?' His eyes searched deep into hers, now the left, now the right.

She looked away; there were so many answers when it came to talking about death. So many shades of intention.

'You do, don't you.' He let out the breath he had been holding. 'You think she did.'

'I don't,' she assured him. 'Dispassionately . . . oh, how can we possibly be dispassionate? But, dispassionately, there's no way to *prove* she didn't. We have to fall back on what we *know* of her. And if you, who knew her better than anyone, can have your doubts . . .'

'Maybe *you* knew her better than anyone. Better than me. I only met her *after* her time in prison – after the priest had got at her . . . brainwashed her. But maybe you saw—'

'Oh man! *Mensch!* Are you torturing yourself with such thoughts now? Oh, God! What devil-spirit put her on the surveying party for the golf course that day? And why didn't I tell her then? Why didn't I *ever* tell her?'

'Tell her what?'

'Because on the surface everything was fine. We could laugh. We could run into each other in Garden City and go for a coffee. It would have been just too pompous to tell her.'

'What?'

'I did once say the half of it – remember? Down in Cornwall. I said liberation did not come for us when we could march freely out of the gates at Ravensbrück. I should have added that it only came . . . I was only completely free when I put my arms around her that first afternoon, when you turned up at the Dower House and met Eric again – remember? She dreaded coming in and joining us. And I went out and dragged her in. I had no idea why I was doing it at the time. But what I didn't realize was that *hatred* was like an invisible chain – a chain out of some witchcraft – stretching all the way from that camp to me, wherever I was . . . wherever I went. And by putting my arms round her like that – it wasn't like *forgiving* her – not an act of *forgiveness* – it was the only way to snap that chain and be free. Free at last! Free at last! Dear God – *there's* a cry that's going to ring down the years now!'

'And she is free in death!'

'Don't even start thinking like that, Billy.' The kettle started to whistle. 'Tea!' She rose and filled the pot. 'Are you sure you wouldn't like something stronger?'

'Tea's fine.' He reached for a biscuit.

'What was the "enormous" favour?'

'Oh, well . . . I came over to ask Eric, but if you're driving down to Wales tomorrow . . . ah . . . I was wondering if *you* could take Peggy and Francis under your wing for the next ten days? They could go to their grandparents but . . . the lure of The Tribe, you know?'

'Of course! Ours will be delighted to have someone else to bicker with. What'll *you* be doing? Milk in first?'

'As it comes. Cynegonde told me there's a huge difference but I can't taste it. I thought I'd go back to Germany, to Frankfurt, to see if *Das Haus Milenas* is still there. I mean, still going.'

She passed him his tea and poured her own, saying nothing.

'You disapprove?' he asked.

'Not at all.' She sat down again. 'It's hardly my place—'

'Also, I was going to ask if you'd like to come with me.'

She froze. He went on – filling the silences: 'Ring down the final curtain . . . You'd actually *see* the good she did finally . . . close a circle for me, too. But . . . they're expecting you . . . Wales and all that.'

'Besides . . .' she said hesitantly.

'Yes? Besides what?'

'Don't you think you ought to take Margaret and Francis there with you? They're both hurting badly – in the way that children hurt, you know. Ten minutes at a time. You can fix it in their mind – all the *good* Inge did. So they'll have that to remember when they come to hear about . . . the rest of it.'

He was startled. 'Who says they ever will?'

'They will. Not in any way we could foresee or predict, but they will.'

He chewed his lip, turning the thought over. 'And you think they're old enough?'

'No, Billy – I think they're still *young* enough.' She took a bite of a ginger snap before adding round the mouthful: 'And as for the invitation – which I gratefully accept – we'll do it sometime this year, I promise.'

'And Felix, too, of course. I should have said that.'

'No!'

'No?'

'We can all go to Frankfurt together and he can go off and look at sculptures or something. *Das Haus Milenas* – that's just for you and me. It will close the circle for us but who knows what it might open for him?'

Sunday, 18 August 1968

Pippin was waiting, as arranged, for her mother at Tewkesbury – plus Jasmine, Alaric, and a young dark-haired stranger, female. Alaric wore the tunic of a nineteenth-century hussar. And Levis. The girls were dressed as women who had not quite finished dressing. And Calley, for it was she, had dyed her hair, normally a deep honey-blonde, henna black.

'Can they come, too?' Pippin asked, with a veiled hint that otherwise she herself might not come.

'Of course they can, darling,' Angela said. 'Just shove all your stuff in the boot.'

'We can crash out anywhere.' Jasmine grinned at Alaric. 'The floor . . . anywhere.'

'All your stuff' was too grand a phrase for what they dumped in the car; even 'all your junk' would have flattered it.

'Was it a good rave?' Angela asked as they piled in, filling the car with the reek of mountain goats and something herbal.

'Yes,' Pippin said as if it was a huge joke. She sat in front but turned three-quarters round and hugged her legs under her.

Her mother thought of mentioning seat belts but chickened. 'Did I say something funny?' she asked as she wound her window open and set off back towards Gloucester.

'No,' Pippin said. 'I did. "Yes" was the name of the main band.'

'We missed them up in Mersey so we caught them here.' Jasmine rolled and then lit a cigarette. 'Chris Squire said The Sinkers and Drifters were cool. But they must decide whether to be just The Sinkers or The Drifters because otherwise it's too long.'

'Well,' Calley said, 'anyone in a band called Yes *would* say that, wouldn't they. Anyway, we all thought Tommy's group was the best of the lot.'

'Especially,' Pippin said archly, 'when *Stained with Tears* got the loudest cheers of all.'

'Yours?' Angela asked her, looking in the driving mirror.

Calley nodded. 'Give or take a couple of dozen rewrites – it's almost gone full circle back to my original.' She refused a puff and passed the cigarette straight on to Pippin.

The open window drew her exhaled smoke past Angela, who said, 'Is that what I think it is?'

'No names – no pack drill,' Alaric warned.

'Felix will go spare if he catches you,' Angela warned back. 'You'd better smoke only in the garden. There's a potting shed and a summer house, too.' She saw Jasmine tickle Alaric below his ear, where the beard met skin. She didn't need to lip read to know that the girl said, 'We could crash there.'

'D'you want me to drive?' Pippin asked. 'Then you could sit here and watch them without risking all our lives.'

Angela pinched a smile and dug her daughter with her elbow;

but after that she kept her eyes mainly on the road. 'Did Tommy's lot use my synthesizer?' she asked.

'Yeah!' All four answered at once.

'No one had ever heard a bass-drumbeat that loud and low,' Calley said.

'Bill Bruford asked for your details,' Pippin added. 'He's the drummer with Yes.'

'Not just loud and low,' Alaric said, 'but absolutely regular and hypnotic. You could see guys almost going into a trance.'

'They could call themselves The Sands,' Calley said suddenly, shaking her head when offered the smoke again.

'Why?' Alaric and Pippin asked simultaneously.

'Sand . . . Ess and Dee. Sinkers and Drifters? You lot want to lay off that stuff – what it's doing to your brains. Or The Sandies. People would ask which ones are named Sandy, or what happened to them? And they could say they OD'd on music. OD – that could be another name. There are millions of names better than Sinkers and Drifters. Zam-Bam-Alakazam. Flyte. Xanadu. Autodestruct. Wallbanger. Cyclops. Nimrod. Alakart . . . I don't need that stuff, see.'

'How many new groups can there possibly be?' Angela asked. 'It's beginning to seem like you've only got to get two lads and a girl strumming together in a pub one evening and suddenly there's another group.'

'But groups are un-forming all the time, as well,' Jasmine said. 'They just put the last of The Monkees in the can.'

'And the Yardbirds . . . gone,' Alaric said, starting a round of casual one-upmanship.

'Cream . . . Little Willie John.'

'But he wasn't a group.'

'He cut wax. He was on some playlists.'

'The Animals – are they going? I heard they were going.'

Pippin had the last word: 'And BBHC won't survive Janis Joplin going – you'll see.'

Or not quite the last word: 'And that's just this year,' Calley explained to Angela.

'And how long d'you think Yes will last?' Angela replied.

'As long as they can stick each other,' Jasmine said.

'No, I think they're too instrumental,' Calley argued. 'And their lyrics are too obscure. And they go on too long.'

'You're just showing your youth, darling,' Jasmine said. 'They're not like The Stones or The Beatles, who will burn extra-bright and then just fizzle out. Yes can go on for ever.'

Alaric agreed. 'They've got it right – everything's crisp. Keyboard there. Guitar there. Drums there. Vocalist dead centre – and crisp, driving rhythm . . . pushing relentlessly. The Sinkers and Drifters are the same – that's why they'll last, too.'

'Sez who?' Pippin asked.

'Sez Tommy?' Angela guessed, glancing in the mirror at Alaric, who grinned back like one caught out. 'You used to be such sweet little children,' she added. Then: 'No. Actually, you weren't. That's just nostalgia.'

'Who were the groups when you were our age?' Calley asked.

Pippin turned on her and drew breath to speak.

'It's all right, darling,' her mother said. 'At your age, Calley, I was in uniform and we were fighting a war. "Group" – or *Gruppe* – meant something quite different then. And when I was Alaric's age – twenty-five, right? – I was being liberated and the BBC was asking for me. The first *bands* I heard were Glen Miller . . . Ted Heath . . . Tommy . . .'

'Ted Heath?' Jasmine was amazed. 'Did he have a band?'

'A different Ted Heath. But the biggest influence on me was Stan Kenton and progressive jazz. Have you heard of The Wall of Sound? That was him. And actually' – she turned to Pippin – 'remind me to speak to Billy Dobson about him. About Kenton. He's doing a lot of work with progressive jazz in American high schools these days – and Billy wants to beef up the music in his school, so he could look into that.'

'Why would you need me to remind you?' Pippin asked tetchily. 'I mean, you don't need any excuse to talk to Billy. How is he, anyway?'

'Yes, how is he?' Calley asked. 'Amanda said he was terribly cut up when she saw him in Bejam's. He was buying dozens of frozen beef bourguinons and chicken kievs. Those children must live on it.'

'Not at the moment. It'll be bratwürst and sauerkraut. He's taking Margaret and Francis to Germany, to see a home, a sort of refuge that their mother set up after the war to help concentration-camp victims.'

There was a silence and then Pippin – all casual-like – said, 'Did Felix meet her there – before he came to England?'

Panic! Angela had prepared herself for a direct question, someday – but not from any of her own children; her mind was suddenly empty of the pat responses. 'According to his records,' she said, meaning to stick to the truth until her *savoir faire* returned, 'he was in a TB hospital in Hamburg. And when he was discharged from there he came straight to London – you remember his story about meeting Adam and Tony again at the Lansdowne Club? I suppose it's *possible* he went via Inge's refuge.'

'Tell us about this house in the Forest of Dean,' Calley said.

'Yes!' Pippin stretched out her arm and gave her mother's elbow a sympathetic squeeze.

But, Angela wondered, sympathy for precisely what? That she had been caught off guard and then was embarrassed into telling an unconvincing lie? That Pippin now believed that Felix and Inge had been lovers and that something had rekindled when their paths crossed again? Or was it just for having been asked to revisit painful memories of the war?

'Well . . . let me see . . . it's down in a valley, right at the western edge of the forest-proper and there's a babbling brook that runs all along one side of the garden, deep enough to drown in if you're already drunk . . .'

'Do we wait up for them?' Felix and Angela stood at their bedroom window, which overlooked the road up to the Speech House, where the ravers had gone for a drink.

'I thought they'd take one look at the prices, buy half a pint each and come home again pretty smart,' Angela replied. 'But they must have earned a fortune sinking and drifting up north.'

Silence drew in around them and she heard it.

It was a perfect evening, warm, with not a breath of wind – certainly not down here in the valley bottom. The setting sun turned the topmost trees on the vast flank of hillside facing them to a gold that almost blinded, leaving the valley in a blue lake of shade. The creatures of the night were waking up and taking over: the rusty screech of an owl, answered from half a mile away (owls, they say, can hear a squirrel's heartbeat). A curious croaking that, by day, would surely be a woodpecker . . . but now just as surely not; so . . . a frog? A deer? Muntjak or fallow? A sudden *crack!* A small-bore rifle? A tree, dying limb by limb? A yelp. A stray dog? Or when do vixens get randy? Crickets singing, unnoticed until noticed.

If you played this slow-motion cacophony in the concert hall, people would get bored and leave; yet here it kept you on tiptoes, filling the infinity of the mind with spaces . . . with pinpointed heights . . . with precise distances that thrilled. How to capture the essence of that? What array of mikes? What mikes for a squirrel's heartbeat? No. It could not be done.

No more could a painter catch that golden canopy . . . now fading . . . now . . . . gone! Snuffed out.

And leave the world to darkness and to me.

'Fancy Calley dyeing her hair like that,' Felix said.

'It suits her, though. I should have done that before anyone got to know me here. Girls with raven-black hair get taken far more seriously than blondes.'

'And I wouldn't have looked at you twice. Shall we sit out there and sip absinthe and watch the world go completely dark?'

'OK.' She opened the French window that led out to the balcony. She raised her voice: 'This is a super house, you know. D'you think we could buy it? Not just for summertime. I can imagine this landscape under heavy snow *and* in spring sunshine. And the autumn colours must be just spectacular.'

Felix came back – amazingly quickly – with a bottle of Pernod, a jug of water, two tall glasses, and a cooler full of ice.

She laughed at his crude subterfuge. 'What if I'd said no?'

'I refrain from pointing out that you never have refused a Pernod on a warm day. Or night. But in that improbable event, I'd have brought it here just the same and drunk it alone.'

He set the tray down on a small rusty wrought-iron table and poured her glass – a tall, flared cone with 'Pernod' stencilled on it in blue. As he straightened up again his eye wandered towards a corner of the veranda, attracted by . . .

'Potted *geraniums*?' he asked.

'I know.' She pulled a face. 'Mrs Harvey's potted "gewaniums – a leetle thenkyou faw letting me pen-gwaze my wabbits on yaww lawn." I couldn't tell her we've got a "thing" about geraniums. They're her prizewinning strain, she said.'

After a pause, he said, 'Maybe it's time we stopped "having a thing" about them.'

She said nothing.

'Mmmm?' he prompted.

In a flat, rather remote voice, she said, 'I'm sure Billy came over to tell me Inge had geranium stains in the palms of her hands when she crashed. She did use to do that you know – crush the leaves and smell them.' There was a silence before she added: 'Stigmata. That's what *you* called them, isn't it?'

He nodded but said nothing as he handed her the glass.

In the dying twilight she watched the shocking-yellow of her drink turn cloudy green; the ice clinked with high overtones. She said, 'Billy once told me there was a fellow in his platoon in the desert who could imitate that clink of ice-in-water perfectly. His brother officers drew lots and one of them shot him at Mersa Matruh.'

Felix remembered an old religious Jew in the camp who spent all his waking hours praying aloud, very quietly but not quietly enough to save his life. He said, 'Another thing – going back to if you had dyed your hair black. Marianne wouldn't have recognized you that first midsummer party. That might have changed all our lives.'

She wondered if at last – at long-long last – this was the moment. *The* moment. What the hell . . . 'I could also have kept it blonde but cut it short.'

She glanced his way. No reaction.

'*Very* short,' she added.

He turned to her at last. 'What's this?'

'Put your glass down,' she warned.

'If this is some . . .' His voice trailed off as he watched her gather her hair and pull it tight to her scalp, bunching as much of it as possible out of sight behind her.

Then, letting it go again, she mimed the act of rowing.

'Have you been sharing their cigarettes?' he asked.

'Don't!' she said quietly. 'You did recognize me – that first day at Schmidt's. You must have.'

He nodded. 'Not immediately. And then I thought a fresh start . . .'

'Anyway, *that's* why I pricked up my ears when I heard Luther talk about your arrest that day at the Wannsee meeting. It drove me frantic. And *that's* also why I didn't really hear the rest of the conference until I played it back. All I could think of was how I could get word to you – and, of course, I couldn't. They'd have shot me and they'd also have made it much worse for you.'

'You said nothing, too, that day.'

'I nearly . . . I could have . . . I wanted to stand up and scream out your name when you walked in with Faith and Fogel.'

'But later – that first lunch we had together?'

'You weren't very complimentary about your rowing partner that day – *if* you remember. I used to dream about you in Ravensbrück.'

'Oh, don't!' He closed his eyes and shook his head. 'These parallels are so . . . embarrassing.'

'Besides,' she said, 'I thought that falling in love in the rose garden in Regent's Park was much better than a long-ago afternoon in a boat on the Wannsee. A fresh start, as you say.'

He reached out and squeezed her arm. 'Absolutely right.' He stretched in the opposite direction for his drink, picked it up, and drained it. 'More?' he asked, rising. 'Can I top yours up?'

'You can top *me* up,' she said archly. 'Later. You on top.'

'I take it that's a yes.' He plucked the glass from her hand. 'Going back to dyeing your hair black,' he said, 'Inge wouldn't have recognized you, either. She might have looked twice but you'd have got away with it.'

It was the perfect moment to explain – what Felix had never understood – why she had been so insistent on befriending Inge. But, just as she had never mentioned their Wannsee boat-outing down all these years, so, too, she had kept her silence over this conundrum.

Funny! She could tell Billy but not Felix – about the chain of hatred that had bound her still to the KL – the chain that could *only* be broken by starting anew with Inge. Their love – hers and Felix's – their children, their wonderfully successful careers, the intensity and absorption of their life in the Dower House community . . . not even those Pierrepoint movies where the Nazis were hanged – none of these had been able to break that chain. They had concealed it, made it seem trivial, distracted her most of the time; but only that hug beyond the haha had been able to accomplish it. And the ritual of that champagne bottle down in Cornwall.

Entlich ist es vorbei – Du!

She had spoken those words to herself as much as to Inge. When a ship cuts its chain, it liberates the anchor as well.

'To turn to more immediate concerns,' Felix said. 'And before they get back . . . I wonder – are we responsible? I mean, Alaric's twenty-six and Jasmine's . . . what? She's had her coming-of-age party. I don't think we can be held responsible. You know what I'm talking about, don't you.'

Angela took a long, slow sip, let it linger in her mouth, and swallowed gently – parsimoniously. 'Oh – you have to admit it's a perfect drink to end a perfect summer day! I did try to have a word with her – though you practically need a crowbar to part her from Alaric. But she just said, "I'm on The Pill, so you needn't worry, darling!" I wonder if Faith knows?' She chuckled. 'I'm sure she'd approve. We're all jealous as hell, of course, that the pill wasn't around when it would have made life a lot more carefree for us! Less of a bingo game.'

'And what about Pippin – to bring it right home?'

'She's on it, too, of course – ever since I caught her nicking mine. But I don't know if she's actually . . . you know. I think it's more in the spirit of Tom Lehrer's boy scout ready to meet a girl scout who is similarly inclined.'

'I hope so.'

She looked at him sharply. 'Why? Why shouldn't they enjoy making love without fear of the consequences. The years we had to go through that – us girls, anyway. That's what paralyzed me on *our* first night – on the train to Cologne. Remember?'

He chuckled.

'All right for *you*,' she said. 'I know *you* weren't out of practice.'

He transferred his drink and reached out to stroke her arm. '*Mmmm?*'

'Patience!' she said.

'Cynegonde has mellowed a lot lately, don't you think?'

'Not having to cook every bloody day. That clubhouse is a godsend.'

Felix said nothing.

'Or don't you think so?'

He covered his silence by sipping his drink and then relishing its after-flavours. 'You asked about buying this house,' he said.

'Yes, but answer my other question first – the clubhouse?'

'This is answering it in a way. I think the golf club has destroyed the community . . . well, not completely, of course, but it has weakened us.'

'What? Willard and Alex playing power games every weekend?

Tony complaining he never *sees* Nicole now? And the last few members of The Tribe running that swindle with the lost balls?'

He shook his head. 'More than that. I know the old parkland was always a bit scruffy. And fallen branches tended to stay fallen a long time. And several children had nasty experiences with horses, cows, and nettles . . .'

'And poor Ruth with that wasp nest.'

'But it was somehow part of the *real world* – the natural world. We could stand out there in our five acres and let the eye run over it and onward into the rest of Hertfordshire. It was seamless. Now we're marooned in the heart of this manicured belt of green and—'

'Parts of it are rough still.'

'Not "still". They're *deliberately* rough – cultivated to be like that. Not simply neglected.' He sighed and fell into thought again. 'It dominates *us* now,' he said at length. 'We used to dominate *it*. We should have seen it when they unveiled that model – the final one. But we forgot the people – those braying, bleating flocks of alpha-males trumpeting their one-upmanship . . .'

Angela burst out laughing. 'You! You're just an unreconstructed old Rosa-Luxemburg communist underneath all that every-artist-for-himself tooth-and-claw stuff!'

'No,' he protested. 'I'm consistent. Capitalism should *only* be applied to art and artists – every man and woman for themselves and devil take the hindmost. Everything else should be managed under communist principles. Eric's right – state patronage has corrupted all the arts beyond repair.'

Angela had trudged after him down this tortuous path too often to make the effort one more time. 'The Lanyons *are* going,' she said. 'He's got tenure at UCLA. Hilary came up and confirmed it to us just after you left. She says they've got a very nice prospective couple lined up . . . someone in advertising. And his wife does the casting of British actors for some Hollywood studio. I wonder if Willard and Marianne will stay on?'

He sat up straighter, surprised. 'I hadn't heard that. Where will they go?'

'Willard's been learning Swedish. Not that he'll need it over there, according to Marianne. She says he's just doing it so people can't pass comments behind his back when he's around. Siri and Virgil are only home in the vacations – if even then – and Peter will turn seventeen this year. Next *month*, in fact.'

'So!' Felix said. 'The old community *is* looking rather the worse for wear. Maybe it wouldn't be an act of outright treachery to buy this place as a second home. We could probably get it for two thousand. Not more than three – the roof looks dodgy over the kitchen end. But I'd also want to buy a chunk of the forest behind us.'

'Really? Why?'

'Wandering through the trees yesterday, I got the idea of burying . . . no – hiding, yes, hiding sculptures in among them so that you glimpse them and are drawn towards them . . . or just stumble upon them. No names. No little brass plaques. I hate those things in gardens.'

'Yes!' Angela became excited. 'And I could hide some all-weather loudspeakers here and there. On a grid pattern. And we could use any two pairs in stereo to make it sound as if something was moving around among the trees, just by changing which pairs. You could sculpt with sounds. Exotic birds – or jet planes – would seem to fly among the trees. Or swarms of bees. Or trickling water that isn't there when you look. You could chase a burglar away at night by playing tiger growls and snapping twigs that always seemed to come from close behind him. We could *herd* him away with nothing but sounds!'

The idea delighted him. 'That clinches it! We'll make an offer tomorrow.' A moment later, he added: 'And it'll mean we're not leaving the community for negative reasons. It will have a future purpose.' He took a gulp of Pernod and said, 'What's that scrap of paper on your bedside table?'

She had to think. 'Oh, yes. I went to put Calley's mattress back on her bed and it was damp so I tried to air it. And I found that bit of paper on her bedside table.' She rose and went to fetch it. 'It's Cornelius's writing, I'm pretty sure. It's certainly in tune with his ideas.'

She passed it to him and he read:

```
showers of impulse
avant-rock
sneering glissandi
shed the faustian urge and join the demotic
collective of europe
```

'What's it mean?' he asked.

'It sounds like Cornelius changing gear. No – changing tack. But what is Calley doing with it? I mean to ask her.'

'Ssshh! Quiet a mo. I think I hear them.'

The full moon had meanwhile risen over what had earlier been the gilded skyline; it was still so low in the sky that most of the road that stretched away from the house and on up the hill towards the Speech House was lost in deep shadow; but here and there the wind had felled enough of a clearing to put a spotlight on the tar macadam and define the unseen stretches.

They held their breaths and faintly on the still night air came the sounds of not-quite-sober voices singing about tears that would not wash away and laughing and screaming girly screams that conveyed not the slightest hint of terror.

'They'll be here in ten minutes,' Felix sighed. 'Unless some misguided idiot stops and gives them a lift.' The words had barely left him when some misguided idiot stopped and gave them a lift. 'I just hope they don't lay a Persian carpet all over his back seat,' he added.

'Talking of Persian carpets,' Angela said. 'The Findlaters seem to have lost touch with that courtier, whatsizname – Rowhali? Rowhani? Faith thinks he's fallen out of favour – that he was only useful to the Shah until that fabulous book came out. It's a shame. I liked her.'

'Or would it be too cynical to suggest that he's seen some writing on a wall somewhere and is building up goodwill with that revolutionary ayatollah in Paris?'

The car shuddered to a halt right in the middle of the crossroads, just below the house. The doors opened and there was a spillage of *jeunesse dorée* – staggering unconvincingly, laughing too loudly, desperate to keep the dying Bacchus on life support.

'Poor things!' Felix murmured as the car set off again in a cacophony of thank-yous and a leaky silencer. 'They think they're the first liberated generation *ever*. They'd never believe how well we understand.'

'Understand what?'

'That moment when you're still more-or-less OK but you know that your mouth will become a rat's nest and you'd like your scalp to weigh less and you wake up in a shop doorway with a dog lifting its leg over you.'

'I must go down and see they don't wake Douglas or Susan.' Angela rose and carried her drink back into the house; over her shoulder she added: 'And after hearing *that,* I'm *so* glad nothing came of our afternoon on the Wannsee!'

The bathroom door opened and out came Calley, wrapped in a bath towel. 'Sorry – you should have knocked,' she told Angela. 'And I'm afraid the water's run tepid.'

She hadn't used the henna on her armpits. 'No, it's OK – I've only just arrived.' Angela thought of adding that the young folks' need for a bath had been greater than that of anyone else in the house. 'I just want to do my teeth. Oh, and by the way, actually . . .' she added as the girl padded off down the corridor, 'in case I forget – is that something Cornelius wrote? That bit of paper on your bedside table? I aired your mattress a bit – that's how I came to see it.'

'Yes.' Calley came back, laughing in anticipation. 'I ran into him one day as he was leaving the Tithe Barn and we got talking and he happened to say that you could make music out of any old sounds and I said it was the same with poetry – you could make it out of any old words. So he dipped his hand, without looking, into his briefcase and pulled out that bit of paper. And he said, "Try that!"'

'And did you?'

'No.' She pulled a naughty-child face. 'I brought it down here to have a go.' She half-turned to leave and then, facing Angela again, said, 'Actually . . .'

'What?'

'Well, I don't know if this is quite the time . . . but . . . well, I'll go and get it anyway. Where's Felix?'

'In the kitchen, setting out our early-morning tea tray. And don't grin like that – one day you'll be just as domesticated.'

'I'll see you down there.' She raced away along the passage.

'Calley wants to show us something,' she told Felix as she came into the kitchen. 'Put the tray down a mo.' They could already hear the girl descending the stairs two at a time.

'First, I have to explain . . .' In her excitement she started speaking before she even entered the kitchen, now wearing men's pyjamas. 'We were talking about family photograph albums – how it's a good way to size up a new boyfriend – either going through his family's and hearing what he has to say, or going through yours and listening to his comments. Or grunts. And Pippin told us that . . . well, for obvious reasons, there's a big blank space in both of yours. So . . .' She swallowed audibly . . . drew breath . . . squared her shoulders . . . 'I sort of thought I'd try to make a poem that was a kind of composite of . . . well . . . ideas, you know . . . to fill *your* photo albums – you could paste it in that gap. I haven't done Angela's yet – and I won't if you think it's impertinent – but this is where I've got to at the moment with the one for Felix.'

She pulled it from her breast pocket, plonked it on the battered old deal table, and fled. 'Tell me what you think tomorrow,' she called out from the hall.

They unfolded the single sheet of paper and read:

When those wounds that opened into Hell
Reeked to your High Heaven,
Where, dear God, was your sense of smell?
Yet there was one could have patterned you:
On a stair made for angels
he wanted for bread
and they – ignorant of
his Old Artificer skill –
gave him a stone.
Of all people, they gave him a stone!
An augury, rather!
About him,
skylarks held their manic daily auctions,
shrapnels of sound
raining reminders to the hope-abandoned . . .
promises of future stairs,
flights of fancy where a child may play,
flights of genius out of common clay,
and a stair that leads to a bedroom warm
and dark with the unquenchable love
that secures posterity
and sequesters it forever safe
from who would turn our daily bread
to a stone

Felix sniffed hard, several times, and took out a handkerchief and blew his nose; tears ran freely, silently, down Angela's cheeks.

'No full-stop at the end,' he said.

'D'you think Calley hadn't noticed that?' she asked huskily.

She took the paper from him, folded it carefully, and slipped it in her dressing-gown pocket. He turned to pick up the tray but she pulled his arms away and wrapped them around her instead. 'Leave it,' she told him. 'We have promises to keep . . . "and miles to go . . ." well, actually, just one staircase.'

'These of pitch-pine,' he said as, arm-in-arm, they went out into the hall. 'One.'

She anticipated him: 'Two.'

He chuckled. 'Three.'

'Four.'

'Five.'

'Six.'

'Seven.'

'Eight.'

'Nine.'

'Ten.'

With the end so near, they both counted aloud in whispers: 'Eleven . . . twelve . . . *thirteen*!'

'Bingo!' he said. 'Lucky for some!'

If this story has left you wishing you knew more about the Dower House community – how Tony and Adam, officers in the British section of the Allied Military Government: Occupied Territories were guests of Willard A Johnson of its American section when the Mauthausen concentration camp was liberated in 1945 and so met Felix Breit, then a prisoner at death's door . . . and how, two years later, the four of them and their wives (or in Felix's case, mistress) became the nucleus of a remarkable experiment in post-war living . . . you can relive it all in *The Dower House*, the first of the Felix Breit trilogy.

And if that leaves you wondering how those first tender, edgy, uneasy relationships were cemented into the bonds of friendship, concern and mutual support that enabled them to commit to the permanence they finally established in *Promises to Keep* . . . the growing pains that turned more than two-dozen children into a Tribe . . . the stresses that forced some to move out and make way for others . . . you can discover each story – tragic, comic, or humdrum – in *Strange Music*, the filling in this stirring and heart-warming literary sandwich.